By the same author :

Land of the Firebird
The Jongleur

Dragons' Pearls

A Fantasy Novel
by
Isabella League

HELENENTHAL
BOOKS

Dragons' Pearls © 2010 by Isabella League. All rights reserved. Printed in the United States of America. No part of this book may be used or reproduced in any manner whatsoever without written permission except in the case of brief quotations embodied in critical articles and reviews. For more information address inquiries to: **Helenenthal Books**, 4191 Bradfordville Road, Tallahassee, Florida 32309-6401.

FIRST EDITION

10 9 8 7 6 5 4 3 2 1

ISBN 978-1-888071-19-1

Artwork by E.E. Coad
Layout & Design by Gregory S. Coad

Dedication

For Hobbes – A gentleman cat
extraordinaire, who will always have a
special place in our hearts.

1989 - 2005

 Prologue

In a Temple of the Most Noble and Honorable Dragon, Southwestern China. In Western reckoning: April 1833

Xiang Lung slept in the pale spring sunlight, his yellow scales reflecting the spring sky. He was an aged *t'ein lung*, a Celestial dragon, the most revered of all the Chinese dragons. Not many would dare disturb his repose, rightly fearing his wrath that might cause an avalanche here in the mountains or even an earthquake if he were angry enough.

But one such daring creature was nearing him, crawling in a humble position as befitted a lowly three-toed dragon before a Heavenly Dragon, the five-toed one.

In spite of his fear the small red dragon – he was an earth dragon, a *ti-lung,* one of those who controlled the rivers – knew that he had to speak to his superior. Something had to be done before they were all destroyed. The Great Ones must not know what was happening – they had to be warned – they had to *do* something about it!

As he advanced respectfully, Qui Lung wished that anyone else save himself had been chosen for this urgent mission. By nature he was shy and retiring. One of the bolder *ti-lungs* ought to have been picked. But the elders of his caste had thought that Qui's humility would please the Great One.

All the same, Qui was far more frightened than he had ever been in his life – he had never been this close to a Celestial. He was not certain how he could dare to wake a Great One.

On his belly he crawled as close as he dared, and found when he opened his mouth to speak that his voice was almost gone. "Please, Great One," he whispered, "I come to humbly entreat you and apologize for ruining your sleep..."

A large eye opened and looked at him. The yellow head had a medallion of gold and the Stones of Heaven hanging down over his eyes, and more gold and jade gleamed on the paler scales at his throat. The whiskers on his face waved slightly. "Why do you bother me?" he demanded in a voice that while not precisely angry, was not friendly.

Qui shrank back and the carefully prepared words of the speech he had memorized yesterday fled as if they had never been. "They are killing us!" he said shrilly. "They are using the caterpillars and sorcery against us! Many have died!"

"What is this you are saying?" Xiang asked, frowning.

Qui flattened himself on the ground in an attitude of greatest respect. "Dragon poachers!"

Xiang sat up so suddenly that Qui let out a squeak of alarm and tried to move backwards.

"Dragon poachers! They dare –" he roared.

Qui winced and went further backwards. "They no longer respect us, Great One! The dragon temples fall into disuse – offerings are few! And now the poachers use sorcery against us! A mighty warlord seeks our flesh and bones – and a sorcerer seeks our pearls of wisdom!" Qui reached up and put a talon on the pearl beneath his throat as if it were in eminent danger.

The Celestial looked about him sadly. This was true, what the inferior dragon said. The people of China no longer maintained the dragon temples, filling them with offerings as was right and proper. These were degenerate times. Even this, his own temple...

"Tell me all," said Xiang to the red dragon. "Tell,me so that I may decide what may be done."

1

Tatya's Dilemma

Trinity College, Dublin, Ireland, May 1834

"The post's here, Dr. Stillfield!" came the cheerful voice of Simon Stillfield's teaching assistant, Séafra Ó Seamáin, as he entered Simon's tiny, crowded office.

Simon had long resisted taking on a teaching assistant other than his dragon Lakota, but at the Chancellor's insistence he had at last done so. And to his surprise, he had found Séafra both helpful and pleasant to work with. A teaching assistant was generally a graduate student who was working for an advanced degree and Séafra was no exception. He was working towards a doctorate in Dracophilology and as, Simon himself had done, would be going to America to study at Harvard, for as yet there was no doctorial program in this subject in any of the Six Nations – Ireland, Great Britain, Scotland, Man, Cornwall and Wales – of the British Isles.

Séafra had a stack of mail, most of which he had opened and sorted. "This one is after being personal," he said, extending a thin envelope to Simon. The rest he deposited on the desk in front of his employer. "'Tis coming a long way by the looks of it," he added as Simon took it, looking at it curiously.

The letter was of some crinkly, fragile paper and had been folded in on itself to make an envelope, in the old fashioned way, and sealed with wax. It was addressed to *Dr Simon Stillfield, Professor of Dracophilology, Trinity College, Dublin, Ireland*. It was stained, slightly torn and from the marks on it had indeed come a long way – from China, by the way of Siam, to Ceylon, through India and from there to the Cape of Good Hope and then to St Helena and finally to London, where it had then been sent on the final leg of its journey to Ireland.

"There's only one person this can be from," Simon said eagerly to Séafra. "Dr Quong Lee! I haven't heard from him in perhaps two or three years."

"The Chinese Dracophilogue?" Séafra asked with interest. "He is being the author of the book we were using in my final term – *The Oriental Dragon*?"

"The very one," said Simon, inserting a letter opener under the red wax and prying it off. "I was beginning to worry about him – he is rather elderly and I really expected to hear from him before this. I sent him a copy of my monograph on the Russian Ice Dragons and asked his opinion and if he had anything to add – he was in a party that actually visited their breeding grounds in Siberia." As he spoke he unfolded the sheet and quickly scanned it. He gave an exclamation and said "Listen to this, Séafra!" and he began to read aloud.

My dear Doctor Stillfield,

As you are among the most eminent in our profession I write to you with a dilemma that this humble practitioner of the ancient study of the honorable and noble dragon cannot resolve by his own self.

It has been many years since I have seen a living dragon. I had thought that many or most of them had retired to the mountains where they would be safe from the depredations of dragon poachers. Dragons are not held in the respect that once they were in the days of my honorable ancestors. The dragon temples, once overflowing with offerings, are fallen into disuse.

Two nights ago, as I was walking in my garden as is my habit before retiring, I was startled by an unexpected visitor. It was a great Celestial dragon, a yellow t'ein lung. I fell to my knees in awe and bowed before him. but he raised me up with one gentle talon and said that he had come to humbly petition for my help! You may imagine my surprise and humility when the Great One spoke of having had read my books and praised them as works of great scholarship. The dragon introduced himself as Xiang Lung. He told me a tale of the deaths of dozens of dragons, slaughtered for their bones, their flesh and for their pearls, which as you know contain both their wisdom and their Tao. He spoke of a sorcerer, who has power over dragons and kills them, not with gunpowder or

9

sword but through a little creature that eats their brains. They are powerless to defend themselves as his magic is more powerful than theirs. An evil warlord is at this sorcerer's side.

The magic of our Chinese Wizards was once powerful – they could level mountains, divide the waters and perform many wondrous acts. But there are few, if any, practitioners of magic left in my country in these days.

I am an old man and I am willing to help the dragons – indeed, it is my honor and my duty. But I cannot do it alone. I have no knowledge of magic or magicians. I therefore beg your help, Dr. Stillfield. Our correspondence and the reading of your books have taught me that you are a man of honor and devoted to dragons. And what is more, you have magic. To help the dragons of my country we need not only a knowledge of dragons but a man schooled in magic as well.

It is not only the honorable dragons we would be helping – it is my country – for our dragons control the rains and the floods and fire. Some of the worst floods in the history of my country were caused by dragons being angered by a mortal. They can also cause earthquakes that devastate the countryside and the cities, causing death, famine and plagues. And the dragons that remain are angry indeed. I do not know what will happen if the dragons were to become uncontrollably enraged or, what might be even worse, disappear forever.

I humbly beg your help before the dragons are all destroyed, or they become so angered that they devastate my country.

Your humble servant, Quong Lee

Séafra's green eyes had widened in surprise as he listened to this letter. He was a short, stocky young man who looked a great deal like a leprechaun, with bright red curls and a snub-nosed face. He was silent for a moment and then said "*Go n-éirí do thuras leat!*"

"You think I shall go then?" Simon said, for Séafra had said in Gaelic "May your trip succeed with you!'"

Séafra spread his hands. "I am thinking that you are having no choice – his letter is being a cry for help. And there is being no Dracophilogue who could be standing by when dragons are in mortal peril."

10

Simon looked at the letter again and read the very bottom line , "This letter has been more than a year coming here! He has dated it Western style – April, 1833."

Simon sat back in his chair and ran his hands through his pale fine hair. He looked very young to be a full professor at University – he was thirty-two but was mistaken for an undergraduate more often than not. "I daresay I will have to go," he mused, on a sigh. "My wife is not going to be happy about this, though. She was rather glad when the Royal Society postponed the trip to China we had been planning for so long."

That had been a severe disappointment. A group of noted Dracophilologists, geographers, and cartographers from the Six Nations, some Americans and the Swedish Dracophilogue Dr. Swensen, had planned a trip to China in the coming year – and Séafra had hoped to go as well. But the trip had been postponed indefinitely, due to the illness of the head of the Royal Society, Dr. Schofield, funding problems and the recommendation by the Foreign Office that conditions were too unsettled in the Far East to guarantee the safety of the participants in the study group.

"And ye've the wee one, too," said Séafra sympathetically.

"Yes – she would not want to leave Alan – he's only a year old – a year old in April. He was born probably at about the time this letter was written," said Simon. "He's a precocious child – he began talking and walking early and he talks in complete sentences and asks intelligent questions – and I can already see his aura, Séafra! It's already tinged with violet! He is going to be a very powerful Wizard!"

Séafra looked impressed. A child's aura did not usually manifest itself until he or she was six or so – then it told a trained eye – an eye with magical Othersight – if the child was magical or not and to what degree he or she would be magical. Magical persons had a blue – to violet range of colour, while those having the talent for magical Healing shone green. Non-magical persons were varying colours of yellow. Orange indicated sickness – either mental or physical, while no one ever wished to see a person with a red or a black aura – for red indicated blood magic, the power gathered by feeding on pain, terror and death, while black was evil incarnate.

"Would that be because Mrs. Stillfield is being a Russian lady and her magic is being different from ours?" Séafra suggested.

Simon shook his head. "I am not certain – we know so little about how and why my wife is magical – for one thing, she's immune to Cold Iron!"

Séafra gave a low whistle. That was indeed an advantage. All Wizards and Witches in the Six Nations, those of the Old Blood, the intermingled Celtic blood with that of the *Sidhe* and the *Tuatha de Danann,* had to avoid this 'death metal' as a non-magical person would avoid poison.

"But Alan is far and away too little to be taken to China, and I know that Tatya will not like to leave him, to go with me," Simon continued "But Tatya will be very unhappy when I tell her that I must needs go halfway around the world."

"Go to China?" repeated Tatiana Stillfield blankly, looking at her husband as if he had suddenly grown two heads. "But I thought that the Royal Society had cancelled the trip until further notice!"

They were seated in the tiny drawing room of the house they were renting in Dublin, near the University. Early in the spring Simon had purchased a sizable piece of land to the south of Dublin and they were even now building a house there. They hoped to have it ready by the autumn.

Tatya Stillfield was from Russia and was a Countess in her own right – the Countess Tatiana Ivanova Kustodieva – and she and Simon had met in St Petersburg three years earlier when Simon had been importuned by the Czar to rescue Russia from a necromancer. She was a slight young woman with gold-brown hair worn in a coronet of braids and had slanted amber eyes. Simon loved her dearly but he did not like the look she now wore – one of mingled anger and reproach. "Why do YOU have to go to China?" she demanded. "Let someone else go – someone who is not in the midst of building a new home and has a wife and a baby! And what about your duties at the University?"

"Listen to Dr. Quong Lee's letter, Tatya," he said coaxingly. "He needs my help – and I cannot in good conscience refuse it," Simon pulled the letter from the breast pocket of his jacket and read it to her.

After hearing the letter she was somewhat mollified, but still said, "I don't see why it always has to be you, Simon! I don't know how Alan and I shall go on without you!" Her eyes filled with tears. "How long will you be gone?"

"I don't know, *mo mhile grá*," he said. "Do you think that I want to be separated from you and Alan, for even a day? But there are some things that have to be done and I think this is one of them. Listen, my heart, I have already spoken to my father – he wants you and Alan and Sacha to come stay with them at Amberwell while I am gone. My mother will love having you and the boys with them and I know that my sisters will love having you as well. Stuart will be home from Edinburgh for the summer – you shan't lack for company – it will keep you from missing me too much."

She wanted to tell him that nothing would keep her from missing him too much . Even his parents and siblings and her own young brother Sacha who lived with her and Simon – all of whom she loved dearly and knew that they loved her – could keep her from longing for him every minute. She could only look at him with her heart in her eyes.

It was a very long night for Tatya. In bed, she had clung to Simon as if she never wanted to let him go. He had said that he hoped to leave within the next fortnight. Trinity Term was about to end – Séafra was more than capable of seeing to the very little that had to be done at the end of the term and the beginning of the Long Vacation.

Of course Simon would be traveling dragon-back. That was the one thing that somewhat relieved Tatya's mind – Lakota, Simon's dragon companion, would look after him. Simon would get to China and return much faster on a dragon than if he had to take ship. And dragon-back was safer as well. Simon had spoken to Lakota about the trip and the dragon was already planning their route.

The next morning, after Simon left for University, Tatya used the scry bowl to talk to her in-laws out at Amberwell and asked if she might come and visit her mother–in-law that day. She was eagerly invited and Lady Diana told her that she would send Lakota to Dublin to fly Tatya out to the estate in the countryside. If it had been a Monday, a Wednesday or a Friday Tatya would have seen her mother-in-law at the charity Sewing Circle to which they both belonged, but on a Thursday, as today, she would have had to wait another day and she simply had to talk to someone now.

Since they lived in the middle of Dublin in a small house that had no stabling or dragon pen, Lakota had to stay out at Amberwell. He was as eager as were Simon and Tatya for the new house to be built so that he could be near 'his' family all of the time.

Less than a half hour after she had scryed Amberwell Tatya, watching in the drawing room window, saw Lakota land in the street outside. The city had been planned years ago for dragon traffic and almost all of the streets were broad enough for even a forty-foot Highland Dhu to land.

Lakota, an American Opal, was twenty-five feet long and a beautiful blue in colour, with his scales, horns and back ridges edged in opal. Tatya had been afraid of him when first they met in St. Petersburg, for dragons were then unknown to her, but she had come to both love and trust him.

Alan would stay behind today, with Nanny Pender, so Tatya took up her Elfin cloak, which she had laid on a chair and went outside to where Lakota waited.

"Hello, Tatya!" said Lakota, when she went up to him. "I am glad you are coming out to Amberwell as I wanted to talk to you about this trip to China." Lakota was now nearly eight years old and was maturing rapidly. When she had first met him he had been rather naïve and child-like, being only five years old at that time, but now Tatya was astonished at how much older he seemed each time they met.

"Oh?" she said, as he crouched low and held out a foreleg for her to climb on. Once she was settled in the saddle he waited until she had done the safety check of the harness and strapped herself in and said "I think you should go with

14

us – you and Alan. It isn't right that you stay here by yourselves – our family should be together. I thought about this all of last night and I am going to tell Simon so. I know that Alan is little but I can take care of all of you! And I daresay that Lady Diana will tell you the same! Is that what you are going to talk to her about?"

"No," she said hesitantly. She had wanted to talk to Lady Diana about how she felt at being left alone.

"Well, you should talk to her about it!" declared Lakota, and then asked if she was settled. When she said yes, he launched himself in to the air and spiraled up until Dublin was a miniature city beneath them.

"I don't know why we don't listen more often to our dragons!" said Lady Diana Delamar thoughtfully. "They have a way of seeing right to the heart of a matter."

Tatya stared at her mother-in-law. Lady Diana was actually Simon's stepmother; her first husband, Captain Jonathan Stillfield. Simon's father, had died during the war with Napoleon. When Diana had married again, to René Delamar, the Marquis of Keir, they had adopted Simon. He never thought of them as anything other than his 'real' parents. And Tatya considered the couple quite the best in-laws she could have ever had.

"You think I should go with him, then?" she said. "But, *belle – mère,* how can I leave Alan?"

"Take him with you," said Diana promptly. She was a tall, lovely woman with curling dark hair and a pair of remarkably lovely violet eyes. When Tatya began to protest, she said "If Alan were a different sort of child I would not recommend it. But he is very intelligent, shows no tendency to get into trouble or wander away from you and has an understanding most unusual in a child of his age. And Lakota is right, you know, he can take care of you. Give Alan a dragon whistle – there is no better guardian than a dragon, after all. In fact, you should all have dragon whistles."

Tatya still looked doubtful. "Would it not be irresponsible of me to take my child on such a trip – so far away from his home?"

15

They had been drinking tea in the Blue drawing room at Amberwell and Diana now put down her delicate Minton cup painted with blue periwinkles.

"Tatya, let us suppose for a moment that Simon was offered a position at some Canadian or American University – an opportunity that was far too good to pass by – would you hesitate to take Alan there?"

"No –" Tatya began.

"Exactly!" Diana said before her daughter-in-law could protest. "And it would be a far more dangerous trip – since dragons cannot fly that far over water you would have to go on a dragon transport ship and suppose the position was far out in Canada, say in the territories? You would have to travel through virgin wilderness and perhaps face hostiles or dangerous animals. To go to China, as René was showing me on a map yester eve, you will be going to Scandinavia and then through Russia, where you and Simon have friends who will help you along. And China is a civilized country, not the uncharted wilderness! What could happen there that a dragon and a Wizard and a Witch could not handle?"

Tatya was to later remember those words and wonder if they had not been tempting fate.

2

Into the Orient

Tatya was surprised – Simon made very little objection to taking her and Alan with him to China. He merely ordered more supplies and bedding. Later, he admitted that the thought of a perhaps lengthy separation was nearly unendurable. In spite of what difficulties might lie ahead he was glad that his wife and son were to accompany him.

The most difficult thing to obtain would be the firestone necessary for Lakota to chew – firestone, which was calcium rich limestone, reacted with his dragon gases and fluids already in his body, to fill his flight cavities with hydrogen and allow him to become airborne. Lakota could only carry so much firestone at a time. Arrangements would have to be made to get firestone frequently. This would not be a problem in their journey across Russia, for Simon had the favor of Czar Nicholas and the firm friendship of his newly appointed Court Wizard, Anatoly Tcherepin. Once they reached China there might be a difficulty, as very little was known about the geography or mineral distribution of this far-off land. What books Simon had been able to find were old and very out of date. The maps were more than likely inaccurate. Therefore they meant to first fly to Canton, to the unofficial Legation of the British Isles and hope to find more current information.

A visit to the Foreign Office in London yielded a letter of introduction to Sir Perceval Barrington-Smythe, the current Consul General, who could further guide them. The FO was far from keen on Simon visiting the Far East – they considered the situation there unstable – for there was much unrest in the area, but they, of course, would not dream of withholding a passport from the adopted grandson of the Duke of Chenevix – a very powerful man, and currently Minister of Magic, and very high in King William IV's favor.

Also accompanying Simon and his family would be their familiars – Janus and Marinka. All Witches and

Wizards possessed familiars – Janus, a black and orange and white cat had been with Simon since he was eight but Tatya, having come late to Witchcraft, had only recently acquired a familiar. Marinka, an orange tabby, was one of Janus's kittens – her father was Vron, a black Tom who was not of familiar stock and had come from Russia with Tatya. Vron was nearly fifteen, which was elderly for a non-familiar cat, and he chose to stay behind rather than undergo the rigors of traveling. He would stay with Simon's parents at Amberwell, where Simon's sister Holly promised to take good care of him.

It took almost exactly a fortnight to gather their supplies, make their plans and say their good-byes. Simon was all impatience to begin the trip – for it was always on his mind that Dr. Quong's missive had been written over a year ago and he did not like to think that the Chinese Dracophilogue might be feeling as if his cry for help had been ignored. Unfortunately there was as yet no reliable way, even magical, that could connect one side of the world to another.

Only since 1811 had it become possible to use a scry bowl over water. The scry bowl was magically charged, purified water that allowed Witches and Wizards to talk over distances and both see and hear one another .This still could not be accomplished over vast distances – to America, for instance, or to Russia. The use of scry bowls was quite common in the British Isles. Even non-magical persons could use them in the many public scry rooms or even in most Inns where each bowl was manned by a *Magus Majori*. It seemed odd, as it had whilst in Russia, to go to a place that had no rapid communication. Other countries and far flung British Isles outposts had still to depend on the Post. The government was currently in negotiations with Russia to allow the hippogriffe express service to fly through Russian territory, This would speed the process of news from the Far East considerably. But for now, Simon would probably reach China before a letter could get halfway there.

Lakota had chosen much the same route that he and Simon had used to get to Russia three years earlier – from Dublin to the Isle of Man, from there to John O' Groats in

Scotland and from there across the wide expanse of the North Sea to Bergen in Norway. They spent one night there and then flew across Scandinavia to Uppsala in Sweden, where the Swedish Dracophilologist, Dr. Lars Swensen, welcomed them. He was most envious of the trip and was insistent that they stop on the way back and acquaint him with all that they had seen.

They spent one night in St Petersburg as well, as the guests of Anatoly Tcherepin and his wife Marushka, the Firebird. Anatoly took them to a private audience with the Czar, who presented them with a safe conduct and a map indicating all of the places that arrangements had been made to obtain firestone. Inquiries had been made amongst the many Chinese merchants in St, Petersburg and Simon and Tatya were gratified to have a list of likely places to obtain firestone – however they were cautioned that it would be best to obtain government permission first. All of the Chinese agreed that it was wisest for the party to first go to Canton as planned.

It was a hot day in June when at last they arrived in Canton. The trip throughout Russia had been uneventful, for Czar Nicholas' vast organization had been used to their greatest advantage. The finest quality firestone and other supplies had been ready at each stop and hospitality had been generous as well.

Alan had behaved beautifully. He was immensely curious as to everything he saw and asked dozens of questions. He adored riding dragon-back and rode, facing outwards in a special sling worn by either Simon or Tatya. Happy laughter was much more frequent than tears and tantrums. Diana had taught Tatya a very useful spell called "Sleep, Baby, Sleep" that could be used to give Alan a nap, sweetly and safely, if he became overtired or fretful.

Lakota had decided to follow the coastline of China down to the South China Sea and then up the Pearl River ninety miles to Canton. He ate as much firestone as he could in their last Russian stop of Vladivostock, a busy port on the Sea of Japan, and Simon loaded several heavy bags of the stone on the rear of Lakota's six person saddle. Tatya and Alan were in the first seat with Simon behind them and the familiars were in a comfortable traveling basket that had been made by Elves and was magiced against any weather and for their security.

Simon was hoping that this firestone would be sufficient until they had official government permission for Lakota to eat Chinese firestone. Lakota informed his passengers that he was going to fly down the coast at top speed, so that he would not run out of dragon gasses before they reached their destination. The old map that they possessed had indeed proved unreliable. The land itself was a far better guidepost.

Accordingly, his riders prepared themselves – all wore insulated flying suits – even Alan – with caps and eye-protecting spectacles that could be pulled down. They crouched low in the saddle, bent over Lakota's back as the dragon took to the air and spiraled upwards.

Hot summer weather was perfect for thermals – the air cells that a dragon could ride in, soaring much as would a gull or a hawk. But as Lakota wanted to make time, he would use his great wings to thrust them along, rather than glide. It was more fatiguing, but he would use less firestone for the action of his wings would be keeping him aloft.

Afterwards, Simon had no idea how far or how fast they had flown. The water and coastline below Lakota went by at a fantastic rate, all blurred, even the enormous shadow of the blue dragon. Simon had meant to look at his watch before they started so that he could gain some idea of Lakota's speed but he had forgotten to do so. And with the cold wind roaring around them he could not even reach into his pocket and withdraw his watch. He had to concentrate on holding tight to Tatya and Alan.

At long last Lakota slowed and began to glide. They were still over the ocean, but Lakota turned to the north and looking down, shortly afterwards, Simon could see a great river estuary beneath them.

In very little time they had followed the river to where a bustling city of narrow, twisting streets and old buildings lay on the north bank of the river. Four miles off a mountain

20

sheltered the city. This, Simon and Tatya later learned was *Pai Yün Shan,* or White Cloud Mountain.

There was no place for Lakota to land in the streets but thankfully the British Isles Legation had a large flat roof suitable for a dragon, as they regularly received hippogriffe traffic from India. Lakota found the Legation by the simple expediency of looking for the red white and blue flag that incorporated the crosses of St. George, St. Andrew and St. David and had, in a shield in the middle, the Harp of Ireland, the seahorse of Man and the pilchard of Cornwall.

Someone had seen then coming, for as Lakota spiraled down to the roof Simon could see a welcoming committee of one. The Legation would have had no idea that they were coming as they had come faster than any message.

A young man stepped forward as Lakota landed – he was obviously well-used to dragons for he came up to Lakota without hesitation and answered Lakota's greeting in a friendly fashion. "Welcome to the British Isles Legation," he said and put his hand up to help Tatya down as Lakota crouched low. Simon followed close on her heels.

"I am Ashton Pendleton, secretary to Sir Perceval Barrington-Smythe," he informed them. "And you are, sir?"

Simon introduced himself and his party. As he spoke with Mr. Pendleton several more people came up the stairs that led to the roof. Among them were several Chinese servants. At the sight of Lakota they stopped and stared and then feel to their knees, bowing and doing homage. One man, more daring than the others, took a good long look at Lakota and then gasped " *T'ein lung! T'ein lung!*" With this the bowing became even more humble and obsequious, the Chinese prostrating themselves before Lakota.

"What are they doing?" said Lakota, puzzled. "Haven't they ever seen a dragon before?"

"Probably not," replied Mr. Pendleton. "For the last hundred years or so there have been very few dragons seen here in China. Indeed, many Chinese people believe that dragons no longer exist. But these people are peasants – they cling to the old beliefs. And they are excited because you have five toes – the mark of a Celestial dragon – the guardians of the Heavens. It is considered extreme good fortune to see a Celestial dragon."

"A Celestial Dragon – that was the type that came to see Dr, Quong!" said Tatya. Simon had begun to unharness Lakota and took the cat basket from the saddle. Janus and Marinka came out when he magiced it open and looked about them with interest.

"Do you mean Dr. Quong Lee, the Dracophilologist?" said Mr. Pendleton quickly.

"Yes," said Simon. "he is a colleague of mine – I am a doctor of Dracophilology as well," he added in explanation. "We have had a correspondence for years."

"I had better take you to see Sir Perceval," said Mr. Pendleton. "And I am certain that you will want a bath and a cool drink – those flying suits must be hot," he added sympathetically.

Even here on the roof the heat and humidity were stifling. Canton had but three seasons – winter, from October to early February, during which the temperature seldom fell below 50°, then a period of transition – February through April – followed, marked by muggy weather and then a hot humid summer. Typhoons were frequent, borne by a south or southwest wind. – none of these seasons were cool by Irish standards. Mr. Pendleton wore a white linen jacket and duck trousers rather than the more formal black wool one would expect to see in a Government House. "This climate calls for tropical kit," he explained as he led them to the stairs. "Sir Perceval feels that dressing for the weather will keep us healthy – and he seems to be correct – the members of this Legation have suffered little illness."

Simon asked for, and received the assurance that Lakota would be fed and given a long draught of fresh water. He promised Lakota to return later and give him a rinse and an oil bath.

An hour later, bathed and refreshed, Simon and Tatya joined Sir Perceval and Lady Barrington –Smythe and Mr. Pendleton on a shaded balcony overlooking the harbor. There was scarcely an inch of water visible in the harbor, so dense were the ships – Simon even saw flags of the countries of the Inquisition – France, Italy, Portugal Spain – and those of

Eastern Europe as well, various German states, the Americas and, of course, the British Isles. It was an international blend of masts and flags and ships of all types – all here for one reason – the rich China trade.

Sir Perceval was a man of late middle years, getting stout and bald, with grey hair and a pair of immense side-whiskers. He was genial, but quite shrewd and seemed to have a good grasp of the current situation in the Far East.

"There is a great deal of unrest, Professor Stillfield," he told Simon as they sat beneath and awning and sipped iced drinks. The ice, from the mountains of Nepal, had arrived that morning, along with the post from India. "Many of the traders here are finding the restrictions imposed by the *cohongs* – the Chinese merchants who control the trading operations – irksome to say the least. In fact, this Legation has no real sanction to be here – the Chinese refuse to open normal diplomatic relations. Most of what I have accomplished here is due to the condescension of a powerful merchant, Zhang Bao. He's a clever old devil, but I would not trust him as far as I could throw him."

"Shall I have trouble getting permission to go into the countryside?" Simon asked. From behind the three men could be heard the softer voices of the two women, playing with Alan. Lady Barrington-Smythe a motherly sort of woman, found him irresistible – she missed her own grandchildren, now being educated in England.

Sir Perceval smiled. "It has all been arranged. I gather that Dr. Quong expected you to come – and someone very, very high up has cleared the way for you. We received permission for you and a party to travel to Sichuan Province where Dr, Quong lives, some six months ago. You will cause quite a stir with that dragon of yours – even now people are gathering in the streets hoping to catch a glimpse of him." His smile faded abruptly. "I gather, Professor, by the fact that you have familiars with you that you a Wizard. May I ask your ranking?""

"*Magus Magistra,*" said Simon. "I am also a fully robed Druid. My wife is a Witch."

"There have been rumors coming to us that there is a sorcerer at work in the mountains," said Sir Perceval. "I am no *magus,* so I do not know if even half the things I hear are so –"

"Most rumor is less than ten percent truth," put in Ashton Pendleton. "Stories grow in the telling."

"Dr. Quong mentioned a sorcerer in his last letter to me," said Simon.

"You may very well have need of every bit of your magic," Sir Perceval said gravely. "And that brings me to another matter. I have a favor I would ask of you, Professor."

"if it is in my power," Simon replied.

"First of all, I would like you to take young Ashton here with you. We would like to see dragons restored to their place of eminence in this country and think that Dr. Quong has the best chance of doing this. We are fully aware of the important role dragons play here. And I should like Ashton to be a sort of observer if you do not mind. He can be very useful – he is fluent in Chinese – in several dialects as a matter of fact."

Simon looked at the young man in question – he was tall and very dark with grey eyes that reminded Simon of his adopted grandfather Chenevix – but Ashton's eyes were full of eagerness, not haughtiness.

"I've a six person saddle on Lakota – there is no difficulty there – but we will need more supplies," Simon said slowly.

Sir Perceval waved his hand. "All will be provided. I am also afraid that I am going to have to ask to keep a eye out for a young fool of an Englishman. About six months ago the Honorable Reginald Faversham came here to Canton, trying to get permission to go into the interior. He had a wild story about a missing jade mine – claimed to have an old map –"

Simon groaned. "A treasure hunter?"

Sir Perceval pulled a face. "Yes – someone is always coming up with some idiotic story about a lost tomb or a mine or a fabulous city of gold or some such rot. Of course Faversham was not given permission but the idiot took off on his own and nothing has been heard of him since. And I have been getting communication after communication from his parents demanding that I do something and find their boy.

24

Fortunately the post is slow, else I think I should have a letter daily."

"Faversham," mused Simon. "The Earl of Hunley's family name. – is that who his father is?"

"Yes – you see my difficulty." Sir Perceval spread his hands in a gesture of helplessness. "A completely unreasonable man – Reginald is his second son but obviously the fair-haired boy of the family."

Ashton had fallen into a reverie and now, looking suddenly alert said "I've only just remembered – Faversham had a fellow with him – a hangdog sort of a chap – as a general *factotum* and dogsbody – by the name of Stillfield – Thomas Stillfield. Could he be any relation to you, Professor?"

3

Cousin Tom

It seemed a long time before Tatya and Simon could be alone together and she could ask him about Thomas Stillfield. First Simon had to attend to Lakota with the promised rinse and oil bath and then he cleaned the dragon tack as well. Dragons wore saddles and packs and most had a net of webbing attached to a breast band for carrying goods and luggage, but a bridle was unnecessary. Sir Perceval offered a servant to do this but Simon always saw to this his own self – particularly when they were traveling. It was critical that it be in tip top shape, for any weakness in the leathers or silver buckles could result in a terrible accident. It was also magiced to stay strong and protect it from rips and tears but the spells had to be renewed every once in a while.

After that was a lengthy dinner with the Barrington-Smythes and plans made for their departure in two days' time, with Mr. Pendleton, to the Sichuan Province where Dr. Quong made his home.

The summer twilight was fading fast when they were at last in the room assigned them, preparing for bed. Tatya was glad that she had packed their lightest summer-weight clothing and night things, for the air was sultry. She was not worried about sleeping comfortably, as Simon could cool the bed magically – indeed she was now far enough along in her Witchcraft studies to do it herself.

Simon had been very quiet the entire evening since Mr. Pendleton had asked him about Thomas Stillfield. From the description given, he had little doubt that it *was* his cousin. He never talked about his Stillfield relatives – in fact, Tatya had only learned of their existence from her mother-in-law, whose opinion of them was very low indeed.

She waited until she had put Alan to sleep in a cot provided by Lady Barrington-Smythe. The cats were at present sound asleep on the foot of the bed she would share with Simon. Once she and Simon were in bed, the two familiars would go and sleep with Alan, keeping him contented. If he awoke feeling ill or lonely they would tell his parents.

Simon had already got into bed and was laying back on the pillows looking thoughtful. Since there was no dressing table in the room Tatya took her brush and went to sit on the edge of the bed and began to brush out her hair.

"Are you certain that this Thomas Stillfield is your cousin?" she asked.

Simon sighed and looked at her rather ruefully. "It certainly sounds as if were Tom," he said. "The description fits – a 'great rough fellow,' Mr. Pendleton said, with brown hair and eyes. The only thing that does not fit is the hangdog air – the Tom I remember was a swaggering bully. But he would be nearly forty now – he was eight years older than I. Mr. Pendleton also remembered that this man mentioned he was from Norfolk – and that is where I was born and lived until I was eight – at Field Grange in Norfolkshire."

"You never mention your cousins," Tatya ventured. "And when we had our third wedding ceremony in Dublin they did not come."

Simon and Tatya had been married three times – once by Elves, then again in a Russian Orthodox ceremony, both in Russia, and once more in an Anglican ceremony in Dublin. Tatya felt well and truly married.

"Living with them is not a happy memory. My birth father, Jonathan Stillfield, left me with his parents when my mother died – shortly after I was born. He was a serving soldier in the Peninsular war – that is where he was killed. All I remember of that early time was being told to be very quiet – as my grandmother Maria was very ill. When I was nearly seven my uncle Frederick – he was the heir to the estate; my father was the second son and made the army his profession – came to live at Field Grange with my aunt Alice and their five boys. Tom was the eldest – he was sixteen, and then there was Dick, two years younger, Robert and John were twins – they were twelve and James was a year older than I. They were all sports-mad, never opened a book if they could help it and made my life a misery. They were always hiding my things, teasing me and hitting me. They were notorious for pranks and malicious mischief in the neighborhood as well. They were expelled from every school to which my uncle sent them."

"They sound horrible!" said Tatya. She too had suffered from unbearable relations. "Quite a bad as my cousins Evgeny, Nadya, and Olga!"

Simon smiled at her. "No one could be as bad as your cousin Evgeny, *mo mhile stór* – he tried to rape you more than once. But my cousins were more than willing for me to go and live with my stepmother when my grandmother became so ill that she must needs go in live in Bath to take the waters daily. However, that was the best thing that ever happened to me – I got what I had always wished for – a real family that loved me. Right from the start *they* were my *real* parents."

Tatya knew that he referred to René and Diana Delamar. "Did your Stillfield relations never try to get in touch with you – were they not curious as to how you went on – if you were happy?"

"I wrote to my grandparents in Bath for a while but I never had an answer. They raised no protest at all when the adoption was proposed and merely signed all the papers the Chenevix attorneys sent them. But then when I was nineteen I was left a very substantial legacy by a godmother I never even knew I had – and then we heard from them again. This lady, Roxanne Holbrook, was a childless widow. She had been a school friend of my birth mother's."

"What was your mother's name?" Tatya asked curiously.

"Elfrida Westhame – I am supposed to look very like her and it is probably from her that I got my magic – for the Stillfields have some remnants of the Old Blood, but no magic," said Simon.

"That name sounds Elfish," Tatya suggested.

"I have always meant to see if Oberon's genealogists know anything about her. The Christian name Elfrida usually is associated with those who have Elfin blood and a 'hame' is what the Elves call their domains, such as Hillhame in the Cotswolds."

"You said that you heard from them again when you were nineteen?" Tatya prompted. "Were your grandparents still alive?"

Simon's mouth twisted wryly. "No, but my uncle Frederick showed up when he learned of the bequest. He said that he was my natural guardian and should have charge of the money as I was still underage. My godmother failed to name a guardian, you see. But legally, the Delamars were my natural guardians as they had adopted me as their son. It was quite nasty for a while until Papa turned the whole mess over to Grandfather Chenevix's attorneys and they sent Uncle Frederick to the rightabout. I have no doubt that Uncle Frederick and my awful aunt Alice just wanted the money – they cared naught for me. I have heard nothing from them since. And I am not happy to hear that Tom is here – and probably in trouble. I wonder why he is acting as a dogsbody to this Faversham? He was the heir and the Grange was a prosperous estate."

"But your aunt and uncle wanted your inheritance – perhaps they were having money troubles?" Tatya suggested.

"They were the type of people who never had enough – with one eye always to the main chance, particularly Aunt Alice" He gave a long sigh. "I really hope that we do not come across them. Faversham sounds a perfect fool and unless Tom has radically improved I have no desire at all for his company."

Tatya lay her brush on the bedside table and slid into bed beside him. The sheets were blissfully cool. "The important thing is to help Dr. Quong with the dragon problem," she said soothingly as his arm came around her. She heard the two familiars jump off the end of the bed and move across the room as Simon doused the mage light that hung above the bed. "With any luck we shan't even see your horrid cousin at all."

Simon and Tatya were awakened abruptly, early the next morning to find Janus prodding them with an impatient paw. "You had better get up now," she said . "We seem to have a situation here."

"What o'clock is it?" Simon said on a yawn. It was not very light as yet – or perhaps it was a dark day, with heavy rain clouds blocking the sun.

"Not yet five," said Janus. "Listen!"

As Simon sat up in bed he could hear sounds coming from out of doors through the open door on the balcony. Beside him Tatya stirred drowsily and said "What is that noise?"

"It's people – the streets around the Legation are full of people – some of them have been here all night!" said Janus. "Marinka and I have been out on the balcony since about 2 AM, listening to them."

"What are they saying?" Simon frowned in concentration, for he could now hear what almost amounted to a roar – one phrase being repeated over and over.

"*T'ein lung*," said Janus "They are all come here to see Lakota, Simon!"

"Good grief!" said Simon with feeling. "Have you spoken to Lakota?" He threw aside the single sheet hat covered them.

"Yes – he's rather upset – he doesn't know what to do," Janus said. "He says he can't understand why they are so excited – he isn't even a Chinese dragon. He wants to talk to you very badly, Simon. I promised that I would send you as soon as possible."

Tatya was now fully awake. "Poor Lakota!" she said sympathetically. "You'd best go to him right away, Simon."

"Alan's waking up, too," said Marinka from near the cot. "I think the noise is bothering him." It was becoming noisier by the moment. As the sun began to rise, more and more people seemed to be arriving.

Simon quickly pulled on trousers and a shirt as Tatya got from bed and went to tend to Alan. The little boy's face was puckered up as if he was going to cry and as Tatya approached he sat up and held out his arms. "Mama! It's loud!" he said clearly. "I don't like it!"

Tatya picked him up and held him close just as a knock came on the door.

"Professor – I'm sorry to disturb you and your wife," came the voice of Ashton Pendleton. "But we're being overrun –"

Simon threw open the door. Pendleton had obviously dressed as hastily as had he, for he wore no jacket, waistcoat or cravat and had not shaved or laid comb to his hair.

"The streets are full of people –" Pendleton began.

"Yes, all come to see the *t'ein lung!*" Simon interrupted. "So my familiar informs me – she says many of them have been there all night."

"It's getting worse by the moment!" said Pendleton worriedly. "Would your dragon mind showing himself to them do you think? Seeing a *t'ein lung* is such good luck – I think, as does Sir Perceval, that if they could all get a good look at him they might be satisfied and go away. We are a little afraid of a riot."

"I shall ask Lakota – Janus says that he wants to see me urgently," said Simon putting on his shoes without bothering with stockings. He followed Pendleton out of the room and went up two flights of stairs to the roof at a run.

Lakota was huddled in the middle of the roof, crouched as low as he could, with his wings tucked tight around him. His head was down and his ruff drooped – a sure sign of an unhappy dragon. He raised his head slightly as the door opened and he said in some relief. "Simon! Oh, I an so glad you are come! What do they all want?"

"They just want to see you," said Pendleton. "As I told you, most of these people have never seen a dragon and the news of your arrival seems to have spread very quickly. We never have dragon traffic here – hippogriffes bring the mail and packages. Hippogriffes do not have the meaning to the Chinese that dragons do."

"But, Mr. Pendleton," Lakota began,

"My friends call me Ash," he said.

"Ash, then. I am not a Chinese dragon – how can I be lucky for them to see?" Lakota said, puzzled.

"I don't know – but they seem to think it is a great honor and privilege to see you," answered Ash.

"What should I do, Simon?" Lakota asked. "Do you think it is right for me to show myself even if I am not a Chinese dragon?"

"I think that it can do no harm, Lakota," said Simon. "Remember when you first came to Dublin how everyone wanted to see you because no one had ever seen an American Opal before? Just think about that – these people are curious and happen to think you one of their Celestial dragons."

"It's just that I don't want anyone to think that they will have good luck from looking at me," Lakota said apologetically. "I would hate to be responsible for someone expecting good luck and not having it."

"You're very conscientious," remarked Ash, "but think of it this way – does a rabbit worry that its foot might bring good luck to people – does the black cat think about it being good luck for it to cross someone's path?"

In the British Isles it was considered very good luck indeed to have a black cat – a true Wizard's cat like Merlin's familiar Pyewacket – to cross one's path. Only in the countries of the Inquisition was a black cat bad luck.

Lakota looked doubtful but when Simon said "Lakota, these people are not going to leave – they are getting very demanding – they might storm the Legation."

The blue dragon was horrified and said "Then you might all be in danger! Oh, no – I cannot let that happen! I will let them see me." He rose to his feet and said "Where should I go?"

It was decided that he should go to the four edges of the roof and show himself in each direction. People surrounded the building on nearly every side.

Lakota walked to the western side of the building and stood there, looking down. Excited screams rose from the street. To Lakota's amazement people were packed against each other, looking up – some holding small children aloft so that they might see. And always they repeated, *"T'ein lung! T'ein lung!"*

Lakota stood on his hind legs and spread his wings, Remembering what he had been told he spread his talons as well so that they could see that he had five toes. The people became almost hysterical with joy and were only silenced when Lakota let out a great bellow which rattled the windows in nearby buildings. He repeated this performance on each direction of the roof and then took off into the sky, flying low over the city. He had just enough gasses left to give out a spurt of flame, which caused gasps of awe from the Chinese on the ground.

"I think," said Ash to Simon , as they stood on the roof watching Lakota in the sky, "we had best leave today. Word of his being here will spread rapidly and the Legation will be besieged."

"We can be ready in two hours," said Simon. He hoped fervently that out in the rural areas Lakota would cause less of a furor. But Canton was the largest city in China and the surrounding areas were heavily populated as well. Given Lakota's reception it began to seem more and more imperative that dragons be restored to China and be once more a part of ordinary life.

4
The Valley of the Yellow Dragon

The "August Personage" – as Sir Perceval called whomever had made it easy for Simon's party to travel into the interior – had supplied directions and several very fine maps. These were in a large portfolio that had been left at the Legation, addressed to Simon. The hand was not Dr. Quong's, for it was obvious that whoever wrote out the directions and labeled the package was not used to writing in Occidental script; there were numerous mistakes – and the maps were completely in Chinese.

Simon and Ash took the maps up onto the roof for Lakota to peruse. As Simon rolled them out and anchored them with several paperweights borrowed from various desks, Ash said apologetically. "I am afraid that although I speak Chinese fairly fluently I cannot as yet read it very well – I shall be of little use in translating the map legends."

"I can read Chinese," Lakota assured him.

"You can?" asked Ash. "Is that something all dragons can do?"

"Oh, no – but Simon and I began studying Chinese four years ago when we thought that the Royal Society would be going on our journey. All of the dragons who were planning to be going studied Chinese." He did not add that since he and Simon had been given the gift of total fluency in the Russian language by Oberon, the High King of the *Sidhe*, that they found any language now came easily to them. Simon had been tutoring Tatya in Chinese as well each evening since they had decided to go to China, and since she too, had been given fluency in language by the High King – in her case English and Gaelic – she was rapidly becoming fluent as well.

"Sichuan, where Dr. Quong lives, is in southwestern China," said Lakota thoughtfully. "I can make almost a straight flight from here in Canton. According to these

34

directions, he lives in the Huang Lung Zhi – that means Yellow Dragon Valley!" he added happily.

"Yellow Dragon Valley is in the southern Min Shan mountain range of northeastern Sichuan Province," said Simon, leaning in by Lakota and studying the map as well and showing that he too, could read Chinese.

"Yes, about 150 miles from Chengdu," agreed Lakota. He could swiftly estimate the exact distance on a map without recourse to measurements. "I could make it in one day, Simon, but I think that it would be better, especially for Tatya and Alan, if we fly a comfortable distance today and get there tomorrow."

Ash had been looking at the portfolio that contained the map and directions and had found two more items in it. "I think whoever wrote these had no idea that you would be flying on a dragon," he remarked. "Here is a list, thankfully in English, of where you might obtain pack and riding horses between Canton and the Huang Lung Valley, as well as the names, I think, of reliable guides. And this was in a corner of the portfolio as well." He held out a little object on the palm of his hand.

It was a small, exquisitely carved Chinese dragon of green jade, complete in every detail. It had a ring affixed to its back so that it might be worn as an ornament.

"What is that?" Simon asked curiously.

"A sign of Imperial favor – your safe conduct through China," said Ash dryly. "Someone very high up indeed wants you to help Dr. Quong! The Jade Dragon may only be used by the Son of Heaven – the Emperor – or Sons of the Dragon Throne – the Princes – and by those who have their favor. Show that anywhere in China and you will be treated like royalty – and woe betide anyone who does not treat you so!" He handed the beautiful little thing to Simon and advised him to wear it on a thong around his neck. "We'd best go and have some money changed," he suggested while Lakota continued to peruse the map

Tatya was busy packing while the familiars were watching Alan – otherwise she would have loved to accompany them. She had tried to see as much of Canton from the balcony in their room as was possible. Simon knew that she was a little disappointed that they had to leave

Canton so quickly – Lady Barrington- Smythe had offered to take her shopping and to sightsee.

They had both been intrigued by the architecture of the buildings of the city – with their overhanging bracketed eaves and tile roofs. Unfortunately "foreign devils", or *fan-qui* such as themselves, were not allowed into the city proper – they were obliged to keep within the 'factories' of their country. But her ladyship had explained that many merchants had set up shop within the environs of the factories, for foreign devils spent freely and this opportunity was too good to miss. One could obtain exquisitely embroidered silks, porcelains, items of jade and semi-precious stone, all sorts of metal goods, jewelry and even trade goods from other Eastern nations such as India, Burma and Siam.

Ash took Simon to a courtyard where money was exchanged. They approached an old man sitting at a table in front of piles of money and an abacus. He also had a scale and weights in front of him. Ash had explained to Simon that in China gold and silver was only used in weighed amounts. Traditional coins with holes in the middle for ease in storing on a string, were made of bronze. New to use were *yuna* , silver coins which had evolved from the silver dollars used by European and American traders. Ash advised Simon to change some of his English gold guineas for both the bronze coins and the silver dollars.

Simon also had a letter of credit from the Duke of Chenevix, which he lodged with a very small branch of Barclay's bank in the British factory. The casher's eyes bulged when he saw the amount of the line of credit. The Duke had given Simon the same on his journey to Russia – Simon had not needed it – he had taken plenty of his own money – but far from home it was good to have this credit to fall back on should it be needed.

The money changer was an elderly man with a wispy, grey beard and a face lost in a thousand wrinkles. He wore a round pill-box hat and a long grey braid hung down his back He wore a black robe over white Chinese trousers and soft black shoes. Although gnarled with age his fingers were nimble on the beads of the abacus and he soon had exchanged a fair amount of the coins in Simon's money belt for bronze and silver coins and several gold bars.

"That's a heavy load," Ash remarked as they headed back to the Legation.

"I shall give most of it to Lakota to carry," Simon said. "A dragon is even safer than a bank! No one would dare to steal from a dragon and they are zealous guardians of any sort of money. He will even keep track of our spending if I ask him to. He'll keep your money belt as well if you like."

Ashton agreed to this at once. He had not relished the thought of wearing a heavy money belt in the summer weather. Since they would be going further north it might not be as hot but it was summer time and was bound to be warm – if not hot and humid.

They made one more stop in the factory marketplace – Simon bought a silver chain for the tiny jade dragon. It had been in his waist coat pocket and he threaded it onto the chain, which he then put it around his neck and tucked it into his waistcoat. He also bespelled it so that if he lost it, it would return to him.

When they returned they found that Tatya was all packed and Lakota was ready to go. Tatya had secured the help of several of the servants who were thrilled and honored to be so near to the *t'ein lung* and had helped her saddle him and stow the luggage. The servant assigned to Ash had brought his cases from his room and put them in Lakota's breast harness. The two familiars were already in their traveling basket and Alan was asleep on Tatya's breast in his special carrier.

After giving Lakota the money belts for safe keeping, Simon did the safety check of the harness, and then they climbed into the saddle to a chorus of goodbyes from Sir Perceval and his lady, other members of the Legation staff and many curious servants.

Lakota sprang into the sky. He was glad to be off – there were still people in the streets about the Legation and he had been obliged to show himself twice more. He had been used to people and other dragons in Dublin being curious about him – there were no dragon breeds in the Six Nations that were blue and the opal tips on his scales and horns were unique as well. He also earned money by being Simon's teaching assistant at University. He allowed students to examine him and answered their questions about dragon physiology and flight. He had never minded that. But the adulation and worship of these people made him uncomfortable. He hoped that in the remote rural area to which they were going that people would be more sensible – or that at the very least there would be less of them to gape and prostate themselves in front of him. Such behavior was embarrassing.

Lakota was planning to go high and relatively fast. He would glide in a thermal whenever he could. The little jade dragon emblem guaranteed them, Ash said, access to whatever they needed, so that firestone should be no problem.

Flying fast and high did not allow them to see much of the countryside, however – but Simon agreed with Lakota. The blue dragon had created such a sensation in Canton that he worried about disturbing the countryside.

Since Ash did not have a flying suit and there had been no time to have one made up they all wore the Elfin cloaks given to Simon by Oberon three years earlier, which were light and warm and fit anyone who wore one of them.

Simon had never clocked Lakota – not even the dragon knew how really fast he could fly – but they were over halfway to their goal when they decided to stop for the night. They had stopped twice for meals and short rest and relief stops – in remote areas – and at last put down in a private, slightly wooded area near a good-sized lake. Lakota estimated that if they started at dawn it would prove an easy flight to the Huang Lung Valley and they would be with Dr. Quong before noon.

And so it proved. Lakota flew lower as they neared their destination and they were all struck by the beauty of the Sichuan Basin – a rich agricultural area of fruit trees, and terraced paddies, rich with the green-gold of ripening rice.

Since they left the Chengdu Plain the landscape had become steadily more mountainous. Lakota glided lower, looking for the landmarks indicated on a smaller map that would enable him to find Dr. Quong's dwelling place. At the slow speed he was flying now he could turn his neck and talk to his passengers.

"There's the entrance to Huang Lung!" he called out excitedly. In a landscape dark green with pointed firs and strange rock formations, stood three old trees, bereft of bark, reaching out thick arms to one another, looking like some of the stone monuments they had seem. Twisted bare branches seemed to supplicate the heavens. Lakota swept past, gasping in awe as the beauties of the landscape struck him. His passengers, too were spellbound.

Some of the mountains were still topped with snow and their slopes were rich with green. There were myriad pools of many colours – some even shone gold in the sunlight. They saw cascading waterfalls and strange, corrugated rock formations caused by the action of the snow melt.

Dr. Quong's house was marked as being on the valley floor, a ways from the nearest village and Lakota found it easily. It was a fair-sized dwelling. A main hall was situated to the north of a central north-south axis, and faced south. The door was in this southern wall, and had banks of windows surrounded in lattice work and covered with translucent paper and carved panels.

Ash, who knew something of Chinese architecture and custom, at once gathered that Dr. Quong was someone of importance, for from the air he could see several courtyards and side buildings, including a very large garden with space for a dragon of Lakota's size or even larger. The house was exceedingly harmonious in plan and execution. The platform of beaten bricks upon which it was built was white, the columns and walls red, while the beams and brackets of the roof were blue. The roof was the curved style so prevalent and was of green tile.

No one was about save a small child playing with a kitten in front of the house. As Lakota spiraled down and landed in the road near the house she looked up and gasped. She gathered up the kitten hastily and ran into he house shrieking " *Yeh Yeh*!! *Lung! Lung!*"

39

Lakota had scarcely landed when the door opened and several people ran out. Most of them wore expressions ranging from amazement to outright fear. Only one, an elderly man dressed in quiet, conservative, but very elegant robes, came forward. He was about sixty-five years old, perhaps more, with a long, thin mustache and very wise dark eyes. He wore a skullcap over graying hair that was still thick, bound in the Chinese queue. He took one look at Lakota and his face lit up. He bowed deeply and said in excellent English "Dr. Stillfield? My humble home and family is honored beyond measure that you and this noble dragon are come to help us."

"The honor is ours," said Lakota, and bowed in return before Simon could utter a word.

5

Likenesses and Differences

Dr. Quong stared at Lakota as if he could not get enough of him. The elderly Chinese Dracophilologist scarcely noticed when Simon and the others slid off the dragon's back and came to stand in the road.

"Ah!" he murmured. "Never did I think to see a Western *lung*! I had dreamed of doing so but never dared to really hope..." his voice trailed off and he turned at last to the human members of the party. "Which of you honorable gentleman is Dr. Stillfield?" he asked, bowing again.

"I am," said Simon. He bowed as well.

Dr. Quong looked startled for a moment and then said "So young to have accomplished so much and to be such a scholar of the noble dragon! But tell me, although I have read all of your books, yet this type of dragon is not mentioned in any of them. I am familiar with the Welsh Red, the Cornish Copper and the others of your nation, yet this beautiful blue is new to me."

"Lakota is an American dragon – an American Opal – I have only just finished the first volume of a two volume work on American dragons," said Simon "and I have brought you a copy of the manuscript, as it will not be published until later this year."

Dr. Quong, highly gratified, bowed again.

A shy and pretty young woman with shining dark hair came forward rather hesitantly and said "*Baba*, I respectfully suggest that our honored guests be conducted into the house and offered refreshment."

"I saw a beautiful garden from above," said Lakota. "May I go into it?"

Dr. Quong bowed yet again. "It would be my honor to entertain you in my humble garden, noble one. Perhaps we might all gather in the garden and converse while we refresh ourselves. I have much to ask and much to tell."

Lakota agreed and leaped into the air, Dr. Quong watching avidly. With one thrust of his wings the blue dragon cleared the house as the young woman, with a pleasant smile, ushered the foreign party into their home.

Tatya received a quick impression of beautifully carved screens, exquisite porcelains and wall hangings before they were all shown outdoors into a Faerie tale garden.

Lakota had landed neatly in a wide space in the midst of a formal garden, quite different from what an Irish or even a Russian garden would have been. White, curving walls enclosed the garden while plum blossom doorways and other geometric shapes allowed a glimpse of the vistas beyond. In the center, a pool in which lotus floated was screened by billowing rockeries – miniature mountains complete with artfully placed stones, shrubs and even tiny temples. There were pots of flowers, in particular the peonies and chrysanthemums so loved by the Chinese, and the three "friends of water" – plum, pine and bamboo. The garden was big enough to encompass large trees such as catalpas and mulberry. Everything was balanced and harmonized on paired opposites – high lead to low, shade lead to sunlight and enclosure lead to open space. Open sided galleries could be seen leading to other parts of the house and other gardens. It was peaceful and serene. There were no straight lines – even the paths zigzagged and curved. It attempted to display in symbolic forms the essence of nature.

Statues of different sorts were also scattered here and there – lions, and other fantastical creatures and of course a dragon or two.

The young woman clapped her hands and servants came running. In no time at all a low table was brought out side and with it low seats, food and drink. Introductions were performed and everyone was seated.

The young woman proved to be Dr. Quong's daughter-in-law, Ping, wife of his son, Jian, and mother to the child they had seen, Mei, Dr. Quong's granddaughter. Jian and Ping had a young son as well, Hai, who was at school at this time of the day.

Jian had attained high rank in the Civil Service at a young age and was at present called away on a matter of business, Dr. Quong explained. He was expected to return in a day or so.

They were served the classic Chinese drink – *Jui,* a fermented grain beverage, and spicy dishes such as Hot Pot and Spiced Duck.

Very politely, Dr, Quong asked questions of both Simon and Lakota about Western dragons, while Ping shyly queried Tatya about Alan and what Ireland was like. Ping spoke English reasonably well and between that and the amount of Chinese that Tatya had managed to learn they were able to communicate. Ash, trained in diplomatic manners, managed to look as if he were vitally interested in the increasingly technical dragon talk.

Beneath the table the two familiars feasted on bowls of freshwater fish.

"This is delicious!" said Janus, after swallowing a large bite.

"I like this sauce!" agreed Marinka.

"What manner of cats are you?" came a shrill little voice in Cat language, which was international in scope.

Janus looked up to see a small, rather indignant kitten regarding them with a hostile glance.

"This is my house and my people!" said the kitten. "Are you come to take my place? I shall not let you!" She hissed and puffed herself up to twice her size – which was not very big – and arched her back in a threatening fashion.

"Am I supposed to be afraid of you?" said Marinka scornfully. "I've seen mice bigger and fiercer than you!"

"Marinka!" said her mother sharply, "Mind your manners – we are guests here." She sat down on her haunches and graciously inclined her head at the kitten. "I apologize for my daughter. We have not come to take your house or your people – those that we came with belong to us and when they leave we shall too. I am Janus and this is Marinka."

Slowly, the kitten relaxed and then said, "I am Xiu – I am of noble birth – my ancestors guarded the sacred temples of Siam."

"Is that why you have blue eyes?" Marinka asked. She had never seen a cat coloured like this kitten – her paws, the bottom of her legs, tail, ears and face were chocolate coloured while the rest of her was a pale cream. The blue eyes were startling in the dark face mask.

43

"Our eyes are the mark of the Gods' favor," said Xiu. "You do not have the favor of your Gods," she stated in some satisfaction.

"Cats don't have blue eyes where we come from," said Marinka, stung by the superior tone in the kitten's voice.

"A heathen and inferior place it must be," said Xiu.

"We can do something you cannot," retorted Marinka, growing angry. As a familiar, she was used to high status amongst other cats and she did not like even the inference that she was inferior. "We can talk to humans!" With this she went out from under the table, followed by both a curious Xiu and Janus.

Marinka went up to Tatya and put her paws on her Witch's thigh and said loudly "I've just met a very rude kitten!"

All conversation at the table stopped and a servant, who had been bringing a tray of *Mapo Dofu* gasped in fright and dropped it on the floor, porcelain bowl shattering.

Even Dr. Quong looked startled and said "What magic is this? A cat that speaks as does a man?"

"I'm a familiar!" said Marinka indignantly. She was only six months old and did not as yet truly realize that what she was used to did not exist everywhere.

"All Wizards and Witches have animal familiars as helpers," said Simon and briefly explained the duties of a familiar and which animals were most suited to the task. But he could not explain why they could talk – no one could, for even after almost one thousand years since the time of Merlin, it was not understood how or even why familiars could speak and read and learn the way they did – or why some cats, ferrets, hedgehogs and owls, amongst others, were able to become familiars and others of the same species were not.

Dr. Quong was fascinated and asked many questions, some of which Janus answered. Dr. Quong was rather surprised to be talking to a cat, but he seemed to adjust rapidly.

"It truly amazes me –" he said when his curiosity had been satisfied about familiars. "There are likenesses between us but many differences as well. I have spent much time in comparing our dragons to one another..."

"Excuse me," said Lakota politely, "But I would love to see an Oriental dragon in flight! I cannot understand how they can fly without wings! I have read your books, Dr. Quong, and I read about the *poh shan,* the growth on top of their heads that pumps air in and out and lifts them into the air. But I am not really clear on how it works. Do they have flight cavities like I do? I wouldn't think that just ordinary air could cause flight – I would think that it would at least have to be helium they pump in. I would love to talk to an Oriental dragon and ask him these things!" he ended.

Lakota was very surprised when Dr. Quong said that he must not do this. The Chinese Dracophilologist insisted that it would be disrespectful to inquire about such things – all his knowledge of the *lung* had been acquired by observing dragons from a distance when he was a young man and seeing a dragon was more common and in reading the ancient texts.

"I'm a dragon too," said Lakota stubbornly. "It will not be disrespectful for *me* to inquire! When we go back home we are going to stop over in Uppsala and I am going to go and talk to the feral dragons so that Dr. Swensen will know more about them. It isn't very scientific not to go to the primary source for information."

"Lakota –" said Simon in protest.

The blue dragon looked slightly abashed. "I'm sorry – I didn't mean to insult you, Dr. Quong, but I really do want to understand how a dragon without wings can fly and the easiest way to do that is to ask. I also want to know why they have those odd tentacles around their faces. Are they like a cats' whiskers and help them navigate or are they decoration? Most British Isles dragons do not have a ruff like I do –"

At this moment an ominous rumble was heard and everyone realized that it had grown darker and the wind was now chill. A thunderstorm was fast approaching over the mountains.

"Oh, Simon, cast a dragon dome!" said Lakota anxiously. He had been struck by lightning on the tip of a wing whilst in Russia and he had never forgotten the experience. He was now more than ordinarily nervous about lightning – all dragons were very cautious about lightning,

45

for if struck, their gasses would ignite and they would die a fiery death.

"Dr. Quong, do you mind if I work magic in your garden?" Simon asked, reaching into his breast pocket for his wand. "I shall have to shelter Lakota from the thunderstorm."

Dr. Quong was very eager to see some magic and readily gave his permission.

Simon stood up and moved away from the table. He stood beside Lakota and pointed his wand straight into the air and reached for the power of the ley lines that ran all over the world. He was surprised at their raw strength. In the British Isles there were so many Wizards using the ley lines that they were constantly having to be replenished. This was practically unused.

When he felt the power surging up from the ground and through himself Simon said *"Tholus!"* in Wizard's Latin and violet light fountained up from his wand. It spread out like an opened umbrella and then fell to the ground, creating an inverted bowl of violet light that covered Lakota and the table at which the rest of the party still sat.

"Now I'm safe!" said Lakota happily.

Ping had taken her little daughter into her lap – they both looked frightened, but were attempting to hide it. Tatya spoke soothingly to them, explaining in a low voice that this was good magic – Simon was a White Wizard and there was nothing evil in it at all. Two of the servants who were left out of doors showed signs of wanting to flee.

Alan gave a great crow of delight. He reveled in being near magic.

Dr. Quong was far braver than his family or servants. He stood up and went to the violet wall that now surrounded them. Outside of the dome thunder rolled and lightning flashed suddenly. "May I touch it?" he said to Simon.

Simon nodded. "It's perfectly safe. If it is struck by lightning the bolt will be absorbed by the ground. If the servants want to leave they can go through that gallery into the house. I left an opening," he added, pointing with his wand to where the violet light ended above a door, for he had noticed that the two servants were wide-eyed and fearful.

At a gesture and a short phrase in Chinese from Dr. Quong the servants fled. "Is everyone in your country able to do so?" the Doctor inquired. "I am was only aware that you were magical because I read of it in your books. I had no idea of what it might truly mean."

"In the "About the author,'" said Janus. "It lists Simon's academic qualifications and magical ones as well."

"No," Simon answered Dr. Quong's question. "Many persons have no magic at all. You mentioned a sorcerer might be involved, sir. Someone has been using magic here – I can feel him in the ley lines, although he is not drawing from them to any great extent."

Ash, who had been very quiet throughout all the dragon and familiar talk said "My cousin Arthur is a *Magus Majori* – he claims that he can tell in many cases who a Wizard is – he leaves a *signature* in the ley lines, Can you tell anything about his fellow from his signature?"

"No, it's a bit different here – for one thing at home most of us know each other," said Simon. Dr. Quong was staring at his wand, so he offered it to the elderly Dracophilogue so that he might examine it. "I am not familiar with the forms of Chinese magic – and this has a different feel to it than what I am used to."

"I have obtained some ancient texts on magic," said Dr. Quong absently, his attention on the wand he now held. It was carved with a design of dragons flying about it , with a silver tip that held a good- sized opal. The handle at the other end was of silver as well. He gave it a tentative shake but nothing happened. "Can anyone work this magic stick?" he asked.

"No – only a trained Wizard – in fact it is a very bad idea to ever use another Wizard's wand," Simon informed him.

Dr. Quong hurriedly returned the wand to its owner. He then sat back down at the table. He looked up over-head at the dragon dome. The rain was now coming down heavily and the storm was at its height. "Remarkable!" he murmured as the rain ran down the sides of the dome, but inside it they were warm and dry. He watched as Tatya threw up some mage lights, for it had grown very dark as the clouds had covered the sky."Remarkable!" he murmured again.

"I have made the correct choice in asking you to come, Dr. Stillfield," he then said "and I will be forever in your debt that you have come so far and traveled so long to help this humble person. And I will never cease to be grateful that I have seen and spoken to a Western *lung*. But now I have much to tell you of what has been happening to our dragons. Four more at least have died since I wrote to you. Some of them are becoming clever at hiding themselves. But I have see the great Xiang Lung twice more and he tells me in tones of sadness that many of the great *lung* do not think that they should fear man and are thus vulnerable to the magic of the sorcerer. And, as we thought, he has the help of a dangerous warlord, in command of many men, all trained in the martial arts and who have no fear nor respect of dragons. She has a fortress –"

"*She?*" interrupted Ash in disbelief, "Excuse me, Dr. Quong – but a *female* warlord?"

"Yes, Mr. Pendleton – such a powerful female is not usual in my country but it has happened in the past. This warlord, they say, is both beautiful and evil. We have found out her name and that of the sorcerer she partners. She calls herself Si Wang Mu – and he is styled Ch'ang Hao. In our mythic history she is the Queen of the Genii and he the King of the Snakes."

6

The Mountain Fortress

To the south of the Huang Lung valley the mountains became steeper, more forbidding. Rather than covered with the rich verdure of pine and bamboo they were huge, stark escarpments of bare rock. It was a harsh, inhospitable country and it was famous for feuding warlords and bandits. Wary travelers stayed well away from the mountains.

At first glance it was difficult to discern why anyone would bother fighting over such a bleak and barren land in high altitude where snow lingered and it seemed as if summer never came. But caravan trails wound through the mountains, the caravans laden with possible plunder. And in this part of the highlands anyone foolish or brave enough to use the old trade routes usually fell afoul of the warlord Si Wang Mu and her band of vicious mercenaries.

She had been a plague to the area for over ten years. The only child of the previous warlord, Zhong Zhou, she had been raised as if she were a son and her father had taught her weaponry and martial arts. When she was but seventeen her father had died – many said by her hand – and she had begun to gather the worst of the bandits, assassins and thieves and make of them a formidable band of marauders. She had changed her name – it had been Zhong Ju – chrysanthemum – and she thought rightly that the sort of man she wished to command would not respect a warlord with a soft, feminine name such as chrysanthemum. Therefore she took on the name of the Queen of the Genii – a powerful name – there were good Genii and bad Genii- she intended to be one of the worst.

The fortress that she and her band called home clung to the steep side of a mountain, with its back right up against a sheer cliff. It was nearly impregnable – its walls were of thick blocks of stone – its windows narrow, with the light coming from high slits under the curving eaves of the red tilled roof. There was but one door – a huge thing of thick wood, bound with copper – the remote ancestor who had built

49

the fortress scorned iron as fit only for peasants. Inside was room for all of her men and the tough little horses they rode – surefooted, iron-hoofed Mongolians. Vast store rooms beneath the fortress, hewn from the rock many years ago, held not only their loot but stores of food, wine and a water well that insured even a long siege laid against them would fail.

About the foot of the fortress, straggling up the steep mountainside, was a village. This provided the other needs of her men – whores, gambling and drink. Some of her men actually were married and had families and these too lived in the village, but these were few. Most of them preferred a boisterous, rough life of freedom.

Si Wang was a demanding commander. The men had to keep tough and fit, as she did herself. They had to practice their skills daily. She employed a weapons-master and a master of several forms of hand-to-hand combat. Discipline was severe – men who shirked their duty, who showed up drunk, did not practice their fighting skills or, worst of all, kept back a choice piece of loot or a woman for their own personal use, were swiftly punished with whipping or in the case of the latter two infractions, beheaded.

But men fought one another to join her band – she was strict and hard but the rewards were great – there was plunder in plenty, equally divided. She provided a safe haven and made certain that her men had the best food and lots of it. Drink, good drink, was available when not on duty or on a raid, and the women in the brothel were willing and pretty. What was even better, the men were not charged for the services of the women or the drink. A fund to which everyone contributed a small share paid for this – a man might go to the village and drink and whore as much as he liked without paying out a coin. Only in the houses of gambling did a man lay down his own money. And SI Wang had no objections to fighting amongst the men – she encouraged it – that was how she chose her lieutenants. The current finest fighter, a nasty young man called Hong Yu, who had killed four other men to obtain his position, currently shared her bed. She took her pleasures as casually as did any of her men, with whomever she fancied.

Several years ago Si Wang had come across a most interesting man – a magician. This had been in Shanh'ai, where she had traveled to invest her money and indulge herself with the purchase of silks and jewels. He was an astrologer as well as a magician and she recognized in him a soul as black as her own. He had been looking for someone like her for a great while and had a most interesting proposition for her – involving dragons.

Si Wang believed in nothing except enriching and pleasing herself. She had no feeling of respect or reverence for her ancestors, tradition or for the dragons. When the magician Ch'ang Hao, had shown her how much money would be paid out for dragon bones and flesh – for dragon bones were ground and used as a variety of medicines and ingesting ground, boiled dragon bones and teeth would calm the spirit and prolong life. Dragon flesh was said to impart many virtues as well to the one that ate of it and again, people would pay handsomely for it.

Ch'ang Hao had spent many years studying dragons and how to overpower them so that they might be killed. They were magical creatures – they could make themselves any size and even make themselves invisible and they could fly. They controlled water and could shake the earth.

But they had their vulnerable points – they could be killed with a splinter of iron or best of all, with a specie of caterpillar that could be introduced into their nostril where it migrated to the brain and began to eat. This was far better than the iron splinter, for iron polluted the flesh, making it useless for sale.

The magician had discovered how to make a net of magical energies that could be cast over the dragon, disabling it and allowing a team of strong men to insert the tiny creature into its nostrils – this did require strong men, for the dragon, seeing its doom, fought hard against this. The magical net tightened around it as it fought, preventing it from flying or making itself bigger or smaller. Even did it turn invisible it could not escape from the net.

Si Wang's greed was such that she instantly agreed to Ch'ang Hao's plans. Her men would be amused by challenging dragons. And all Ch'ang Hao wanted was the pearl of each dragon that it wore beneath its chin.

These pearls were useless as such – for they were not actual pearls, but the source of draconic wisdom and had

51

many special powers as well. And Ch'ang Hao wanted those powers for himself. With the powers of the pearls he could be a sorcerer as great as any of those in the old legends. Even the Emperor would bow down before him. He had no desire to be Emperor, but he saw himself at the Emperor's side as a trusted and much respected advisor.

Even though it was now June the mountain air was cold. Snow still adorned the peaks. Fires of dried dung burned in the round brass braziers set about in Si Wang's private hall in several spots, but the air was still chill. There was little furniture – a table and some stools, for wood was difficult to obtain and furniture had to be brought up the steep mountain paths by pack animals. Rather than chairs there were piles of cushions here and there that served as chairs and bedding.

Ch'ang Hao had been summoned to Si Wang's presence by her servant – an old man who had served her father. The magician increasingly disliked the female warlord but she was serving his purposes. As he entered her private sanctum he said "Cover yourself, woman! Have you no decency?"

A low, throaty laugh greeted his protest. The naked woman on the pile of cushions stretched and ran her hands down her body. "Do you like what you see, sorcerer? I would take you to my bed save that I know you to be practically a eunuch – or is it boys you like?" She laughed again, this time derisively.

He did not like what he saw. She was as hard as any man – with small breasts and a taut body. He liked a woman to be soft and rounded and what was more important, compliant and submissive with small, bound feet. Si Wang's feet were large – he could not even look at them without shuddering. And she was currently glistening with sweat as well. She had probably been with Hong Yu again – she liked to practice fighting with him – naked – and then fall upon him voraciously for an exhausting bout of lovemaking. She was beautiful in her own way, he supposed – her black waist length hair gleamed like a raven's wing and she had a perfect complexion of ivory while her dark eyes gleamed like two chips of obsidian. But for him she lacked all charm – and he disapproved of her immodesty. She thought nothing of appearing in front of any of her men naked and even bathed with them in the bath house or called any one that took her fancy to her bed.

Now she sat up in the makeshift bed and stared at him. She made no effort to cover herself in spite of his admonition. She found his discomfort amusing. "My men have found another dragon," she said. "We will ride out tomorrow and take it. It is becoming more difficult to find these creatures," she said "but the amount of those wanting their bones and flesh increase daily." She rose from the bed, stretching again in a sinuous motion that reminded Ch'ang Hao of a panther he had once seen in his travels in the land of Hind. She clapped her hands and the little manservant scuttled in. "The Great lady desires?" he said with a deep bow.

"Bring my bath," she ordered and moved to the table as he bowed deeply and backed out of the room. A bottle and porcelain wine cups stood on a bamboo tray. She poured herself a brimming cup of rice wine but did not offer a cup to Ch'ang Hao. A bright-eyed glance over the rim of the cup seemed to mock him. "You see, Ch'ang, I remember that you do not like drink as well as not taking women."

Ch'ang sighed. He had given up correcting her impressions of him. Because he did not find her sexually alluring did not mean that he did not like women – and he was avoiding both sex and drink for a reason. He was convinced that he had to be 'pure' to access the wisdom of the pearls. For so far, he had been unable to tap their virtues. There had to be some secret to it. He had read – he had read extensively – how some sorcerers remained chaste and sober and this increased the potency of their magics. Si Wang could not seem to understand this. Nothing was more important than gaining the wisdom of the pearls.

Si Wang looked at him appraisingly. He was not an unattractive man – he was perhaps as much as fifty years old but still strong and fit. He wore a small beard on his chin and his hair was still thick and dark. He was rather thin, with a scholar's stoop and long thin fingers that she could imagine stroking her body. She could not understand why he did not want her – if she appeared like this before any of her men they were instantly aroused and would fight for the privilege of claiming her. And in truth, she wanted to take the sorcerer as a lover. All the men she had taken – for she was the aggressor in most cases – had never given her what she wanted – a son. She wanted a son who she could train and mold. A daughter would do but a son would be more respected – a daughter would have to fight as hard or harder than she had to lead these men.

Lately she had become enamored of the idea of the sorcerer as a husband, not just a lover. With her as mother and the sorcerer as father her son would be invincible – magic combined with her fighting skills and ruthlessness! Her son could have an Empire such as Genghis Khan's. Ever since her father had told her the story of the Queen of the Genii she had dreamed of a dynasty, with a consort renamed Tang Wang Kung – the King of the Genii. She had even begun to call this fortress Kwen-Lum, after the mountain home of the two Genii. But the sorcerer stubbornly refused to cooperate. She felt that if she flaunted herself enough and taunted his manhood he would one day lose his temper and take her.

Now she flung herself into a low chair and sat in a most immodest fashion. She laughed to herself as a blush ran up from the sorcerer's collar. He wore red robes, heavily embroidered, that she had obtained for him. She herself had no womanly skills such as embroidery but there were women in the village who did such things. She had had the embroideress embellish the robe with the symbols for long life, surrounded by five bats on the front back and sleeves. This meant 'five blessings – for bats were very lucky as everyone knew. He should realize that this was a sign of her favour.

"Why will you not lay with me, sorcerer?" she queried. and poured herself another cup of wine. "I could give you very great pleasure – I know how to give as well as take pleasure."

He ignored this as he always did and said. "Have you heard anything of persons asking questions about the dragons? On my last trip to Canton I heard rumors that many people – highly placed people – are becoming alarmed that

54

the dragons are disappearing" Some of the magical supplies he needed were obtainable only in Canton.

Si Wang gave this the contempt it deserved She made a rude noise into the wine cup."Do you think that anyone cares about dragons in these days?" she asked, scorn dripping from her voice.

"One of the sons of the Dragon Throne – Prince Tuan – is said to be very interested," Ch'ang Hao informed her.

"The one they call the Scholar Prince? if he were ever to take his nose from out his scrolls he would fall flat upon his face!" She tossed back the rest of her wine.

The door opened and the elderly manservant, followed by four men carrying a bath tub and cans of hot water, entered.

Si Wang waited until the tub had been filled with hot water and she stepped into it. She flaunted her bare body at the four men, who gazed at her in admiration. She could see the desire written on their faces. She took a quick glance at the sorcerer to see if this display of lust made him jealous or even aroused him, but he was frowning, and staring at nothing. "I heard," he continued, "that the Prince is seeking help from a great scholar of dragons."

"Another scholar?" she scoffed. "What shall they do, Ch'ang, attack us with their calligraphy brushes?" She laughed at her own joke and the four men who had watched her splash water on her body chortled as well while the little old man said "Hee! Hee!" in a gasping chuckle. "The only thing I worry about is that we may not find enough dragons to kill," she said confidently.

But Ch'ang remained abstracted and ignored her, chewing thoughtfully on his lower lip.

With an angry sigh she beckoned to the largest of the four men. "You – shed your clothing and join me. We will pleasure each other."

The man eagerly stripped and stepped into the big tub. She closed her eyes as he began to eagerly fondle her. But when she opened them to see if Ch'ang was looking on, the sorcerer was gone, without receiving her permission to leave.

What did she have to do to make that eunuch see his future as her consort and the father of her son? She sighed again and then gave herself over to the pleasures of the moment, uncaring that her manservant and the three other men were watching. Of course, they had not had permission to leave either.

7

The Large Bear-Cat

The next morning Lakota was growing bored. Earlier in the day all the talk had been of how to help the dragons and Simon had indicated that he needed to talk to Xiang Lung, the dragon who had contacted Dr. Quong. Dr. Quong, it was planned, would leave an offering in the dragon temple on the hillside, with a scroll humbly entreating the Celestial *lung* to call upon Dr. Quong and his guests. This was written and a servant dispatched to take it to the temple.

Lakota thought this very silly. He could not understand this awe that the Chinese had for dragons. He didn't like it – he thought it unnatural. Dragons, in his view, were meant to work with and live with people. He could not imagine life without Simon and the others in 'his' family and furthermore, did not want to imagine it. Dr. Quong had expressed amazement that the 'noble one' was willing to carry people on his back and be saddled like a horse. Lakota was taken aback by this. That was what dragons did! That as well as many other jobs, for dragons enjoyed working; they enjoyed making money as well.

While the discussion had been about dragons Lakota had been very interested, but once the topic turned to magic and Dr. Quong brought out a number of ancient scrolls about magic...that was of no interest to the blue dragon. Magic was for Wizards and Witches and even familiars. Lakota appreciated all the things that Simon did for him that were magical such as the dome that protected him from lightning and the power drawn from the ley lines at home that warmed the sands of the dragon pen, but he had no interest in the theory and practice of the arcane arts.

Simon had brought a gift for Dr. Quong – something brand new – a portable translation table. Until very recently the translation tables were huge, found only in large libraries, and needed the constant attention of a Magus to keep the spells intact. But a friend of Simon's, a research Wizard at Columbia University in America, had developed this – a small, portable tray that held a book or a manuscript. and allowed the user to read, in any language he wished, any book, no matter what language it was printed in – and the spells were good for twenty years. Simon's friend had sent several to him and Simon had brought one to Dr. Quong.

The Chinese Dracophilologist was delighted with this gift and at once, he put it to good use and the three men, Simon, Ash and Dr. Quong, began to study the old magic manuscripts to see if they could find out what type of spells the sorcerer could be using against dragons. They were archaic in text and style and the table was a great help.

They were out in the garden again so that Lakota could participate, as well as the two familiars. Tatya was occupied with Ping and Alan was playing with Mei – Hai, of course had reluctantly gone off to study with the scholar who ran a small school in the valley. He had wanted to stay at home and watch the strange *lung* and the foreign devils. Both his mother and Grandfather were horrified when he respectfully requested to remain at home that day. Education was too important to be missed! The guests would still be there when he returned home. As Hai respected his elders and their wisdom, he obediently went to school. Only the recollection that the other boys would hang on his lips when he told them what was happening at his home enabled him to go off to his small school reasonably cheerfully.

Now Lakota said, in a lull in the conversation, "Simon, could I go look around the valley? I would like to stretch my wings and there is nothing I can do here if you are all going to talk magic." His tome was a little wistful.

"Would that be all right, sir?" Simon asked Dr. Quong, who could see no reason why Lakota could not explore the valley of the Yellow Dragon. He merely cautioned Lakota to stay within the valley – since it covered some 270 square miles there was a good deal of area to explore – but Dr. Quong felt that the area away from the valley was not safe. They had no idea how near the depredations of the warlord and the sorcerer extended.

Given permission, Lakota launched himself and spiraled up into the clear air. After the storm of yester eve it was a bright, clear day and every thing stood out in sharp relief.

The valley was truly a beautiful place. From up in the air Lakota could see the tree-covered slopes – with some trees he did not recognize – and the terraced pools. There were so many pools! Lakota tried to count them but soon gave up – there were just too many. They were lovely multi – colours too – and unable to resist any longer, Lakota landed near one of them.

This particular pool gleamed pale gold. He wondered what made it such beautiful colours. Perhaps a taste of the water would give him a clue.

He put his muzzle in the water and drank – it tasted of minerals – not like the spring water he was used to at home. He had heard other dragons and people speak of taking the waters in Bath or at one of the other mineral water spas in the British Isles, but he had never visited a spa but no one had ever told him the waters tasted good.

The more he drank the better he liked it – he had thought it rather nasty at first – and the taste reminded him of something.

It was firestone! That's what it reminded him of – the limestone he chewed to ignite his gasses. He had noticed that this valley was full of limestone – there could be no difficulty in getting firestone here!

He took another long draught – really, it was quite delicious when one got used to it! – and then took a long breath – and rose several feet off the ground.

Surprised, he let out some gasses in a whoosh and settled back on the ground. He felt extraordinarily buoyant. Experimentally, he took another deep breath and again rose from the ground. This time he extended his wings and gave a tentative flap and popped up straight into the air!

Lakota felt so insubstantial – unlike when he chewed firestone he was not aware of the calcium churning in his stomach. He felt lighter than air.

And he *was* lighter than air, for he noticed suddenly that he was beginning to float up very high indeed. Slightly panicked, he let out a long stream of flame, and found that expelling his gasses brought him down nearer the earth. Emboldened by this he practiced raising and lowering himself by breathing deep and then expelling flame or gas. He felt as if he were one of the balloons he had seen once in Phoenix

Park when the family had gone to see aeronauts flying in a basket hung beneath a huge balloon. Lakota hadn't seen the need of this – if people wanted to fly they had the choice of a dragon, a hippogriffe or a flying horse – but he was always interested in flight so he had asked many questions. He now seemed to be flying on somewhat the same principles as a balloon. He went higher in the air and did some head over heels flips and rolls – much like the moves in dragon-ball – and he marveled at the effortless flight. This was wonderful! He could hardly wait to show Simon! Was this what made Chinese dragons able to fly without wings?

However, the effects began to wear off quite shortly and he was obliged to land. And below him, squinting up into the sky and watching him, was a creature the likes of which he had never seen.

It was rather like a bear, but it was marked so strangely. Its forelegs and hind legs were black, as were its ears, and a band across its shoulders,. A black patch covered each eye The rest of it was white.

"Well!" it said in Animal as Lakota landed near him, "That was quite an exhibition! What sort of creature are you any way?"

"I'm a dragon," retorted Lakota, stung, for its tone was not friendly, but rather belligerent. "And I was about to ask you the same question!"

"I belong here –" stated the creature, "but you don't! And I don't for one minute believe that you are a dragon – I have a dragon friend and she looks nothing like you!"

Lakota sighed. Were all the animals here so aggressive? Janus had told him of the hostility of the kitten Xiu. Lakota was a friendly soul by nature so he said in a pleasant tone " I am an American dragon – there are many different types of dragons in the world."

"What's American ?" the animal asked, frowning at Lakota.

"It's a land far over the sea in that direction –" Lakota pointed to the East where the Pacific ocean lay. "But you haven't told me what you are," he added hopefully.

"Humans call us large bear-cats but among my folk we call ourselves Pandas," the creature said.

60

A large shadow passed overhead and Lakota looked up. Against the brilliant blue of the sky he saw a large white shape, dazzling in the sun.

It came lower and lower and he could make out that it was an Oriental dragon. It undulated like a snake through the sky.

"*Ni hao*, Chao!" the dragon called out as it approached the ground.

"*Ni hao*, T'a Ming!" called out the panda.

"She'll soon set you straight!" the panda said to Lakota. "You're no more a dragon than I am! A big lizard, perhaps..."

The white dragon landed quite close to Lakota and looked at him in some surprise.

She was different than the pictures and drawings of Chinese dragons that Lakota had seen. Truthfully, he found some of these representations very ugly, with large goggling eyes, and all the extraneous 'whiskers' on their faces. This dragon's were not like his – his were blue with a cat-like iris, while hers were rather human-like, with whites and a round, dark pupil. She did have whiskers, but they were not as many as he had seen in pictures and actually rather attractive. They were short, like a fringe on her upper and lower lip and several longer ones waved about her face – she even had eyebrows of these whiskers. Her spinal ridges were small compared to Lakota's and his in turn were smaller than those of the dragons in the British Isles. Her horns were very small and were behind her ears, rather than in front as his were. The biggest difference lay in their bodies.

She was much more like a snake – her body was long and lithe and very slim, and even on the ground she continued to coil up and then uncoil again as if she still moved through the air. Her scales were very large and even her face was scaled. Her tail ended in a tight coil and seemed to remain that way. And she was brilliantly white. Lakota had only seen white dragons once before – the Ice Dragons of Siberia – but she was nothing like them. She had four toes on each foot.

"Who is your friend, Chao?" she asked of the panda.

"He's no friend of mine," growled the panda. "He claims to be a dragon! I told him how ridiculous that was! He claims to have come from across the ocean!"

"You fail in your duty to a guest, Chao," she said in rebuke and bowed to Lakota. "I humbly beg pardon for my friend's ill manners. He has a good heart, however rude his exterior may seem."

Lakota returned her bow – he had never seen such people for bowing but when in Rome..."I AM a dragon, " he said, "An American dragon, and I am here with my friend Simon, who is a magician, to help Dr, Quong Lee save the dragons from extermination. My name is Lakota." He bowed again.

"Ah!" she exclaimed and her whiskers began to wave – Lakota was to later find out that this was a sign of pleasure, much as the tail of a dog wagged when it was happy. "This humble person, T'a Ming Lung, acknowledges the great honor you have done us." She then looked at his talons – her eyebrows went up and she bowed still lower. "A *t'ein lung*! I humbly crave pardon, Great One! I did not realize –"

"Oh, stop it!" said Lakota, a little peevishly, tired of all the bowing and scraping. "I'm not great or noble – I'm just Lakota! Lots of dragons have five talons – why, in America, Simon tells me, the Savannah Silver has SIX toes! I do not understand this business about toes at all!"

"You do not have rank in your far away country?" she queried, startled. "How do you then know which of you is superior, if you will excuse my impertinence?"

"Ask me anything you like," Lakota returned. "And where I come from, dragons don't have rank unless for a talent such as a dragon bard or maybe a police dragon has rank."

"I would say this is all very interesting, except that it isn't," said the panda sourly. "T'a Ming, we were going to walk to the Shitazheenhai. I caught some swallows for your luncheon –"

"And I have gone up on the slopes and found the nicest bamboo for you," she returned. She then turned to Lakota and asked very politely if he would condescend to join them.

62

Lakota accepted but he gave an internal sigh. There was such a thing as too much politeness. Dragons, like Elves, believed in and appreciated good manners but he felt that this form of genteel behavior was overdone. He began to think that the Celestial dragons must be intolerably conceited and swelled up in their own importance if this was how everyone – human and dragon – deferred to them.

He walked along with the undulating dragon and the lumbering, rather sullen panda, who obviously did not want to share his friend.

But Lakota was too curious to withdraw. Here was his chance to find out about flying and have his questions answered. If she was in awe of him she would not object to answering his questions. In this case, he could use this excessive respectfulness to his advantage.

8
T'a Ming

"He can breathe fire," said Chao suddenly as they walked along.

T'a Ming turned to look at Lakota. "Truly? Only the very old can breathe fire, or have wings. These are gifts that the gods have granted only to the very honorable elderly of our kind, who have the wisdom and the stature to properly use them. You must be far older than I, for your horns are much developed as well. I have but recently attained the state of *kion-lung*, or horned dragon."

"I am seven," said Lakota. "I have only once seen a dragon that could not breathe fire – the Ice dragons in Russia spit ice. I've never seen a dragon without horns."

"You are seven millennia in age?" she asked, her eyes widening.

Lakota looked at her in surprise. "No, I am seven – seven *years* old!"

"This is strange indeed," she said. "Among those of us in this land, it takes one thousand years to hatch from our egg, another thousand years to grow scales – it has taken me over three thousand years to become as you see me now."

"I was two years in the egg," said Lakota, "But that was only because I was waiting for Simon."

"Who is this Simon?" asked the panda crossly. Lakota wondered if he was always in a bad mood.

"My human friend – we're bonded to each other – actually, he is more like my brother. American dragons have a bond with one human, usually a Wizard, and we are together for as long as we live," Lakota explained. "We can feel the presence of the one who will be our particular friend and that is when we hatch."

"Most curious!" remarked T'a Ming. "In the usual way of things we have but little to do with humans. Many times human scholars will come and read philosophy to an egg but once we are hatched we see but little of humans, unless there is some great task to accomplish that requires us

64

to help humans. Or we might see our worshippers at a temple, making offerings. In the days of my honourable ancestors the Emperor had always a dragon adviser at his side."

"The less we have to do with humans the better," Chao growled.

"How do you fly without wings?" Lakota asked curiously, ignoring the curmudgeonly panda. "I know about the *poh shan* but I don't understand how it works."

"How do *you* attain flight? " she asked in return. She seemed to have recovered from her awe at him having five toes.

Lakota gave her a brief explanation at the conclusion of which she nodded and said "We too have what you call flight cavities. And these fill when our *poh shan* is raised and lowered."

"The oxygen in the air must combine with some chemical in your cavities," Lakota mused. He was amazed when she did not know the chemical composition of her body gasses. She accepted the fact that she could fly .She did not seem to care about how it was accomplished, unlike all the dragons of his acquaintance who could reel off chemical formulas like any Oxford Don.

"It is also our pearl that makes us fly, for it is filled with ancient magics," T'a Ming raised her head so that Lakota could see the large milky globe at her throat.

It was the strangest thing that he had ever seen. He thought it looked very uncomfortable. He had not really noticed it before, for it was the same shimmering white as her scales.

"This is our Pearl of Knowledge," she explained, and took it from beneath her chin with the talons of one foreleg. "It allows us to ascend to heaven, and keeps our wisdom in it. It is also shows that we dragons are the keepers of the Tao."

Simon had told Lakota of the Tao – the Yin, the dark feminine side, represented by the moon, and Yang, light and male, representing the sun – perfectly balanced in a circular symbol. He understood this simplified explanation but still thought it very strange.

"You have lost your pearl?" inquired T'a Ming sympathetically.

"We don't have pearls," Lakota answered as he studied the shining object she held in front of him,

"But then, where do you keep your wisdom?" the white dragon said, puzzled.

"In my head!" he said shortly. Her tone seemed to imply that he was somehow lacking in dragonly attributes – that she felt sorry for him. This rankled.

"Are we going to stand around here all day discussing philosophy?" Chao demanded. "I'm hungry!"

"I most humbly beg your pardon, honorable Chao," said T'a Ming, replacing the pearl beneath her chin. *How did it stay there?* Lakota wondered, for she did not seem to hold it in place. "I allowed my curiosity to overcome me, and I most humbly apologize for this lack of manners." She bowed to the panda.

"We are nearly to the pool," the panda said in a surly fashion.

The pool was worth the trip – it was a lovely thing of many hues. Once again, Lakota could sense firestone and he had little doubt that if he drank of this water as well, he could easily become airborne.

At the edge of the pool lay a large pile of bamboo stalks and roots. And in a wicker cage were a quantity of swallows.

"What are those birds for?" Lakota said as Chao hurried eagerly to the bamboo pile and with a brief thank you to T'a Ming, began chewing with his powerful jaws. His manners were not nearly as polished as were T'a Ming's

"Chao has kindly caught them for me for my meal," T'a Ming said.

"They were quite easy to catch," said Chao through a mouth full of bamboo roots. "They're quite stupid."

"You're going to eat those birds?" exclaimed Lakota, revolted. "But they're alive – and they are not cooked!" Simon had told him that they must not be judgmental about customs in other lands, but he found this sickening. He could not bear the thought of eating anything that was still living. He refused her offer to share them, as politely as he could and wandered away to look at the pool so that he would not have to watch the grisly meal. It quite destroyed what appetite he had. He was glad that he had had a large breakfast.

When she had finished she dipped her muzzle in the pool and washed the blood and feathers from her whiskers and teeth.

Chao was still busily eating. "He will eat for quite a while. Pandas need a great deal of food," she said to Lakota. "Will you fly with me? I will show you more of the valley."

Lakota was agreeable to this – perhaps studying how she flew would make him forget seeing the blood on her jaws.

She raised an lowered the *poh shan* on her head that reminded Lakota of a bellows. It looked like a hard growth of some sort. Watching carefully, he could see that she swelled slightly as her flight cavities filled. Perhaps Dr. Quong would know what chemicals were combined with the oxygen to enable her flight.

T'a Ming watched him quite as critically as he crouched down and sprang in to the air after taking a draught of the waters in the pool.

She rose straight into the air while he spiraled up, catching a thermal cell. With the buoyancy from the water he was able to begin gliding almost immediately. Usually the weight of the firestone in his stomach made him a little heavy until it had been converted, before he could glide.

"What is this you do?" she asked as they flew side by side, him with stiff wings, riding the thermal, while she writhed in the air, her body bending from side to side. Again. Lakota was reminded of how a snake moved. He, however, had to coax her to fly beside him – for she kept insisting that it was not proper for a four-toed Imperial to fly alongside a five-toed Celestial. he found this ridiculous and told her so, shocking her sensibilities.

"I'm gliding in a thermal," he now said in answer to her question. "It's marvelous!"

Again, he was surprised. She did not understand him; she had no knowledge of aerodynamics at all and said simply that she 'just flew' He found it incomprehensible that she did not know how flight worked and seemed to have no interest in it. These dragons were a strange lot, he decided, although he rather liked her – save for her disgusting eating habits.

She showed him several more beautiful pools – one from which the valley took its name – it looked as if a yellow dragon lay sleeping in its depths. This, T'a Ming explained, was the manifestation of a yellow Imperial dragon who had vanquished a fierce demon long ago,

She next took him to a pool called Zhuanhua, which meant 'whirling flower'. This pond was crystal clear and the spring in it never ceased to well up. She showed Lakota how it got its name – when flowers or leaves were thrown into it they whirled round and round with the flow of the water.

They then went to the Zhaga waterfall, which was about three miles of water flowing over a cliff face. Here the current flowed around trees growing in water. At the bottom of the waterfall was a round shaped stone on which the water cascaded, sending splashes of liquid up into the sunlight. This looked like jade, which earned the platform its name – Jianya Tai – spattering jade platform.

Lakota was thrilled with this – he flew in and out of it many times, enjoying the cool water on his scales for the day had grown very hot. Dragons such as he did not feel, as humans did, the extremes of heat and cold, but all the same the water was refreshing. And it was so beautiful! He had to bring his family here – they would enjoy splashing in it too – Alan would be delighted with it.

T'a Ming watched him in amazement. She was well used to water – her lair lay at the bottom of a lake in a palace of crystal and pearl and Chinese dragons spent the first stage of their development as carp-like fish, but it never occurred to her to play in it as he was doing. Indulgently, she thought of him as very young – he ought not to be even hatched as yet, in spite of his wings, horns and fire breathing abilities.

A voice like the jingling of copper pans said suddenly, "What is this creature that flits about in the water as does a bird?"

T'a Ming turned about and immediately made a deep obeisance. "O, noble one!" she said, eyes properly downcast. "This humble four-toed one brings to your lordly notice the American dragon La-ko-ta."

Lakota, hearing his name, looked up and left the water fountain when he saw another dragon standing on the bank with T'a Ming. he flew over, landed, and bowed his head politely and said, "Hello!" But he did not abase himself as did T'a Ming and he refused to lower his eyes.

The new arrival was a great yellow dragon, a five-toed *t'ein lung*. That he was of some importance was immediately apparent, for besides having the Celestial talons, he wore jewelry – on his stag like horns glittered gold and jade and his talons were covered in sheaths of the same. A collar of carved jade, in a design of a carp passing through the Dragon Gate on its journey to becoming a dragon, known as the *li lua lung* rested on his yellow scales. A jade and gold ornament hung down on his forehead and rested between his eyes. Lakota recalled reading in Dr. Quong's book that a yellow dragon was considered superior, a symbol of the very center of the earth. Only the Emperor and members of his family were allowed to wear yellow robes embroidered with dragons. A white dragon like T'a Ming symbolized the direction of the West, the season of autumn, mourning and death.

"You come from far across the sea," said the yellow dragon. "Are you one of those of whom the scroll spoke – here to help us against this evil sorcerer and the warlord who abets him?"

"Yes," Lakota said simply.

"I would meet this sorcerer of whom the honorable Quong speaks so highly. He says that this sorcerer, although not of China, is a great scholar of dragons and has mighty magics as well." the yellow *t'ein lung* continued.

"Simon is a Master Magician," said Lakota proudly. "I will take you to him."

"It is well," said the yellow dragon. "I am Xiang Lung, great dragon of heaven" He turned to T'a Ming, who crouched even lower to the ground. "And you are, *kion – lung*?"

"This humble person calls herself T'a Ming Lung, O Great One," she said in low, respectful tones.

"You will accompany us, for news of what is to be done must be carried to the inferior dragons as well," Xiang commanded.

Inferior! Lakota thought in anger. How did these dragons stand this endless bowing and scraping and why did they not resent being called *inferior*? T'a Ming seemed pathetically grateful for Xiang's condescension.

When they took flight she stayed in the rear of the group.

Lakota thought briefly of the panda. Would he wonder where they had gone? Surely it was rude to not notify him that they were going elsewhere?

But T'a Ming made no mention of Chao as they as they flew in the direction of Dr, Quong's house. Therefore Lakota copied her. He did not understand the whys and hows of these dragons' behavior, but he was a stranger here and he would do as they did.

9
The Stone of Heaven

"Face up to it, Faversham," growled Tom Stillfield. "We're bloody well lost! This idiot guiding us has no more idea of where we are than we do ourselves."

Even here in the heavily forested mountains it was hot. Although it was not quite ten-thirty in the morning, Tom had removed his jacket and was carrying it slung over his shoulder. He was drenched with sweat and had to keep wiping his face with a now soaked handkerchief, for the sweat ran down into his eyes.

Reginald Faversham looked at him in trepidation. "Oh, I say," he bleated. "Do you really think so? He seemed as if he knew the way so well – hasn't hesitated one minute!" He looked toward the stocky guide, Gao Kun, who like them was at present sprawled on the ground, a little way from where they sat, refreshing himself from a water bottle.

"We've passed this same damned rock formation three times," said Tom sourly. "We're going in circles! And if you ask me, it's deliberate."

"Surely not!" Faversham protested. "Why, I'm paying him good money to guide us to where the map claims the jade mine is!"

And you're a simple minded looby, Tom thought, *"fair game for any Captain Sharp that comes along.*

If Tom had been capable of being honest with himself, he would have added "Including me", for he had gulled Faversham quite as thoroughly as he had accused the guide of doing.

He had sold his services to Faversham as an experienced adventurer and mercenary, a dead shot, expert in armaments, who had been in India, and Africa and had shot tigers, lions and elephants and fought desperate battles with hostile natives. But all that Tom knew of India and Africa had been gained by listening to some prosy old bores at his club in London. He had never been out of England. True, he was a crack shot – it was one of his very few skills – and he knew what he was doing with the rifle that was slung across his back. He had brought down some game on this trek – otherwise they might have gone hungry. Faversham was paying him a fantastic wage for his expertise – and Tom had no compunction in taking it. He had long ago decided that he would take whatever came his way, and the hell with right and wrong or what means he took to get what he wanted and needed.

He despised men like Faversham – aristocratic, rich, and silly fools who let themselves be taken advantage of by someone more intelligent and cunning. Faversham even looked like a fool – he was a long, thin young man who facially resembled a sheep – he even had light, wooly, curling hair and was given to vocal bleating – Tom fully expected to hear his employer say "Baa!!" one day soon. Faversham affected a monocle and had a tiny, barely discernable mustache. In Tom's opinion the fellow should have grown a beard to hide his lack of a chin.

Tom himself was big and burly – his hair was thick and brown and he easily passed for ten years younger than he was – his habits of drinking, smoking and womanizing had not as yet caught up to him. He had cultivated an air of competence that impressed such fools as Faversham but Tom had the uneasy feeling that certain people, such as Barrington- Smythe and Pendleton at the Legation, saw right through him. He always felt distinctly inferior around people like that – and he hated the feeling.

Now Tom raised his voice and said "You, Gao Kun! Get your arse over here!"

The guide was on his feet at once, and was bowing before them with a wide grin that showed crooked teeth with a gap in the middle. He was dressed in strange fashion – with padded and quilted jacket and a hat rimmed with fur. How he could stand it in this weather Tom did not know. Gao Kun claimed to be from Mongolia, quite near to where they were headed.

Tom stood up, took a hand gun from his belt and idly cocked it." Have you any idea where you are going?" he said in a smooth, silky voice, aiming the gun right at the guide's middle.

72

The smile faded from Gao Kun's round face. His English was reasonably good – he understood Tom's words and he understood Tom's actions even better. "Map is wrong!" he blurted out. "No landmarks like on map! Trying to find landmarks, honored sir, but not there!"

"In other words, we're lost," Tom cocked the pistol and squinted down the barrel. "This is a remarkably lonely place, Gao Kun. If I were to shoot you, no one would ever know."

"Oh, I say, Stillfield!" protested Reginald Faversham.

Gao Kun fell to his knees. "Please, honored sir, will find right road! Been here before but map landmarks are not here – maybe map is old – maybe there was earthquake – change how land looks!'"

"Where are we then?" Tom asked sharply. "Do you know that much?"

"Min Shan Mountains – in Sichuan province," he said eagerly. "Maybe we find old peasant – can tell us if earthquake or mountain slide made landmarks disappear!" He looked very pleased with himself for thinking of this idea.

"Oh, I say! Look, Stillfield! It's providential!" came Faversham's sheep-like tones.

Along the mountain path came an elderly man, a younger man and a heavily laden water buffalo. They all moved slowly – the animal was not noted for its speed – and at the sight of the party on the road in front of them the little cavalcade stopped and stared.

Gao Kun jumped up and ran to them, gabbling excitedly. The old man talked just as excitedly to him, the younger man remaining respectfully silent as his elders conversed.

Fifteen minutes later Gao Kun retuned. "Peasant says that ahead is Huang Lung Valley – much good water, and foreign devils like you have come there too! Has not seen landmarks but people in village might know!"

Tom frowned. "Other white men?" Were they after the jade as well? "Did this old man see the foreigners?"

Gao Kun bowed. "No, has heard of them from sister's nephew, who has had it from uncle's cousin, who was told by –"

"Never mind," said Tom impatiently. "How far are we from this valley?"

"Two, maybe three day," answered the guide. "Honorable sir, he has rice and tea for sale..."

Faversham fumbled at his pocket. "Here, go and buy some from him." He pressed a bronze coin into Gao Kun's hand. "Running low on supplies, what? Perhaps you could get a bird for the pot, eh, Stillfield?" he asked hopefully. "I daresay these woods are full of birds!" He waved a long, thin hand at the forest of mixed deciduous trees and bamboo.

Tom frowned. "They may also be full of bandits." He really had no idea if there were bandits or not – but it impressed Faversham who looked as if he had never thought of the possibility. "And we'd be a prize for them, would we not?" he said in trepidation.

In truth Tom thought that the bandits would give them a wide berth. All of the people they had met so far had acted as if they had the plague – *fan qui* – foreign devil – was the one Chinese term that Tom had come to understand, as everyone murmured it or shouted it as they passed. Even this old man and his party were going well around them as they went by on the road, with a wary eye as if they were a threat of some kind.

Besides that, if the little traffic they had seen was any indication there would be nothing worth a bandit's laying in wait for the unwary traveler on this road unless he was a tea or rice bandit.

"Gao Kun, go and see if you can find some water," Tom directed. "We'll make camp in that meadow we passed and rest until tomorrow and then go on to this valley. We can get directions and stock up on supplies there."

"Oh, famous notion!" approved Faversham. "I own, I am considerably fagged and should be glad to rest for a while. Catch up on my sleep, what? And if we can find enough water, perhaps take a bath!" he added, looking down in distaste at his wrinkled, soiled and sweat-stained linen suit.

A bath, a nice, cool bath sounded good to Tom as well. It was considerably hotter and more humid here than it ever was in England.

And then he could relax and dream about how rich he was going to be when they found that enormous jade mine. It was the purest form of jade, the map claimed, the Imperial

74

jade itself so prized here in the Far East. Just selling it to the Chinese alone would make them impossibly wealthy.

The Chinese called jade 'the Stone of Heaven" and finding a rich strike of it would allow Tom to have his own version of heaven – the life of a gentleman of leisure with no need to ever worry about the future again – and even to pay back that conniving son of a bitch, his own brother Dick, who had stolen from Tom his birthright.

Tatya had spent an interesting morning with Ping. Although the Chinese woman had a cook in the kitchen she was very much in charge and saw to the stocking of her pantry and the shopping her own self so that everything was of the highest quality.

She showed Tatya the many different foods that went into Chinese cuisine – things far different and more exotic than anything Tatya was used to. Before she had married Simon, Tatya had lived most of her adult life in St. Petersburg, in Russia, a most cosmopolitan city, and had thought herself sophisticated when it came to food, but Ping showed her things she had never imagined could taste so good. They sampled such things as *Jook soon* – bamboo shoots, *dow foo* – bean curd, *lien gee* – dried lotus nuts, and *heung bew fun* – five flavor powder. The food they had eaten last night was spicier than either she or Simon was used to but they had enjoyed it – more than Mr. Pendleton did, she thought. He had drunk a great deal of water during the meal!

Ping explained that the cooking of Sichuan was a great deal spicier than that of the Canton area and showed her guest the chili paste that was the basis of the flavor of many of the dishes they had eaten.

Simon, busy in making plans and talking shop with Dr, Quong, did not miss Lakota until after the noon meal of clear soup, fish braised with bamboo shoots, red peppers, hot peppers and black mushrooms, and twice-cooked pork with rice. The most difficult thing was learning to cope with the chopsticks but he asked for instruction and watched carefully how it was done and was soon using them adroitly.

After the meal Simon began to become uneasy – the blue dragon had been gone a long time. Surely he could have come to no harm in Huang Lung Valley! Worried as he was, Simon was certain that his bond with Lakota would have told him if anything bad had happened. All the same he hoped that Lakota would return soon.

They had retreated to the garden again, to sit beneath the shade of a pavilion that overlooked a pool of lotus. And there they sipped a very fine cup of tea – a green tea called 'Silver Needles' that was perfect for summer weather, served from a thin porcelain pot with a green glaze that looked as if it had been made from bamboo, with handless porcelain cups to match. The tea was drunk without milk, sugar or lemon. Dr. Quong discussed the book of the *Ch'a Ching*, the *Tea Classic*, which told of the Emperor Sh'en Nung, who discovered the goodness of tea some two thousand, seven hundred and thirty seven years before Christ.

Dr. Quong had just begun to talk of the Chinese belief that tea gave one vigor of body, contentment of mind and determination of purpose when taken over a long period of time. "As the honorable Li Yu said 'Better to drink such a beverage than wine which loosens the tongue,' " Dr. Quong was saying when suddenly a great dark mass obscured the sun and three dragons landed in the garden.

"Thank the Lord it's a large garden!" said Ash beneath his breath as the occupants of the pavilion stood up – the Chinese bowing low as they recognized a *t'ein lung*. They bowed almost as deeply to T'a Ming for they recognized in her a four-toed dragon – an Imperial dragon.

"You honor my humble garden, O Great One," said Dr. Quong to Xiang with another deep bow.

The yellow dragon inclined his head graciously. "I have come, honorable Quong, to meet this magician you tell me of – and to tell you that the Dragon King grows very angry – another of the earth dragons was killed this morning by foul magics! I do not know if I may restrain him any longer!"

Dr. Quong brought Simon forward. "Here is Dr, Stillfield, the magician of whom I spoke, noble *lung*."

Simon bowed politely but not with the reverence shown by Dr, Quong and his family. "I shall be glad to help in any way that I might," he said in Chinese.

Xiang looked faintly taken aback. "A *fan qui*, and a very young one at that! What can such a youth know of magics? In the time of my ancestors magicians were old, venerable and learned men!"

"Simon is a *Magus Magistra!*" said Lakota indignantly. "And if you really knew anything about magic you would know that that means Master Mage! It isn't easy to become a Master Mage and he is a fully robed Druid as well! It isn't the age of the magus – it's the talent! Show him a dragon dome, Simon!"

T'a Ming had looked shocked when Lakota spoke to Xiang in such a fashion and had sunk down on the gravel path, trying to hide her face. She had introduced this rude dragon to the great lord! His misconduct would be on her head!

Simon exchange looks with Dr. Quong and then withdrew his wand and pointed it in the air. In a few moments all the humans and the dragons were covered in a dome.

Xiang blinked in surprise. "What does this do?"

"It is a shield to protect us from lightning," Simon explained. "It can also keep you from leaving here unless I wish it."

"I think not," said Xiang rather contemptuously and walked right into the violet wall. He bumped his nose hard when the wall did not let him pass. He was not stupid – he did not continue to try to get through the wall. "Where did it come from?" he asked, turning back to look at Simon.

"Magic – I draw my magic from the power lines of the earth," Simon explained.

"Ah!" said Xiang. "Perhaps you *will* be able to help us – I spoke in haste, for I am impatient and in despair. Every day it seems that I hear of another death. When will this stop – will there be any of us left?"

"Please, tell me everything you know of what has happened to the other dragons," Simon urged, lifting the dome with a flick of his wand. He sat down on the pavilion steps in front of the yellow dragon. Tatya and Ash resumed their seats on the cushions as well, Tatya pulling Alan into her lap. The cats had never risen but they had missed nothing, watching through slitted eyes. Dr. Quong and Ping did not sit until the *t'ein lung* invited them to do so.

"It began some two years ago..." said the yellow dragon.

10

The Dragon's Anger

"It seems as if I am going to have confront yet another necromancer," Simon said on a sigh. "I was afraid of that."

He, Tatya, with a dozing Alan in her lap, Ashton and the cats were still seated in the pavilion. The dragons, save for Lakota, had left, as had Dr. Quong and his daughter. The old man felt in need of a restorative nap and Ping had household duties.

"Do you know how he is trapping these dragons?" Ash asked. "You were speaking Chinese too rapidly for me to follow – and what was that other language the yellow dragon spoke? You seemed to understand it as well."

"That was Dragon," Simon explained. "When he became extremely agitated he reverted to his own language. I can understand Dragon well enough, but I can not speak it because my vocal cords are all wrong for the sounds one needs to make."

"That's why you need me!" put in Lakota.

"Yes, indeed," said Simon, with an affectionate look at his dragon friend. "As far as I can tell, this necromancer is using black, not blood magic."

"Which is good," Tatya put in. The last time Simon had faced a necromancer he had been a practitioner of blood magic, the magic that drew its power from pain and death of the necromancer's victims. It was a powerful and dangerous magic.

Xiang had explained that an inferior dragon, an earth dragon, a *ti-lung*, had actually seen the capture of an Imperial dragon. The *ti-lung* had hidden, afraid of the men and the power he felt and had watched as the sorcerer called the other dragon to him – impelled it to come to him was the way that Xiang put it – and then cast a black net of energy over it. Men had then forced it to accept a caterpillar in its nose. This seemingly harmless creature, pushed by magic, made its way up into the dragon's brain and immediately began to feast. Within hours the dragon was dead. The men then stripped the flesh from its bones after hacking it to pieces. They boiled down the remains and took the bones as well. leaving nothing behind. And the sorcerer took the pearl.

"Why is a caterpillar so dangerous?" said Lakota. He had not understood the horror that the Chinese dragons felt for the caterpillar. "If one ever got up my nose I would just fry it to a crisp!"

"Don't forget, Lakota, these dragons can not breathe fire as you can," said Simon. "Even though you don't have to worry about caterpillars, I am going to cast a protective spell on you that will repel any net anyone tries to throw over you and an anti–compulsion spell as well. No one will be able to call you, save one of us with our dragon whistles."

"I'm going to give you and Dr. Quong dragon whistles as well," Simon added, turning to Ash. "If we become separated and in danger, Lakota can hear the whistles from over fifty miles away."

"I'll protect you just as if you were part of my family," Lakota assured Ash.

"Did Dr. Quong's magical texts tell you anything, Simon?" Tatya inquired.

Simon shook his head. "Very little – they dealt more with mythology, such as the Creation story and tales of dragons and phoenixes. Magic seems to be tied up with religion and the texts are not only written in flowery language, but are rather obscure to one who has not been raised up in any Chinese religion. Dr. Quong has been trying to help me understand, but what I had hoped for was a book of spells such as we have at home. There doesn't seem to be such a thing. There is a magic square that might be able to decipher and one scroll talks of *shu shu* – an ancient system of divination, astrology, dream interpretation, and the active and passive principles of the universe. Dr. Quong insists that I start practicing *tai chi* – exercises that he claims will help to put me in touch with the *chi* of the earth, which sounds as if it may be much the same as ley lines, although I shall have to study it quite a bit more before I can say for certain that this is so."

Better you than me, thought Ash, suddenly glad that he had no magic. When he was a boy he had wished fervently to be magical. What a lot of study it was! Magic looked so effortless when done by a talented mage, but it required years of study and practice for proficiency. Little wonder there were no as many mages as there were used to be, particularly top-ranked mages such as Simon.

"When are we going to leave?" said Janus. The familiars had been very quiet so far but they had missed nothing. Janus, having been gifted by Oberon as well, had rapidly picked up Chinese.

"Probably tomorrow," said Simon, "Tatya –" he began.

"I know," she said on a sigh. "You want me to stay here with Alan where it is safe. And if it were not for Alan I would insist on going with you. But I cannot call myself a good mother and take my small child into danger." She tried to smile at her husband. " I keep telling myself that at least I will be here, in China, not on the other side of the world, should anything happen to you."

Lakota stretched out his long neck and touched her hair with his sensitive muzzle. "I'll take care of him, Tatya! And if he needs you I will fly back as fast as I can and fetch you!"

"I know you will," She smiled in a rather watery fashion and touched his nose lovingly. "I've discussed it with Ping and she will be glad to have me stay – if Dr. Quong is to go with you she will be alone here, save for the servants, for her husband is frequently called away. We've found that we have a lot in common and are fast becoming friends."

Simon smiled at her in return. He was grateful for her good sense and proud of her that she was putting such a good face on being left behind. It was very hard on her, he knew and they would discuss it further when they were alone together.

"It looks as if we are in for another thunderstorm," Ash interrupted, pointing to dark clouds that were massing overhead. "We had best get inside."

Even as he spoke two servants came hurrying towards them to gather up the silken pillows in the pavilion and the tea things.

Since thunderstorms were a frequent summer feature in this mountain valley Simon had scouted out a long gallery that connected to the house. It was large enough to accommodate Lakota and would allow him to put his face in at a door that opened into the main sitting room of the house. The dragon's protective shield could be cast over this. Simon knew that the blue dragon would be most unhappy shut up in a dome away from his human friends and this way he could still keep them company.

Now Lakota hurried to this gallery as a sudden peal of thunder rang out. Simon took Alan from Tatya and the little party quickly followed the scurrying servants to the house as large drops of rain began to fall. The storm was coming up very fast indeed.

Ten minutes later Lakota was safe and dry and they were all in the house. Shutters had been secured and fires lit in brass braziers. The temperature had plunged dramatically and the wind had begun to scream about the eaves. It became violent very quickly and immense peals of thunder shook the house and lightning flashed in great blue white sheets. Lakota, who could see the sky through the dragon dome, reported that the clouds were nearly black and looked as if they were boiling. The lightning, he said, was cloud to cloud.

"Is this usual for this time of year?" Simon asked Ping.

She shook her head. " We have had so many storms lately! There are usually a few in the summer when it is very hot and sultry but it seems now every day we have a bad storm and they are just getting worse all of the time!"

Dr. Quong, who had risen from his bed at the first clap of thunder and rejoined them, looked grave and said "It is as the honorable Xiang Lung declared – the dragons grow angry at the murders of their kind. It is they who raise the storms."

"I would like to know how they do that," said Lakota from his doorway. He was resting his head on his outstretched forelegs. "I should have asked T'a Ming! I can't make it rain. Not even Simon can make it rain."

"You cannot do so?" Dr Quong queried of Simon.

It took a moment for Simon to answer for an incredibly large thunderclap nearly deafened them all and rolled heavily over the house.

"All we Wizards can do is guide the weather," he answered finally. "With the right spells we can push a wind along, or guide the rain where it is needed or push it away from a flooded area. We can also clear clouds away. But no one has yet figured out how to call rain, wind or snow. There is even some question as to whether doing so would not interfere with the natural cycles of the earth. It's an ethical debate that has been going on for almost one thousand years."

"Some people say that Merlin could control the weather," Tatya remarked. Alan did not like the noise of the thunderstorm and was hugging his mother tightly around her neck. Ping, too, had her young daughter in her lap and even Hai, a sturdy bright-eyed little boy of nine, who had managed to get home from school just before the storm broke, sat quite near his *Yeh Yeh*, his grandfather, trying not to flinch at the savage barrage coming from out of doors.

Marinka was hiding against Janus' stomach and after Janus had seen Xiu jump in the air at the sounds of the storm, the older cat motioned to the Siamese kitten to join them and Xiu had crowded against Janus gratefully.

"Merlin?" queried Dr. Quong. "I have not heard this name."

Simon, thinking that it would take everyone's mind off the storm had just begun to explain about the most famous Wizard in the history of the Six Nations when a pounding came at the front door. almost as loud as the reverberations of the thunder peals.

A servant ran to the door and flung it open just as another lightning flash illuminated the sky. The rush of wind shrieked into the house and blew out the lanterns. In the sudden darkness the figure in the doorway was large and menacing and Ping uttered a piercing scream, clutching Mei to her breast.

Simon and Tatya almost simultaneously threw up Mage lights which flooded the room with brightness that the wind could not harm.

"It is I, Jian!" came a voice – he had to shout over the thunder, for it seemed as if there was a a double velocity of noise – two bolts of lightning, one right after the other and two immense peals of thunder.

The servant had to struggle to close the door, such was the force of the wind Simon gave it a magical push which closed and locked it.

Ping put Mei on the floor and ran to Jian. Her husband was soaked to the skin, his quilted jacket and blue trousers wet through, his shoes sodden wrecks. A puddle began to gather around him as he stood in the doorway.

"Come at once, honorable husband, and dry yourself!" she cried. "You will take your death!"

"My horse – our guests –" he began with a tired gesture.

"A servant shall tend your horse and our guests will still be here once you have dried yourself," said his father.

"I crave forgiveness for any rudeness on my part to our honorable visitors," Jian bowed in the direction of Simon and Ash

Simon bowed as well and said courteously. "It would grieve us to keep you from obtaining comfort and perhaps becoming ill," he replied.

With more bows Jian allowed his wife to escort him from the room.

"He could probably use a cup of tea!" said Lakota. He had raised his head in interest when Jian had entered. "I would like a cup myself. The tea here is very good!"

Ping had found him a large porcelain bowl to use as a teacup. He was quite dexterous with his talons and was able to pick it up and sip at his tea, although he found the lack of a handle a little awkward. But even the teacups the humans used, he had noticed, lacked handles. However the cups were some of the most beautiful porcelain he had ever seen. Like all dragons, he appreciated beauty, whether it was in jewelry, art, music or chinaware.

"I'll tell the servants," said Tatya and handed Alan to Simon, who took the little boy into his lap. Alan was nodding sleepily in spite of the noise and Simon rightly discerned that Tatya had decided to use Lady Diana's sleep spell on him.

Jian made short work of drying off and joined them just as two servants bore in a laden tea tray. Outside, the storm still raged.

Jian was a tall young man, very slim and straight with a long face in which humor mingled with intelligence.

His glossy dark hair was tied in the traditional queue and he had donned casual robes of blue silk, heavily embroidered with phoenixes.

They all sat at a low table on top of the *kang*, a raised platform of bricks. Channels ran inside this dais and heat ran through these channels, from a hearth on the outside wall. A *kang* was in many of the rooms of the house and was used for sitting and sleeping mats were placed on the bedroom *kang* as well.

After introductions and much bowing had been exchanged, the tea was poured – this time a *Wu-l* tea, a black tea used to treat colds – in this case, to prevent one. If Jian was at all discomfited by taking tea with a dragon or even with foreign devils, no one would ever have known, for he was a courteous as his parent.

"It has been raining like this since I left Chengdu!" Jian informed them, wrapping his hands around the paper-thin cup, reveling in the heat. Beneath the low chair on which he sat the comforting heat of the *kang* slowly crept up his feet and legs. "It was said that reports had been received from the north of heavy rain as well – many people are afraid of flooding."

Dr. Quong nodded his head wisely. "It is, as I have said, the dragon's anger. They control the rain and the wind and they are telling us that the slaughter of their kind must be halted. Too many have died."

"Prince Tuan is much concerned. He arrives tomorrow, Father, and he hopes to go with us to confront these thieves and murderers. I left him in Chengdu and came ahead so that we could prepare for the honor of his coming to our home."

"It will indeed be an honor," agreed Dr, Quong. "Prince Tuan, although young in years, is a scholar of repute."

"And a formidable warrior as well," added Jian. "He has rare skill with the blade."

"Ah –" Dr. Quong began, but was destined to never finish his remark, for with a shriek, Janus leaped to her feet just as Lakota bellowed. The two kittens shrieked as well and dived under the table.

"Simon!" Janus screeched, every bit of fur on her body standing on end. "Earthquake! A bad one!"

85

And the entire house gave a sudden lurch and ripple. Pictures fell from the walls and porcelain crashed to the ground. The *kang* buckled and they were thrown from their chairs as the wall nearest them began to tumble.

11

 The Wall of Water

There was no time to pull out his wand. "*Desistĕre!*" Simon shouted at the wall, his hands out-flung as he hit the floor.

The wall, and the ceiling it supported stopped in their fall, hanging in the air mere feet above the bodies of those who had been seated at the table.

Simon came to his feet and took out his wand. "*Resistuĕre, reparare,*" he commanded. With amazing speed the wall moved backwards and put itself back together again.

"Is everyone all right?" he said, turning to the others who still lay on the floor.

The adults had each sheltered a child – all three of whom were crying. Ash had grabbed Dr. Quong and protected the elderly man with his body. All were considerably rumpled, but safe, even the familiars and the kitten Xiu.

Jian stood slowly, Hai in his arms with the little boy's face pressed into his father's neck. Jian looked at Simon wide-eyed. "What was that you did?" he said in awe. "You saved our lives! We would have been killed if that wall fell on us! How – "

"That was *magic*, my son!" said Dr. Quong proudly. "You may see now why I sent for Dr. Stillfield!"

"Simon!" Lakota interrupted. "Get everyone out of there! Another shock is coming! Everyone should come into the garden!"

The three cats streaked out of doors ahead of the humans. Simon dropped the spell that covered Lakota's gallery and they all followed the dragon out into the middle of the garden. Thankfully the rain had stopped.

There they found the six servants employed by Dr. Quong's family. One man was dazed looking, blood streaking his forehead. He was supported by two others. The cook and two of the maids were weeping. One of the maids clutched her arm, which had been injured.

"Simon – I can feel the safest area," said Lakota anxiously, His ruff, a sure gauge of his emotions, was tight against his neck. "Have everyone get as close to me as they can and I will shelter them with my wings from falling debris."

No sooner than this was done did a huge ripple and wrench tore the ground. Trees shook and fell, the garden wall tumbled in places, and the house twisted and buckled. Ten feet away from Lakota a huge crevice opened in the ground and swallowed a section of the garden.

It seemed as if the ground would never stop shaking but in reality, the tremor lasted but a few minutes. When it passed, Lakota said confidently, "That will be it for a while. There will be some little shocks later."

"How can you be certain?" Dr. Quong demanded as they came out from beneath Lakota's sheltering wings.

"I seem to have some connection to the other dragons for some odd reason," Lakota said. puzzled. "From the minute the earthquake began it was as if I was there with them. I don't understand it at all – and I don't understand why they want to hurt people by doing this! I shall have something to say to that Xiang when I see him again!" he added, his tail lashing angrily. "There is no excuse for this! I don't care how mad they are! They might have hurt or even killed you!" he looked at Simon and Tatya and Alan and nuzzled each one of them. "If you had been killed I would have found out who was responsible and killed them!" he added fiercely.

Everyone's attention had been on listening to Lakota or surveying the damage. Only Hai, still in his father's arms, had been surveying the sky where black clouds stilled rolled angrily, swollen with yet more rain. "*Baba!* Look!" he called excitedly, tugging at his father's shoulder to gain his parent's attention. "Look up in the sky!"

Jian turned to look, for experience had taught him that Hai, a sensible boy, would not call his attention to childish foolishness, and he gasped in shock at what he saw.

The sky was full of dragons of all colours and types. There were earth dragons, the *ti-lung*, the underworld dragon, the *fu ts'ang lung*, and the treasure dragon, the *fu-can lung* – the latter two seldom emerged from beneath the earth. In colour they were white, gold, green, azure, scarlet and yellow. There were also, in smaller numbers, Celestial and Imperial dragons. Lakota recognized T'a Ming and Xiang.

Dr/ Quong pointed to a brace of scarlet dragons flying together. "Those are the spirit dragons – the *shen lung*. They are the dragons of the storm, for that is what their colour symbolizes. I see azure dragons as well – dragons of the clouds, sky and wind. It is the scarlet dragons who control the ill weather and they must be appeased."

"Appeased, is it?" Lakota growled, his ruff standing straight out. "I'll give them appeasement!"

Before anyone had time to protest his actions the blue dragon had launched himself into the sky and with a mighty thrust of his wings brought himself to the group of bright red spirit dragons slithering through the sky. They were a terrifying and dramatic sight against the black of the storm clouds.

They ignored his loud "Stop! I want to talk to you!" as if he was invisible and slid on past him. That is, until, with an enraged bellow he let loose a mighty wall of flame that singed the end of their coiled tails.

The air was full of shrill dragon screams and they stopped in mid-light to turn and stare at him in horror and consternation.

"*A t'ein lung*," the phrase ran through the masses of dragons. "A *t'ein lung* who breathes fire! "

A very aged black Celestial dragon said in a voice so loud that all those on the ground could heart him plainly, "He is winged, as well – he is a *ying-lung*. He must indeed be venerable and honored by the gods for only those so favored are to be granted wings and horns – and none amongst us can breath fire – and all of this in spite of his odd appearance. What do you wish, aged one?"

Lakota did not correct his misconception – he was more than a little tired of all this nonsense about toes and age – he just wanted this bad weather to stop before it hurt any humans.

"These earthquakes and thunderstorms and rain are at an end!" he thundered."You are hurting people! There may be many dead from this earthquake and the heavy rain will destroy crops and cause yet more people to drown! It has to stop!"

"What do we care for humans?" said one of the scarlet *shen-lung* scornfully. "They are killing those of our kind. There is not a *lung* here who has not lost a relative or a friend to these dragon poachers! Humans, who claim to revere us and make us offerings at the temples, have done nothing – and it is humans who are harming us!"

"And our temples fall into disrepair and there are few offerings!" another red dragon interrupted passionately. As far as Lakota could tell, he was a young dragon and hot-tempered.

This observation was borne out when the leader of the spirit dragons said in rebuke "You forget yourself, Zhen Lung, to speak so before your elders. And you as well, Yun Lung," he said to the first dragon who had spoken."These are matters for older heads than yours."

Both Yun and Zhen hung their heads. "We stand rebuked, honorable Jin," said Yun, as Zhen bowed in agreement. "We meant no disrespect."

The venerable Celestial announced himself to be Ning Lung, the eldest of the Celestials. As he spoke, Xiang joined them.

With a reverent bow, Xiang said "I know this dragon, honored one. He is come from the West, with a magician, who with the noble Quong, the scholar of dragons, has pledged to help us."

"This is so?" Ning turned to Lakota. "A magician will stop these predators?"

"Yes, Simon is a powerful magician and a Dracophilologist!" said Lakota quickly. To his surprise he was able to hover as long as they did in the air. He could hover for only ten minutes or so ordinarily but he supposed it to be the strange water he had drunk earlier. He had not eaten any firestone in the last two days, yet he could easily fly and hover and even had produced an enormous flame. Perhaps drinking these rich mineral waters made these wingless dragons able to fly?

Ning wrinkled his brow until his whiskers knotted. "Dracophilologist? I know not this word."

"A scholar of dragons. The word means a lover of the study of dragons – it's a word scholars in America created," explained Lakota "Such as Dr. Quong is. Simon teaches Dracophilology at Trinity University at home in Ireland."

"Much of which you say is strange to me," said Ning, "And I would speak of it further so that I may understand. But now – do you promise that this magician will help us – that the deaths will stop?"

"Simon will do everything he can to stop the people who are hurting you – he loves and respects dragons. Dr. Quong will help as well and Prince Tuan is to arrive tomorrow –"

"Ah!" many of the dragons murmured in satisfaction.

"The Prince is well known as a friend to dragons!" said Ning approvingly. "We are honored that he has left the Forbidden City and comes to our aid."

"But none of them can do anything," Lakota pointed out "if it is pouring rain and there are earthquakes! They will be hard put to survive. This weather must cease so that we can help you!"

"This is true," Ning agreed. "I have the ear of the Dragon King – it was he who instructed the *shen lung* to make this weather to show our anger. I shall tell him of your pledge and he will agree to stop the ground shakes and the rain."

"Excuse me, honored Ning," said the leader of the *shen lung*, with a reverent bow. "But the rains are creating a torrent that has caused the streams to swell and the banks of the rivers to fall. There is a wall of water heading towards the Valley of the Yellow Dragon." He raised a talon and pointed to the far end of the valley.

Lakota swerved about abruptly in the air and gasped in fright. It was as if an immense wave were coming their way. Lakota had once been in Brighton, sea-bathing with his family, when a rogue wave, caused by a storm out at sea, had knocked several people off their feet, away from the safety of the bathing machines. He had helped rescue them, for he swam very well. But he had never forgotten how fast and deep that wave had been, nor how easily the humans had been swept away and nearly drowned.

Without a word to the Chinese dragons he spun in the air and plunged down towards the garden of Dr. Quong.

He was shouting even before he landed. "Simon! Simon! There is a huge flood coming! We must get everyone to higher ground at once before you all drown!"

"Where?" Simon demanded.

Lakota understood that he meant in which direction the water was coming from and raised a talon and pointed.

"That end of the valley is full of people!" said Dr, Quong in horror. "And they will be in shock from the shaking of the earth. Can they be warned in time?"

"No!" stated Lakota. "It is coming so fast!" he added piteously. "Oh, those poor people!" Tears stood in his eyes. "And the animals too!"

"We'll just have to stop it, Lakota. Can you take me there, as fast as you can?" Simon asked.

"I don't have my saddle on –" Lakota protested.

"It doesn't matter – I'll hold onto a spinal ridge." As Simon spoke he climbed onto the foreleg that Lakota automatically extended and onto the dragons' back. Riding dragon-back without a saddle was both dangerous and far from comfortable. "Get everybody up on the roof if you can," he said to Ash and Jian. "Tatya, cast a dome around all of you and the stable as well once everyone is on the roof. I don't know how it will hold against that much water but I can't think of anything else to do."

Tatya nodded, clutching Alan to her breast. Unlike most Witches who were taught the magic of the moon and of crystals she had learned to use ley lines, for Simon, not another Witch, had been her first magic teacher. He had taught her early on how to cast a dragon dome to protect Lakota in case she and the dragon were out by themselves.

"Simon!" Tatya ran forward and pressed herself against Lakota's side. Simon leaned down and kissed her and Alan quickly. "Take care of yourselves, *acushla*," Simon said. "I'll be back as soon as I can."

"Godspeed," she whispered. She had scarcely stepped back when Lakota leaped in to the sky and headed towards the end of the valley. They could now hear a faint roar in the distance.

Behind her, as she stood watching the dragon fly away, she could hear Ash and Jian, organizing the servants and ordering ladders fetched.

Dr. Quong touched her gently on the arm. "Come, my child," he said. "We must do as we are bid. He is a great and powerful magician. If anyone can save this valley it will be him."

Tatya nodded and turned and walked away with him. Her first responsibility was to Alan and to these people she might be able to save. But another part of her wanted to go with Simon.

The Chinese dragons, still hovering above, watched with interest as Lakota took off again, carrying a passenger. "That is the magician the Western *lung* carries," Xiang explained to Ning.

"Ah!" said the aged Celestial. "Do you think that he will work magic? I wish to see this! Come," he called to the others. "We will go to observe."

With this they turned in mid-air and streamed after Ning in the same direction Lakota and Simon had gone, looking like a multitude of colourful banners in the sky against the now clearing clouds. For Ning had kept his word – there would be no more bad weather. But what was done was done and the dragons could not stop the wall of water. Even Simon had serious doubts that he himself could save the valley from inundation and many deaths.

12

☽ Family Reunion ☾

Tom Stillfield stood on a mountainside and cursed. With a spy glass he surveyed the scene below. A raging cataract of water was rushing down towards the valley below, which was already damaged by the earthquake.

First they had had to seek shelter form the violent rain and lightning in a shallow cave, but not before they had become soaked to the skin. Then had come the earthquake and common sense had dictated that it would be wise to get out of the cave. Tom and Gao Kun had to drag a protesting Faversham from the cave shelter – the idiot thought they would be better off in there! Tom could only too well imagine being buried alive in that cave by the force of the earthquake.

Faversham listened in amazement to some of the most virulent language he had ever heard. "Oh, I say!" he protested. "What ever is the matter, pray? The earthquake seems to be over with, what?"

Tom snapped the spyglass closed and looked at his employer in exasperation. The amiable, sheep-like face wore a look of confusion. He honestly did not understand.

"The valley, where we hoped to find supplies and some hint of as to where we might be going, is about to be flooded!" he growled. "With that destroyed God only knows where we shall find what we need in these damned God-forsaken mountains! I checked our packs – we're down to a little rice and tea and we need blankets and dry clothes as well. Everything in our packs is wet and will soon sprout mold in this heat! And you ask me what is the matter!"

"Oh!" said Faversham blankly and then said "Bad show, old chap! What are we to do then?" His tone indicated that Tom should provide a solution.

Gao Kun tugged at Tom's shirtsleeve. "Look, honorable sir! Look!" Excitedly he pointed to a shelf opposite them "A strange *lung*!"

A blue dragon was landing opposite them, with a rider. Tom, like most people who lived in one of the Six

94

Nations, was well used to dragons over-head and in the streets – they were quite common. But he had never seen one this colour before. He had not been particularly interested in Chinese dragons – only if they were *objets d'art* in precious stone or metal that he could filch – and he assumed that this was a Chinese dragon. But as the rider slid off the dragon Tom realized that he wore Western dress and moreover, he was hatless and had a head of flaxen hair unlike any Chinese Tom had ever seen. Tom opened the spyglass again and leveled it at the pair. What were they doing?

The Chinese dragons stayed high in the air, higher than they had flown earlier. They thought themselves safer from the magic up her. Although interested and curious they were also nervous. Therefore they were unobserved by those below, but with the long sight of dragons, comparable to that of a bird of prey, they could see all the events below clearly.

Simon felt a tightness in his chest and a lump in his throat as he looked at the wild water below – they were well in front of it – Lakota had picked an excellent place to land. The water was further away then it had seemed but coming very, very fast.

But what could he do about it ? Something had to be done – that was for certain! Simon had noticed how many homes and several well-populated villages lay directly in the path of the wall of water. These people would be killed if nothing was done. But looking at the power of the water he was uncertain that any spell he knew could stem the flood. Not only the people of the valley but his wife and child were in imminent danger.

"Do something, Simon!" Lakota urged as Simon took out his wand.

Simon reached for the ley lines and opened himself completely to their force – and was startled at the depth of that power – it almost swept him away . He leveled his wand at the flood and shouted "*Sistĕre!*"

95

And to his surprise and profound relief it halted, acting as if it had hit an invisible wall, splashing high up into the air and then subsiding.

"Oh, wonderful!" enthused Lakota "Will it stay there for good?"

"No," said Simon shortly. Already he was feeling the strain of holding back what must be tons of water. "We have to get rid of it, Lakota, but I don't know how."

"Let me go up in the air and look," said Lakota and leaped up. He was only gone for a minute and he said eagerly as he landed "Simon! On both sides there are channels which could be enlarged for the water to drain away! One leads to one of the ponds and the other goes into a different valley that looks uninhabited! If you could magically cut one channel I will go and dig the other with my talons. Opposite us it looks as if it would be easy digging – it is mostly boulders. But I shall have to get those men off the ridge – they are standing just where I want to dig. How stupid they are to be up there!"

"They probably climbed up to get away from the flood," Simon said. "Lakota, go and do what you need to – I am going to try to hold this water and cut a channel at the same time."

He sounded strained and Lakota gave him a worried look but took off and landed near the three men who stood in the other cliff side.

Lakota was somewhat surprised to find that only one of them was Chinese – the other two looked as if they were European. Therefore he said in English, very politely "I'm afraid you are going to have to move – I need to dig a channel in this rock right where you are standing."

"Oh, I say!" said Faversham with the air of one making a great discovery, "You're an English dragon! Didn't know you chaps came in blue, what? And is that gentleman an English Wizard? Who had thought we'd all meet up so far from home, what?"

"Get on my back and I'll take you over the water where it is safe," said Lakota. "Hurry!"

Both Tom and Faversham had been dragon-back before and trusted an English dragon, but they had to drag a shivering and terrified Gao Kun onto Lakota's back. The blue dragon jumped across the watery divide, scarcely needing to flap his wings even once. He waited impatiently as the passengers slid of – jumped in Gao Kun's case – and went back across where his powerful talons at once began digging, flinging earth and boulders right and left.

Tom strode forward as if to speak to the Wizard, but Faversham grabbed his arm. "Never interrupt a Wizard when he is doing a Working, old chap! The magic could backfire, what? Wizards in my family – I know!"

While Lakota was ferrying his passengers to safety Simon had been rather feverishly searching through his memory of every spell he knew for one that would accomplish what he needed to do. He needed to sustain the halting spell for at least ten minutes and then dig a deep channel in rock to divert the water.

The sustaining spell was the simple command of "*sustinĕre*" and with luck, would last at least ten minutes, twenty if he was extraordinarily fortunate.

But how to cut a channel in rock all by himself? That was something that was usually undertaken by a team of Wizards – who were specialists in geomancy – the magic of earth. That was not Simon's field. He had taken his Mastery in general knowledge, like his father had – a much more difficult discipline that it sounded, for someone taking *Magistra* in general knowledge had to demonstrate arcane intelligence in many different disciplines of magic.

Simon suddenly remembered a conversation he had had with his father and great grandfather, Lord Lyonshall, who at one time had been Arch Druid of Britain. Lord Lyonshall held that a truly talented mage could visualize what he wanted to do and if he had a firm picture of what he wished to accomplish in his mind, a simple 'create' spell would be enough. He was experimenting with the theory in his laboratory at his home in the Cotswolds and claimed to have several successes.

Simon could think of nothing else to do – the 'dig' – *fodĕre* – command would not even work as quickly as Lakota could. He could not possibly have a channel ready before the sustain spell failed.

Only vaguely conscious of the men behind him, Simon began visualizing, with his inner eye, blasting a channel out of the rock and pushing the water through it to a safe location. When he thought he had a good clear image, he pronounced "*Creare!*" and leveled his wand at the rock face he wished to cut away.

A violet light shot out of the end of his wand and hit the rock like a bomb. Stone and dirt spewed in a high arc as the magic went through the stone as if it were soft butter, cleaving a deep channel for the water. Almost at the same moment Simon heard Lakota shout "It's through!" and with an immense rushing sound the water began rapidly to dissipate, safely, in two directions, leaving only a small amount to flow into the Huang Lung valley as the invisible wall broke up and faded.

Lakota was beside him a moment later. "You did it, Simon!" he said enthusiastically.

"*We* did it," Simon corrected his friend. Gratefully, he leaned against Lakota's dirty foreleg. He was so tired ....

Tom shook off Faversham's restraining hand and came forward. "Damn it, if it isn't my little cousin Simon! You haven't changed much at all – just gotten taller!" he said, with a twisted grin.

"Tom," said Simon, looking at his cousin, who hadn't changed all that much either. But he seemed to be wavering strangely – was there another earthquake going on?

"Tom," said Simon again and fainted dead away.

When Simon came to himself again it was to find Tatya's anxious face hanging over him. He seemed to be laying in a soft bed made of many pillows with warmth coming up beneath him.

"What happened?" he asked. His head felt as if it were stuffed with cotton and he felt so weak!

"Oh, Simon!" Tatya cried, and flung herself on his chest, sobbing.

Lakota's blue face came into view. "You're awake!" he said happily, his ruff standing out on both sides of his head. He bent his long neck and nibbled at Simon's hair and then touched Tatya's hair as well. "Don't cry, Tatya!" he implored. "I told you he would be all right!"

Tatya sat up and wiped her nose inelegantly on the sleeve of the loose cotton wrapper she wore. "When Lakota brought you back here I thought you were dead! He had to carry you in his talons and you were so limp – we couldn't revive you! But Lakota knew just what to do!"

"Cerridwen taught me!" Lakota said, proud of himself. Cerridwen was the Welsh Red dragon who had worked for Simon's parents for many years. "Professor René taught her what to do for magical backlash and I told Tatya what she taught me!!"

"Does this happen a great deal to Wizards?" Tatya asked worriedly. "We followed Lakota's directions – he said we had to keep you warm and we spoon fed you strengthening broth and a herbal concoction Lakota knew but, oh, Simon – it's been a day and a night!" She looked ready to cry again.

"I did a Great Working," Simon found he could only whisper. "This is the usual outcome of a Great Working...."

"Then I don't want you doing any more of them!" said Tatya fiercely. "I thought you were dead or dying!" she shuddered. "I couldn't have borne it –" she bit her lip and turned her head away, determined not to cry any more.

"Cerridwen told me that it was the power of the ley lines leaving the Mage that makes the backlash. The more power drawn the greater the reaction," Lakota said. He lay his muzzle on Simon's pillow and confided "I was worried too, but I remembered that Cerridwen said Professor René was sick from magical counterblast for days when they were in Egypt."

"I had forgotten that," Simon murmured, closing his eyes.

"Could you eat something?" Tatya asked anxiously. "All that you have had for two days is broth."

Simon suddenly realized that he was very hungry indeed and opened his eyes again. "Food would be good," he agreed with much more animation.

Tatya helped him sit up with many more pillows and Simon saw that he was in one of the galleries, which accounted for Lakota being able to be with him. Unfortunately in front of him lay the heavily damaged garden, much changed by the earthquake.

Tatya helped him into a robe. "I helped Ping repair some of her porcelain and furnishings with the new repair spell that Grandmother Ninon developed. She'll be so pleased to hear that they worked beautifully!"

Simon looked down at the robe she was drawing over his shoulders. "This isn't mine," he said, staring at the blue Chinese silk embroidered heavily with gold dragons, seed pearls and semi-precious jewels.

"It's just one of the many gifts that people have been bringing to us!" said Lakota excitedly. "I have a collar of mutton fat jade! It's beautiful!"

"Gifts?" repeated Simon, feeling rather dull and stupid.

"Everyone in the entire valley is so grateful, Simon!" Tatya explained. "They have been coming with gifts ever since you stopped the flood. As soon as you are better you will have to see them in person."

"I've been thanking them," said Lakota. "There was a delegation from the village and they wanted to thank you in person."

"Were many people hurt in the earthquake?" Simon wanted to know.

Tatya sobered instantly. "Yes – unfortunately. There were too many deaths and some serious injuries. But it would have been much, much worse if that water had swept through the valley – most of the populace would have drowned. That is why they are hailing you as a hero, Simon! This beautiful robe is a gift from Prince Tuan. He arrived yesterday with some soldiers – they are doing what they can to help the people recover from the earthquake. This robe is a mark of his admiration and esteem."

"He gave me the jade collar," put in Lakota. "I like him – he is going to go with us when we go into the mountains to find the dragon poachers. Ning, the oldest Celestial, also wants to talk to you. He saw the Great Working and was very impressed. And Dr. Quong and Ash want to see you too."

"Not until he has eaten!" said Tatya firmly. "People and dragons will just have to wait! Lakota, you watch over him and don't let anyone bother him until I get back with a tray. Ping has had the cook make strengthening invalid food."

"Where's Janus?" Simon asked Lakota, suddenly anxious, for it seemed strange that his familiar was not at his side.

"She offered to watch Alan while Tatya stayed with you," Lakota answered. "They're both fine," he added, seeing the look on Simon's face. "Everyone here is fine – Alan was a little weepy and wanted someone familiar to be with him which is why Janus said she'd stay." Lakota unconsciously made a pun.

Simon smiled and lay back on the pillows. He was still very tired and for now more than content to let Tatya fuss over him. He would quickly recover now, with good food and good care. But tomorrow they had to make plans

And he suddenly remembered – the last person he had seen before he fainted was his cousin Tom. He would have to be dealt with as well.

13

Prince Tuan

Tom Stillfield was not at all certain that he was pleased with the current situation. It was pleasant to be warm and dry and well-fed again – even if the food was too spicy for his taste. But in spite of his broad hints and outright demands, nothing was being said about when he and Faversham would be able to go on with their quest for the jade mine. They had been told by that officious Prince that they must remain where they were for now. And yesterday soldiers had arrived to enforce this edict. He and Faversham were virtual prisoners in Dr. Quong's house.

Tom was certain that he did not like meeting up with his cousin Simon again after all these years. He had practically forgotten about him – only remembering how much he had disliked the other boy when they were both children – how jealous he had been of him, for their grandparents had always held Simon up as the example of a 'good boy' – one who was quiet, studious and obedient. Tom's jealousy and hatred were fanned every time that he heard "Why can't you be more like your cousin Simon?" particularly when Tom had got into yet another scrape. At the age of sixteen, when he considered himself quite grown-up, it had rankled to be compared to an eight-year-old – and to be found lacking when held up against that eight-year-old was even more galling.

And Simon seemed to have fallen on his feet – he was obviously wealthy – one look at his tailoring and the fact that he was able to keep a dragon told Tom that, although Tom had no idea where the money came from. Cousin Simon had a beautiful wife – a Russian Countess no less! – and what is more he was a Wizard. He could obviously have anything he wanted and yet in Tom's point of view, he was wasting all these gifts.

To Tom, money was power. Wizardry was power. Money could bend people to your will, as could Wizardry – here Tom's thoughts showed that he had no real understanding of what it meant to be a Wizard. And what was dear cousin Simon doing with all of his power? Teaching at a bloody University! Helping the Chinese to save a pack of useless dragons – nothing he had learned about Chinese dragons since arriving at Dr. Quong's had impressed him – he could not help but learn more about Chinese dragons as that was all these people bloody well talked about! At least at home the dragons were useful – they carried the Post and transported people and goods, amongst other needed functions, but these foreign creatures seemed only to create havoc and, in Tom's view, were better off dead and gone. Creatures who could create an earthquake ought to be eliminated.

When he was finally allowed to see his cousin Simon he was going to talk some sense into him – show him that he and his dragon would be better employed helping them to find the jade mine and making them all rich – or, in Simon's case, richer. It had been Tom's observation that no matter how rich a man was he always wanted more. Cousin Simon would be no exception to this rule.

In the meantime he would bide his time and perhaps indulge in a little dalliance. On the whole he found Chinese women unattractive, but one of the maids here had a saucy rear end that appealed to him – and it had been too long since he had had a woman – not since that brothel in Canton.

Tatya had taken an instant dislike to Simon's cousin. She found him loud, coarse and crude – unlike the refined gentlemen in the rest of Simon's family. Nor did she like the way he looked at her and every other woman in the house. She was more than a little dismayed that Dr. Quong had offered the hospitality of his home to Tom and Faversham – Faversham at least was a gentleman, albeit a rather stupid one – but Dr. Quong, who seemed sweetly naïve at times, was certain that any kinsman of Simon's could be nothing but a man of honor. Tatya was too well aware that many people had relatives that they would hesitate to introduce to the local dustman – dirty dishes, as Simon's adopted great grandfather Lord Lyonshall would have called them. Certainly her horrible relatives in St. Petersburg would be a source of shame and consternation if she had to introduce them in Dublin!

She had no worries about Tom's lascivious looks – if she caught him bothering any of the maids in the household or he tried his tricks on her or Ping she would administer a sharp lesson. Defense was the first magic she had learned and she had used it successfully more than once to defend her honor. She would enjoy putting him in his place, for the more she saw him the more she disliked him.

However, Prince Tuan, who had arrived just after Lakota had brought Simon home, she *did* like very much. Gentle, courteous and even a trifle shy, the Prince was obviously a thoughtful, kind person, who immediately put everyone at their ease. There was no height in his manner at all, considering that he was the third in line to the Dragon Throne and he treated Dr. Quong with great reverence both as a scholar and as his elder. Tuan at once sent his soldiers out to see how they could help the victims of the earthquake and personally inspected the damaged valley with Jian. Food, clothing, doctors and anything that was needed was forthcoming and somehow the Prince managed to see and offer sympathy to all those who had lost loved ones in the earthquake. Poor people were given money for burial and for temple offerings.

Tuan was also a quiet, unobtrusive guest who made few demands on the servants and graciously expressed his gratitude for the Quong hospitality at such a time of difficulty.

Between the two of them, Tatya would have thought Tom the Prince, for he seemed to expect, just because he was English, that his needs and want should come first to these 'heathen Chinks' as she had heard him refer to his hosts more than once. She knew what Simon would have to say to that! And she could tell that Ash disliked Tom as well, although he was too much of a diplomat to say so.

It took Simon a full day and another night to recover enough so that Tatya and the local doctor would let him see either Tom or the Prince. Tom was loud and obnoxious in his protests at this Turkish treatment but the Prince was understanding, saying that he would not wish to jeopardize the honorable sorcerer's recovery by insisting upon an audience. Even the Celestial dragon Ning, who frequently came to the garden, was content to wait, speaking to Lakota and asking him many questions about magic and the dragons of the West. Janus answered many of the elderly Celestial's inquiries about magic, since she was Simon's helper in many magical undertakings.

For two days all Simon did was eat and sleep. Three days after the Great Working he at last woke up clear-headed and feeling ready to rise from his bed. Other than Tatya and Alan he had seen only Dr. Quong and Ash very briefly.

Over Tatya's protests he dressed and went into breakfast, where he found the Prince and Dr. Quong deep in a discussion of one of Simon's own books – the manuscript of his new work on American dragons.

"Is it true, then," said Dr. Quong eagerly, after Simon and the Prince had exchanged bows and greetings and Simon had taken his seat at the table "the Savannah Silver dragon has six toes?" He looked up from a picture he had been perusing from the manuscript. "The American dragons do not much resemble our Chinese *lung.*"

"This Silver must be revered amongst its own kind," said the Prince.

Simon smiled."As a mater of fact the Silver is rather looked down on by other dragons, most of whom revel in working and making themselves useful. Of all the dragons I know it is the laziest. It spends a great deal of time sleeping and trying to get out of work. Most Silvers blame this on the hot temperatures in the American South – saying the heat makes them lethargic And yes, they do have six toes."

Prince Tuan looked rather startled. He was a young man of only twenty-four, with a slim, very athletic build, but a scholar's manner. His eyes, behind Western wire-rimmed spectacles, were warm and kind and full of intelligence. "I have noticed, Dr. Stillfield," he said quietly, "that your books make no mention of the rankings of the dragons. Which are considered superior?"

"The only superiority, if you can call it that, is in size – the Highland Dhu of the British Isles is the largest, with the New York Gold of America a close second. Our Western dragons do not have a hierarchy as do those here." Simon said 'thank you' in Chinese to the servant girl who put a full plate of *jook*, the usual breakfast food, in front of him. *Jook* consisted of boiled rice and dried scallops or dried shrimp, boiled with chicken bones. Simon actually found it quite palatable. *Jook* was a dish from southern China, but that was where Dr. Quong had been born and raised and he had brought the recipe with him when he came to the valley many years ago.

"Your command of our language is excellent," said the Prince, "as is your wife's. You have obviously studied long."

"And may I commend your Highness on your command of English?" said Simon, for that was the language in which they spoke at present.

At this moment Ping, bearing a bowl of *Don Mein*, came into the room. She had prepared these noodles for The Prince and Simon with her own hands. With her came Tatya and Faversham, followed by Tom slouching along.

Tom was in no good humor, and when he heard the talk was again turned to dragons he nearly groaned aloud. These people were damned bores on the subject! Faversham, the idiot, looked as interested as any of them and immediately began telling a long story about the Cornish Copper his family had employed for years and the interesting things (to him at least) it had said and done in the time he had known it. He even told the Prince about Dragon Day, when all the children were taken to meet the Post dragons and get rides and feed them dragon treats. The Prince was much struck by this and by the fact that dragons worked for their keep, and were not objects of veneration and worship.

"Talk to Lakota, your Highness," Simon suggested. "I am certain that he will tell you that the dragons of the British Isles would rather work – they like to be busy and useful. Merlin, when he changed them almost 1,000 years ago, implanted that desire and the love of mankind in them. Before that they were dangerous creatures indeed. Most modern dragons are ashamed that their ancestors were so savage and uncivilized."

The Prince nodded "And you speak to and work with dragons regularly!" he marveled. "I would give much to speak with one of our *lung!*" he added wistfully. Even though Ning had come to the garden several times to speak to Lakota, Tuan was too much in awe of the venerable Celestial to even approach him.

Tom, getting more irritated by the moment, played with his *jook* – there were bowls of fish with ginger, soy sauce and scallions, chicken with the same, and beef as well, to spoon over the *jook,* all of which were delicious – but he wanted none of them. He wanted a nice beefsteak, with a baked egg and some fried potatoes – perhaps a slice of a nice York ham, and a yeasty bread fresh from the oven. He noted with annoyance that his cousin manipulated those damned sticks which the Chinese used for utensils with perfect ease. Tom had bought knives, forks and spoons for himself and Faversham in Canton where one could still obtain such things – in his opinion chopsticks were just another sign of the complete lack of civilization in this heathen country. Inedible food, no proper beds, incomprehensible language, strange customs – he despised it all. And to his further annoyance cousin Simon spoke Chinese! Perhaps that was some sort of Wizard's spell. Tom's knowledge of magic was not very extensive.

"Why are you wasting your time on this dragon nonsense, cousin Simon?" he now said loudly, interrupting Dr. Quong's question about a point in Simon's manuscript concerning the Maple dragon of northern New England, a shy, rather reclusive creature.

"It is not nonsense!" Simon said, irked by Tom's rudeness and the graceless way he was slumped at the table and his clear indication of his dislike of the food in front of him, as well as his boredom with the topic of discussion. He was a strong contrast to Ash, who politely listened to everything that was said, even though he could have but a minimal interest in the more esoteric and technical dragon talk he was hearing. Even Faversham, although a mental lightweight, was at least pretending to look interested. It had been nearly twenty five years since Simon had seen Tom – and time had obviously done little to improve him.

107

"Dragons are my life's work – and restoring the dragons to their place of honor in Chinese society, as well as saving their lives, is very important to all of us here," he said in answer to Tom's protest.

Tom ignored the anger in his cousin's voice. "I have a far better use for a Wizard and a dragon – help us find the jade mine and we'll cut you in for a share! We'll all be fabulously rich!" He smiled knowingly at his cousin – who could resist such an offer?

Before Simon could respond to this proposition the Prince said quietly."I must beg to disappoint you, Mr. Stillfield. You and your companions are not to precede any further into my country. You are here without permission. This is a grave crime and were it not that you are related to Dr. Stillfield, who is an invited guest, I should be within my rights to have you imprisoned and perhaps executed. Tomorrow my soldiers will escort you back to Canton, where they will see you on a ship bound to the British Isles. Mr. Pendleton has authorized funds for this ship. The jade mine you seek is the property of the Dragon Throne and shall remain so."

Tom looked at him with blazing eyes as Faversham bleated "Oh, I say!"

"I understand that your father, Mr. Faversham, is of no little importance in your country. That is the only thing that saves your life as well. I do not wish to have – what is it you called it, Mr. Pendleton?" the Prince turned politely to Ash who supplied the phrase "a diplomatic incident."

"Yes, "repeated the Prince in satisfaction. "A diplomatic incident." He might look kind and mild, but his voice was strong and commanding. He expected to be obeyed. "You will do well to consider yourselves fortunate that I am inclined to clemency."

As Tom began to sputter the Prince put up his hand. "Do not try my patience further, I beg of you, or I shall have to have you removed."

Foolishly, Tom began to speak, which suddenly changed to a gasp of pain as a very sharp pang made itself known in his ankle.

Outraged, he looked down and saw a black and orange cat looking up at him. She had bitten him! Janus had done this to give this foolish man a little hint that he ought to keep his mouth closed before he did further damage. But before she could move back he drew back his foot and kicked her, sending her sailing out from under the table.

And the next thing he knew he was picked up by a whirlwind, tossed into the air and slammed against the wall. Dazed, he looked up to see his cousin standing over him with a white, set face in which his eyes burned with anger. "Don't you dare ever to do that again if you want to keep on living!" Simon said through clenched teeth.

"I kicked a bloody cat!" said Tom, defensively. What the hell was wrong? "It bit me! It's only a bloody cat!"

"Janus is my familiar!" Simon retorted. "Even if she were not, I don't allow any animal to be abused by you or anyone else!"

The Prince had watched wide-eyed as Simon, without touching him, had picked up his cousin from across the length and breadth of the table and spun him around, tossing him so hard against the wall that all the porcelain in the room rattled —not even using the magic stick that Dr. Quong had told him of. Magic was both wonderful and terrifying, the Prince decided. The air in the room crackled with power.

As Tom tried to stand, Simon pushed him back down on the floor with another burst of magic. "Is she all right?" he asked over his shoulder.

Janus lay on her side where she had landed, quite a distance from the table. Her eyes were closed and her breathing seemed a little ragged. Tatya had jumped up and gone to kneel beside her. She lightly passed her hand over the cat. As she did so, Marinka, closely followed by Xiu, came into the room.

"Oh, what has happened to my mother?" Marinka cried out. The Prince stared, for he had not yet been in company with the familiars. They had mostly stayed near Simon while he was in bed, lulling him to restful sleep with purring and keeping his bed warm with their furry bodies.

"I think she has a broken rib, Simon!" said Tatya worriedly, for the cat merely looked at her through glazed, half-shut eyes and meowed, rather than spoke, as if the effort of speech was too much.

"You had better pray that I can Heal her or you will need all your prayers for your own preservation!" Simon threatened Tom and, turning away, finally let his cousin rise.

"Oh, bad show!" Faversham said as he hurried forward to help Tom to his feet. "Never hurt a Wizard's familiar, what? It just isn't done, old boy!"

"It's only a damned moggy!" Tom snarled, pushing away Faversham's helping hand and heaving himself to his feet. "You people are all insane!"

With the aid of the traveling medical kit and book that Stuart, a medical student at the University of Edinburgh, had given Simon before his trip to Russia, Simon was able to set Janus's rib and make her comfortable. He could not completely heal it for he was not a natural Wizard Healer and lacked the training to be able to 'see' the broken bone the way a Wizard Healer could.

But this meant that Janus would not be able to accompany the party that would leave, perhaps as early as tomorrow, to find and stop the dragon poachers. Marinka, of course, although she bitterly resented it, would be staying behind with Tatya. And now it looked as if Janus would remain behind too.

Prince Tuan put two guards on the door of the room that Tom and Faversham shared. They would be put on their way south in the morning, closely watched until they reached Canton and then seen onto the ship.

But the next morning, when a tray was taken to the room, laden with breakfast for the two prisoners, they were gone. They had discovered a weak spot in the wall, made, no doubt, by the earthquake, and had enlarged it into a man-sized hole, making good their escape. A search of the surrounding countryside failed to find any trace of them, for they had stolen two horses from the stable as well.

14

 **Strange Companions**

It was decided that helping the dragons was of more importance than finding Tom and Faversham. Prince Tuan would send a detail of his soldiers to hunt for them, but it was felt that with little ready money and no supplies they might well return to Huang Lung Valley in defeat. They had not even taken Gao Kun with them. He was allowed to go on his way, home to Mongolia, for accepting the guide position with Tom and Faversham had been a way for him to get there, as he had few funds of his own.

Accordingly, the next day Simon began packing up to start on their journey and readying Lakota and his gear.

Prince Tuan and Dr. Quong were fascinated with every aspect of the preparations. The Prince was as excited as a small boy at the thought of riding a dragon high in the sky. He had expected to go to the areas where the dragons had been taken on horseback – a rather lengthy and difficult trip into the mountains.

In preparation, Simon first gave Lakota a good oil bath, for it could be a good while before this might be accomplished again and a dragon with itchy skin was not happy and his saddle and breast harness might even chafe. Dr. Quong was full of questions about the necessity for this and wanted to know if this was obligatory for American dragons as well. It was, Simon explained, for most of the dragon breeds in the Americas were the result of dragons from the British Isles mingling and mating with the few native dragons. Dragons had gone to the New World with the very earliest settlers. So powerful was Merlin's spell that the characteristics of the British dragons had dominated in the breeding.

Lakota always loved an oil bath – it made him wiggle and sigh in delight as Simon used a soft brush and a cloth to get the oil in between his scales and wiped it carefully around his face. Even his talons were well oiled.

Then the dragon tack was cleaned. Prince Tuan marveled at the dragon saddle. It had six seats – Simon explained that a big Highland Dhu, who sometimes could be forty feet long compared to Lakota's twenty-five feet, could carry as many as twenty or thirty people if necessary.

"I can carry ten or twelve, and their baggage, if I had to," Lakota told the Prince. "But six is more comfortable."

A dragon saddle was not one piece, but several – technically, it should be called 'saddles' for each separate unit had two seats, with a hole in the center between the seats to fit over the spinal ridge – the triangular shaped 'fins' on a dragon's back. Each saddle had to be custom-made for each dragon, and in the course of a draconic lifetime, this had to be done several times as the dragon grew. Each saddle had a girth, like a horse's saddle, but for added security a dragon always had a breast-plate, that each saddle was connected to beneath its belly, as an added   safety precaution. On this breast harness on the dragon's chest was hung a tight knit mesh bag in which the dragon carried the bulk of the luggage. Panniers could also be attached to the saddle.

For the rider's safety, harness hung from each saddle. A belt went around the waist and another went over the shoulder. These were always magiced to adjust to the rider perfectly and on a saddle made for a Wizard, the buckles and rings were of silver, copper or brass to avoid the danger of Cold Iron. All dragon saddlers kept a Wizard on staff to do this bespelling as it was an absolute necessity. A Wizard such as Simon could renew these spells his own self but non-magical persons had to take the saddle back to the saddlery every year or so for a spell renewal. If the person forgot to do this the dragon would remind them. Lakota explained that dragons were very concerned for the safety of their riders and insisted on frequent safety inspections and the timely renewal of the strap spells.

Each saddle also had built into it a pull out handle – sturdy and thick for timid riders to hold onto, and the rear saddles had pull out leg rests so that the rider's leg would not interfere with the wings.

There was no bridle to the dragon tack. When the Prince remarked on this Simon said "Lakota knows where he is going better than I do – why would he need a bridle, which is after all for commands and control – he has no need to be controlled or commanded."

By ten in the morning of the next day they were packed and ready. Lakota's web harness contained foodstuffs, a tent and bedding, a traveling Wizard's kit, the Wizard's medical kit, a box for money and weapons. It was not necessary to carry much water, for a dragon could find water in a sand-filled desert. Ash had brought enough rifles and pistols with him from Canton for all of them and extra ammunition was stored in a waterproofed, magiced case. Simon also had his Elfin bow and arrows, with which he was proficient indeed. Ash looked doubtful when he saw these last – old fashioned weapons he considered them – but Lakota laughed and said "Wait until you see what Simon can do with those ! They can reach distances a gun cannot!" Prince Tuan had a sword as well.

Lakota carried only the minimum of firestone. These hills were full of it and after discussing the matter with Simon, he had decided to drink the water from the pools and see how far that would carry him. He had been drinking it regularly since his discovery and had noticed that the more often he drank, each time he drank it, the effects lasted longer. It seemed to have a cumulative effect on his capacity for flight and flame. Simon intended to do a chemical analysis of the water when they returned.

Jian was to stay behind, with several of the soldiers, in case Tom and Faversham did return. Dr. Quong did not like to leave the women unprotected and looked at Simon in surprise when Simon declared that Tatya was more than capable of protecting the entire household. The Chinese Dracophilologist was too used to thinking of women as tender plants that needed constant care from males. "My wife is a very powerful Witch," Simon explained. "Her defensive magic is particularly strong. She came to Witchcraft late but has learned rapidly and is already nearing the top levels of her craft."

But neither Dr. Quong nor the Prince, nor Jian himself could be comfortable leaving the women, children and servants alone and Jian was the logical one to remain behind.

Simon was explaining to the Prince and Dr. Quong how to mount and secure themselves in the saddle – each was both a little nervous and also elated – when T'a Ming dropped out of the sky. And on her back rode the panda Chao, with one paw clutching a back ridge and the other covering his tightly shut eyes. A large lumpy bag was tied to one of her spinal ridges.

The white dragon bowed low before Lakota, "If it pleases you, noble *t'ein lung* La-ko-ta, my honorable superiors desire that I accompany your expedition to see and observe. I may also be of help, they feel, for I have been made privy to the location of all the places that our *lung* have died and have some idea of exactly where the evil warlord has her lair. They desire me as well to make you known to the *lung* of that region." As she spoke, she remained in a humble position, her whickers writhing, not in happiness but in agitation.

"That is a bear cat!" Dr. Quong said in surprise, looking at Chao, who growled at him.

"And why are you here, Chao?" queried Lakota of the panda. He or T'a Ming would have to serve as translator between the panda and the humans, for although Chao understood human language well enough and even could speak Chinese, it was animal Chinese and not under-standable to human ears, not even Simon's.

"To protect her!" the panda spat. "Can't you see she's terrified of this trip? Those idiot Celestials ought to have picked someone different, someone braver – or better yet, gone themselves!" He obviously lacked the reverence for the Celestial dragons that everyone else had.

Lakota told this to the humans and then said very gently to T'a Ming "I will protect you. Simon is giving dragon whistles to everyone – you and Chao shall each have one and I shall fly as fast as I can to help you should we become separated. But stay with me and you shall be safe."

The look of gratitude she gave him was piteous – she was indeed terrified out of her wits. But from his observations of her Lakota knew that she was too much in awe of the Celestials ever to question or protest anything they told her to do. Again he thought what a stupid system these dragons lived under. He would never put up with it, that was for certain!

114

"Chao does me great honor, to come with me and be my protector," she offered timidly. "For he is much afraid of heights –"

Chao interrupted this with a roar and demanded "Why did you tell him that? He doesn't need to know that!" On his furry face was an expression of mingled rage and chagrin.

"But don't pandas live at high elevations?" Lakota said in surprise. Her had learned a little about the great bears from questioning Dr. Quong and the other members of the household. Pandas lived in dense bamboo and coniferous forests some 5,000 to 10,000 feet up in the mountains, so high that they were cloud or mist shrouded much of the year. Bamboo was their primary food – the stalks and roots – but they also fed on gentians, iris, crocus and fish, with an occasional small rodent. Lakota had learned that it was very unusual to see a panda on the valley floor.

"I don't live there! My home is in the valley," said Chao brusquely. "Don't tell those humans I'm afraid!" he added, for they had been speaking in Animal.

Lakota agreed to this and merely told the humans that Chao was T'a Ming's friend and wanted to help the dragons too.

Both Dr, Quong and the Prince bowed respectfully to the panda. Ordinarily, people had little to do with the great bear cats, although they were much revered in China – artistic depictions of them went back for centuries and they were a much-loved figure. But they were shy and there were not all that many of them.

Ash reflected that one never knew what was going to happen in the company of Wizards, and looking at the panda's size – he was almost six feet long and probably weighed close to 25 stone (350 pounds) – and at his powerful jaw, Ash decided that if there was fighting, Chao would be a formidable opponent. Simon, of course, was far too used to all sorts of Faeries, leprechauns, and such to cavil at a panda's accompanying them.

At last every one was ready – goodbyes were said, embraces exchanged and the two dragons went aloft, Dr. Quong, the Prince and Chao all with their eyes closed.

115

Lakota was careful to watch out for T'a Ming. He insisted that she fly by his side – she had a tendency to want to hang back in respect for his status as a *t'ein lung*, but he could not keep a proper eye on her if she was behind him. Besides, if he needed to talk to her it would be much easier if she flew next to him than shouting backwards over his tail. He was concerned about Chao as well – the panda's seat seemed none too secure and he still kept his eyes firmly shut, covered with one paw while he held on to her spinal ridge with the other. Both Dr. Quong and Prince Tuan had long since opened their eyes and were exclaiming in wonder at the views below them and marveling over the smoothness of Lakota's flight. They both held the handles of their saddles tightly, though, where Simon and Ash did not. But Simon and Ash had grown up riding dragons – it was nothing new to them.

While they were in Russia Simon had bought toys for Lakota and Tatya's young brother Sacha. Made in China, these toys depicted in painted tin and clockwork a Chinaman with a long pigtail riding a Chinese dragon. These were mechanical toys, meant to be wound up and then 'fly' along a table top or a floor, but Simon had magiced them so that they actually flew in the air. Lakota still treasured his.

Lakota saw now that the attractive little toys were wrong – humans did not ride dragons here – it was a very rare occurrence, found only in myth. Most of these dragons considered it degrading to carry a human and wondered at Lakota being willing to do it. He though this a stupid, narrow-minded attitude. He loved carrying his people and going places with them!

At Lakota's rate of speed – which was not overly fast - the party soon landed at a place high in the mountains to the south near to where most of the dragons had been poached. Lakota had picked a spot large enough for both dragons to land and have a comfortable campsite. Simon left these decisions up to him. Lakota knew what was needed and could sniff out water as well.

It was rugged terrain – above the tree line where the air was thinner and much cooler and the landscape consisted of little other than boulders, and stony soil. It would be a cold night but it would not be dark for hours yet – time enough to make a comfortable camp and perhaps scout the area.

Prince Tuan's soldiers were to follow them on horseback. Lakota estimated that this would take at least three to four days, if not more, depending on the weather and the ground conditions. He was confident that he and Simon between them could handle a necromancer and a band of bandits.

The Prince and Dr. Quong were loud in their praise of their first ride dragon-back and marveled at how quickly they had arrived at their destination. They were still a bit nervous about being up in the sky so high but both had been brave enough to open their eyes.

The Prince, looking about at the bare rock of their campsite worried aloud about how they would be warm and cook their food, for there was no wood or dung to make a fire.

While Simon had put up the tent, Ash had busied himself making a ring of large stones. This he filled with smaller, dense rocks.

When Simon had finished with the tent, he walked over to this small cairn and said approvingly "I see you've been camping with a Wizard before!"

Ash grinned. "Yes, with my cousin Arthur – the *Magus Majori* I told you of – our favorite holidays are walking tours and Arthur always makes a ley line fire for us to cook on and keep warm."

"Are you going to do more magic?" the Prince asked eagerly as he overheard this exchange. He hurried over to where Ash and Simon stood near the pile of stones.

He watched breathlessly as violet fire seemed to run off Simon's hands and an answering blue-white burning seemed to come up from the earth to meet it. The two sets of flames mingled and then spread over the rocks, seeming to ignite each one, until within minutes, it subsided into a steady glow, looking like burning lumps of charcoal. But unlike charcoal, these would not turn to ash. They would burn until Simon desired them to quit, providing even heat for cooking and sending out a reliable, steady warmth. As the

117

Prince looked the colour changed from the blue-white and violet to the normal reds, yellows oranges and flashes of blues found in a fire. Simon explained that this was purely cosmetic – many non-magicals found a violet/white fire disconcerting, so mage fires were always coloured by the Wizard to look as if they were ordinary wood or coal blaze.

"Your Highness!" came Dr. Quong's voice, rather breathlessly. "You must really see this – it is extraordinary!"

He had gone into the tent when Simon had finished erecting it – he had been certain that four men could not fit into such a small tent – at least not comfortably – and had poked his head in – and been amazed.

It was so spacious! It was as large as a house! There was furniture in it and separate rooms with soft beds – even a room with sanitary facilities. Twice he went inside and looked at it and then went outside to look at the outside, trying to reconcile the interior with the exterior. But this was impossible – they bore no relation to one another.

Prince Tuan was equally stunned and declared that he wished they still had Wizards in China, when such miracles were possible. He said that when he returned to the Forbidden City he wished to ascertain why there were no Wizards that he knew of, in his country, when the old tales from the days of his ancestors were filled with Wizards. Surely Wizardry should be encouraged and studied!

He had many more questions about magic. Tea was made and the men sat about the campfire, discussing this and their plans for tracking the dragon poachers as a stew made with dried vegetables, meat and stock from Simon's stores began to bubble away in a very large pot.

Chao, who had slid from T'a Ming's back and nearly kissed the ground in gratitude, went quietly, staggering a bit, to one side and drew some bamboo shoots from the large bag he had tied to one of T'a Ming's spinal ridges and began to chew. He looked out of sorts and ill-tempered but that, Lakota suspected from the little he knew of the panda, was not unusual for him, and the blue dragon judged it best to leave Chao alone. Perhaps a good meal would sweeten his temper.

Lakota was worried about T'a Ming. She had been uninterested in the magic performed, and even as the savory aroma of the stew began to fill the air she neither lifted her head and sniffed nor appeared hungry. She remained low on the ground, crouched down as if to hide herself and shivered involuntarily every once in a while.

Lakota went to sit beside her, bearing a dragon-sized mug of tea for her and asked very kindly what was wrong.

She gave a tremendous shudder and said "I am certain that by going on this journey that I am heading to my own death, noble one. Pray forgive this lowly four-toed one for inflicting her fears upon your honorable self!" she added hurriedly, afraid that she had offended him.

"I'm your friend – I want to help you," he replied, reaching out to touch her nose to his. Among Western dragons this was a greeting and a gesture of caring and comfort – he hoped it would be interpreted as such by her. "Why do you think that this trip will be your death?"

"I cast the *I Ching* – the Book of Changes – yester eve and I did not like what I saw there," she answered.

Lakota had studied, with Simon, this aspect of Chinese beliefs. The *I Ching* was an oracle, based on the belief that the universe followed fixed laws and patterns, which made the future entirely predictable. Lakota found this idea rather amusing – as if anyone, even a very talented Augur, could know the future so precisely! To him, it made no sense at all. But he could see that Ta Ming firmly believed it. Lakota had more faith in the Tarot cards, used by a genuine psychic Talent, than in the three coins or yarrow stalks used in the *I Ching*. And he had even more faith in his ability or Simon's to protect the white dragoness from harm.

But however foolish he thought her fears, they were very real and he had to soothe her. If she were too frightened to function, she might be a serious liability.

"I'll asked Simon to put a protective spell on you," he suggested, urging her to drink her tea. He thought it might soothe her nerves. But the cup shook in her talons and a great deal of the fragrant brew spilled on the ground.

But to bespell her proved impossible, for as Simon explained to a frustrated Lakota, T'a Ming was as terrified of his white magic as she was of what she believed to be her eminent death.

"White magic, magic of the Light, cannot be *forced* on anyone," he explained to an interested Dr. Quong and Prince Tuan. "T'a Ming cannot, of her own free will, *accept* the magic. I took an oath to do no harm and that means I cannot force her to be bespelled, even though it is for her own good."

Lakota understood this – he had been around White magic since he had been hatched. But it was difficult for him to understand her fear of it. And he became incensed again at the arrogance and stupidity of the Celestials, who had sent this poor, timid creature into danger. That egotistic Xiang ought to have been the one to come on this expedition instead of sitting at home in comfort! And Lakota would be the first to tell him so when they reached Huang Lung Valley again. But for now he would have to exert himself to protect T'a Ming as best he could. She would not be able to do it herself.

15
Pearls Of Wisdom

Prince Tuan lay awake a long time that evening after everyone had retired. He had much to think about – both the plan for action against the dragon poachers and the magical things he had seen that day.

He had been much struck by what Simon had told him about magic – the Wizard had explained that magic was not static – it was always changing and that there were Wizards, at the great Universities and in independent laboratories, who were continually working on and developing new spells. Even the ley line fire was a relatively new spell. Thirty years ago it did not exist – then, one could only draw the heat of the ley lines in a holy or sacred place. Now it was possible to tap it almost anywhere. And in his father's day a mage had to be standing near or on top of a ley line to use its full potential. Simon had even spoken of how the methods of teaching magic to young students had changed since his father was young.

This seemed almost incomprehensible to the Prince. In China, tradition was everything. Little had changed in thousands of years – the way of life, the way things were done – it remained the same.

He burned to reintroduce magic to his homeland. At first his first thought was that it would make his country invincible in war but Simon had told him that Wizards took an oath NOT to kill – magic was for defense only – not to wage warfare. Even in the late hostilities with Bonaparte the only magic used had been that of Augury – and that largely to predict the weather for Lord Wellington and his troops.

Prince Tuan was startled to learn that in spite of their flaming abilities and tearing talons, dragons did not go to war. Aggression was no longer in their nature and they found it impossible to hurt human beings – unless protecting their immediate family – and they preferred not to have to kill.

Only in the case of a black or blood magician, Simon had explained, would he use magic to eliminate someone – he had a duty, as a practitioner of the White magic of the Light, to rid the world of those who used Dark magics for evil purposes. Like his oath to do no harm, he had sworn to do away with malevolent magics and those who practiced them.

Before the Prince finally fell asleep – he had to get used to the Western style bed – he daydreamed about restoring magic to the Chinese Empire – and what if he himself could practice magic? It was a heady thought!

At the fortress of Kwen-Lum, one day before Simon and his party arrived in the mountains, Ch'ang Hao sat brooding in the room that Si Wang had given him to use as his magical laboratory.

It was very late on a dark and moonless night. Overhead, the remnants of a fearful storm swept by at speed. Clouds black as the inks ground for calligraphy were carried away rapidly by a fierce and strong wind.

Everyone else was sleeping, save for the guards Si Wang always posted. Even the warlord herself lay sleeping in the arms of her current favorite.

Once again Ch'ang sat in front of the dragons' pearls. He now had a significant amount of them. They were not all bluish white, as was a true pearl, for some were red and others were gold.

The pearls before Ch'ang seemed somehow diminished. When worn under a dragon's chin they had a luminescent quality, seeming to shoot little flames visible to the discerning eye. These had faded – much like a string of pearls that needed to be worn against human skin to keep their quality.

He still had not been able to unlock their secrets. The dragons' pearls were, among other virtues, rumored to multiply anything they touched but repeated experiments with everything from gold to silk had failed to yield so much as a shadow representation.

And so much was locked in the pearls! Not only the wisdom of the dragons, but many old scrolls said that the pearl held the secrets of truth and of life itself and that everlasting life was available to those who understood the truth.

The pearl was called the image of thunder, the image of the sun, of the moon and even of the egg emblem – which symbolized the duality of nature. It was also called the 'pearl of potentiality'.

But whatever potential the pearls had Ch'ang had failed to realize.

He had tried every spell he knew – all of the black magics he had spent so many years studying. He had some mastery over the five elements – fire, water, air, earth and metal, but none of those had made any impression on the pearls. He had tried the dagger magic he had learned in Tibet from the forbidden black Buddhist monks. Consultation of the *I Ching* was equally fruitless – what he read there was more confusing than helpful and usually the *I Ching* spoke clearly to him.

There was no help for it. He would have to summon one of the *Kuei*.

The *Kuei* were demons – some scrolls claimed that they were demons that may have developed from the souls of humans who were not properly honored at their deaths or perhaps the victims of murder – those who died under mysterious circumstances. Others said that they were ghosts or spirits. Some called them the Hungry Ghosts.

Whatever they actually were, they were dangerous. They could inhabit animate or inanimate objects. They could assume the aspect of a member of one's own family and could mimic every thing in nature, visible and invisible. And, as well, they could become hideous monsters. They sought revenge for the ills they perceived humankind had done them – not merely on those who had failed to honor them, or had killed them, but on *all* of humankind.

Summoning them and controlling them called for an elaborate ritual and a sacrifice of a goat or a sheep or even a human being. Preparations would have to be made – not something that he could do this night – he needed rest to summon and control a demon – particularly control it.

The ceremony would have to be two days hence, for Si Wang's men had found another dragon and they would leave early the next morning to catch and kill it. Ch'ang would need energy for the spells he used upon the dragon as well.

Over the glass bowl of pearls Ch'ang cast a cloth of blue silk, depicting stylized blue dragons playing with a pearl.

Ch'ang pushed back the stool on which he sat and, with the aid of his magical staff, pushed himself to his feet. He was no longer as limber as he once was.

Without his staff of consecrated bamboo he could work very little magic. He had not been able to precede much beyond the level of sorcery of the *Use of Magical Tools*, for he had been self-taught. and as all the texts he had read said that to be a Master required the teachings of a Master – the Master would find the pupil when the time was propitious. But no Master had ever found him, as the scrolls had said. He had come to realize that there *were* no Masters any more.

Tomorrow he would consult the *Shang Shu, the Book of Ancient Texts*. Much of it was useless to a black magician such as himself, but there were small kernels of truths he could use to his advantage.

He waved his staff and the lights, which consisted of several bowls of oil furnished with twisted pieces of rope to serve as wicks, went out abruptly. He then sought his bed – a thick mat on the top of a *kang* which was heated with dried water buffalo dung. He thought little of the coming dragon slaughter – it had become almost too commonplace. What he thought of as he slid into sleep was the demon – would it finally help him to unlock the secrets of the pearls?

Lakota was the first to awaken in the morning. The temperature had fallen during the night but the ley line fire still burned. Lakota, T'a Ming and Chao had all curled up next to it.

T'a Ming had finally gone to sleep, utterly worn out from emotion. Lakota had heard he, sobbing quietly far into the night as Chao had growled imprecations against the Celestials until he too had fallen asleep

Lakota yawned and stretched, spreading his wings and to his surprise heard someone say "Ah!" in tones of delight.

He turned his head sharply and saw an extremely elderly man sitting on the opposite side of the fire. His face was a mass of wrinkles with wise, dark eyes. His hair was snow-white, as was the wisp of beard on his chin and his sparse, long tails of mustache. He wore robes of scarlet, embroidered with phoenixes, set in circular designs on the front panels and in bands about the hem and sleeves. A matching cap topped his head.

"Hello," Lakota said in Chinese, surprised to see this man. Simon had warded the campsite last night – no one should have been able to enter. "How did you get here?"

The man smiled. It was a sincere, friendly smile that made his eyes crinkle and Lakota warmed to him instantly.

"I am Feng Hu," he said, as if the mere announcement of his name explained everything. He inclined his head in a reverent bow. "And you, most honorable dragon, are not only a *t'ein lung*, but have attained the status of a *ying – lung* as well. Even in my long life I have never seen a winged dragon and I am honored that I should live to see one."

His Chinese was strangely accented. Oberon's gift though, enabled Lakota to adjust to it easily.

"What is this star that blazes on your forehead?" Feng Hu then asked.

Lakota was astonished. "You can see that?" he exclaimed in surprise. No human he had ever met had been able to see that mark of Elfin favor. Simon and Janus bore it as well. Even other Wizards and Witches sometimes failed to notice it.

How to explain it to a Chinese person? As far as Lakota knew and had studied, there were no Elves, as they knew them, here in China. For some reason Lakota did not understand, there was an air about this man that spoke of only good – and Lakota had no reservations in trusting him, even though in his family they spoke only to one another of their visits to the Hollow Hills.

"It is a mark of favor from the High King of the *Sidhe* – who are magical, immortal beings who live in the Hollow Hills at home in the Six Nations," he finally settled on.

"Ah!" said the old man again, as if he understood.

"How did you get past Simon's wards?" Lakota then demanded.

125

"You do not know of me?" the elderly man returned.

"No," said Lakota "But then I am not Chinese – I'm an American dragon, but I now think of myself as Irish, since I have lived in Ireland since I was hatched."

"I am a magician," the old man said. "When I felt a deep stirring in the *chi* I woke from my long sleep. I must be needed."

"How long were you asleep?" Lakota asked curiously.

"I went to my rest when the House of the Han sat upon the dragon throne."

Lakota had studied the dynasties of China – the Qing were the present rulers. There had been more than one Han dynasty – all were ancient, even the most recent was almost 1,000 years ago. As the blue dragon remembered – and dragons had remarkable memories –the first Han dynasty had begun about 206 B.C... "That's over two thousand years ago!" he protested. "If you are speaking of the first Han dynasty..."

"There has been more than one?" Feng Hu inquired with interest.

Lakota stared at him in consternation. He still liked the old man but was beginning to wonder if he was slightly mad.

"You have not as yet told me your name," the old man said gently. "If I am to be your guest, I should be honored to know the names of my host."

"I'm Lakota," the dragon replied. He pointed a talon at T'a Ming and Chao and pronounced their names. "When the humans awake I shall introduce them to you as well, but Simon is going to want an explanation as to how you were able to overstep the wards he set."

"It was not a simple task," Feng Hu admitted. "The magical barriers were strong and well-set. This Simon of which you speak, Lah–ko–ta, is he the magician? Is it he who I can feel in the power of the earth?"

Lakota nodded. "And there is also a black magician who is killing dragons. Simon is a White magus. We are here to help the dragons"

"Yes, I could feel his good intent," said the old man almost to himself. "But his magic is different from mine own.

126

We must meet and talk. Perhaps we might help one another. I have been called from my sleep for a reason."

"They should be stirring soon," said Lakota, eyeing the sun as it came up over the mountains. Even though it had been light for some time the sun had not as yet peeked over the stony crags. "While we wait, may I make you a cup of tea?"

"That would be much appreciated," said Feng Hu, with a bow of his head. "And will you be so good as to tell me of the magician and his companions?"

Lakota agreed to this as both T'a Ming and Chao began to awake. Simon would be quite surprised to find a Chinese magician at breakfast.

They had risen at sunrise and mounted up to ride long and hard to where the dragon had been seen.

Ch'ang Hao was no horseman. He had never become used to riding on horseback and felt that the horse knew it and scorned him, even the fat, gentle mare that Si Wang provided for his use. It was three hours of rough riding through rocky and treacherous terrain before they reached the small, hidden valley where the dragon came to drink. There were few trees and but sparse vegetation in the valley pocket.

Si Wang's best scouts had observed a dragon here almost daily at about the same time each day. It came to drink the crystal water and nibble upon an elderly, stunted fruit tree.

Chen Bo was one of Si Wang's most trusted and valued officers. He was completely devoted to her – particularly since he had been allowed to share her bed on numerous occasions. He was one of the most assiduous dragon killers and delighted in trapping and butchering the creatures. He nearly always won the honor of putting the caterpillar in the creature's nose his own self, for he had found most of the dragon victims.

In appearance he was a short, stocky man with a block-like head and face. Ch'ang had originally thought him rather stupid – but that block like exterior hid an astute and ambitious brain.

They had to wait an hour before the dragon appeared.

It was a *shen–lung*, a Spirit dragon, azure in colour, which indicated it was of the sky or the clouds. It was three-toed, and relatively young. It was female, Ch'ang guessed.

"Sorcerer!" hissed Chen Bo *sotto vice*. "Look at her sides! I think that she is with egg!"

Eagerly, Ch'ang peered at the dragon from their place of hiding.

There was a distinct bulge in its slim sides and Ch'ang grew dizzy for a moment. Dragon eggs were worth a fortune and they could cut this one from its mother's womb when she was dead.

Dragons were fatally easy to compel. Ch'ang cast an illusion that was guaranteed to ensnare them – their own greed and arrogance entrapped them. Many of them believed themselves invulnerable to magic or death and would not heed warnings.

The dragon looked around her, saw nothing and smelled nothing. Si Wang's men were clever hunters – they were downwind of her and well hidden amongst the rocks in their dark armor of rhinoceros hide. Reassured, the dragon put her head down and drank deeply.

Ch'ang lifted his staff. From its tip burst a swarm of illusory swallows, all chattering in their high-pitched voices.

The dragon looked up sharply and lunged for them as they passed close to her head. No *lung* could resist swallows – the birds were their favorite food. While she was most vulnerable, her attention elsewhere, with swift motions of his staff Ch'ang cast his net of black energies that held her fast against the earth.

The properties of this net prevented her from using the few magics dragons had – that of changing size at will and becoming invisible.

Once she was caught fast Si Wang's men ran forward with wooden pegs and hammers and staked her down so that the web held her flat against the ground. As she screamed in rage and terror they went about their work with grim efficiency.

Then came the most dangerous part. Her jaws were snapping ineffectively against the restraints where her snout protruded from the widely spaced mesh of the web and her teeth, although not as long and as sharp as those of a Western dragon, could still do considerable damage to a man.

Several of Si Wang's younger followers had become quite dexterous at throwing a looped rope over the dragon's muzzle and then pulling it tight. Sometimes it took more than one try but in the end they always accomplished their task. Today was no exception. One, then two, and three ropes encircled her snout, making it impossible for her teeth to be at all useful and muffling her loud shrieks as effectively as a gag.

Si Wang, clad in gleaming black armor trimmed in silver, strolled up to Chen Bo and handed him a small lacquered box. "You have the honor, Chen," she said.

Eagerly, he opened the box and took a small caterpillar in his hand. He approached the dragon with a malevolent look on his face. holding out the caterpillar so that she might see it.

She gave a great muffled scream when she saw the tiny creature, for she knew that it meant her doom. Uselessly, she fought against the restraints, trying to lift her head so that he could not reach her face.

Three of Si Wang's strongest young men held her head down with the ropes, their strength augmented by the black magic if Ch'ang Hao.

She had no chance at all. She cried aloud in despair as Chen Bo placed the tiny caterpillar in her right nostril and Ch'ang pushed it along with a burst of magic.

It reached her brain within ten minutes and began to feast immediately, for the brain of a living dragon was quite its favorite food.

It took three hours for her to die – the caterpillar had no need to eat the entire brain – the section he favored was the one that governed the nervous system and that caused a quick death – but unfortunately not a painless one. The men watched her death throes without a twinge of guilt or compassion.

Ch'ang was more than a little disgusted by Si Wang's behavior at these times. The death of the dragon seemed to arouse her sexually and she always picked four men to fight one another while they waited for the dragon to die. The winner was allowed to take her – and what sickened Ch'ang even more, the losers got a turn as well – right in full view of all the others, who made ribald comments and urged their comrades on with laughter and cheers or jeers. Ch'ang wondered that they had any respect for her at all, behaving like a common whore as she did. But somehow she was well respected and even feared by the men.

Ch'ang deliberately turned his back on this disgusting activity and walked away to be by himself.

Thus he was alone when he felt it. A tremor, not unlike an earthquake but invisible to the others ran through him. A tingle ran up and down his spine and into this fingers and head. It came up from the ground into his staff.

He knew at once what it was – someone else was using magic. But WHO? he thought, puzzled. As far as he knew he was the only practicing magician left in China. Only the monks – but they never ventured from their mountain fastness in the land of Bod! Who could it be? He had to find out! And find out quickly!

Behind him, Si Wang's display of her charms over, the men began their grisly task of cutting apart the now dead dragon.

16

The Han Magician

Shortly after Lakota had made tea for himself and Feng Hu, T'a Ming and Chao came fully awake.

The white dragoness awoke heavy-eyed, looking as if she had been plagued by ill dreams and was completely unrefreshed by her sleep. Chao, as usual, was in a bad temper and he did not look happy to see yet another human. Sending a low growl Feng Hu's way, ignoring the magician's courteous bow, he lumbered off to where he had left the bag of bamboo the night before and took enough from it to make a breakfast. He then flopped on the ground and began to eat, keeping his eyes on the group at the campfire.

T'a Ming bowed to the old man, addressing him as 'Venerable *Wu.*" She seemed to know of him, but then she was even older than he was, Lakota reflected, if indeed they were not both mad.

"What does *Wu* mean?" he asked curiously as he poured tea into a dragon-sized cup for T'a Ming.

"Sorcerer," said T'a Ming, looking at Lakota in surprise. "You do not know of the honorable Feng Hu, who studied at the magic mountain of Taishan, where heaven and earth meet? It is said that the venerable *Wu* ascended all 6,300 steps to the Temple of the Jade Emperor and from there he passed through Heaven's Gate!"

"In my time," said Feng Hu mildly, "I was considered one of the outsiders – the *fangshi* – a person of technique – for I deviated from the path laid out for such as I by the Dragon Throne. I did not always take the path of official doctrine," he added, with a twinkle in his eyes "for the official doctrine did not always allow for the truth behind the natural laws that I sought all of my life. It was one reason why I took my rest – and at the time of the Han, sorcery was coming under suspicion and many of the *Wu* were accused of charlatanism. After the conductor of souls, Li Shou, was executed as a fabricator of portents, many of us judged it best to leave our homeland or to sleep away the years until we should be needed again."

Lakota nodded. "Like Merlin," he said. Of course, this meant as much to his listeners as all the talk of *Wu* had meant to him. Likening Feng Hu to Merlin made sense to the blue dragon, for everyone in the British Isles knew that Merlin, like Arthur and his knights, lay sleeping, in a secret place, waiting until the time came when he was sorely needed.

They had been talking quietly as the sun mounted into the heavens. It was still early, for midsummer was drawing near. Movement at the door of the tent caught Lakota's eye and he said happily, "Here is Simon!"

Simon was the first up – both Dr. Quong and the Prince still slept while Ash was just beginning to stir. Simon was indeed surprised to see an elderly Chinese gentleman at their fireside.

Lakota hurried toward his friend and low-voiced, told him of Feng Hu and all that he had learned of the Chinese magician as they walked to the camp fire.

Feng Hu stood up as Simon drew close and bowed deeply. "Do I address the honorable maker of magics?" he inquired.

Simon returned his bow, inclining his head in assent. "Lakota tells me that you are a magician as well," he said.

"And as I have learned," Fen Hu remarked. "one of considerable antiquity." A small, warm chuckle escaped him. "I felt you in the *chi* and it woke me from my long sleep."

Simon sat down at the fire's edge where convenient rocks made handy, if rather hard, seats. He poured himself a cup of tea after replenishing Feng Hu's cup.

"Lah-ko-ta has told me of the dragon poachers," said Feng Hu, sipping slowly at his tea and savoring it as he had the first. "I should like to offer my services. Perhaps that is why I was awakened."

Like Lakota before him, Simon found the old man's Chinese a little different than what he was used to and he soon realized that it was archaic – in two thousand years there had no doubt been a linguistic shift. Fortunately, he had Oberon's gift as well and he found himself quickly adjusting to what the other magician was saying. The others would not be so fortunate.

"That would be much appreciated," Simon said "for I am unfamiliar with Chinese magic and I have no idea of the power of this necromancer who is aiding in the deaths of so many dragons."

"I have many questions for you, young *Wu*," Feng Hu said, putting down his cup. "I am eager to talk of magics – of yours and mine, to compare them. and to find if we might work well together. But now," he added, sounding rather wistful, "after two thousand years I am more than ready for a little food!"

Ch'ang Hao had spent the night after the death of the spirit dragon in fasting and meditation.

The demon had to be called at a precise moment when the balance between the *ying* and *yang* – the dark and light – of the day was equal. This was best done in the long twilight of the summer evening or the lengthy summer daybreak. Since they were to go after another dragon today Ch'ang chose the early morning hours.

Incense burned in the darkened room as Ch'ang prepared for the summoning. The door was locked and the windows closed with shutters firmly in place. On a low table where the smoke of the incense curled up into the air sat a small brass gong and a baton with which to strike it. On this table sat a yellow candle in a cylinder, in the semblance of a man holding a bowl over his head which was filled with earth. Another covered bowl of fine porcelain sat on the table as well.

With his staff Ch'ang inscribed a tight square about the table. This drawing left a visible black line. Moving outwards, he inscribed another black-lined square.

To the north he placed a bowl of water in which floated a black candle. The bowl was tortoise shaped. To the west he put a white candle in a metal bowl which was a representation of a stylized tiger. At the southern end of the square was a red candle in a bird-like vessel. And at the east side of the black square was a blue-green candle in a wooden candle holder carved to look like a dragon. These candles and colours and animals represented the Five Activities, or elements – earth, water, metal, fire and air. The four outside areas also represented the seasons – clockwise, these were winter, spring, summer and autumn. Altogether, these were also the five primary colours and the five sacred animals.

Ch'ang sat down behind the low table on a yellow silken cushion. He wore robes of brilliant yellow, embroidered with Celestial dragons. Yellow was the ultimate colour of power and symbolized the earth itself from where he would draw his power. This honour was supposed to be reserved for the Emperor and his family, as was wearing a depiction of the five-toed *t'ein lung*. But this robe would show the demon he wished to summon his authority over it.

With a wave of his staff Ch'ang lit the center candle and then lit one after another, widdeshins, or counterclockwise. As they burst into flame, one by one, the room seemed to fill with menacing shadows.

Ch'ang removed the porcelain lid from the bowl on the table in front of him. A dark red liquid caught the light of the candle, its surface rippling slightly as if something living lay within its depths. The bowl was full of blood. Earlier in the morning hours just after midnight with a special dagger, Ch'ang had sacrificed a goat.

Now he lifted his staff and dipped the head of it in the blood. As he began a low, monotonous chant he sprinkled blood in each direction, pausing over each candle to make certain that, at the very least, one drop of the blood touched the candle flame. Lastly, he poured the blood on the floor in front of the table, facing north, where it remained in a perfectly round pool, not seeping into the floor at all but remaining on the surface.

He continued to chant as a low hum began to fill the air. The candles flickered and flared out as a wind suddenly seemed to fill the room. Ch'ang spoke a sudden WORD and banged once, twice on the gong. He then returned to the chant until, without any warning, the puddle of blood was sucked into the air. seeming to vanish into nothingness.

Ch'ang spoke another WORD and struck the gong again.

134

Above the section of floor where the blood had been an amorphous mass began to boil, bearing a startling resemblance to a storm cloud. As Ch'ang continued to chant it thickened and darkened and eyes of malicious intent were visible in it, shifting rapidly from place to place.

Ch'ang said yet another WORD – this time striking the gong three times.

The mass thickened, steadied and formed into a human-like image, but one distorted and exaggerated in a horrible fashion.

The creature was broad and rather squat, clad in ragged white robes – the colour of mourning. It had a face of dead white as well, with a look of such evil intent and malice on its fleshy features that even the bravest man might well shrink from it. Wild locks waved about its head and when it smiled, as it did now, its teeth were seen to be long and pointed as were the fingernails of its thin and bloodless hands.

"I am Wu Chang Kuei!" it thundered. "Who dares to summon me?"

"I do – the sorcerer Ch'ang Hao," said the necromancer in a firm voice. "I desire your service and have sacrificed a living animal for the blood you drank. Furthermore I will sacrifice again for you when you have done my bidding."

A look of cunning came over the demon's ugly face." I shall do your bidding, sorcerer, but only if you agree to my price – *I* shall name the sacrifice!"

"What do you desire?" Ch'ang asked. "If it lays within my power –"

"I want a child – a nice plump male child – not above ten years of age – and fresh-killed – not a corpse dug from the ground." The demon licked his lips in anticipation, his eyes gleaming with unholy fires.

This requirement did not bother Ch'ang. The brothels in the village were full of illegitimate brats that no one cared for – one would not be missed. "Done," he said. "When you have done my bidding I shall sacrifice a child to you."

"What is it you require of me?" the demon asked.

"I wish to know how to unlock the secrets of the dragons' pearls," said Ch'ang.

135

"Is that all?" scoffed the demon."I thought that you had a task of some difficulty for me! I have the best of the bargain – a juicy child to eat for but a bit of information!"

Ch'ang was taken aback. Surely it was not simple – or he would have stumbled on it long since!

"There is a certain book that you need – and you black sorcerers do not read it as a rule, which tells me that you are not as intelligent as you like to think you are!" the demon gave a great bellow of nasty laughter. "You must read the *T'ai Ping Kuang Chi* – and there will be your secret, O foolish one!"

"*The Great Records made in the Time of Peace and Prosperity?*" Ch'ang repeated in surprise. The demon was right though – it was not a book ordinarily found in the library of a practitioner of the black arts. He had thought the book only a collection of records of fantastic animals, heroic tales and defeat of evil. The mere title alone – mentally, he chastised himself. He had never thought to look in the books of white magics, thinking that the dark was the road to his desire.

"I want that child tonight, sorcerer! Remember and do not forget – a nice plump young boy – or I will come in the night and eat you – even though you are probably stringy and tough!" The demon smiled again, a smile that promised death.

"I awoke this morning at dawn," said Simon to the elderly Feng Hu, "from a dream of darkness and convinced that something dreadful had happened." Something in the Chinese magician inspired his trust – goodness and simplicity of spirit shone from him as if he was lit from within.

They had talked of the differences in their magics for a while – and discovered many similarities as well, as the others emerged from the tent. The Prince and Dr. Quong were delighted with the offer of help – they had no trouble believing that he had slept for 2,000 years. Ash, Simon could see, was reserving judgment. But as Simon had thought, he, Lakota and T'a Ming (who had been alive for 3,000 years at least) understood him best. The other humans in the party had a bit of trouble with his archaic speech.

136

"I, too, felt something this morning as I journeyed here," admitted the old magician. He had not said where he had come from – only that it lay far to the West. He had also not mentioned how he had traveled. There was no sign of a horse or other mode of transportation. "It felt of evil sorcery. You say this black one uses magic to entrap the *lung*?"

"Yes –" Simon began but was interrupted by Lakota's excited voice "Simon! Look! We have company!"

Two dragons were landing – one an immensely fat spirit dragon of azure hue and the other a gold Celestial.

"My daughter is dead!" the Spirit dragon roared. "Dead, and profaned and her egg – my grandchild – stolen!"

The golden one bowed. "Honored magicians," it said "We do most respectfully request that you rid us of this plague!"

"Request!" said the azure *shen lung* angrily. "We DEMAND!" His voice shook rocks loose from the mountain side and he glared at the humans and their accompanying dragons. Then as they watched, his face twisted and great tears slid down his cheeks. "My daughter! My blossom!" he sobbed and put his head down to cover his face with his talons.

"We believe that the egg still lives," put in the Celestial quickly. "Please, before any more die, while the egg can still be saved – I beg of you!"

"We will leave as soon as we break camp," said Simon. "If you will be so good as to take us where the egg was last seen?"

"An honor," said the gold dragon, bowing its head. "I most humbly thank you."

"Wait and offer gratitude when we have rid you of this plague, honorable dragon," said Feng Hu. "The task is not as yet accomplished."

137

17

The Watcher In Shadows

Above the campsite, high amongst the dark rocks of a steep mountain side, lay Chen Bo, Si Wang's best dragon scout, hidden from sight by his position in the deep shadows, and downwind. His eyes gleamed with greed as he took in the sight of four dragons all at once – and four dragons who seemed to have no fear of humans at all – for they spoke to and interacted with people.

He had seen the fat dragon and the gold one flying their way purposefully toward a destination and by dint of whipping his horse viciously had managed to follow them. This was much better than the small dragon the other scouts and located! He dismissed the people as of no account They could be easily dealt with – a quick sword thrust and all of that lovely dragon flesh and bone was the band's for the taking.

But the longer he looked at the scene below he began to realize that there was something very strange about this group.

At first he had seen only two elderly Chinese men talking to the that azure dragon and the gold one. They had been joined by a man who looked as if he were some sort of nobleman – that fact did not bother Chen Bo – a nobleman could be killed as easily as a peasant - but then two more men emerged from the tent, carrying saddles (although there were no horses in evidence) and Chen drew in his breath sharply. *Fan qui!* Foreign devils! They had to be foreign devils for they were definitely not Chinese! Chen had never seen a foreign devil but he had heard tales of them – these did not seem to have tails or horns as he had been told – but they were probably dangerous none the less.

And as he watched, he realized that they were indeed very dangerous – for at least one of them had magic. He watched as one with hair the colour of thistledown waved his a stick and the tent folded up as if a team of men were taking it down. He put out the glowing campfire with a similar wave....

This was enough for Chen. Carefully squirming backwards so that he would not be seen, he left the ledge to slide down the hillside on a grassy slope to where his horse stood waiting for him, out of sight of the ledge he had spied from. Si Wang must know of this immediately!

Perhaps she would even reward him, he thought as he mounted his horse and swung it around with a tug on the bit. He would ask for another night in her bed, he decided. He had more money and goods in the storeroom than he could spend in a lifetime and he had found the occasions he spent with her more exciting than any of those spent with the whores in the village, for she was a hell-cat and he much enjoyed their sexual tussles.

He whipped the tired horse yet again. It was a long ride to the fortress of Kwen-Lum. They were having to go further and further afield to find dragons, which was why he had been this far out this morning. Fortunately, he knew of a place where he could halt and commandeer a fresh horse. No one would dare oppose one of the officers of Si Wang's band of brigands.

It was done – the demon was appeased. Ch'ang had gone down to the village and visited several of the brothels. As he had thought, there was a superfluity of illegitimate brats in each of them. It was not difficult to find one of the whores who cared more for money – and opium – than her child. A handful of brass coins and a block of pressed opium paid the greedy bitch for her boy.

The boy was plump and healthy as the demon had ordered but from the glazed look in his eyes he had been given the opium pipe by his mother or one of the others in the brothel. And one part of Ch'ang, where a little kindness still lingered, made him painlessly stop the boy's heart, rather than dispatching him with a knife. Only after the boy was dead did Ch'ang use the knife, for the demon would expect and want blood.

The demon did not need to be summoned – he was waiting and graciously asserted that the sacrifice was acceptable. To Ch'ang's relief he disappeared in a cloud of sulfurous smoke, bearing the sacrifice with him. Ch'ang was not squeamish but he did not relish the idea of watching the demon feasting on human flesh.

He had just put all of his arcane impedimenta in a locked, lacquered cabinet when a knock came at the door and Fan Heng, the old manservant of Si Wang, called out in his cracked, wheezing voice."The Great Lady desires your presence, sorcerer!"

What now? Ch'ang thought, sighing under his breath. He hoped it was not another attempted seduction.

To his relief she was completely clothed when he entered her hall. With her were her first lieutenant, Hong Yu, and the scout Chen Bo.

"Well, Ch'ang – it appears as if you have competition!" she said, with a short hard laugh. "Chen has seen a sorcerer – a foreign sorcerer! – this very morning! "

A chill went down Ch'ang's spine – yet somehow he was not surprised – he had felt someone else in the earth's energies.

"Tell Ch'ang what you have seen, Chen," Si Wang directed. She was bright-eyed and keyed up – traits Ch'ang had observed in her when they were to raid a caravan or go after a dragon.

Chen, his eyes gleaming greedily, told of the four dragons and the men he had seen with them. He related exactly the magic he had seen.

Ch'ang was not certain whet to think of this. "Was this foreigner young or old?" he asked of Chen.

"I cannot say, sorcerer – he was a foreign devil after all, but If I were to guess I should think him young in years," said Chen after careful reflection.

Hong Yu was in full armor and carried his helmet beneath his arm. The other hand was on the hilt of the sword that hung at his side. He was a handsome young man but with cold, expressionless features and hard eyes. "His youth argues that he cannot be far advanced in magical skills," he stated. "And what real skill can a foreign devil have?" he added in scorn.

Fan Heng shuffled into the room with a tray of rice wine and three cups. He had obviously been listening at the door. "My sister's son says that there are foreign devils in the Huang Lung valley," he cackled. "You remember, Great lady, the man who came with his son and the water buffalo, bearing tea and rice for us? That was my sister's son. He saw three *fan qui* with his own eyes both in the valley and two more upon the road. One of the foreigners was a female."

Si Wang looked thoughtful. "And Chen saw but two. That argues that there may be three left behind."

She came to a quick decision. "Hong! Take a troop to Huang Lung! Ride day and night – take all the horses you need from the countryside. I want those *fan qui* brought here – all of them! If this foreign sorcerer proves to be a threat we shall have his friends – and perhaps his woman – as bargaining pieces. I want them all alive, Hong," she added, for she knew well that Hong enjoyed killing.

"I will be honored to do your bidding, lady! Hong bowed low and left at once." A few moments later he could be heard shouting for his troop to assemble.

Si Wang smiled, a slow predatory smile. "There is another dragon, close by," she informed the sorcerer. "We will leave within the hour."

"But it is late in the day!" Ch'ang protested. He needed to rest after the ritual of demon summoning and the sacrifice. It had tired him more than he had expected.

"So?" she said, lifting one shapely brow. "We will make camp in the hills." Seeing his discomfiture she laughed. "You are too used to soft living, Ch'ang! Sleeping on the ground will do you well!"

"But now," she smiled even deeper at Chen Bo, "You have done well and deserve a reward." She shrugged off the cotton tunic she wore to reveal she wore nothing underneath it. "You can stay and watch if you like, sorcerer," she said over her shoulder as she advanced on Chen, who was already eagerly fumbling at his clothing. "You might learn something!"

Ch'ang fled the room, followed by the cackling laughter of old Fan Heng.

Feng Hu was intrigued by the dragon saddle and was surprised to find that they were all going to ride upon Lakota's back.

"But surely the noble *lung* will not wish to so demean himself?" he said, watching Simon and Ash saddle Lakota.

Lakota gave a long sigh. He was very tired of all of this noble dragon and five toes nonsense. He wished fleetingly that he were again at home in Ireland where there was no doubt about what a dragon did and everyone was friendly and informal. China was interesting – in a way – but there was no place like home.

"I LIKE to carry riders," he told Feng Hu. "I like being with people – especially my family – there's nothing demeaning about it! All the dragons at home carry riders!"

Both the fat Spirit dragon, Chin Lung and the gold Celestial, Ru Lung, had remained and watched the proceedings with interest but it was clear that they were appalled that Lakota was going to take on riders.

"This is dishonorable and unseemly!" protested Ru as Simon place the three sections of saddle on Lakota's back. Ash was well used to saddling dragons and slipped the breast harness on over the blue dragon's head as Lakota obligingly ducked his head and lifted his front legs so that Simon could slide the girths through the long piece of leather that was the belly strap from the breast plate. Each of the three girths ran through a 'keeper', a loop in the leather that Simon tightened right up against each of the girths so that Lakota could not get a talon in it by accident.

Lakota gave Ru a pained look and then said defiantly "I don't care what you think! You are not going to keep me from carrying my people!" He turned his long neck and dropped his head on Simon's shoulder for a moment. "All of this noble dragon business is a lot of rot!" he said quietly.

"Lakota –" said Simon, in reproof.

Lakota lifted his head. "I'm tired of all of this, Simon," he said in Gaelic. "I'm tired of being told everything I do is wrong and have these lazy lay-abouts, who expect to be waited on hand and foot and be worshipped as if they were gods, tell me that I am lowering myself to carry you and our friends! From what I have heard they haven't even *tried* to defend themselves from the dragon poachers! They just expect humans to take care of it for them and blackmailed you into it by sending earthquakes and floods! No dragon in the Six Nations would behave like that – we would only come to you if we could not solve the problem our own selves! I don't like any of them except maybe for T'a Ming and I think I feel more sorry for her than anything!"

"We promised to help them, Lakota," Simon, in the same language, reminded him. "I can't say as I am overly enthusiastic about these dragons either, but they do need our help."

"Oh, very well, but they're big *babies!*" Lakota muttered. "If one more of them tells me I am demeaning myself I am going to flame him!"

No one else understood this exchange, for even Ash did not have speak Gaelic, being English born and bred.

The look that Lakota cast at the other dragons was enough for them to cease their protests for although his countenance normally reflected good humor and intelligence, there was a look of resolution in it that now gave then pause as he said "I don't want to hear any more about what dragons should and should not do. I will do as I wish!"

"It is always a mistake," said Feng Hu mildly, "to force our own ways upon others who may not be of our country or our persuasion."

This mild rebuke had much more effect than anything Lakota had said.

"I meant no disrespect, venerable sage," said the gold Celestial Ru, bowing his head. "I merely hoped to guide this unenlightened one into the proper mode of behavior."

"Surely you are aware," continued Feng Hu in a deceptively gentle tone, "that as a winged *ying lung*, Lah-ko-ta is a Proper Conduct Dragon?"

If dragons could be said to blanch, the two did so, gold and azure colours fading. They both looked stricken. "Forgive us, Great and noble *ying lung!*" Chin faltered. "It has been many millennia since we were honored by the presence of a *ying lung* and this humble *shen lung* had forgotten all that he had learned of the powers of the great *ying lung!*"

"I shall forgive you on one condition," said Lakota, seeing an advantage in this "Never again address me as 'noble dragon'!"

In a few more minutes after the packing of the tent and supplies and a careful check of the safety harness, they were ready to go. There were more protests from the azure and the gold dragons when they saw that T'a Ming proposed to carry the panda Chao.

Lakota let out a small flame, which frightened them, and said sternly. "If I am the Proper Conduct Dragon I hereby declare that is perfectly acceptable for her to carry Chao!"

Simon had rigged up a safety harness for Chao using the extra leather he always carried and, with Lakota translating, secured the panda and his now much diminished bag of bamboo on the back of the white dragon. Ash, meanwhile, was making certain that their Chinese passengers were safely harnessed in their seats.

Simon was the last to mount. As he fastened his harness he said to Ru and Chin "Do you have any idea what they would have done with the egg? Would they have destroyed it?"

"No," said Ru, "for eggs are much prized. The shell is valuable and –" he swallowed hard and said almost in a whisper "and roast dragon child is considered a delicacy."

"As we flew here we saw a caravan heading south – and by the stench of death that rose from the pack saddles I could tell that they carried dragon bones and flesh!" said Chin.

"Then that is where we will go," decided Simon. "We may be able to rescue your grandegg, Chin Lung."

"I pray that it will be so!" replied the azure dragon and raised his *poh shan* to begin pumping in air. Within moments the three Chinese dragons rose straight up into the air while Lakota crouched low to the ground, sprang up and snapped his wings open with a mighty crack.

And heading north, Hong Yu, with a company of mounted soldiers at the heels of his war horse, moved swiftly towards the Huang Lung valley, eating up the miles, going as fast as he dared push them over the rough terrain.

18

The Grandegg Rescue

Feng Hu watched the ground beneath him with mild curiosity.Unlike the Prince and Dr. Quong, who were exhilarated by riding on the back of a dragon, the elderly *Wu* was only interested in a detached fashion. He had lived too long to be much surprised by any new experience.

Of far more concern to him was the shocking evidence of modern depravity – dragon poachers who blatantly, in what amounted to blasphemy, took the lives of the noble creatures that were such a part – an important part – of Chinese culture. In his day, only the most desperate criminals, the lowest of the low, would even dream of harming a dragon. Then, the dragon temples were many, filled with offerings of cream and caged swallows, and the position of Imperial Dragon Feeder was much sought after. It was a high honor. According to Prince Tuan, no one filled this post at the moment. The Prince had also told Feng Hu that the dragon temples were largely ignored. And what was even worse, no dragon was in resident in the Forbidden City to advise the Emperor.

Feng Hu was further disturbed by the news that the only sorcerer in China was a *dark* magician. What had happened to all of the sorcerers of the Light? Why had things gone so wrong? He liked Simon and found him interesting to talk to, but it stung that his country had to depend upon a foreigner to rectify a situation that should have never taken place.

But Feng Hu knew that he alone could not correct this problem. He had been powerful in magical skills but he was old and stricken in years – he had been elderly when he went into his long sleep. Now he was ancient indeed, and he felt every year as a burden. The foreign magician was young and strong and Feng Hu had been surprised by the depths of the young one's knowledge and power. True, much of his magic was different from what Feng Hu was used to, but the more they talked the more Feng Hu realized that there were many similarities – they often called the same thing by a different name or arrived at similar results by a varying methodology. In Feng Hu's time a magician studied by himself or with an acknowledged Master of the craft. It had astonished him when Simon explained about the schools and universities in his land where one could study sorcery – or as the young one always called it, Wizardry.

And now he was high in the sky, riding a foreign dragon, a dragon who was as different from the Chinese dragons as night was from day. Feng Hu had been equally intrigued by his conversations with Lakota.

Feng Hu was pleased, though – both strangers (and even the other young foreign devil) seemed equally committed to helping stop the dragon poachers and to restore the dragons to their rightful place in China. He was equally pleased with Dr. Quong, a wise and eminent scholar, and the Prince. If all of the members of the ruling family were as Prince Tuan, the Empire was in excellent hands.

T'a Ming flew close to Lakota. He had refused to let her fly in a subordinate position behind the Celestial *t'ein lung*. He wanted to keep an eye on her. Nothing had lessened her terrors – not his reassurances, or those of Chao, nor the presence of two other dragons. He could see that she could barely concentrate on her flying. To take her mind from her fears, he swung his head close to hers and said in a low voice "Why is Chin so fat? He is the first fat dragon I have ever seen!"

"He is an arsenic eater," said T'a Ming, looking at him in surprise. "Do you not have such in your land?"

"Arsenic is a *poison!*" Lakota exclaimed in shock.

"Not for dragons," she said. "It is indeed delicious and some of us cannot do without it, much as humans use opium. His heaviness is a result of over-indulgence."

"It's poisonous for *this* dragon!" he retorted. "I would have to ingest a lot more of it than a human would, but it would kill me just as surely. And I cannot imagine enjoying eating arsenic and calling it *delicious!*"

"Your ways are very strange," she said.

147

From her back Chao made a rude noise. "Nothing is worth eating save for bamboo!" he stated."It is the best, most satisfying food there can be!" He still had his eyes tightly closed and maintained a death grip on his dragon friend's spinal ridge, in spite of Simon's safety harness.

"How much longer are we going to be sky- bourn?" he demanded.

Lakota looked ahead and turned his neck to speak to Simon "I see a caravan ahead!" With his long dragon sight he spotted it long before Simon could.

From behind Lakota came Chin's rumbling voice."That is it! That is the caravan that bears my Grandegg!" He had taken up the British Isles term of 'Grandegg' enthusiastically.

Simon leaned forward. He sat in the first seat, so that he could speak with Lakota as was necessary. "Are we able to land somewhere ahead of the caravan, where they may not see us?"

"I'll scout a suitable place," Lakota promised. They were relatively high in the sky and Lakota had noticed more than once that people tended *not* to look up above their heads. The sun was in front of him and if he were careful he would neither cast a warning shadow, not allow the caravan to see him. His sky blue scales helped camouflage him as well.

Lakota directed the other dragons to stay in the air as there was little they could do and it would be safer for them. And he and Simon were counting on the element of surprise to stop the caravan. Lakota was afraid that the Chinese dragons would be more concerned with who landed first and proper protocol than in taking command of the situation. This was absolutely necessary as the caravan consisted of over twenty pack animals with a man walking beside at least every other animal and six mounted guards who looked competent and heavily armed.

Lakota, staying high until the last minute, found a place somewhat ahead of the caravan route and landed behind some of the strange, almost square rock formations so common in the area. This worked well for the plan that Simon had discussed with the Prince and Ash before they had broken camp that morning. With two of the high powered British-made rifles Ash and Tuan would keep close watch on the caravan once it was halted, ready to shoot anyone who even looked as if he was threatening to oppose Lakota and his party.

Dr, Quong, who had spent much time in his youth in archery practice and hunting with a bow, was given Simon's Elfin bow and quiver full of arrows. "The range is too great," he protested, when he saw the place that they were to conceal themselves. "Even should the caravan be directly below us the arrow will fall short of its mark."

"Those are not the arrows that you are used to," Simon explained. "They are magic."

"Ah!" said the elderly Dracophilogue, satisfied and happy with this explanation.

Feng Hu insisted that he ride Lakota with Simon and help with the magic. The Prince protested at this, citing his age, but Simon knew that magic prolonged life and health and many very elderly magicians were capable of just as much as the younger.

When the three riflemen were in position, Lakota, carrying Simon and Feng Hu, leaped into the air, went high and then dropped like a stone to land in front of the caravan on his hind legs, wings outstretched and his maw, with its huge teeth, showing open. He let out a fearsome roar and a sheet of flame high above their heads.

The effect was instantaneous. The pack animals. mostly donkeys, tried to flee as the men screamed and tried to follow them as well. The caravan guards' horses were maddened with fear and tried to run or rid themselves of their riders with violent bucking.

Simon cast a violet barrier that prevented any of the animals or men from escaping and Feng Hu sent a rope of jade green energies after one donkey that had managed to evade the violet light It was caught and captured by this energy. A guard at the rear of the caravan who regained control of his mount attempted to level his rifle at Lakota, but from above, Ash shot it out of his hand.

It was all over in the space of a few moments. The caravan quickly surrendered, certain that they were to be robbed and murdered. There astonishment was great when Simon told them that all his party wanted was the dragon flesh and bones and the egg. The caravan leader was still not happy with this – he would lose a great deal of money by giving over the dragon remains – and the egg was worth a great deal of money. His master, Zhang Bao, would not be happy to hear of this and would very likely retaliate.

"Would your master be happy with the equal value in silks and jade?" Feng Hu inquired in his tranquil tones.

"I must see the quality of the goods," said the leader greedily.

"Look then," said Feng Hu and smote this staff upon the ground.

A pile of bales and crates appeared out of the air, all open and spilling out exquisite silks and items of jade of the most cunning artistry.

"You will find the goods to be of the first quality," said Feng Hu as the leader and several of the other men ran to the piles.

As soon as their attention left him, Feng Hu suddenly sagged and Simon caught him under his elbow to steady him.

"I thank you, young *Wu*," Feng said, closing his eyes and suddenly looking rather frail. "It has been many, many years since I was called upon to perform such magics and I fear that I am out of practice."

"That was quite impressive for someone out of practice!" said Simon in admiration.

"Is he all right?" Lakota asked, quite close.

Feng Hu assured him that but a few moments would see him restored to his old self, but nonetheless he kept a tight hold on Simon's arm.

Lakota continued, "Simon, how are we going to get the egg and the other dragon *materials*?" The blue dragon avoided saying dragon *flesh and bone*.

"I shall call it," Simon said and leveled his wand at the pack train. "*Dracones – os, caro, exire! Dracones – ovum, pellis, exire!*"

As the packs began to open and the parcels and casks began rushing towards them to pile upon the ground at Simon's feet, Lakota, who knew enough Wizard's Latin to understand what Simon had said, moaned, "Not the dragon skin too! How *could* they?"

He looked up just in time to see the missing egg flying at them and caught it neatly in outspread talons. "At least we've saved this dragonet!" he said fervently.

Feng Hu let go of Simon's arm. "So many dragons!" he mourned, for the amount of plunder was not inconsiderable. "They must be given honorable internment, my young friend. Have you any experience with tomb building?"

By the end of the day on a ledge overlooking the valley below, a new tomb stood. It was a splendid edifice with a crouching Chinese dragon on top, carved by magic. It was impossible to discern how many toes this dragon had, for about its feet were bands of peonies and plum blossoms. This was Lakota's idea.

Lakota had completely lost his temper when Chin and Ru had begun to argue that inferior dragons could not be buried in the same place of honour as a Celestial or even an Imperial.

Steam coming from his nostrils in great puffs, he had exclaimed angrily "You are all *dragons* – now matter how many toes you have! And all of these dragons DIED from the same cause in the same fashion! And I would like you to explain to me exactly how you are going to tell which flesh and bones are Celestial, Imperial or whatever! And I don't know about you but I have no wish to look at the remains to try and determine which is which!"

At the very thought of this T'a Ming began to cry and Chin and Ru both looked grave. "It would be most dis-respectful !" said Ru. Chin, who had kept his Grandegg clutched tight against his chest since Simon had returned it to him, nodded in agreement.

The tomb covered all the remains, then, indiscrim-inately. It was impossible to tell how many dragons were even represented, for the hides had been tanned and in that process, dragon skin uniformly turned a dull brown. losing all the vibrant colouration of the living animal. All of the talons had been cut off and were separate from the skins as well – talons were in much demand as weapons or defensive points for heavy armor. The flesh was packed tight into ceramic jars and the bones jumbled into boxes.

The sides of the tomb bore the names of all of the dragons that the three Chinese *lung* could remember of those that had fallen to the poachers. Feng Hu excised them in Chinese characters, divided by their ranks.

Dr. Quong grew sad and pensive as he saw the long list of names. "Shall we be left with enough *lung*," he queried Simon, " to bring back their glory? So many have died! And it will be one thousand years before this egg hatches!" He gestured towards the blue marbleized egg that Chin still clutched.

"Your sorrow does us great honor," said Ru, the golden Celestial. He turned to look at Simon and Feng Hu. "And there will be much honor in telling the others of our kind of what you have done for us this day."

"We shall shortly be able to do far more," Simon promised, "for I obtained the exact location of the warlord's fortress from one of the caravan men. He said it lies but three days' ride from here – probably a day's flying or less for Lakota."

"Please, honored sirs, take care," begged Chin. "This woman has a fearsome reputation and her band of men are said to be fierce fighters! I know that you have much magic but –"

"To be cautious is to live another day," said Feng Hu. "We thank you for your concern, noble *lung*." So saying he bowed low to the two dragons.

Goodbyes and expressions of mutual pleasure were exchanged. Ru and Chin then departed.

Simon wished that he might have seen the arrangements that they made for the egg, but Lakota was able to satisfy his curiosity on that point, for even Dr. Quong did not know. Lakota had asked Chin what would happen to his Grandegg. "The egg will spend one third of the time in the next one thousand years in the water, one third in a cave high in the mountains and the last one third of the incubation in the company of man, usually in a temple where the monks will read to the egg and discuss philosophy in the same room where the egg is kept so that the dragonet may benefit from the knowledge it hears. But, Simon, no one can mind-talk to the egg!" the blue dragon finished in amazement. "Imagine that – one thousand years in the egg and not to be able to talk to anyone! I am so glad that I did not hatch like that! I was only in my egg for two years before I came to Ireland and hatched in the Incubatory," he added. "That was quite long enough!"

Both Feng Hu and Dr. Quong began to ask questions of Lakota, for this information was new to them.

Ash came to stand near Simon and said quietly, " Well, do we attack this fortress head-on?"

Simon shook his head. "We shall want to do an exploratory flight to get some sense of what we are up against – we have no idea of how many men or what type of weaponry she has. And I might be able to get a feel of this necromancer if we can get close enough. I don't want to go into this blind."

"Will Feng be up to this, do you think?" Ash looked doubtful. "You said that he almost buckled at the knees after conjuring up that silk and jade."

"I don't know," said Simon carefully. "Age ,as you know, means but little to a magician, but even magicians age differently. He was asleep for a long time – the more he is exposed to the energies of the ley lines the stronger he may become."

"I thought that use of the ley lines drained a magician," Ash frowned.

Simon smiled. "It's rather paradoxical – for the ley lines do drain our energies as we use them but Wizards also feed on the energy. One of my professors at the Tara Druidry explained it like this – the energies in nature are like that of a tree – which draws much of the goodness it needs to grow from the earth – but then returns goodness to the earth with its dead leaves that become nutrients in the soil."

"If you say so," said Ash doubtfully, not certain that he really understood, but more grateful that ever that he had not had to study magic.

Simon grinned at him. "Let's set up camp," he suggested. "I think we're all ready for some food and tea."

Ash could agree to this with no doubts at all.

153

Suddenly remembering something the caravan leader had said, Simon inquired, " Does the name Zhang Bao mean anything to you? The caravan leader said that Zhang Bao was his employer and the name sounded familiar to me."

"Good God!" Ash swore. "Zhang Bao is the merchant in Canton who is most cooperative with the foreign traders! And *he* is the contact for these dragon poachers?" He laughed, a short, mirthless laugh. "Once we tell the Prince I shall be doubtful if Zhang's life is worth a farthing! His Highness tells me that his father has just handed down a degree that trafficking in dragon skin, flesh or bone or any part of a dragon is punishable by beheading! Zhang is a wily devil but I do not see how he can get out of this! He is as good as dead!"

19

Tiger in the Valley

Hong Yu's men were proud of their leader. He was strong, fierce and ruthless – a deadly fighter. The men called him "the Tiger" and were proud to ride in his troop. Only the best were accepted to his command.

They followed him eagerly to the Huang Lung Valley, knowing that there would be plunder, women and destruction. No one of them complained that they rode almost the entire night and day, commandeering fresh horses as they needed them, over the owners' protests. If the erstwhile owner protested too loudly, they were soon quieted by a sword in the gut.

The troop slept and ate in snatches. They were hard and fit and would still be able to fight once the valley was reached – if there was actually much fighting. They expected the valley to be full of peasants – poor farming folk who would have little defense against them.

Tatya missed Simon badly. They had hardly been apart since they had been married and she had grown used to sleeping against his comforting warmth or cuddling after a bad dream. She tried not to think of what might be happening in the mountains, and tried to place her trust in Lakota and in Simon's magical skills.

She had brought a small traveling icon of the Virgin of Vladimir with her. Simon had purchased it for her before they left Russia. In the new house that they were building outside Dublin she was to have an iconostasis, a wall for her icons, which would be painted red before the icons were hung upon it. Red was a favorite Russian colour. Although she could not worship in her faith – there being no Russian Orthodox church in all of Ireland – she was comforted and felt a link to her own land by praying in front of her icons. Unlike some autocratic husbands of whom she had heard, Simon did not require her to give up her religion for his. She worshipped with him on Sundays at the Anglican church, since there was none other, but she had her icons at home, and kept her own saints' days and kept religious holidays in the Russian manner, with her young brother Sacha.

Several days after Simon left she awoke with a feeling that something was wrong somewhere and danger loomed. She checked Alan – he was still sleeping peacefully and the familiars were all well – Janus sleeping quietly. The calico was still suffering some pain from Tom's brutal kick but she was on the mend and Marinka was being very solicitous of her mother. Even the kitten Xiu was being friendly and helpful.

Therefore, it had to be Simon who was in trouble. The only thing that she could do was to offer up prayers. He had scryed her last night – they had agreed on a time that he would do this each evening as long as he was able – and things had been fine then. He had told her of the Chinese magician, Feng Hu, and of how they were scouting the mountain fortress of the warlord. Something must have gone wrong, for the feeling of dread was not abating.

She knelt before the icon of the Virgin of Vladimir, a fine copy of the original, which dated from the 12th century, and prayed for Simon's safety. It never occurred to her that it was her own safety she had to worry about.

Comforted by her prayers, she then went about the tasks of readying Alan for the day and seeing to Janus and Marinka's care.

Ping was quite glad that Tatya was staying with her, for Jian had been called away again. He was a magistrate and was such, administered the affairs of the district. He had done well in his Civil Service examinations and had turned down, modestly, a higher position, an action which did him no disservice in the eyes of his superiors in the government. His family was quite confident that he would rise in importance very shortly, especially since he had the favor of Prince Tuan.

Ping found her new friend fascinating, especially when Tatya performed magic. She had been awestruck when

Tatya restored some of the damaged porcelain and pictures ruined by the earthquake. Try as she might, Ping could not see how they had been repaired. She was glad that they had been mended, for many of the broken things had been in her family for many years and she had brought them with her when she came from Macao to marry Jian. It had been an arranged marriage – her family was distantly related to her father- in-law, who had originally come from Macao. But she had loved Jian from the first and she had no doubt that her feelings were reciprocated.

Today she planned to teach Tatya how to make spring rolls. These were a delectable blend of black mushrooms, bean curd, shrimp, rice wine, ground pork, bean sprouts, bamboo shoots, water chestnuts, snow peas and *gow choy* (Chinese chives), cut fine and seasoned with soy sauce, salt, pepper, both peanut and sesame oil and sugar. This filling went into a delicate flat roll made of flour and water and then was pan fried until crisp and golden brown. These spring rolls came from East China, not Sichuan, but had been introduced to her family in Macao by Ping's mother, who came from Shangh'ai.

Those, with some chicken and vegetables, would serve as luncheon for the household.

Yesterday they had spent a pleasant day working on their embroidery. Ping had been embroidering a dark pink robe with mandarin ducks amid lotus blossoms for herself, but decided to give it to her new friend. Tatya had brought her workbox with her, of course, and had been stitching a Russian style shawl for her mother-in-law's birthday but had decided to present it to Ping before they left China. The two were avid needlewomen and had a good time comparing techniques – many of the stitches they did were the same, only known by different names.

Today, Alan and Mei played beneath their feet with Marinka and Xiu as they worked in the kitchen, chatting companionably with the cook and one of the maids. Every day Tatya's command of Chinese grew, and she found she could follow even rapid conversation easily.

"Our children play well together," Ping observed as she chopped the wedges of bean curd into small sticks. The

157

two children, despite their age difference, for Mei was five to Alan's one year, had struck up a friendship.

Tatya and the cook were shredding the bamboo shoots, the water chestnuts and the snow peas. Tatya looked down at the two children who were playing with a top of Alan's that Simon had enchanted for him. Once started it spun endlessly all over the floor and was guided by a stick. The two children were laughing and pushing it here and there with their sticks.

Running feet were heard and the door to the kitchen burst open to reveal a panting, sweating young man with a look of alarm on his face, "Mistress!" he gasped, looking to Ping.

"What is it, Fu?" asked Ping. Fu was the last born son of one of their tenant farmers. Dr. Quong owned much of the land hereabouts, which he rented to tenants, some of whom lived on the land while others lived in the village and went out to work the land daily.

"There are warriors coming this way! Men on warhorses and with swords! They are killing people and burning the houses! They seek the *fan qui* lady!" He cast a quick, frightened look at Tatya. My father sent me to tell you ! You must hide!"

"How many men?" Tatya inquired, for Ping had gone quite pale and could not seem to speak.

Fu had no real idea – there seemed to be hundreds of them. He was only fifteen, but already considered a young man. He had never been out of the valley and the most danger he had ever faced was the recent flood and earthquake.

"What shall we do?" whispered Ping, a hand going to her throat and eyes wide in shock. "We cannot fight! Oh. I wish that the soldiers of the Prince had remained here!"

"The first thing we do is make certain that the children are safe. And Fu, you go and warn the rest of the valley," said Tatya briskly. "There is a storeroom in the back where we shall put the children." She stooped and picked up Alan as Fu took off at a run, heading down the valley .

The cook and the maid were beginning to wail in terror and looked up on shock as Tatya ordered them to be quiet. "I want you to stay with the children," she said, leading the way to the storeroom. "And Janus," she added, for all

158

three cats had trotted after them, "I'm putting you in charge. I shall seal the door and give you the Word for it. If for some reason I cannot come and let you out you can judge for yourself when it is safe to come out."

Janus nodded and nosed Marinka and Xiu into the storeroom. Alan and Mei were looking tearful as they were handed over to the servants. "Let's get some of their things and anything of value," suggested Tatya.

Ping called the other maid and with the cook's help, they gathered a good amount of the more fragile household goods, clothing and food and water for the rooms occupants. Tatya magically lifted Dr. Quong's entire library and her own things, what Simon had left behind, and Alan's. It was a large storeroom and at this season the winter's stores had been largely used and not as yet restocked.

With Tatya's magics, the room was ready in no time at all. "Go on in," Tatya said to Ping when they had finished. and she had given Janus the Word of release.

"But are you not coming as well?" Ping faltered.

"No. I have many defensive magics I can use against them."

Ping looked hesitant for a moment and then said, with a quick up-thrust of her chin, "Then I will stay and fight too! There are knives in the kitchen – and this is my home!"

"Are you certain?" Tatya looked at her searchingly.

"Yes!" said Ping.

Tatya gave her a hug and said "Let's make certain that the children are safe." She gave Alan a quick kiss and Ping did the same to Mei. They both left the room and Tatya closed the door behind them.

She stood back from the door and took out her wand which she kept in a skirt pocket. At the tip was a huge diamond, a focus stone that Simon had given her when he first began to teach her magic.

She raised the wand and leveled it at the door and silently commanded it to seal and lock. A bolt of sapphire blue leaped from the tip of her wand and ran all around the door, sealing it tightly. From inside the room they could hear the maids and the children crying.

"The warriors will hear them weeping!" said Ping worriedly.

"No, they won't," said Tatya and with another spell silenced the noises coming from behind the door. All was then as quiet as if nothing but stores lay behind the door. "If they manage to break into the house we shall tell them that the door is blocked by a beam that fell during the earthquake and that it is dangerous to go into that room."

Ping looked at her in awe. "Truly, you are wonderful, honorable Tatya! Are you often attacked in your homeland?"

"Not recently," said Tatya dryly.

They could now hear noise – particularly screaming – coming from the valley. Smoke was also born on the wind.

"What if they set fire to the house?" Ping worried as they hurried about, closing the shutters and barring the doors. "The children, the servants ...."

"They are as protected in that room now as if they were in a locked lead vault," Tatya assured her. "but unlike in a vault they will have air."

Even as she spoke she was looking about her This house would not be easy to defend. The doors were not sturdy and the windows were but of oiled paper with relatively flimsy shutters. The walls were not as sturdy as they had been before the earthquake. Determined men could easily gain access.

They would not go down without a fight. Tatya opened herself to the ley lines as Simon had taught her and began to draw power. She had learned to throw the Elfin weapon, levin bolts, beneath the Hollow Hills At one time in her life she had been helpless – but with magic she was helpless no longer and needed nothing but her own wits and her own skills to defend herself.

They did not have long to wait. Hooves pounded outside and men's voices came in through the windows, somewhat muffled by the shutters.

Ping was terrified. Tatya could feel her shaking as they stood together side by side. The young Chinese woman held a huge kitchen knife in one hand. She was muttering beneath her breath – probably a prayer, Tatya thought.

Tatya had a firm grip on her wand. When the men found the at the door was locked, she heard a brusque voice give the order to knock it down.

160

Tatya steeled herself. As she had guessed, it took but a few blows with a heavy log to knock down the door and then the men were in the room.

Tatya had only the time for a quick impression of Chinese warriors in black and silver armor, with red tunics and trousers before she began firing levin bolts. Three of them went down immediately, surprised looks on their faces.

Bravely, Ping struck at one man who tried to come from the side and plunged the knife into his shoulder.

After that Tatya lost sight of Ping. The men seemed to be coming from everywhere and she was hard put to stun all of them. She was vaguely aware that other figures in peasant black had joined the fray, armed with axes, pitchforks and hoes.

For one moment she thought they might actually do the trick but then a voice cried out "HOLD!" and she looked up to see a hard faced young man with his arm locked about Ping's neck and a sword to her throat. Ping's kitchen knife, red with blood. lay upon the floor at her feet.

"Stop your enchantments, Witch, or she dies!" the young man said in the coldest voice Tatya had ever heard. As Tatya watched, he pressed his heavy curved sword against Ping's throat and a trickle of blood leaked down onto her blue robe. Ping's eyes were huge and terrified as she whimpered a little.

Tatya dropped her wand arm and at a nod from the young man two of his men sprang forward and twisted her arms behind her back, binding her hands with a stout rope. One of them took her wand.

"You are responsible for the life of this one," said the man holding Ping. "If you do anything wrong she will die – painfully. Do you understand?"

"I understand," said Tatya. She could do nothing that would hurt Ping. She had no doubts that this man would carry out his threat. He seemed utterly ruthless. He reminded her of her cousin Evgeny, who had been just the same.

The peasants had dropped their makeshift weapons when they had seen their mistress threatened. They huddled together in a miserable group, five of them, from an elderly man down to a boy of about ten.

"Shall we kill them, honorable Hong?" asked one of his men, raising his sword and advancing on the peasants., wearing a smile of pleased anticipation.

Hong Yu frowned. "They are not worth dulling your blade upon," he said curtly. He pushed Ping into the arms of another warrior. "Guard her well, Lui. She is the guarantee for the *fan qui* Witch's good behavior."

"What are you going to do with us?" Tatya demanded, as she was prodded into walking forward in the direction of the door.

He smiled slowly, a smile that did not reach his eyes, and made his handsome features even colder. "Why. you are to be the guests of my mistress, Si Wang Mu. She will decide your fate!"

20

⚪ Captives ⚪

"Why did I listen to you?" Reginald Faversham moaned. "Could have been on a ship heading home to England by now!"

"And give up that jade mine?" Tom snapped, irritated.

"Rather give it up than be like this," Faversham insisted. "How are we to get out of this pickle, pray?"

"I 'll think of something," Tom muttered.

They were indeed in a pickle. They had escaped from Dr. Quong's easily enough through the damaged wall. Tom had had to drag a protesting Faversham with him. It had been a bit harder to steal two of the horses in the stable, for guards from the small group of the Prince's soldiers were patrolling the grounds.

But from there everything had gone wrong.

Only one of the horses was saddle-broke – the other, a cart horse, had never bore a rider and did not want to start now. Tom ended in riding that one – Faversham proved to be a poor horseman – and it took all the skill Tom possessed to keep it from throwing him. He was riding bareback as there had not been time to steal saddles as well as bridles. The horse seemed to spend all its spare time thinking of ingenious ways to toss, scrape, and knock its unwanted rider off. Tussles with the stubborn horse impeded their progress considerably.

They had no food and no weapons for defense or for Tom to hunt with. Neither one of them had much Chinese and in spite of the fact that Faversham still had a good amount of money in his money belt they could not approach any of the natives to buy food. As 'foreign devils' they would be remembered too well. Tom had no doubt that the Prince's men were more than likely in pursuit of them.

He had resorted to sneaking into villages at night and stealing food. This had unleashed an avalanche of protest from Faversham who insisted Tom at least leave a few coins behind to pay for the stolen goods. An English gentleman did not steal! Tom took the coins, but left them in his own pocket. Why waste money on peasants?

Then the saddle-broke horse had gone dead lame. The cart horse could not be brought to carry both of them, so they abandoned the horses and went back to traveling by shank's mare.

Tom could tell by the sun that they were going in roughly the right direction. He still had the map, carefully folded in a hidden pocket in his jacket. He had no idea how long it would take to get there at this rate. He seethed with anger when he thought of cousin Simon, whose dragon could have had them to the site in hours, and, with those great talons, dug up enough jade to make them all wealthy. Simon was just the same as he had been – a Goody Two Shoes – and selfish to boot. Why did he care more about Chinese dragons than he did about his own cousin?

And that Prince – already rich – yet he wanted the jade mine for himself! Of course, Tom saw nothing immoral in exploiting a mine in a land not his own to which he had no legal right. It was finders keepers as far as Tom Stillfield was concerned.

The weather had continued hot and sultry to add to the misery of insufficient food and the biting and stinging insects of summer. Water seemed to become scare as well.

Yesterday had been the worst disaster of all. They had run afoul of a small band of robbers.

They had been dozing, during the heat of the day on the bank of a small stream. The cool water had been as ambrosia and they had drunk deep and splashed liberally in it, even taking off shirts and boots to cool down. Faversham spent some time talking wistfully of a spot of tea, but at last fell into a light doze. Tom, too, tired, hungry and sick of listening to Faversham complain, fell asleep and woke with a start to find three men standing around them. Three men, armed with swords, pikes, and old fashioned pistols.

Tom and his employer could not understand what they were saying, but their intent seemed clear. Faversham and Tom were their prisoners.

They were allowed to resume their shirts and boots, but their hands were tied behind their backs and they were each slung over the backs of pack animals, face down, and were tied roughly to the packs. It was a hideously painful position, particularly when the horses began moving at a faster pace.

The robbers stopped but seldom – to eat some tasteless, dry meat and cold rice, washed down with strong tea and to relieve themselves. Tom and Faversham were fed and allowed the same privilege, but their feet remained tied and they were guarded every minute. Then it was back on the pack animals again.

Tom took careful note of the sun when they stopped. He guessed that they were moving steadily south. He could not imagine why the robbers had kept them alive. They had relieved both himself and Faversham of all the monies and valuables they possessed. Nor did he have any idea where they might be going. For the first time he wished that Gao Kun was still with them. At least the guide would have been able to translate. Not knowing what was happening was worse than anything.

Now he looked at Faversham, who was trying his best to keep a stiff upper lip, but was prey to anxiety of the worst sort. The Earl's son proved to have a lurid imagination and had already conjectured everything from being held for ransom to white slavery and being forced to become opium addicts.

Their captors had let their hands free so that they could eat their evening meal. Once again it was very tough dried meat, rice balls – this time fired in grease – and tea.

A stolid guard, busily shoveling food into his mouth as if it were actually tasty, sat on a rock near them. He was a huge man, strong and powerful – and well-armed. He never took his eyes off them. The ropes that bound them were thick and well-made. One they had eaten and used the bushes as a latrine they would be bound hand and foot again, and they would be watched all night. Tom could see no chance of escape.

How soon would they reach wherever the bandits were taking them? And what would happen when they got there?

165

Ping was so frightened that darkness roared in her ears and in front of her eyes. She wanted to faint, to go away from the fear and be blissfully unconscious, but she could not. She could only watch helplessly as the warriors ravaged her home, stealing, breaking and destroying. She was glad that the female servants and the children were hidden and listened as Tatya coolly explained that the door to that store room could not be opened as a large timber from the ceiling had fallen down and blocked the door and that the roof was unsafe. Only food stores, ruined by the earthquake, were in that room

Hong had a few men try to open it but it was as Tatya said, unable to be opened, and they gave up trying. There had been enough loot – they were already burdened down with food, jewelry, silks and porcelain and a few girls they would take with them, to use and discard as if they were unwanted packages.

Hong also questioned them closely as to the whereabouts of the other foreign devils, Tom and Faversham. Tatya told him that they did not know – that they had run off. He only believed her when this was confirmed by the only male servant – a stableman – that they had managed to catch.

Ping was also terrified for Hai. She did not know what had happened to her small son – for he had been with his teacher at the little school that met in one room at the local Buddhist temple. She could only pray that even these violent men would respect the sanctity of the temple and that the monks would shelter the children.

And Jian! Jian would think her dead when he returned to these scenes of destruction! Dead – or carried away to be dishonored by the bandits. Ping had no illusions as to how she and Tatya would be treated by the robbers – raped and left for dead, more than likely. She shivered as she imagined it. Her foreign friend would be irresistible to those barbarians! They would be wild to see if a foreign woman was somehow 'different' to lay with than was a Chinese woman.

Hong, however, had his orders from Si Wang – 'unharmed' she had said – and that included leaving the foreign woman inviolate. What his men would do to her could not be construed in any way as 'unharmed'. She might be left alive, but just barely.

And the foreign devil woman was a Sorceress. She seemed to care for the Chinese woman who was mistress of the house. Hong would see to it that she was not touched either, to insure the Sorceress's good behavior.

However, once Si Wang had used the Sorceress for whatever purpose she had in mind, Hong intended to ask for her for himself and his men. They had all talked about having the foreign woman and what they wanted to do to her. Hong would make certain that he was the first to use her – it was his right, after all, and he found her strangely attractive, tall and large-footed as she was. The colour of her hair and eyes was striking and odd, and she was bigger than a Chinese female but womanly in shape. She also seemed to be completely unafraid of him – even a bit contemptuous. He had only before met one other woman who did not fear him – Si Wang herself. And the warlord was too free with her favors... The whores in the village bored him with their fear and all too often when he wanted and needed a woman, Si Wang was occupied with someone else. Her appetite was too great for exclusivity. Perhaps he might keep the foreign woman as his mistress.

When they had taken everything they wanted from the house, Hong ordered his men to mount up. Tatya and Ping were tied to the saddles in front of two separate men, while the other women they had stolen – mostly young girls – were herded into a group and tied together in a long line, as they screamed and cried in fear.

Hong did not continue ravaging the valley – he had what he had come for – a foreign devil – even though he knew that Si Wang would be much displeased that he had only been able to obtain one of the foreigners. Still, perhaps she was enough.

Ping could not help crying as they left her home at a canter. Behind her she heard the ominous crackle of fire – and prayed that Tatya was right – that the children and the servants would be safe in that room.

Tatya heard the sound too – that was one thing she could do that the horrible Captain of this band of cut throats could not even discern. She knew a fire smothering spell from the book of *101 Useful Household Spells for Both the Magical and Non-Magical Person,* written by Simon's great grandfather and great grandmother, the Marquis and Marchioness of Lyonshall. The fire smothering spell was a simple one – it only worked on small fires – and the fire had not taken hold as yet. Casting the spell silently, using the power of the ley lines, she stopped it before it spread too far. And none of the men bearing them off noticed.

As they rode on down the valley she was to wish that she knew the larger spells that the firefighting Wizards of Dublin knew. Wealthy people had their homes bespelled to repel fire – and both her husband and her father–in-law, argued that poorer persons should have access to this service as well, for many of the poorer parts of Dublin, particularly the non-magical parts that depended on fire as lighting – were subject to frequent fires. Both Simon and his father gave generously of their time and power to help make the city safer.

Tatya now wished that she had studied the fire dousing spells, for she watched in horror as they rode up the valley. The bandits seemed to have fired much of it. Everywhere was death and destruction. People were screaming and crying – she saw a mother, wild with grief, holding the body of a child, and two old people, dazed looking, outside a burning house, holding one another and their pet cat. A few people had organized a bucket brigade to try to deal with the fires.

As Hong's troop swept by, the tied girls running to keep up. shouts and curses followed them from some of the braver souls, but many of the inhabitants of the valley fled in terror, thinking they were returning. And not a few said nothing, for they were dead and what had happened would never matter to them again.

It was ironic, in a way, Tatya thought, that Simon had saved the valley from flood only to have it pillaged by these outlaws. And she could not help but know that the bandits might have never come here if it were not for the presence of herself and Simon. The hard-eyed leader of this band had made it clear that he had come looking for 'foreign devils'. What was not clear was how he had learned of their being here in the first place. She had spoken to Simon by scry last night – and all had been well then. From what she overheard the men had been traveling for several days – that meant that they had not learned of her being in he Huang Lung valley from Simon himself or some member of his party. Who had told them? Had the necromancer Seen them?

And what did this Si Wang want with them?

Tatya knew that she had to protect herself and Ping from rape and violence or even worse. Her heart sank when she thought of the other girls, now stumbling breathlessly behind the trotting horses. How could she save them as well? Could she even manage to do *anything* for them?

And always, always in her mind was her worry over Alan. She was thankful that he was safe for now, as was Mei. Janus was a sensible cat who could be trusted to watch over the two children. The servants did not seem sensible – they were more the type to indulge in hysterics. And would they listen to the orders of a cat? She could only send a silent prayer to her favorite saints that Jian returned home soon, or that Simon would rapidly conclude his business and go back to find her missing. He would turn China upside down if needs be to find her. In the meantime, she still had her dragon whistle, and the next time her hands were freed she would blow upon it. Tatya had no great hopes that Lakota was close enough to hear it, but she had to try. And in the meantime, perhaps she could use subtle, minor magics that the outlaws could not see, to ensure her safety and that of the other women. She just was not quite sure what she could actually do.

21

Dragon In Danger

Simon, with Ash and Prince Tuan, lay high on a ledge on the mountain above the fortress of Kwen-Lum. For the past several days they had been scouting the forces of the warlord Si Wang Mu. Lakota, too, had spied upon the stronghold from very high in the sky where he would not be noticed.

The Prince had borrowed Simon's English binoculars. The Galilean optics had been augmented by magic and allowed a greater field of vision and higher magnification than was possible with a non-magical instrument.

"I think that our estimates are indeed correct," the Prince said , very quietly. "She has at least one hundred men and they are well armed and very well trained."

"Their guns are very old fashioned," Ash pointed out in the same low voice. "We have seen very little target practice other than with bow and arrow. That might argue that ammunition for the guns is scarce."

"There is no way to tell if this is indeed true," said the Prince on a sigh. "I shall have forty men here shortly and we have two magicians and a dragon who breathes fire. Will this be enough to combat these people?"

"The full compliment of men is never sent out at one time to one location," Simon pointed out. "The expeditions after a dragon are never more than twenty men, from what the witnessing dragons have told us. With the necromancer to capture the dragon, twenty are more than enough."

"And when they go out to rob and steal as few as ten go out," Ash added. In the past few days the warlord's band had not taken a dragon but they had preyed upon unwary travelers twice.

"They must be stopped!" muttered the Prince. "Not only the dragons must be saved but it is unacceptable that travelers cannot pass through this region in safety. Such cannot be tolerated in the Empire! The robber band must be dispersed and their leaders beheaded."

170

"Tell, me, honorable *Wu*," he continued, turning to Simon, " Will the venerable one, Feng Hu, be able to help us? He seems frail – and he is much stricken in years."

"Quite honestly, your highness, I don't know," Simon admitted. "His magic is different from mine. Although magic prolongs life – my great grandfather is nearing 100 years of age and is still hale and hearty – Feng Hu is far older than any Wizard I have ever met. The magic he performed at the caravan site seemed to exhaust him. But it was quite impressive magic – he later told me that he had magiced the silks and jade from his old home. Dematerializing goods, even in our Western tradition, is *not* simple magic – it requires a good deal of skill and knowledge. Many Wizards are never able to master even the simplest dematerializations. My father teaches dematerialization at Trinity and two thirds of the applicants for his class fail to qualify. I shall have a long talk with Feng Hu, your highness, and sound him out." Unspoken in Simon's mind was the worry that the elderly – extremely elderly – magician would be more of a liability than an asset.

Feng Hu had declared himself not up to the rigors of climbing to the ledge and Dr. Quong had begged off as well. The two elderly Chinese gentlemen had remained at the hidden camp site, with Lakota, T'a Ming and Chao. Simon had not only warded the camp but had used what was called a 'look the other way" spell. There was no spell as yet that could make anything or anyone invisible but the spell Simon had used made it very difficult for anyone to focus on what was to be hidden. It was a form of minor compulsion, ordering the observer to look away   It was quite effective, and when combined with the smokeless ley line fire it was almost as good as being invisible.

Feng Hu had been much taken with the spell and had asked if it had been in place the night he had come to them.

It had not – they had been far enough away from the warlord's territory that it had not been necessary. Simon had just used the usual wards that would warn him of an intruder. But now, on her doorstep, they could not afford to give themselves away.

The Prince passed the binoculars to Ash, who adjusted them and said "We've seen little of the necromancer. Do you suppose he is still here?"

"Oh, he's here all right!" Simon said grimly. "I can feel him!"

"Does it then not follow that he can feel you?" the Prince queried.

"No," Simon answered. "I've raised my shields to the maximum. If he does know how to shield himself he is not bothering to do so now. He will be able to feel me in the ley lines, or the *chi*, as you call it here – I cannot shield that – but where I am and who I am and how powerful I am he will not be able to tell. Feng tells me that this Ch'ang will not be able to discern him either unless Feng is actually working magic. I daresay he felt both of us when we raided the caravan."

"I hope that this has not warned him," said the Prince worriedly as Ash lowered the binoculars.

"Excuse me, your highness," said Ash, "but something is happening down there. A rider has just entered the fortress at great speed and it looks as if orders are being issued to saddle up."

The Prince reached for the binoculars and, focusing them on the scene below, said excitedly "Yes – they are in a great hurry! Far more so than when they went out to rob! Perhaps they have found another dragon!"

"We'd best get back to camp," said Simon. "Once we are behind this cliff I shall whistle for Lakota." The three of them slowly backed off the ledge, keeping low, even though a look-away spell cloaked their movements.

Lakota arrived promptly with news of his own.

As his passengers strapped themselves onto the saddle Lakota turned his head and spoke softly. "There is an Earth dragon waiting back at the camp. I saw him circling overhead and went up to meet him. His name is Ah Lung and he says that his mate is in grave danger. He saw what he thinks was a dragon scout spying upon her and she is in no condition to fly away as she has just produced an egg. It is her first, and she is very weak. And of course she cannot pick up the egg and take it with her."

"Why not?" the Prince asked curiously.

Simon answered. "For the first twelve hours a dragon egg is very soft and could easily be pierced by her talons if she attempted to lift it. In an Incubatory new eggs are never moved except by magic Wild dragons know enough to leave the egg alone until it hardens sufficiently. Piercing the shell would kill the dragonet."

"Ah Lung is waiting to show us where she is," said Lakota. "If we can get there before the poachers, Simon, we can save her and the egg!"

"My soldiers are not here as yet," said the Prince, looking troubled.

"I saw them from above this morning," Lakota said. "They are still fifteen or so miles away. We cannot wait for them! Poor Ah is beside himself! We cannot let another dragon die!"

"No, we cannot do that," Simon agreed. "Back to camp, Lakota, if you please. Everyone is properly harnessed."

Ch'ang Hao did not want to go after another dragon, for he was troubled by the fluctuation in the *chi* that he had felt. And almost daily since then he had felt the same thing – a one point it had nearly knocked him from his feet.

He had tried every trick he knew to See the other magician but there seemed to be something in his way, as if the Sight was clouded by some sort of mist that was impenetrable. Neither blood divination nor water divination worked. Always was that frustrating absence of anything identifiable. At times he thought he could catch a glimpse of *something* but when he tried to narrow in on that something, it slipped away from him. He could not tell where or who was using the energies, nor even how close this person was. For all he knew, the person was across the sea in Japan, or in Bod or Burma or Siam. The *chi* traveled a great distance. He had even seen and felt it used in his youth, when he had traveled far to the south, to the land of Hind, a land with few sorcerers and but most of those that existed of the blackest sort. But here in his own country, no – and feeling it now disturbed him.

But Si Wang insisted that he come and capture the dragon, She pointed out that she had been otherwise pleasantly occupied – in bedding a new recruit whose size and virility had appealed to her – and as Ch'ang was doing nothing better, he had to come. They would not be able to take the dragon without him. She refused to listen to his tales of a strange stirring in the *chi* when she called him to her room. The new recruit, carrying his clothing and wearing only a look of satiation on his face, was just leaving.

"You are an old woman, Ch'ang," Si Wang said scornfully as old Fan Heng finished laying out her red tunic, trousers and armor and then began to scrape the sweat from her body. A strenuous bout with the quarter staves had proceeded the sexual tussle in the cushions.

This time Ch'ang did not look away from the sight of he nudity as he usually did. He scarcely saw her. "You are not a magician – you can not possibly understand –" he began.

"Why do you worry? You say yourself that you cannot see anything! If you spent more time in manly activities such as mounting a woman, drinking and fighting you would not be prey to these foolish fears!" Si Wang interrupted.

"Perhaps I should be as manly as *you* are?" he said sarcastically.

She was not insulted, but gave a crack of laughter. "Why not?" she replied. "I have appetites, Ch'ang, and I indulge them. What good does your celibacy and abstinence do you? Has it made you any wiser or richer? No, *I* have done that for you, and yet you scorn me for taking my pleasure with any man I fancy – the men I so honor do not scorn me, you may be assured. No, they pant for my favors and fight to see who will mount me first! Never forget, Ch'ang, when I found you, you were performing magical tricks in a brothel to amuse the customers too drunk to make proper use of a woman! *I* have provided the monies for you to study your dark magics, and have made certain that you will die a wealthy man!"

Old Fan Heng cackled in delight as Ch'ang winced. He would prefer never to be reminded of how low he had sunk before he had joined Si Wang. The scrolls and books he had needed for his esoteric studies were difficult to obtain and expensive – for they were forbidden by law. Ch'ang's background was not one of wealth and privilege. His father had been a mere craftsman and not a master of his craft at that.

There was no doubt that their partnership had allowed him to study, without worry about where he was to lay his head or how he was to fill his stomach. And his personal share in the storerooms was considerable – money, jewels, and other goods – he could retire tomorrow and live the life of a noble.

"I do not want to see or hear any more of this reluctance in you," Si Wang continued as Fan slipped her shirt over her head. "Nor do I want to see the look you put upon your face when I am taking my pleasure. If you will not take your pleasure of me yourself, as is *my* wish, you will at least stop behaving as if you see something unpleasant!" she commanded fiercely. "Now ready yourself! Even if you do not wish to enrich yourself further, I do and so do my men! We shall have no more of this ridiculous talk of someone in the *chi!*"

"As you desire, lady," said Ch'ang, in resignation and left the room. He would go and catch another dragon for her. Perhaps he was being overcautious. And yesterday, he had found in the long disused library of this fortress – if one could call a box of dusty, mouse-nibbled scrolls a library – a copy of the *Tai Ping Kuang Chi,* the book that the demon said contained the secret to unlocking the wisdom of the pearls. He would begin studying it this very night. And, he decided, as he headed out to the courtyard where his placid mare awaited him, when he was all-powerful and wise, he would lay with Si Wang and put a spell upon her that would make her crave him and only him – all others would fail to satisfy her. Then he would deny her his body and watch her weep and wail and tear her hair while she begged him to come to her bed. It would be a fitting revenge.

The Earth dragon Ah, a *ti-lung*, was a beautiful jade green, with a white underbody with red whiskers and back ridges. As he talked to Simon and Lakota his whiskers writhed furiously and his tail coiled and uncoiled repeatedly.

"My mate, Fen, is quite near here," he said, anxiety filling his voice. "I am certain that the human I saw this morning when I was fetching her something to nibble upon was a *lung* killer! He wore armor and had a look of evil intent upon his face! He took care to remain hidden. A human who, as is proper, reveres dragons, would have a look of worshipful respect!"

"And give offerings, as well," put in T'a Ming, her eyes wide in fear as great as Ah's.

Ash was occupied in checking the rifles – modern repeaters of the very latest technology, far superior to anything that Si Wang's men carried. He gave the Prince a rifle and an ammunition belt as well as Simon continued to speak to the *ti–lung*.

"Thank you, Mr. Pendleton," said the Prince. "These weapons are most excellent. I much admired your prowess with your gun the other day. You are an excellent shot. I hope that you will put that skill to good use today and eliminate as many of these bandits as is possible."

"I shall do my best, your highness," said Ash. "I've readied a rifle for Simon as well. Do you think that the venerable Feng – "

Tuan shook his head. "In his day men fought with swords and lances. And he is a scholar as well, not a soldier. Our other scholar, Dr. Quong, had informed me that although he has a small talent with the bow, he never has yet fired a gun."

To Ash's surprise, as they went to mount upon Lakota, Simon refused the rifle. "I've never fired a gun," he said, "I'd much rather trust my magic."

"Never fired a gun?" repeated Ash blankly. "But surely you've gone hunting – why your grandfather Chenevix, owns one of the largest hunting estates in Scotland – deer and grouse – and salmon fishing too!"

"I don't like to kill animals," Simon said. Indeed, neither he nor Lakota had any intention of killing *humans* – Lakota would intimidate them and Simon would stun them for the authorities to deal with them as they saw fit. People would probably die today, but not by his or his dragon's hand.

176

Both he and Lakota had been forced to kill – once, whilst in Russia and both still had nightmares about it.

Ah was halfway off the ground, his *poh shan* pumping as he impatiently waited for the balance of the party. "Come, oh, come!" he implored, his eyes filled with fear. "Fen awaits us! "

Dr. Quong, armed with Elfin bow and arrows, was to remain behind with T'a Ming and Chao. The white Imperial was to go up every once in a while to see if the troop of the Prince's soldiers was near and direct them to the probable place of attack, should they arrive in time to be of use in the coming conflict. Chao, growling fiercely, declared that he would protect T'a Ming.

Feng Hu insisted upon going with them. Although he looked as frail as a paper door his spirit was strong and Simon could not gainsay him.

With Lakota's speed they should be able to get to Fen much earlier than the dragon poachers and perhaps lay a trap for them.

Simon soon realized that he was the only one who seemed at all concerned about the strength and skills of the necromancer they were about to face. Even the Prince's worries about their numbers had been assuaged by the extreme confidence of Feng Hu, who seemed to feel that no black magician could possibly be his equal, particularly when he had the added strength of the young *Wu*, Simon. Out of the entire party, only Ash seemed to have the slightest trepidation and even he seemed to labor under the common misapprehension that one Englishman was equal to five foreigners in a fight.

As Lakota took to the sky behind Ah Simon could only hope that their confidence was not misplaced. He had a feeling that the coming confrontation would be neither quick nor easy.

177

22

With the Robber Band

Ping had never ridden a horse before. Like most Chinese women of her class she was accustomed, on the rare times she traveled, to being in a covered cart, or perhaps sailing in a boat. When she had come from Macao to marry Jian, it had been on the sea and then on the river, followed by a short distance in a wagon. She was more than a little frightened of horses – they were so big and made sudden moves and noises – and being tossed up in front of a strange man, and tied to the saddle like a parcel, unable to use her hands for balance – she could feel the man's hard body pressing up against hers and when he grabbed at her breasts and she cried aloud in protest he laughed in a nasty fashion. She was suddenly afraid of more than the horse.

Fortunately she was not dressed as she would usually be in delicate silk robes but in cotton garments – a long, loose tunic over blue trousers, such as the peasant women wore – only her garment was of much higher quality and adorned with embroidered peonies. Since they were to spend the day in the kitchen making spring rolls and then had planned to work in the garden she had deemed this attire far more suitable. She was glad of the trousers beneath her tunic, for otherwise her thighs would have been badly chafed. As it was, before they had gone too far she was in some discomfort. She could hear the village girls behind her, crying in their distress, having to run to keep up with the trotting horses. She feared for them. Already the men were talking and laughing about what sport they were to have with the girls. Fortunately for Ping, as a gently raised upper class female, she did not understand many of the things they joked about. She not only worried about her own fate and Tatya's, but that of the village girls, for she was the lady of the village and they were her responsibility. How could she face their families (if she ever saw them again) if the girls were raped and dishonored or killed? And what would Jian do if she was dishonored by these men? She had no doubt that they meant to use her, for the man behind her kept touching her, in spite of all the wiggling and pulling away from him that she could manage. All her efforts just made him laugh the harder. Jian would probably put her aside, repudiate a wife who had been defiled – it would be well within his rights. It was all that Ping could do to keep from crying like the village girls.

Tatya, in front of another man was less comfortable– she wore a white, Western style linen gown and nothing underneath it but a light camisole and short knickers. The lower part of her bare thighs rested on the saddle. She was well used to riding both bareback, astride, sidesaddle, and used to riding dragon-back as well. All the same, it was far from comfortable, and the man she rode in front of had actually dropped the reins of his horse and was guiding the animal with his knees so that he could use both hand to grope at her body.

"Oh no you don't!" she thought and used a trick she had learned from her mother-in-law – she sent a pulse of energy through her body – it made her tingle but as the force was expelled outward it affected the rider behind her as if her had stuck his hands into a tank of electric eels. He had a terrific shock and gave a loud yell of pain.

Hong, who had been riding his horse a little ahead of him, swung the animal around and demanded sharply "What is it, Lui? Why do you shout?"

"This bitch stung me!" Lui answered. He raised his hand as to hit Tatya.

"Leave that!" Hong commanded. "The lady wants her unharmed. And keep your hands from her! There will be time enough for that later. If you want a woman that badly I shall give you one of the village girls – a virgin. There is no telling what might happen to a man that lays with a sorceress." He did not really believe this but he had decided that he wanted her for himself. Once Si Wang was done with her, the Witch was his. He had heard old tales that a sorceress could provide pleasures far beyond mortal reckoning and he was eager to find out if this was true.

Obediently, Lui picked up his reins and slid back on the saddle, moving away from Tatya. He had not thought of the fact that she was magical, only that she was female and he had not had a woman for nearly a week. It might indeed be dangerous to have intercourse with a Witch – a man was weak and exposed at that time and who knew what she could do to him?

Tatya heard the note in Hong's voice that indicated his interest in her. She was confident that either Simon or Lakota would come to her aid before it came to that but she was also confident that she could repulse any advance he made towards her. Her one real worry was Ping and the village girls. How could she save them? Out of the corner of her eyes she could see the man holding Ping was subjecting her friend to rough fondling and she knew all too well what the fate of the village girls would be. Some of them were just babies – ten years old at the most! They would never recover from the brutal handling they would receive from these men. Some would even die and many would rather be dead after the men had their way with them. What could she do to help them? She took a deep breath as she thought of a spell, a simple but effective escape spell. She only hoped that it would work at this distance and that she could make it work slowly enough so that it would not be noticed.

Jing Mai was the first to notice the strange behavior of the rope.

She was the eldest of the village girls – sixteen years old and well-used to fending for herself. She was tough and hard – she had had to be, for she and her widowed mother, who was ill, lived by themselves and it was up to Jing Mai to provide for them both. The Quongs were very kind to them and bought, for an excellent price, the fish that the Jing Mai caught every morning and took from door to door in the rush baskets carried by her donkey Po. In all the world Jing Mai loved only her mother, her donkey and her little dog, Lim.

And now all of them were dead – killed by these robbers, She had seen them all die – her mother by the sword of a robber who cut her down with a careless swipe as if she were a thing of little account; Po when his braying annoyed another robber and brave little Lim, when he had tried to defend his young mistress.

Jing Mai knew all too well why these men had taken her and the other girls. The men had been taking turns circling back and riding by, calling to the girls and making crude comments, laughing in a coarse way. She had heard them say that they would draw lots to see which of them had which girl first. All of the girls would be used more than once, as there were only nine girls and some twenty men.

Jing Mai could not bear it. The youngest girl, little Shi, was only ten and quite small for her age. How could she survive? None of the girls, as far as Jing Mai knew, had ever been with a man – she had not, even at her age.

Most of the others were crying, and wailing, begging for mercy, and praying as well. Not Jing Mai. She busied herself in calling encouragement to the others, exhorting them to keep on their feet so that they would not be dragged. And all the while she was looking about her for a means to escape.

That was why she noticed the very odd actions of the rope that bound them together.

First of all, it began to ease its tight hold on her wrists. They were tied in two lines, then tied together and led by a man on a horse. She was the second from the front behind twelve-year-old Ya who was crying for her mother, and in front of fourteen-year-old Wen, who was praying to the lady Kwan Yen for aid.

Their wrists had been tied brutally tight and were being rubbed raw by the dragging. And yet Jing Mai's bonds were slowly becoming easier. And then she saw that the rope itself between them was unraveling.

Perhaps Kwan Yen had answered Wen's prayers – she was known as a most devout and pious girl! Wen would kill herself if she was dishonored.

Jing Mai dared to steal a look at the other girls she could see – yes – their ropes seemed to be doing the same thing as well! What was causing this? It had to be magic! And involuntarily Jing Mai looked up to the front of the line where the *fan qui* lady was on a horse with one of the bandits. It was said in the village that she was a Sorceress and her husband was a Sorcerer. The Quong servants had told her, when she had delivered her fresh fish that morning, that this was indeed true and not a rumor. Had the Sorcerer not saved the

181

valley from the flood? Had he not saved the lives of all the Quongs when a wall threatened to collapse upon their heads? And the cook had seen for her own self the Sorceress repair shattered porcelain with but a flick of her magic stick.

Jing Mai hoped that no one else noticed the rope's decay, for she had to talk to them first. The sun was declining – they would stop soon. The bandits had stolen food and drink as well as goods and from what she overheard, they planned to drink and feast before the girl lottery. If luck was with them , perhaps she could lead them in an escape.

It was not long before Hong called a halt for the night. He knew that his men were hungry and thirsty – and they were eager to share out the girls. Their appetites for food and drink and sex were always sharp after pillaging and killing. He could understand this, for he felt the same way. After a raid, he would go to Si Wang's tent and they would drink and couple for hours.

But now that he had seen this amber-eyed Witch he wanted no one else. The village girls were comely enough – one or two even beautiful – but he would not be satisfied with them. They were all afraid of him.

Hong's was the only tent set up and he thrust Tatya into it, leaving Ping with Lui. "Remember," he said threateningly to Tatya, "If you use your tricks she dies!"

"If one hair on her head is harmed, or she is raped," Tatya said coldly. "I shall make all of you sorry you were ever born." She gave him a long look that left little doubt that this was a promise she would keep.

If she had but known it this defiance aroused him further. What a bed partner this woman would be! Fearless and proud – and if he took her as his mistress, unlike Si Wang, she would be available to him at all times – his alone. Although he had always found Si Wang intensely exciting and satisfying he resented having to share her with all of the others she favored. The thought of having this exotic woman all to himself excited him and he resolved to have her even if he had to pay Si Wang for her.

182

Tatya was aware that he, for some perverse reason, wanted her – probably because she was foreign – but was unaware just how inflamed he had become – not could she guess at the plans that were going through his head for her future. She was determined to find a way to escape.

"What are you going to do with those little girls?" she demanded when he had finished tying her to the center tent pole.

"What do you care?" he said. "They are only peasants and not even of your race. When my men have finished their feast and drinking they will be stripped so that my men can take their choice. Then there will be a lottery as to which man gets to have the first turn on each of them. After they each have spent their lust , which is only fair and right, it is anybody's guess what will happen." He smiled, a cold chilling smile that did not reach his eyes. "My men have large appetites – for food and drink and women. You are fortunate, Sorceress, that you are not out there as well – my men relish the thought of a foreign woman!" Most Chinese men would consider it a defilement to lay with a non-Chinese woman, but these considerations did not weigh with the bandits. A woman was a woman – and theirs to use.

"Your men also seem to have large appetites for blood as well," said Tatya. "I would have come with you if you had demanded that I do so – It was not necessary to kill and burn and rape in the valley."

"But it was necessary, lady!" he said. "You see, that is what satisfies us – we are hungry for the smell of blood – it excites us and makes us feel as if we are alive!" He chuckled as she drew back slightly from him. "Do you fear me, little Witch?" he whispered, putting his face close to hers.

It took all her nerve not to shrink away from him. His eyes glittered so strangely and she wondered if he were quite sane. If she only had not to worry about Ping...

"You speak excellent Chinese," he said, and began to stroke the side of her face with one finger. "Tell me, when you are writhing beneath me, will you cry out in Chinese or in your own *fan qui* tongue?"

"You will never find that out!" she said forcefully and turning her head swiftly, bit his finger.

183

As quickly as a striking snake he lifted his hand and slapped her hard, so hard that tears came to her eyes. Then he ripped her dress from her shoulders and tore the chemise under it, down to the waistband, causing it to fall away until only the ropes around her wrists prevented it from falling off entirely.

"Beautiful!" he said, gazing upon her breasts. "So pale and pink! – like a peony flower. I shall write a poem about your breasts, Sorceress. And rest assured – I shall have you – and you will beg me for my attentions before I am through. Even Si Wang, the warrior lady, weeps with delight when I mount her "

Tatya was too proud to let him see that she was in the least shamed or embarrassed by what he had done. She did not lower his eyes, nor did she flinch when he began to touch her. She thought of Ping – how she had to protect her friend – and of Simon and Alan, and of home, anything rather than what he was doing.

A few moments later he sat back, getting no response from her – neither fear nor anger, nor even the pleasure he had felt certain that he could arouse in her.

"You are cold – I do not envy your husband. But I will change all that – you have never had a lover such as I." He rose to his feet and looked down at her. "I shall leave you uncovered – it gives me great pleasure to look at you like this. I cannot wait to see you completely uncovered and in my bed awaiting my pleasure."

He stood in thought for a moment and then seemed to make up his mind. He went to the opening of the tent and called for Lui.

When his gaze was off her Tatya shivered. What a strange and frightening man he was! To speak of blood and killing with enjoyment, to threaten rape and in the next breath to speak of writing poetry!

Lui entered the tent and looked at Tatya curiously.

"Has she not beautiful breasts, Lui?" said Hong mockingly. "See how pink her nipples are! She is so beautiful that I cannot wait to claim the rest of her body. I will take her immediately to Si Wang so that she may get what use she wants of her first and then she is mine. We shall ride all night, you and I – you with the other woman whom I shall

184

give you when we reach Kwen Lum, for your own use. She is a noble – have you ever taken a noblewoman, Lui?"

"No, honorable Hong, only whores and peasants. I have never even been fortunate enough to have the warrior lady. I must be the only one in Kwen Lum she has not coupled with," said Lui, licking his lips as he gazed at Tatya.

"That is very wrong of her, Lui. You are a good and faithful soldier, and deserve the same reward of her body as the others have had," said Hong. "Perhaps having a noblewoman to play your games with – I hear that your tastes are a little unusual – will make up for that lack."

Lui, a big, thickset man with eyes too close together, nodded in agreement, never taking his eyes off Tatya.

Hong turned back to her and swiftly untied the rope from the tent pole. He pulled Tatya to her feet and said roughly " We shall ride all night. Once my mistress, Si Wang Mu has done with you I will have you, Sorceress – have no doubt. Old Ch'ang shall prevent you from using your magics upon me and I will make you mine. Until then, do as I say – the woman you are fond of is hostage to your good behavior. If you use any of your magic at all I will give her to the lowest of the men at the fortress and they will use her until she dies. Until we reach Kwen Lum she will ride in front of Lui and he will cut her throat if you offer me any resistance. Even should you have your magic revenge on me she will still be dead!"

Tatya was suddenly afraid. She had no doubt that he was telling the truth. He was quite mad, she was convinced of it.

With her dress still hanging about her wrists he propelled her out of the tent and waited until Lui rode up with another horse in tow. Ping was already tied to his saddle and like Tatya, her garments had been torn to shreds and she was exposed. Lui had obviously copied his Captain's action. Lui, chuckling, held her in front of him by grabbing one breast. "She tried to bite me!" he laughed.

Roughly, Hong threw Tatya up on the saddle, and tied her wrists to the pommel. "Punish her when we reach Kwen Lum," he said carelessly. "Ask old Fan for a bull-hide whip. Women must learn, even if they are bitches, that they cannot bite." He swung up behind Tatya and like his underling, grabbed her breast, "You will soon learn to please me," he hissed in her ear.

"You can go to hell!" she thought and thought of the many ways she could send him there, once Ping was safe. And she could not even begin to imagine what Simon would do to this man when her husband knew how she had been treated. Lakota too .... Hong's days on this earth were numbered.

23
The First Confrontation

The female earth dragon, Fen, crouched low on the banks of a swift-running mountain stream. She had crawled from the stream only moments before, weakened by the labor of laying her first egg. Unlike her Western counterparts who laid their eggs in warm sand, the *lung* of China produced their eggs in water, where the egg then spent the first third of its existence. *Lung* also mated in the water, or in the air.

Her mate, Ah, had left her. He had seen what he was certain was a dragon poacher and had taken to the air, agitated and fearful, hoping to find the Sorcerer that was in the area, supposedly to save dragons from the terrible fate that had overtaken so many of their kind recently.

Fen feared not only for herself but for her egg. At this stage it was fragile and vulnerable. Even she could not move it, for her talons might puncture the still soft shell and the dragonet within would die. The cold water would help harden the shell but until that happened in the next twelve hours the egg was in danger.

It was a beautiful egg – jade green, with streaks of red running throughout the almost transparent surface. The dragonet would look like its parents. At this stage, she could almost see her child through the soft, fragile shell. But she could not speak to it mind to mind as did Western dragons.The dragonet could understand what it heard, but could not communicate with its parents or anyone else.

The older dragonesses had told her that the laying of the next egg would not be as painful, just as her first intercourse with her mate had been almost torture for her. She had been raised to offer the strictest duty and obedience to her mate and one did not neglect one's duty, no matter how one suffered – but to her surprise each time she had mated it had become easier and now she enjoyed sexual congress quite as much as her mate – and he was very eager for it indeed. If the laying of eggs became as easy and enjoyable as their union she looked forward to laying many, many eggs.

But now this one had to be protected. So that it would not be swept away by the swift current of the mountain stream she had laid it in a naturally deep pool. In spite of the fact that it could not be easily seen by prying eyes she knew that the poacher had seen her in the act of laying it – a *lung* laying an egg was unmistakable – for just as it did when they mated, the waters grew agitated and caused flooding and sometimes the ground shook. This was particularly true for the earth dragons. Here in the mountains the moments of birth and mating had even caused avalanches

If only Ah would hurry! She thought, shifting her position slightly on the grass. She was sore and felt so tired! She doubted if she could fight if they came upon her now. She had heard that they had magics which prevented a dragon from using their own magics – such as shrinking or enlarging themselves, or in her case, opening the earth to swallow them up or causing a mountainside to fall upon the heads of the dragon killers. She was too exhausted to summon up any magic, even the slightest. A flight of swallows could go by at the moment and she would not even snap at the delicious birds, a *lung's* favorite food.

Her head jerked up as her sensitive ears heard from far off the sounds of horses' hooves, and jingling bridles. She gave a convulsive shudder. They were coming! Oh, where was Ah?

Fen had laid her egg far too close to the fortress of Kwen-Lum. But it could not be helped. Fen was still young and inexperienced in these matters – a dragoness who had had more eggs would have realized how close she was to the birthing time and not left her lair in the earth. But they had been out in search of food, which was practically the only time an earth dragon left the underground lair. In the old times they had not had to search for food – it would have been offered at the dragon temple in the hills but the temple had fallen into disuse and no tempting offerings were seen there any more. When the birth pangs had come upon her it was all they could do to ground themselves and find a suitable stretch of water. Their lair, an immense cave, had a stream running through it – ideal for the egg. It was there that she had expected to birth the egg. It had been immaturity and ill luck that had decreed otherwise.

It did not take Si Wang and her band long to get to where the dragoness and her egg were – it was on the other side of a small mountain from the fortress and the path over it, one frequently used by travelers, was relatively easy to traverse. The sturdy little Mongolian ponies made nothing of going up the incline and down at a full gallop. They made excellent time and arrived at the site before Simon did.

Si Wang much regretted the absence of Hong Yu. The taking and killing of the dragon always excited her, quite as much as did the robberies – particularly when there was a killing. She found that she had to have sexual release, and even after she had lain with the men she chose to fight for her favors, she still needed more stimulation. Hong's mother had been a prostitute and he had grown up in a brothel. He knew tricks to pleasure a woman that other men did not. He was still her favorite lover. Too, he was her match in fighting with sword and staff and she was as stimulated by their naked practice fights almost as much as what followed. But she could not find satisfaction with but one man.

Ch'ang, riding beside her, saw the look that came over her face. She was licking her lips in anticipation. He shuddered at the thought. Si Wang was unwomanly – it was not for a woman to seek out men to stimulate her Jade Chamber – a woman should be submissive and obedient, for after all, woman was the property of man. He could hardly wait to remove himself from her presence and find himself a proper woman, one who would submit to his desires with downcast eyes and low voice, who would have small bound feet and be soft and rounded in shape. And she would be one who embraced his own religion, Taoism, and had studied the sex manuals such as "Important Matters of the Jade Chamber" A compliant, willing, modest wife, who kept her tiny feet properly covered...lost in these beatific dreams Ch'ang did not notice that they had reached the site until Si Wang kicked him in the leg and said "What do you dream of, Ch'ang?"

189

"Not the joys of the peony blossom!" jeered one man close to him and Si Wang, using a common name for the female genitalia.

Si Wang and the other men – there were about twenty of them – laughed raucously, as Ch'ang slid awkwardly from the saddle. He ignored them – he did not wish to show them that their words rankled. "Where is this dragon?" he demanded.

The scout who had found her pointed towards a small depression a little ways off where Ch'ang could hear the noise of a rapid stream running over the rocks in its bed. "She lies there, sorcerer. She has just made an egg. She is weak and tired."

A murmur of satisfaction ran through the group. A dragon egg would add considerably to their profits and this was the second egg they had found recently. Dragon egg was used not only as medicine but as an aphrodisiac and the dragonet was in much demand as food for rich men with jaded palates. Eating of a new-born dragon, even one forced from the shell, was thought to impart wisdom and perhaps immortality.

Ch'ang stalked forward and saw in the small valley a jade green dragon on the banks of the stream. He was wise enough in the ways of dragons to know that the egg was no doubt in the water.

Fen was so panicked that she could not think what to do. Should she shrink and fly away? But that would leave the egg unprotected! Should she let them have her and hope that they were satisfied with that and leave the egg alone? She heard the horses arrive and the men's voices and their rowdy laughter.

In absolute terror she watched the magician, for she at once discerned that it was a Sorcerer who came towards her – and prepared to face her death.

"Please," she choked out. "Please do not harm my egg! I will let you have my life, if only you will not harm my egg!" All of her maternal instincts compelled her to protect the egg at any cost, even that of her own life.

Ch'ang paid no attention to her pleas. This would be very easy – she was more fearful than any dragon he had seen as yet. She obviously knew what he meant to do with her.

From behind him Si Wang said "Very well, if you submit yourself to us I shall leave your egg untouched."

Ch'ang ground his teeth. Did that woman have to interest herself in everything? Dealing with the dragons was his task, not hers. And why bother to make a promise she had no intentions of keeping?

Fen bowed her head and whispered "I thank you,Gracious lady. Do with me what you will."

"You could have stayed at home, Ch'ang," said Si Wang carelessly, pushing by him. "I shall apply the caterpillar myself." She slid down the slope to where the *ti-lung* lay, resigned to her fate.

Si Wang walked up to the dragoness who looked at her with dull eyes.

"Lower your head, *lung!*" Si Wang commanded as she removed a box from the pocket of her breeches and opened it to reveal a caterpillar.

Fen shuddered the length of her body. How much would it hurt? She hoped that Ah would tell the egg how much its mother had sacrificed for its sake and that they would honor her spirit properly.

Obediently, she put down her head as Si Wang took the wriggling caterpillar between two gloved fingers and began to lift it towards Fen's nostrils.

A thin stream of flame shot from the sky between the *ti-lung* and Si Wang.

With a oath and a scream the warlord jumped backwards. Her hand was burned, even through the protection of the glove. The box and the caterpillar fell to earth, burning, as her men began shouting in warning. Si Wang slipped on the grass and fell onto her bottom, thus allowing her an unimpeded view of an immense winged creature hanging in the air above them. As she watched, more flame came from its nostrils, igniting the grass on the hillside, the resulting fire cutting her off from her men. Violet light flared from a point above it and she saw that four men rode

191

the beast – two of them foreign devils. Gunfire crackled and she heard screams of pain.

Ch'ang sent a quick bolt of black energies up towards the sky, which was countered at once by another surge of violet light. The two arcs of power met in the air, bursting and spreading wildly, like am immense firework, with a noise like thunder.

"Ch'ang!" yelled Si Wang. "Put out this fire!"

He heard her and turned quickly, pointing his staff at the conflagration. It died as if it had been doused by water.

Holding her burned hand to her chest Si Wang scrambled up the hillside to stand by Ch'ang. Her hand was not too badly burned – she had been wearing the heavy gloves she always wore with her armor – but it did hurt and the pain made her angry.

"Who is that that dares to challenge me?" she demanded of Ch'ang, her eyes flashing.

"I know no more than you do!" he retorted as another burst of violet light came towards him. A lift and twist of his staff spun out a black wave of energy that caught and burst with the light from above, making another violent display of pyrotechnics.

The creature overhead whirled in the sky and sent another long burst of flame towards where Si Wang's men tried to defend themselves on the rim of the valley. She heard men and horses scream in fear. They were shooting both their guns and bows at the creature but not only did it dart and roll too quickly for them to aim properly but there seemed to be an invisible shield of some sort protecting it. The arrows and bullets met a barrier and fell to earth.

Was that a dragon? she wondered furiously as she watched its gyrations in the sky. She had never seen a dragon with wings except in old sculptures, nor had she ever heard of a dragon that could spew fire. And it, from what she could see, did not look like the dragons she knew.

Jade green waves of pure energy suddenly joined the violet that was attacking them.

"There are two of them!" Ch'ang exclaimed in disbelief.

"Two of what?" Si Wang demanded.

Ch'ang did not answer. Instead he raised his staff, knocked it upon the ground, causing an audible crack to reverberate through the valley and disappeared in a pinwheel of spitting sparks.

"Coward!" Si Wang screamed "Come back here and fight!"

One of her men galloped up to her, dragging her horse behind him. Both horses were wet with sweat and terror. "Come, lady! gasped the man. "We cannot fight these Sorcerers! Six men are dead already!"

SI Wang was forced to agree. She vaulted onto her horse, and took off at a gallop. The balance of her troop was already fleeing over the mountain at high speed, leaving the dead and dying behind.

Bitter, angry thoughts filled her brain as they fled. Ch'ang would be fortunate if she did not have him beaten within an inch of his life! She was paying him well and allowing him a very generous share in their loot and plunder. And now he had failed in his primary duty and left her and her men to face a Sorcerer alone!

"Shall I go after them?" Lakota asked eagerly, turning his long neck back to talk to his riders.

"No, my friend, we shall wait for my men to arrive before we attack again. And I shall send my lieutenant, Wang, to the garrison in Chengdu for reinforcements," answered the Prince. "Our two Sorcerers can do a great deal but I would like to have more warriors before we assault the fortress."

"In the meanwhile," said Ash, "we can keep them bottled up in their rat-hole with magic and Lakota's flames. At least they can take no more dragons or unwary travelers."

Simon said nothing. He wished that the Necromancer had not conceded so early in the fight. He would have liked to get a better feel for the man's power. The fact that he could dematerialize argued that he was a talented Sorcerer but Simon's unfamiliarity with Chinese magic made him uncertain. He would have to confer with Feng Hu.

Why had the man given up so easily? Was it because he felt himself defeated? Or did he leave to summon help – such as demons? Black magicians, Simon knew, depended on demons and evil elementals for their main sources of power and, at least in the Western tradition, one did not summon those up easily – particularly when taken totally by surprise.

While the Prince and Ash exulted over the easy defeat of Ch'ang and the eventual defeat of Si Wang after a short siege of her fortress, Simon felt that it would not be as easy as they thought. The Sorcerer would not be defeated until he was totally stripped of his powers or dead. And he would lay odds that old Feng would feel the same.

Jing Mai lay in the grass, watching the man who had been set to guard them. The man who Hong had left in charge had stopped the troop as soon as their leader rode away carrying the foreign devil woman and her friend with him and Lui. The men were eager to drink, feast and avail themselves of the girls.

The girls, panting and sobbing, had fallen to the grass where they had halted. They had been given no food or water and an obviously reluctant man had been set to guard them. A little ways away a camp had been set up and already the campfires were lit and the smell of food was wafting through the air. There were bursts of rowdy and lewd songs, and the splash of rice wine into basins could be heard. The guard glanced wistfully towards the camp more than once. They had drawn lots to see who would guard the girls and he had lost. He had been told just to watch them – he was not to take one of them – that was for later.

Jing Mai watched him from under half-closed eyes. He had lit a fire , a small one, to make tea, for, of course, even in this band of robbers, it was a dereliction of duty to drink whilst on guard.

She had checked the ropes. They were now loose about her wrists and they were continuing to disintegrate. She had but to get rid of this man and they could escape. The rest of the camp was paying no attention to them, intent on feasting and swilling down rice wine.

Jing Mai had always been curious and sought information wherever she could find it. One never knew what would come in useful and she had had her mother to care for, as well as herself.

She had made a friend of the son of one of the village pleasure women, a boy who most of the others avoided. And he had taken her, at her request, to spy upon the activities in the House of Pleasure.

At first, when she was younger, what she saw there struck her as both amusing and undignified. As she grew older what she saw caused in her a great scorn for men. Could they not see that the women were manipulating them and furthermore, did not really sigh and moan in ecstasy but feigned each sound? It struck Jing Mai that this information might one day be of some use to her, so she had kept returning to the place of hiding with her friend and watching the goings-on at every opportunity.

Now it gave her an idea. The man set to guard them was relatively young – not much older than she was and from the looks he cast at the girls and back to the camp, he was quite frustrated, wanting both the food and the drink and a girl. He was also quite unprepossessing in looks and manner. To judge by what she had observed in her village, he was unlikely to be able to lay with a girl unless he paid her or took her by force. Most girls favored good – looking or wealthy young men when they gave their favors.

Feeling about beneath herself and trying not to move too much she found a rock. She eased it from the ground, sighing in satisfaction as she felt the size of it. It should just serve her purpose. Carefully, she put it by her side where it would be close to hand when she needed it. Then she set about the rest of her plan. She lifted her hand and untied the cotton cord that held on her trousers and wiggled her hips. At the same time she used her still bound hands to pull her blouse up to her chin. She had to make certain the at the rope did not completely fall off.

"What are you doing Jing Mai?" came a horrified whisper from Ya.

"Rescuing us," Jing Mai said angrily. "Keep your voice down, fool of a girl!" She kept wiggling until the trousers were below her knees and she could slide one leg and then

195

the other from them. It was impossible to move her blouse but she rolled around until it was pushed up enough so that she looked as if she was almost nude.

Then she moaned and began moving her hips up and down as she had seen the women in the House of Pleasure do when they wished to excite a client.

The guard had been staring wistfully at the camp fire, hoping that someone would bring him some hot food. They had been in the saddle most of the day and he was hungry. It smelled so good!

When Jing Mai began to moan he turned quickly to look at the girls and his eyes ran out on stems. "What are you doing?" he demanded. He put his cup down on the ground abruptly and stood up, going to stand over her.

"I long for a mighty Jade Stalk!" she said, moving suggestively. "Can you not pleasure me? I am certain that you can give immense pleasure to a woman – you are very large, are you not?"

"Jing Mai!" said Ya in outrage.

The guard was flattered, although somewhat suspicious. "Are you not a virgin?" he asked uncertainly, watching the gyrations ofher body.

"I work in the House of Pleasure," she lied. "Bend down and I will tell you what talents I have. Here, place your hands on my breasts – they ache for your touch. I am certain that you are a marvelous lover. Oh, hurry! I must have you!"

If she worked in the House of Pleasure, he thought, she was no virgin and the other men could not be angered that he had deflowered her. Having this obviously eager girl would somewhat make up for missing the wine and food. And he would have intercourse tonight before he was too drunk to enjoy it.

He knelt down beside her and grabbed her breast.

"Not there – between my legs!" she hissed. "How can the jade stalk enter the peony chamber from there?"

Obediently, he moved to between her outstretched legs and bent over her breasts.

As soon as he was positioned, the fit and agile Jing Mai twisted and kneed him hard in the groin. He gasped and clutched at himself. Before he could yell in shock she had

196

grabbed the rock and bashed it into his skull. And, like a rock, he fell across her body.

She was very strong for a girl of her age – the outdoor life of fishing and walking the valley to sell her wares had made her so. With contempt, she pushed the body aside. "You will never rape a girl again!" she said in satisfaction.

She then pulled the ropes from her wrists and picking up her clothing, shrugged into the blouse and trousers.

The other girls stared at her with wide eyed surprise. "Come!" she said. "The *fan qui* Witch has loosened out ropes and no one watches us!" She went down the line, helping the others to shed their bonds. "We shall run while the rest of these men feast and get themselves drunk. By the time they come for us we shall be on our way home!"

24

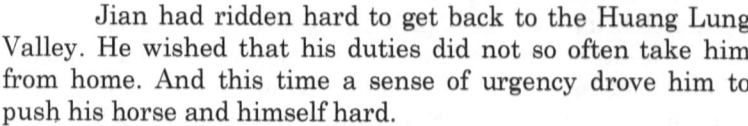

The Secret Entrance

Jian had ridden hard to get back to the Huang Lung Valley. He wished that his duties did not so often take him from home. And this time a sense of urgency drove him to push his horse and himself hard.

His horse smelled the smoke before he did, throwing up his head and snorting. "Quiet, Zun," Jian said, pulling up and patting the sweating bay neck of the horse. "What disturbs you?"

Then he too smelt the heavy, acrid odor, far more thick and dense than would come from cooking fires. Suddenly frightened, he put his heels to Zun and they took off at a gallop.

He was completely stunned and shocked by the devastation of the lower end of the valley. Buildings were burning, people were screaming and crying and everywhere was death.

He stopped an elderly peasant who was dragging a cart. To Jian's horror the cart held the body of an elderly woman who was dead, the breast of her gown covered in blood.

"What has happened here?" Jian cried.

"Robbers," said the peasant shortly. By rights he should have answered Jian's inquiry with more respect for the dignity of the district Magistrate, but he was angry and too tired to care. "Robbers from the mountains. My wife tried to prevent them from taking our granddaughter so they killed her. They took girls from the village and several women with them."

Several women! With his heart in his mouth Jian whipped the tired Zun and galloped on down the valley, ignoring the people who called out to him as he passed, as if a demon were at his heels.

His home had been looted – he could see that even before he jumped from Zun's back as they slid to a stop in front of the house. The door hung from one hinge and the oiled paper of the windows had been torn. "Ping!" he called hoarsely "Hai! Mei! Where are you?"

"Baba!" came the voice of his son and a small figure, followed by a saffron-robed monk came from around the back of the house.

Jian dropped to one knee and gathered his son to him."Where are your mother and sister? And the servants and our foreign guests?"

The monk came closer and bowed. "I have just brought him here from the school, honorable Magistrate. The bandits did not venture as far as the temple so the children were safe."

"Baba, I cannot find Mama!" Hai said, sounding as if he wanted to cry.

"Have you been in the house?" Jian demanded of the monk.

"No, there was no time –"

"Stay here with the boy," said Jian harshly. "I will go in."

He was very afraid as to what he would find. He called for Ping and Mei as he went through each room.

Everywhere there was signs of a bitter struggle. Scorch marks on the wall, broken porcelain on the floor and even traces of blood. His heart almost stopped when he came to the kitchen and found a dead body, face down. But it proved to be that of a young man he did not know. He was dead of a knife wound to the chest.

He had gone to the back of the house, calling and searching, seeing everywhere the signs of malicious damage and looting. He smelled smoke as well and noted that part of the roof smoldered.

As he reached the area of the storage rooms a door suddenly turned blue in front of his startled eyes and then opened by itself, to reveal his daughter, two maidservants, the foreign boy Alan and three cats.

"Baba!" cried Mei and rushed to her father He picked her up and hugged her close. Many Chinese cared naught for girl children but Jian loved his small daughter as much as he loved his son. "Where is your mother?"

The cook, Zhi, bowed. "The foreign Sorceress sealed us in this room, Magistrate. From what we could hear the robbers carried her and the lady away."

Janus with the acute hearing of all cats, had heard more than the cook had, even though the woman had had her ear pressed to the door. The familiar now said, "They took your wife to insure Tatya's good behavior. She was fighting them with magic."

"Why wasn't I here?" said Jian in anguish.

"It's a good thing you were not!" said Janus crisply. "You would be dead by now and what good would that have done? What you need to do," she continued, "is to find Simon. Alan has a dragon whistle but Lakota is too far from here to hear it because we have been blowing it for hours on and off and there is no sign of him. Its range is only fifty miles."

Jian put Mei on the floor. He looked a little startled to be receiving instructions from a cat.

"But how can I leave my children?" Jian said in anguish.

"We will take care of your children, and Alan as well," said Janus, as if it were a foregone conclusion. "We shall all go to the temple, as this house is no longer habitable."

Jian found himself agreeing to this plan and together he and the cats walked out to where the monk waited with Hai, Jian amazed at the alacrity with which the two children obeyed Janus' 'nanny' voice. "Come along now! Don't dawdle!" Marinka and Xui trotted along with the two children.

Hai had gone to pat an exhausted Zun. The horse stood with his head hanging. Jian was guiltily aware that he had ridden the faithful creature nearly into the ground and had ignored his needs.

"Are there any other horses left in the valley?" he asked the monk. "My horse is spent and I must go after my wife."

Before the monk could speak hoof beats were heard and Jian looked up to see a young man, not much more than sixteen or seventeen, riding towards him, leading another horse. The youth looked vaguely familiar to Jian.

"Magistrate!" the young man called out. "I saw you arrive. You will wish to go after the bandits. I wish to come with you. I watched – I know in which direction they have taken their prisoners."

"Who are you?" asked Jian.

"This is Gui," the monk supplied. "His mother is one of the pleasure women. No one knows who his father is."

Gui flushed and bit back a hot retort that sprang to his lips. "They have stolen your wife, Magistrate, and they have stolen my friend Jing Mai as well, and eight other girls. I know all too well what those men will do to them."

Without a second thought Jian hugged his children good-bye, bidding them to show proper respect to their elders. He swung onto the horse, noting in some surprise that the two animals were of good quality, not the very small rabbit horses, usually used as pack animals, that he would have expected from a youth who resided in a House of Pleasure. Gui wore a sword as Jian did himself.

"The men who were using these horses will need them no longer," said Gui, understanding Jian's glance.

No more words were exchange as both riders bent low over the horses' necks and lifted the animals into a gallop. Behind them, the monk took up the reins of Zun and asked the children to show him to the stable so that he might take care of the horse.

Hong was a cautious man. Leaving Tatya with Lui some distance from the fortress he crept forward almost invisibly, to see if it was safe to enter.

Below he saw signs as if the fortress prepared for a siege. The two cannon were wheeled into position. Arrows and gunpowder and ammunition were being laid in rows along the ramparts and men scurried to and fro, intent on various tasks.

He could not imagine what had happened but he decided that discretion was called for. They would go the longer way around – through the waterfall that fell from the stream that passed behind the fortress. The stream supplied water for the fortress – and from the front of the huge pile their enemies could not see the source of water that made a long siege possible.

There was a secret entrance to the fortress behind the waterfall coming up under the building. Hong judged it most judicious to come in this way. It would be more time before they could enter Kwen Lum. Hong regretted that. He wanted to show Si Wang the foreign woman, and have the warlord do what she wished with her, then take the Witch to bed. He had become thoroughly aroused having her tied on in front of him, massaging her bare breasts while he guided his horse with his knees. He had whispered in her ear everything that he would do to her once she was his. She had not reacted at all to his touch nor to what he had said and he had become obsessed with seeing her cry out in pleasure. He was certain that her foreign devil husband did not know how to please a woman the way he did. He had heard, from his mother, who had worked in a brothel in Canton frequented by foreigners, that foreign men had little knowledge of a woman's body and no idea how to give a woman her own pleasure.

He carefully returned to Lui and the horses and noted with annoyance that Lui now held both the noblewoman's breasts as he himself had held the Witch woman's. Lui admired him – Hong was well aware of this – but it was irritating that the big man copied his every move.

Quietly as possible they went back down the mountainside and followed the almost indiscernible track around to the waterfall.

Si Wang had returned to Kwen Lum in a towering rage. She had called for her bath and told old Fan to go and fetch Ch'ang from whatever hole he was hiding in. She also ordered that the fortress be prepared for a siege.

The doctor she kept for the men came and bandaged her hand while men with buckets of steaming water filled her bath. She shed her clothing rapidly, not waiting for Fan to undress her, cursing loudly as the sleeve of her shirt caught upon the bandage covering the burn.

She had just slipped into her bath when Ch'ang appeared, following Fan, who bore a tray of rice wine and porcelain cups. He immediately poured a cupful for her and taking it, she downed it in one gulp.

She looked at Ch'ang coldly. "I would be well within my rights, Ch'ang, to have you whipped for the coward you are," she said coldly.

"I might be able to fight and defeat one Sorcerer," he said equally coldly "but not two."

Before she could speak he held up a hand to forestall her. "There were two Sorcerers there, Si Wang. The foreign devil with the violet magic and the jade green of an ancient Chinaman. I was not prepared to fight two of them and combat dragon flame as well. I was beginning to gather more power when you sent for me," he added, rather peevishly.

"See that you do gather more power!" Si Wang snapped. "I want them all destroyed! We shall take that odd dragon as well!" She lapped her hand emphatically on the surface of the water, sending up a heavy surge of spray.

The door to the room flew open and Hong entered, dragging a woman with him.

"The *fan qui* Witch," he announced, throwing Tatya down in front of the tin tub. "The others had left the valley by the time that we arrived." Briefly, he outlined how he had taken the Witch and the magic she had used.

"That is most excellent, Hong! She is the one I most wanted!" said Si Wang in delight. "*You* do not fail me!" she added with a sly look at Ch'ang.

"Are you the woman of the foreign Sorcerer?" she demanded of Tatya.

When Tatya did not immediately answer Hong grabbed her hair and pulled her head back. "Answer the warrior lady!" he commanded. "Lui, slice the noblewoman!"

"No!" Tatya shouted. "He is my husband. I will answer all your questions if you do not harm my friend."

Ch'ang had been studying her. "I cannot detect much magic. If she has any, it is very little," he announced.

That's because I have my shields up, you stupid bastard, Tatya thought. Calling these people names, even just mentally, was a relief to her feelings.

"Strip the rest of those rags from her," Si Wang ordered 'I wish to see her. Have you had her yet, Hong?"

"No, great lady, you said she was to be unharmed," he answered.

203

"Coupling is not harmful, Hong!" Si Wang said with an evil laugh as her lieutenant pulled the last of Tatya's dress and knickers off her, leaving her clad but in stockings and shoes.

Why does everyone I meet wish to strip me naked? Tatya thought in irritation.

Si Wang stood up and exited the tub and came to stand over Tatya, dripping water. She looked at her captive so closely that Tatya was tempted to ask the warlord if she wanted to examine her teeth as well.

"What is this?" Si Wang said sharply, suddenly alert. She squatted down by Tatya and reached out a finger to touch her stomach. "You have borne a child," she said.

Even the most talented of Wizard Healers could not eradicate all of the stretch marks of pregnancy. It was this faint remnant that Si Wang now traced with a fingertip.

"Yes," said Tatya shortly.

"The father is this Sorcerer?"

"Yes."

"Is it a son?"

"Yes."

"Where is he?"

"At home in Ireland with his grandparents." Why was this of any interest to the warlord? Tatya was certainly not going to tell her that Alan was here in China.

"Are they Sorcerers as well?" Si Wang wanted to know.

"We're *all* of us Sorcerers," said Tatya a little sarcastically. "Everyone in Ireland is a Sorcerer."

"I shall have you whipped if you speak to me like that again and then I will give you to my men for their amusement," said Si Wang, standing up. "Ch'ang, this woman is yours. You should be happy to couple with another magician."

"I don't want her!" Ch'ang said in horror. "It is well known that a Witch gets her power by draining a man's seed! If her husband still has power after laying with her, he must be very powerful indeed!"

"Yes," said Si Wang, her eyes gleaming, " and potent as well, to put a son in her womb."

Tatya studied the warlord, and was puzzled by her. It did not seem to bother her that she was stark naked in a group of men, still wet from her bath. Even naked she commanded the situation. But what did this woman want? What did all of her questions mean?

Si Wang looked at Tatya again. The dragon whistle hung down between her breasts. Si Wang bent over again and took the dragon whistle in her hand. "What is this?" She gave a tug and the silver chain broke.

"A token of some sort," said Ch'ang.

Old Fan snickered. "A love gift!"

"Rings on both fingers..." said the sharp-eyed Si Wang. "Take them off and give them to me."

Hong bent down and wrenched the rings – her Elfin wedding ring and the *Cloddagh* ring Simon had had made for her when he first brought her to her new home in Ireland – from Tatya's fingers. "Offer me no resistance – your friend dies else wise," he whispered threateningly.

"What to do with you?" Si Wang mused, looking down at Tatya as she shook the rings and the dragon whistle in her hand. "Take her to the brothel in the village – tell them to put her to the lustiest men who use women roughly."

"I should like to have her," said Hong quickly.

As if I were beads in a bazaar to be bargained over! thought Tatya indignantly.

"Si Wang looked at him, her eyes narrowing. She felt a spurt of anger, an emotion she did not recognize as jealousy.

"You want *her*, Hong, when you can share *my* bed?" she said softly.

"But I cannot always share your bed, lady. You have other lovers, which is your right. This one will do for when you are otherwise occupied. And to have a foreign devil to couple with will make my men admire me even more," Hong explained.

Si Wang looked at him for a moment and then said, "Very well. You may have her. I can see the lust you have for her in your eyes. But you will have to wait to slake that lust until we return. We leave, you and I and Chen Bo, to spy upon this Sorcerer. Ch'ang will accompany us as well. We need to ascertain how much magic this foreigner has and what threat the old Sorcerer with him might be. Rape her

205

when we return. For now lock her in the cellar with the other one. Lui may guard them. Ch'ang, has she enough magic to overpower Lui and escape?"

Ch'ang shook his head. "Whatever magic she had is gone. As I told you, she feeds upon her husband and steals the power from him. She probably lay with him the night before she threw blue thunder bolts at Hong Yu. That power is all gone now."

Keep on thinking that way, Tatya thought. *You're in for a surprise, you arrogant male thing!*

Si Wang gave a crack of lewd laughter. "Then to defeat this foreign Sorcerer all we must do is to place him in a room of forty Sorceresses and make certain that he couples with all of them! His powers will be gone! What are you doing, Lui?" she turned quickly as a movement caught her eye.

"Taking the rest of this woman's clothes off, great lady," he said, somewhat abashed as Ping struggled in his huge hands.

"I told Lui that he could have this noblewoman to play with," Hong explained. "Lui told me that to his regret you have never lain with him. He insists on copying everything I do," he added *sotto voce.*

Si Wang laughed again. "When we return, Lui, we shall go and watch Hong rape his Witch. Then you shall play your games with the noblewoman and I shall lay with you! I do not know why I have neglected you for so long!" She looked pointedly and admiringly at the front of his breeches.

And I thought my cousin Evgeny was bad! Tatya thought to herself.

Hong hauled her to her feet. "I shall take her to the cellars. We have cells there that no one has ever managed to escape from." He ran his hands down her body as he pulled her up. "I am glad that you are not a timid shrinking virgin," he bent and whispered to her in satisfaction.

Tatya, again, made no sign that she had even noticed he touched her in such intimate fashion. What he said or did to her now did not matter. It would be the last time her ever touched her. And if he thought her compliant and powerless, so much the better. One guard would be easy to overcome. And if Ping was thrust into the same cell...

And one day she would repay that warlord woman for taking her rings and the dragon whistle – all gifts from Simon. Losing the dragon whistle would make their escape more difficult. But Tatya already had the glimmerings of a plan.

25
The Rescue of Ping

Giving the rope that bound Tatya's wrists together to Lui for a moment, Hong took a lantern from a table in Si Wang's room and lit it from a nearby oil lamp.

He took the rope back exclaiming angrily at Lui as the big man, holding a struggling Ping in one hand, tried to fondle Tatya as well. "Leave her!" Hong exclaimed. "She is mine! I have given you a woman of your own – feel *her* body!"

Ping was sobbing hysterically and began screaming when Lui ran his big hand over her.

"Stop that noise!" ordered Si Wang. Fan was busily helping her into her clothing and armor. Si Wang reached out as if she would strike Ping, who shrank away, wisely stopping her screams.

"Fool of a woman!" said Si Wang in contempt. "I pity your husband if this is how you greet his advances! *I* will not shrink from Lui's caresses! He will probably give you greater pleasure than you have ever known."

"And you, *fan qui*," she said, turning to Tatya "You are fortunate indeed that I have given you to Hong. I have seldom lain with a man who was able to please me more. Remember, I could have sent you to the brothel where you would have been taken by many men. Instead you will have one lover. But he is very lusty!" she added with a ribald laugh. "You both have cause to be grateful to me! I am certain that you both will thank me tomorrow."

Tatya looked at her, incredulous. She expected to be thanked for being raped, for being taken away from husbands and family?

Hong grabbed Tatya and swung her up on his shoulder like a sack of flour. He grabbed at her buttocks to steady her as old Fan opened the door.

Lui copied his idol and they went out into a hall, lined with weapons of all types. Hong opened another door which led to a dark stair.

208

Tatya lost track of how many flights they descended. The stair was circular. It was a tortuously long descent – or so it seemed, slung over Hong's shoulder with her only view the steps they traversed.

As they descended it became colder and Tatya could hear water dripping. She thought that they might even be lower than the level they had come in on under the waterfall. This place was much bigger than she first had thought – and a lot of it was below the surface of the ground.

Just when she thought that she could not stand being bounced around like a sack of meal any further the stairs ended. Hong went down a long dark corridor, lit only by the bobbing light of his lantern.

At long last they arrived at the end of the corridor. To Tatya's dismay Lui went on by them carrying Ping.

Hong took a ring of keys from his belt and unlocked the door. Once inside, he hung the lantern on a wall hook and threw Tatya to the floor.

He tied her hands to a ring in the wall and once more ran his hands over her.

"While I am gone, little Witch, you may dream of our union," he said and, grabbing her hair which was by now loose and streaming down her back, forced her head back and kissed her once again grabbing her breast with his free hand.

Ah!" he cried in triumph "Your nipples are hard and firm – you warm to my touch."

"Don't flatter yourself," said Tatya coldly. "It is chill in here and that is a natural reaction of any woman. Your grandmother would be just the same."

He let go of her hair. "I will discipline you so that you will speak to me only with honeyed love words, Witch. I would take you now but Si Wang will not wait," he said in regret. "You will soon learn how to please me and bow before me with respect as your lord and master. You will beg me to mount you."

"When hell freezes over," Tatya said giving him a look as if he was less than a clod of dirt.

He flushed with anger, raised his hand as if to slap her and then instead roughly ran his hand through her most intimate place and cursed as she showed no reaction. "Just you wait!" he hissed.

209

He got to his feet and, taking the lantern down, left the room, plunging it into blackness. The door he shut firmly behind him and she heard the key turn in the lock.

"Bastard! Just *you* wait – you'll regret ever having touched me!" Tatya said under her breath as she heard his steps go down the corridor.

Tatya made herself wait for fifteen minutes before she magically untied the rope around her wrists and threw a mage light up so that she could see what she had to deal with.

It was a small room, without a window. It could not have been much more than 6 by 8 in size and other than the hook for the lantern and several rings (one of which she had been tied to) on the wall there was nothing in it at all. It was probably a store room of some kind. She had hoped that if this room had been used for prisoners there might be a bed and blankets, something she could use for a garment.

It was very cold and the walls ran with damp. Keeping a steady mage light on the tips of her left hand fingers, she wasted no time in unlocking the door with a spell. It was a simple lock and well-tended, for it opened beneath her magic quite easily with no sound of grating, nor were there any creaking hinges. She slipped out into the corridor after listening carefully for a moment and sending out a magical probe that told her the corridor was empty. She did not like that – Lui was suppose to be guarding them – she prayed that this did not mean he was raping Ping at this moment.

All of the doors – and there were many – in the corridor were locked. Tatya muttered some Russian curses to herself. She could sense Ping's presence but where exactly she might be was not readily apparent. She would have to look in each room.

She had looked in two rooms, both empty when she heard Ping scream.

Ping was so frightened at this point that her mind felt numb, as bruised and as battered as her body.

The ride here, with that big man squeezing her breasts until they hurt, had been awful beyond belief. She was unable to get away from him at all, for he was so strong and the more she tried to draw away the harder he pinched and grabbed until she was certain that she would be black and blue. Her mind went round and round with thoughts of the girls, what would be done to them but most of all, what would be done to her and Tatya.

And she was ashamed on top of her fear. For her breasts to be bared for all to see! To have this man fondle and pinch her in front of others – to know what he intended to do to her!

And then he had pulled off her clothes in front of all of those people! Ping had been so shamed – she had tried to cover herself but he would not let her. He looked at her with lustful eyes and had touched her. She could not help screaming. And then that horrible unnatural woman had said that they should be grateful! Grateful!

How Tatya could be so calm when that man had handled her in such indecent fashion, how she could not be shamed and crying to be seen naked by all of those people? Tatya had seemed unemotional, so composed and con-temptuous of what was being done to her. Was this what possessing magic did for a person?

Ping did not wonder why Tatya had not rescued them with magic, She really had no idea how powerful her friend was and in the back of her mind she supposed that she did not have the power that Simon did, for after all, she was a woman and men were the powerful ones in every way. Everyone knew that.

Ping had been raised to be obedient and subservient to men. That was the proper way of things, according to the principals of the writings of the honorable Lady Pan Chao, a Confucianist who had lived 1700 years ago. These principals held that a woman must be gentle and orderly, chaste and sedate, and must not listen to lewd talk nor look at unseemly things, and not be slovenly in the house. And, Ping thought in flat despair, she herself was no longer chaste and had listened to lewd talk and seen unseemly things. And unseemly, and horrible, terrible things had been done to her as well. All of these thoughts raced through Ping's mind as she was jolted down the stairs on Lui's shoulder, his huge hand covering her buttocks, copying exactly his Captain's hold on Tatya.

Ping had hoped that they would lock her up with Tatya but Lui continued down the dank and dark corridor to the end, past where Hong disappeared behind a door with Tatya. Lui carried a lantern also and set this down on a table in the room before lowering Ping to the floor.

He grunted in satisfaction as she stared up at him, her eyes full of fear. She was too frightened to move. He reached into a pocket and withdrew a handkerchief, with which he gagged her. "I do not want you to scream too soon," he confided, "There will be time enough for that later."

Ping tried to shrink away from him. The lantern light was feeble, but it showed her a room full of strange things that she did not understand what they might be. There were tables with odd items attached to them and chains hung from the ceiling with shackles on the ends of the chains. What she took to be a rope bedstead stood upon its side close to her. Before she had time to really look at the contents of the room he picked her up again and deposited her on top of a table.

When he began to tie her down she fought him, kicking and shrieking through the muffling gag, trying to hit him with her bound hands.

He laughed at her. He was so strong that he could hold her with one hand. Everything she did was completely ineffectual. It took him but a few moments to spread-eagled her on the table top.

Then he went to a nearby brass brazier and, taking a flint from a nearby shelf, kindled a fire in the charcoal. Ping was very much afraid that he was doing that so that it would be comfortable for him when he removed his clothing to take her. She was shivering in terror as much as from the dank, creeping cold and the darkness.

When the fire was burning steadily he came to stand beside her and began to run his hands up and down her body. "I have never had a noblewoman before," he said. "The peasant women and the whores scream loudly when I use my toys on them. Will you scream too, noblewoman?"

Ping strained against the bonds that held her. She must get away! She must! She felt filthy and degraded that he

212

was touching her in such fashion. And what was he talking about?

Lui laughed. "I know how to tie a knot, little noblewoman. You will not escape from Lui. I will go and fetch my toys and then I shall enjoy you. The Captain has given you to me and you will be my woman, my own, from now on. We will spend much time in this room."

He moved away from the table and Ping heard the door open and close.

She was filled with utter dread and panic and had no hope – she knew what would happen to her. What did he mean by 'toys'? There could be no escape from this – she would be despoiled, if not killed. The look in his eyes just now frightened her profoundly – it was lust – and something else – something she did not understand, but it made her stomach clench with fear.

He returned some fifteen minutes later. She heard the door open again and turned her head to look at him. She gave a muffled gasp of horror.

He was completely naked and carried a canvas wrapped bundle which he lay down on the table beside her. It was long and slim, as if it might contain a sword. He unwrapped it tenderly and said, talking to himself "They did not say that I could not take her now. The lady wants to watch what I do and I should know how this one will react so that the lady is pleased with what she sees. I cannot wait to have her."

This was obvious to Ping. She watched, fearful eyed as he finished unwrapping the bundle and took what it contained out and showed it to her.

"See, little noblewoman? See my rods?" he said in a pleased voice. "I shall put these in the fire and then I shall touch you with them – here and here –" he touched her breasts and stomach "and here as well." He put a hand on the inside of her thighs. "Then, while you scream with pain, I shall take you."

He turned and put the three rods in the fire.

Ping struggled and pulled as hard as she could against the bonds but she was tied too tightly. She could not move. No, oh no! This could not be happening! *Kwan Yen, save me!* she begged.

213

Lui turned back to her. "They will be hot very soon," he said, smiling a smile that made Ping sick to the depths of her soul. "Are you afraid? I want to hear you scream now. Perhaps you will beg me to spare you." He ripped the gag from her mouth.

And Ping screamed.

The door to the room seemed to explode in a bright blue light. Lui turned quickly towards it as another brilliant flash of blue in the shape of a huge ball followed it and caught Lui full in the chest. He was slammed backwards into the wall, an expression of shock and surprise on his face. He hit the wall with such force that his head snapped back and struck the stone. There was a sound like a ripe melon falling to the ground and he slumped to the floor.

The blue light cleared and there was Tatya. She hurried at once to Ping's side. "What did he do to you?" she asked fiercely, bending over her friend.

"He was going to burn me!" Ping could only whisper, her throat raw from the strength of the scream and her voice choked with tears.

"Did he rape you?" Tatya demanded as she took care of the ropes that bound Ping to the table.

"No, but – oh – he touched me! He touched me!" Ping cried, her teeth beginning to chatter.

Tatya helped her sit up. Ping was shaking so badly that she was almost helpless.

Ping gave a wild look at her friend. "We must run before he awakes!" She said urgently, wrapping her arms around herself. "We must find clothing and run."

"He won't be waking up," said Tatya matter of factly. "I killed him."

Ping looked at her, shocked, "You killed him?" she repeated blankly. "If he is dead, was it not an accident?"

"Don't you think he deserved death for the way he treated you?" said Tatya. "I knew exactly how much power to use to drive him against that wall in order to kill him. And I have no guilt at all about doing it. He was a loathsome piece of excrement. And judging by what I see here, I have done every woman in this area a favor! One down and two to go," she added to herself.

"What is this room?" Ping asked, shivering. "It feels evil."

"It is a torture chamber," Tatya answered 'And from the look of this equipment it looks as if this Si Wang uses it frequently – and has a taste for Western torture devices as well." There was a rack and an Iron Maiden as well as things Tatya did not recognize.

"Let us go," Ping said, shuddering. "Have you found clothing for us?"

"Unfortunately, no," said Tatya. "I had hoped to take his uniform, enormous though it would have been, but where he left it is anyone's guess. We don't have time to search for clothing, Ping, I am sorry. What I have found down here is empty rooms – and it is so damp that I doubt anyone would store cloth or clothing here. We're going to have to leave here as we are. But find your shoes and put them on."

"Leave here naked?" Ping said in shock. "To go outside like this? What if someone sees?"

"If we are clever about it no one *will* see," Tatya replied. "We can't stay here, Ping!" she said, becoming a little exasperated as the Chinese woman began to cry, moaning that she could not go out unclothed. "There are worse things than being naked! Such as being raped or dead! When they come back and find him dead and us gone they will come hunting us!" Tatya continued forcefully. "I am only one woman with magic – I can not protect us against an entire garrison! And I have no way of getting in touch with Simon or even Lakota, since that bitch took my dragon whistle. I have an idea – a magical idea – to protect us and even defeat that horrible Hong but I have to find a temple in the mountains so that I can do it. We have to get out of here and climb into the hills."

Ping, her eyes full of tears, arms crossed over her breasts, just looked at her. "I am not as brave as you," she whispered "And I feel so much shame to go about thus –"

"It isn't as if you made a choice to walk about with no clothing on –" Tatya was sympathetic but she was also practical. First things first – and that was getting out of this fortress and escaping into the hills. If it had to be done nude - well, that was what would have to be done.

"How will we get from this evil place?" Ping asked, trying to wipe the tears from her face without uncovering herself. Tatya hoped that she was not going to be so missish for the entire time. Her excessive modesty might be a problem.

"I am almost certain that there will be one more lower level to this fortress," Tatya explained. If it was anything like the fortresses she had seen in the British Isles and in Russia . She increased the magnitude of the mage light so that it lit the way more clearly for them. "If what I suspect is true, we can slip right out under the guards' noses. But first we have to find another stair – one that leads down."

26

The Swim

To Ping's surprise, Tatya insisted on taking the ropes that had bound her to the table. "We may have need of these when we climb into the hills," she explained. To Ping's further amazement as the ropes slid through Tatya's hands the four pieces became one. Tatya was able to coil a good length of rope and sling it over her shoulder.

Tatya ended in putting on her friend's shoes as Ping was shaking so. "Can you walk?" Tatya asked Ping in concern.

"I must, I must!" Ping said through chattering teeth. "I am so cold!" she apologized. "Are you not cold?"

"I'm Russian. In comparison to a St. Petersburg winter this is a balmy summer day," said Tatya. "Ping, I promise you that when we get to a suitable temple I can warm us with magic. I know this is hard for you and I am sorry that I cannot take the time to find us clothing but we have to get out of here *now*. I have no idea how long they will be gone and I can guarantee that the horrible Hong will be down here as soon as they return. He is determined to have me. And he holds the threat of harming you over my head."

"Would you have allowed him to – to – *take* you to keep me from harm?" asked Ping in wonder.

Tatya had been kneeling to insert Ping's small feet into what were going to be woefully inadequate shoes for what they had to do. She looked up at her friend and said "Yes."

But your husband –!" Ping faltered. "He would rid himself of such a wife!"

"Not Simon – he isn't like that. He would understand that I had to do what was necessary." Tatya was absolutely certain of this for she and Simon had bared their souls to one another when she had been nearly raped – twice – by her cousin Evgeny.

Ping looked doubtful – what kind of a husband would want a wife who had lain with another man, even if it was by force or by threat? But she said nothing.

She had to lean on Tatya as they left the room and went down the corridor to where they had come down the stairs. Tatya was hoping that there would be a short flight of stairs to the lower level she hoped to find.

A very small door stood opposite the main staircase. It was probably a servant's stair. Tatya opened it cautiously and was at once gratified to hear the sound of running water.

"What is this place?" Ping whispered, tightening her grip on Tatya's arm.

"When they brought us in under the waterfall I noticed another stream flowing through the bottom of the fortress that went on out doors to come out under the waterfall," Tatya answered. "It is probably the water drainage for the fortress – used for the bath water and the kitchen –. "

"A midden?" exclaimed Ping, revolted.

"No, it is not sewage," said Tatya soothingly as they began down the stairs. "Once when we were visiting Scotland, Simon and I were in a castle that was built very much like this fortress, with a secret entrance beneath a waterfall. They did not drain the castle garderobes into the water – places made to withstand siege cannot take the chance of polluting their water supply and I am willing to wager that the cesspit is on the far side of this fortress. Smell the air – it is not fetid. I daresay that the Necromancer has put a purifying spell on this water. We will be able to swim in it easily."

"Swim!" Ping stopped dead on the stairs. "I cannot swim!" she said in shock. "I will drown,Tatya! I have never been in water deeper than my bath! Women do not swim! How can you suggest such a thing? We will *both* of us drown!"

"I can swim and swim very well indeed," Tatya said firmly. "Not only are these ropes for the climbing we must do, but I shall tie you to myself and all that you will have to do is hang on. And we will NOT drown," she continued as Ping opened her mouth to protest. "I know a spell for breathing underwater. It will be perfectly safe and we will slip right past any guards – and I shall use a don't look at me spell."

"We will be invisible?" Ping asked hopefully. Then no one could see her shame!

"Not invisible, no, but the guards will be compelled to look elsewhere," Tatya answered, disappointing Ping.

They had reached the bottom of the small flight of steps. The noise of the water was quite loud now and far ahead they could make out a faint light that was the curtain of water from the water fall, open to the air but effectively hiding the entrance to beneath the fortress. A rough, unfinished road, wide enough for horse traffic, that led up to the main enclosed courtyard on a steep slant, ran beside the water. Beside this road it fell off ever more precipitously to the water below.

"Can you stand by yourself for a moment?" Tatya asked. "I need to investigate this water and see where it leads."

Ping nodded. She backed up until she was leaning in the damp wall. It was unpleasant on her bare skin but she needed the support.

"You'll need a light," Tatya said matter of factly, and took Ping's hand. She put the mage light in it.

Expecting heat, Ping drew back, automatically, flinching. To her surprise the light was cool and unlike an oil lamp, burned with a steady blue-white light.

"I'll be right back," Tatya promised and eased herself into the water. It came up to her shoulders. "Oh, good, it's nice and deep!" she said. "We can remain underwater most of the time. I hope it stays deep." She paused for a moment and Ping heard her murmur to herself and then her head disappeared underwater.

It seemed an age to Ping until Tatya returned. Every noise, even the slightest, made her shy and shrink. She was certain that she heard rats scrabbling about and as well as the rush of the waters at her feet and the thunder of the waterfall, there was a steady dripping from several places. In her fancy she heard footsteps on the stairs.

After a long time Tatya's head popped up from the water. "We're in luck!" she said in satisfaction as she climbed from the watercourse. "The water joins a river that very close to here goes underground. I followed it until it came up. It then heads downhill to the village below but where it comes up again it looks as if it cannot be seen from either here or the village. And best of all, there is a temple on the side of the mountain that will be perfect for what I want to do. It is going to be a rough climb. I shall do my best to help you but

219

we are not really dressed for scaling rocks!" she added ruefully. "It's going to be a long swim underwater as well."

Ping looked at her with misery and fear mingled on her delicate features. Her glossy black hair, usually worn high with decorated combs, now hung halfway down her back, a tangled, heavy mass. She had guessed rightly – Lui's huge hands had left black and blue marks on her breasts and arms and she was sore where his fingers had poked and pried. All she wanted to do was lay down and cry forever, thinking of her home and how she was certain to lose Jian's respect and regard and how she would probably not be allowed to ever see her children again. Two days ago she had been a happy, treasured wife and mother and now she was a naked fugitive, having to do things that were beyond her capacity. She was ready to give up.

But Tatya was not. Even as Ping watched, her friend was knotting the rope about her waist and looked both serious and capable. "I'm going to tie you to me," she explained, "up under your arms and then you may hold onto the rope. I am going to tow you – you won't have to do anything – let me do all the work. If you like, you can even keep your eyes closed."

Ping could not meet her in the eyes. "You shame me," she whispered. "All that I have done is cry and whimper like a small child and I have done nothing to save myself." A tear slid down her cheek. "I will try to be less of a burden," she said.

Tatya, overcome with pity, hugged her. "I know you will. I've had had to do things like this before. I learned to be self-reliant and made up my mind that I was not going to let anyone or anything take advantage of me. I've learned to do what I have to do – I learned a lot of that from Simon. He's an unusual man – he gives me the compliment of knowing that I can take care of myself and can make up my own mind."

"Now," she added briskly, "lift your arms and I shall tie this rope around you. And I shall put the spell on you for underwater breathing – it won't hurt – you won't even know I've done it until you find that you can breathe as a mermaid does."

Five minutes later, after Tatya had doused the mage light, they were in the water, roped together, Ping clinging tightly to the rope with both hands. She was trying bravely to copy Tatya and disregard her nakedness, although it grated against the principles of modesty she had been brought up to. But she could not keep an arm over her breast and a hand above her female parts and hold onto the rope at the same time. She did not want to be a drag on Tatya. And she resolved to keep her eyes open as well.

Ping's girlhood home had been near the sea and a river which flowed into it. She had seen boys and men, even peasant girls, swimming. She had never seen anyone swim as Tatya did. She did not kick her feet, no did she flail with her arms, but wiggled her body as if she were a fish and slid through the water at a fantastic rate. Ping did not know that Tatya had been swimming since she was a small girl and when she had married Simon, had gone with him to visit the Merfolk off the coast of Ireland, with whom he was very friendly. Tatya had learned how to swim as they did.

It was strange – like a dream – to move beneath the water, breathing easily. The water was cool against her skin and if she had not been so frightened it might have been enjoyable. When they emerged from beneath the fortress sunlight made dancing ripples through the water, caused both by the refraction of the water and the strong rippling current of the stream. The channel was surprisingly deep – it had been carved not just by the stream itself over the years but by the snowmelt each spring that came rushing down the mountainside.

The sunlight disappeared abruptly as they swam into a cave opening, most of which was underwater.

That was not enjoyable. Even though she could breathe Ping was still frightened by the darkness that now surrounded her. She missed the mage light and was happier when she saw Tatya send out a beam of light in front of them. The rocky walls of the underground river, however, seemed dark and menacing.

It was an eternity before they at last broke the surface of the water to find themselves in a little bowl of a valley. The water grew placid here, broadening out into a small pond before it drained on down towards the village. A few stunted trees, much bent by the wind, were in this exposed area.

Tatya helped her friend climb up the bank and then untied the rope that bound them together. "I think it is mid-afternoon," she announced. "I saw some fish in that pond – I shall try to catch some. We haven't had a thing to eat since yesterday morning and we cannot climb with no food in our stomachs. And if I do much more magic without food I am going to collapse!"

"But how will we cook fish?" Ping asked worriedly. "We have no way to start a fire!"

"Ley line fire – it will cook the fish and warm us too, without smoke. Simon taught me how to make one," Tatya answered. She sat down on the grass beside Ping and began to twist her long honey brown hair, wringing the water from it. "I truly regret losing all my hair pins," she said, squeezing a long strand.

Ping did the same. It was warmer here than it had been in the fortress but it was still strange and embarrassing to be sitting out in the open, naked, with her friend, discussing cooking fish. Had it really been only yesterday morning that her world had changed so radically?

Tatya had been looking about her and now pointed to an outcropping of rocks. "We can shelter there – we should try and get a few hours sleep. I did not sleep a bit on that wild ride last night."

"Nor did I," said Ping in a low voice. "I felt so dishonored. He never took his hands from me."

Tatya could see clearly now the bruises on her friend and said sympathetically, "Try not to think about it any more. He is dead and will never harm you again. We must think only about escaping."

Tears welled up in Ping's eyes and she bent her head, folding her arms across her chest once more. "It would be better if he had just killed me, for Jian will want me no longer. And he told me once that I would just not be First Wife, but only wife – he has brought no concubines to my quarters, as is his right, nor gone to the Houses of Pleasure! He said that he wanted only me. And I was happy – oh, so happy ! – and proud that I was the only one he wanted. Many women have to share their husbands with concubines – and watch as he takes her, as is advised in the old books -"

"What!" exclaimed Tatya. "Ping, that cannot be right! Surely you misunderstood!"

"But my father read to me the advice and told me this is how I should comport myself when my husband took a concubine. When first the newcomer comes to the women's quarters the man must control his desires and have the newcomer stand at attention near the Ivory couch where the First Wife or other concubines please their lord. After four or five nights he may take the newcomer to bed but only in the presence of his other wives and concubines. My father said I was to be attentive and see what the other women did to please my husband and copy them. He said in this way , and by strict obedience and bowing to the will of my husband, that I would be a good wife."

"What did your mother say to this advice?" Tatya asked, a little sarcastically.

Ping looked at her, startled. "She agreed with it, of course! Women are inferior and we are here but to please our husbands. My father had three wives and ten concubines. Would you not behave so if your husband brought a concubine to the women's quarters?"

"No," said Tatya bluntly. "I'd kill both of them. Thank goodness, concubines are against the law in Ireland and men have but one wife at a time. Not that it prevents some of them from having other women – we just don't have to give the other women house-room and watch them lay with our husbands!"

"Your customs are very strange," said Ping.

Tatya was glad to change the subject and very glad that she was not a Chinese woman – she would not want to share Simon. Tatya stood up and stretched. "I'm going to see if I can catch some fish gypsy style," she said and waded into the pool, with scarcely a ripple on the surface of the water.

27

 Around the Campfires

Jian and Gui rode until they were reeling in their saddles with weariness and their horses were stumbling with fatigue.

They were forced to stop as the sun was beginning its decline. Darkness would have caused this necessity eventually, but by stopping earlier they were able to set up a snug camp.

Jian was surprised. The youth Gui had thought of everything. Packs, which Jian had not even noticed in his haste to be mounted and away, were tied on the back of each saddle. The packs yielded rice, dried meat, dried vegetables and tea, a cooking pot, a tea pot and chopsticks as well as blankets for sleeping. There were even brushes and curry combs for the horses as well as a little grain sack to supplement their grazing. Two small coils of rope made hobbles for the two animals.

Gui knew how to set up a campsite as well. In very little time he had a fire going and tea and food steaming on the fire. He had chosen a spot well off the road, near a little spring, and sheltered from the view of the road.

"Where had you all these things?" Jian asked. "Do they keep such things at the House of Pleasure?"

Gui gave him a look in which exasperation and a tinge of contempt were mixed. "I took what I needed," he said shortly. "I do what I must to rescue Jing Mai and the other girls."

Jian looked into his tea cup and said slowly, "You said that you knew what those men would do to the women…"

"Are you so naïve, Magistrate, as to pretend you do not know that they will be raped many times? Your wife and the *fan qui* lady might be saved for the officers – but then again they might give the foreign devil to the men, as they will be eager to find out if she is different from a woman of our race. But they all will be raped. The bandits will be full of blood lust, which makes them want a woman very badly –

they will be very rough with them. All they will care about is satisfying their lust. They will not care if the woman is a noble or a peasant or even a small girl who is a virgin."

The boy spoke bitterly, staring not at Jian but into the flickering firelight as if he saw unpleasant things there. "I do not want Jing Mai to end in a House of Pleasure," he added almost to himself.

"But what else is there for her – she will be defiled – taken by many men – what man of honor will want her then?" said Jian.

Gui gave him a mocking smile. "You go to rescue your wife. By the time we find them she will most assuredly be dishonoured – probably by more than one man. Why do you not leave her to her fate?"

"Naturally I will put her aside if she has been so used –" said Jian stiffly."

"Oh, naturally!" Gui said sarcastically.

"But since she has been my First Wife for almost ten years I have a duty to see that she is properly taken care of –"

"And do penance for the rest of her life, perhaps returned to her parents' home, where they will never cease to berate her for having allowed herself to be raped and dishonouring her husband? They will be shamed before their neighbors for having their daughter returned to them and you will keep her dowry!" Gui looked straight into Jian's face and once again Jian was startled by a flicker of recognition.

"My mother has told me, Magistrate, that you were a frequent visitor to the House of Pleasure before your marriage. But they have not seen you since then. And it is common knowledge that you have no other wife, not have not taken any concubines. Your wife had no sisters to bring with her as secondary wives for you. This argues that you think highly of your wife, perhaps even love her. And this is how you would treat her – to put her away for something she could not help?"

"A woman of honour," said Jian stiffly, "would not let herself –"

Gui burst into laughter, laughter which had a hard, scornful edge. "*Let herself*? Magistrate, I called you naïve – I now see that you are *stupid*! Have you ever seen a woman raped? I have! There is not 'letting' about it. When young girls

225

are purchased for the House of Pleasure they are tied down for their first time. Their struggles are nothing against several full-grown men. Ours is not a House where the girls are trained, like those of the Green Bowers, to sing and play and exchange views on philosophy! The men who come to where my mother works are merchants and drovers and traders – many of them rough men who cannot remember the next day what the girl they lay with looked like, much less remember her name! To those men, a woman means as much as a jar of bean curd – a receptacle for their seed. The bandits will not say to your wife politely "Please, lady, we would like to lay with you?" and she is free to refuse! Does your wife have martial skills so that she can fight them off? They will take her by force and they will be cruel. In what way is this her fault? Was she at fault to allow herself to be taken from your home?"

"You do not understand – you are a nameless man of no family and cannot know what honour means," said Jian stiffly.

Gui threw the dregs of his tea into the fire, causing it to sputter. "I may be a nameless bastard," said Gui evenly, "but I know this – I care not if Jing Mai has been mounted by all twenty men in the troop of bandits. When I find her we shall be married. If she is with child I shall raise the child as my own, and never let that child know that he is not my get. Nor will I ever berate Jing Mai for something that is not her fault and she was powerless to prevent. I love her too much. I will be too grateful if she is alive and not lost to me, to worry of such inconsequential things."

With this he arose and went to one of the blankets that had been spread on the ground. He wrapped it around himself and lay down, his back to Jian. In a few minutes he was asleep.

Jian sat for a long while staring into the fire. In imagination he could see Ping's face in the flames and he thought of her pretty, affectionate ways, what a good mother she was, how she honoured his ancestors as her own and how his father treasured her. He thought of being in bed with her, of her eager response, how completely she satisfied him and how the thought of another woman had become repugnant to him. He remembered how eager he was to arrive at his home

226

after each trip, how they would lay in bed talking after making love and realized suddenly that the growing sickness inside was not so much anger that she would have allowed herself to be violated, but that he must lose all of her warmth and her charms and put her aside. To send her back to her parents, to never see her again, to try and explain to his children why their mother had been sent away... He put down his tea cup and sunk his head in his hands. Ping! He was swept by a wave of longing so profound that he nearly groaned aloud.

And then, in the usual irrelevant fashion of the mind, he suddenly remembered where he had seen Gui's features before. He saw them every morning in the shaving mirror. Gui was the image of himself at the same age.

"You must allow me, Young *Wu*, to deal with this sorcerer," said Feng Hu quietly. He raised his tea cup to his lips and took a reflective sip.

Simon looked at him in consternation. They were all sitting about a ley line fire, having a final cup of tea after the evening meal. After the encounter earlier that day with the warlord and her troops Feng had been exhausted and had gone to the tent to rest when they returned to the camp. He had not emerged until supper was ready. To Simon he looked paper-thin and frail, as if a slight wind would blow him away. And here he was speaking of taking on the necromancer by himself!

Trying to be tactful and diplomatic Simon started to say "Perhaps we should discuss this –" but Prince Tuan interrupted him, saying in shock, "Surely you jest, venerable one! You are very old; you have admitted this to us and just the events of this day have wearied you! How can you hope to do battle with a formidable foe such as this black magician?"

Feng looked at him, frowning slightly. "That is *my* concern, Prince. I know what I am doing and it must be me that takes on the sorcerer. He is of the Middle Kingdom and it must be a man of the Middle Kingdom who defeats him," he said, using the old name for China.

227

Simon and Ash exchanged glances, both uneasy in face of the old man's stubbornness. Would they have to prevent him from confronting Ch'ang? He would be throwing away his life for no reason.

"I had thought that both of us, acting in concert," Simon began, not wishing to hurt his elder's feelings by expressing doubts of his abilities.

"No," said Feng decidedly. "I must do this thing myself. There are reasons for it – they will become apparent – and there is the fact, young *Wu*, that you do not like to kill – and this black magician must be killed. I will delight in destroying him. He is a stink in the nostrils of all Sorcerers. To kill dragons – to call up demons – these are acts of the most profound evil. They cannot be allowed to continue."

"But–" Tuan began.

"I will hear no more!" stated Feng, holding up a hand. He stood – not easily – and said "You have many plans to make for tomorrow. I, too, have plans to make. Plans that I can make laid down on my bed." With great dignity he stalked off to the tent.

As Ash and Tuan looked at him Simon shrugged. "I can't stop him," he said. "I am not certain how powerful he is – he seems frail but some of the things that he has done have surprised me. He is not frank with me as to what his powers are or as to his limitations. We have a warlord to defeat as well and no time for me to brangle with him and perhaps get into a Duel Arcane. The best I can do is to stand by, close at hand, in case he needs me."

Tuan looked helpless and exasperated. "The venerable one flouts my authority," he said.

"I think, Highness," said Ash slowly," that Feng Hu is still in the service of a Han Emperor. I think that he does not truly recognize your authority."

Tuan let out a long sigh. "My men arrive tomorrow," he said. "The good La-koh-ta saw them encamped close by and I shall ride out to meet them in the morning. I shall send to Chengdu for reinforcements and we shall lay siege to the fortress. We shall also execute the prisoners."

Simon was aware of the necessity of this – but at the thought of the three prisoners being killed he grew sick, Four others had been killed and Lakota had dug a mass grave for them with his talons. Realistically, Simon could not expect to get through this campaign without deaths. Still, he hated the need of killing.

Tatya and Ping had feasted on fish Tatya had 'tickled'. Her father-in-law had learned this skill when he was young and had no money for hooks and lines and had taught it to her one day during a picnic on the banks of the Liffey.

That day, Tatya, skirts kilted above her knees, had been seen in the water by a local starched-up matron, who had been scandalized by the length of limb displayed and had registered shocked disapproval as she had been driven by in her barouche. What would the same matron say now if she were to go by with Tatya and Ping as bare as the day they were born, eating fish with their fingers by a ley line fire? Tatya smiled at the thought. She remembered what her father-in-law had said when she told him that Mrs. Giddings had gone by and been shocked. "She probably is wishing, *n'est – ce pas*? – that her legs were as well turned as yours," had said René cheerfully.

Ping was liking the last of the fish from her fingers. "I did not know that I was so hungry!" she said. There had been no salt or seasoning for the fish but it still was delicious to appetites sharpened by hunger.

Tatya lay back, with her arms under her head. "It is amazing how much better everything looks when your stomach is full. Before we ate I was worried about scaling this mountain. But now that I look at it with a meal under my belt – I have every confidence that we can do it."

Ping tried not to look at her friend. The ways of the West were every strange. How could she lay like that, all exposed? The thought of climbing this cliff side thoroughly daunted Ping, especially the thought that she had to do it in the nude. All she worried about was if someone was to see them. She would never recover from the shame.

Watching in the lowering sun how Ping could not look at her Tatya sighed inwardly. She wanted to be patient with Ping, and could even understand how she was the way she was, considering how she had been raised, but sometimes

Tatya wanted to slap her. What did it matter whether they had clothes on or not at this point? There were other much more important matters to attend to – Tatya would far rather be naked and out of the hands of those awful people than completely clothed and still in their custody. Of course, she had had the advantage of spending much time with the Elves, both in Russia and in the British Isles. The Elves regarded clothing as optional and encouraged their guests to participate in their religious rites, all of which they insisted had to be performed *au naturel*. The Elves were so natural about being completely unclothed that after a time one became accustomed to it and soon learned to relish in the freedom of it. Ping had had no such advantage.

And at any rate, what Tatya had planned as a snare for Hong involved a Witch's ritual, one, moreover, that had to be performed sky-clad, as fully two-thirds of the Witches' rituals were. She suddenly wished that it were Simon with her – he would not be making all this fuss over a lack of clothing. He would probably enjoy it, even in a desperate situation such as this.

"We had better try to get an hour or two of sleep," she said to Ping. "We have time – it is better to wait until the sun is lowering further before we start to climb, and we do not need to be at the temple until moonrise. The moon will be full tonight and that is ideal for what I need to do."

Near another campfire, well hidden, with its smoke magiced away by Ch'ang, Si Wang lay back on a blanket, frustrated and angry. They had been unable to find the campsite of the foreign magician. Ch'ang kept trying to find it, but finally had to admit that there was a barrier in the way. He could not see it at all, only feel that ripple in the *chi* that so disturbed him.

She watched through narrowed eyes as Hong paced back and forth, one hand on the hilt of his sword and the other clenched into a fist.

"You are like a hungry tiger, Hong," she said. "Sit down and have some tea."

"I don't want any tea!" he snarled. "I want her – the amber-eyed Witch! You insisted that we come and spy upon these people and what have we seen – nothing! I could have had her twice by now!" He was so incensed that he forgot to be tactful.

Si Wang stared at him. She felt as if a knife twisted in her gut and again she did not realize it for the jealousy it was. "We shall stay here the night and in the morning I shall go out with a flag of truce. I wish to speak to this *fan qui* Sorcerer," she said sharply.

"I want to go back!" Hong blurted out, sounding more like a boy eager for his first woman than the experienced man she knew him to be. "All I can think about is her – I burn for her and I must, I shall take her! Her white breasts, her long legs – I dream of them wrapped around me!" He stopped suddenly, breathing fast as he saw Si Wang's furious face.

She sat up abruptly."Go then to your Witch and lay with her! But you shall never take me again if you go to her now! I promise you that!"

To her complete consternation he turned on his heel and ran towards the horses, vaulted on the nearest one without benefit of a saddle and took off at a gallop.

She never thought that he would do it.

28

Drawing Down the Moon

Hong lashed the horse that he rode unmercifully with the ends of the reins. All he could think about was that amber-eyed Witch and how badly he needed to possess her. One part of his mind wondered if she had enchanted him but he did not really care if she had. He wanted her so much that his entire body was one vast ache of yearning. He thought of how she had looked naked, her arms tied above her head, bringing those magnificent breasts into prominence, and how she would look, spread out in his bed – if she fought him at all he would tie her down until she acknowledged his right to do anything he wished to her.

By the time he reached the fortress the horse was lathered and heaving. Vaulting off the animal and flinging the reins to a passing bandit, Hong ran into the fortress, his desire at white heat. Soon, very soon, he would take her! He had never felt this way about a woman before, never felt that he had to have her and only her.

Lanterns hung on a row of pegs by the door to the cellars for the convenience of those who had business below. A brazier burned nearby and with a handy pair of tongs and a coal from the brazier Hong lit the lantern, his hands shaking so badly that he could scarcely accomplish the task. Anticipation made him fling open the door and run down the stairs to the cellars in dangerous headlong flight. He began shedding his armor and sword belt as he ran, heedless of them clattering down the stairs. He only retained hold on the keys that would unlock her cell and the lantern to light his way. And he wanted the lantern so that he could see her.

By the time he reached the corridor he was completely unclothed. He held the key in his hand as if he were going to put it in the lock at any second. He was panting, his heart was racing and he was ready for her. He would leave her hands tied, he decided as he neared the cell where he had left her. He would force her legs apart and mount her immediately, for he was almost in pain from desire. Later,

232

there would be time to take her again and again, and teach her to please him, as well as see her cry aloud in pleasure, for he knew in some strange fashion, that his desire for her would not be easily diminished. She was so different from other women and her indifference, her contempt of the way he had handled her beautiful body was a challenge of which he would not soon tire. He anticipated many, many hours of intense gratification with her. He had never wanted even Si Wang this badly. The Witch would be his, all his. He would share her with no one, but he would see that she was kept very, very busy, for he had a large appetite.

At long last he reached the door and put the key in the lock, his hand trembling so that it took a few minutes to accomplish this task. When at last he heard the lock tumblers click open he dropped the keys to the ground and jerked open the door. "Your master is here, little Witch!" he called out as he lifted the lantern to illuminate the room "Open your legs for –" he broke off with a gasp as the lantern light spread throughout her prison.

The room was empty.

Hong began to curse, his anger overwhelming. Where was she? Had some other man dared to take her? Was some other man even now enjoying her?

Then he realized that he had not seen Lui in the corridor. The big man should have been guarding the two women. Cursing again, Hong though that Lui was probably riding the noblewoman, unable to keep from taking her.

Hong knew Lui's tastes – that he wanted to hurt a woman before he took her. Personally, Hong thought this a waste of woman flesh – they too often died beneath the pain Lui liked to inflict and what good was a female corpse?

But he knew where Lui would have taken her and he ran down the corridor to the torture chamber and flung open the door.

He recoiled at what he saw there in the flickering light of the lantern.

Lui, the indestructible Lui, lay with his head and shoulders against the wall, his eyes open and staring, an expression of surprise upon his face, The big man was naked – he had obviously meant to take the noblewoman, although there were no ropes on the table that was used to interrogate prisoners and that Lui used for his tortures. The fire in the brazier had died out but Lui's little 'toys' as he liked to call them were still in it. There was no smell of burning flesh as was usual when Lui played with a woman – for he often brought whores from the village here – one could hear their screams all the way to the topmost floor, where they were completely ignored by everyone.

What had happened? Hong was bitterly enraged – and disappointed. Damn Si Wang! If she had not insisted on him accompanying her on that abortive mission he would have had his release by now, perhaps even taken the Witch again – and she would have not escaped – she would have been too occupied for that.

For he was beginning to think that she *had* escaped and taken the other woman with her. How or why he did not care. Perhaps she had promised someone who came to look at her nakedness a rich bribe, or given him her body to insure his cooperation. Perhaps Ch'ang was wrong and she still had magic. How else had she killed Lui, a giant compared to her?

None of that mattered. All that Hong knew was that he had to have her back. He still wanted her – more than ever. When he had her back he would chain her to the table and use her until she would obey him.

Grimly, Hong set about picking up his discarded garments and armor. There was only one place she could flee – into the hills. She would be too conspicuous in the village and she would find no one to aid her – they were all too afraid of Si Wang's retaliation. The Witch was a foreign devil, after all – too different from the villagers not to be noticed.

And Hong smiled to himself, a mocking smile, at the thought he that came into his mind.

They were naked, the two of them. There was no place that they could obtain clothing. They would be ashamed to be seen – most likely they would find a hiding place rather than trying to run where eyes could feast on their nudity. There was no place that they could hide from him – he knew this area too well and all the likely hiding places that two frightened, naked women might go.

Yes, he would find them – and very soon he *would* have her.

The climb was a nightmare.

After a few hours of sleep Tatya roused Ping and told her that it was time that they left.

Tatya had had some experience in climbing. When they had first come back to Ireland Simon had taken her to the Scottish Highlands for a honeymoon, which they had not had when they first were wed.They had spent time in the Hollow Hills with the Elves – there seemed to be openings into Oberon's kingdom everywhere – but they had also spent time exploring Scotland. This included some climbing in the Cairngorms. She had discovered that Simon enjoyed mountaineering and she quickly became fascinated with it as well. The views were spectacular and the climbs challenging – even with magic to help. Magic also made it completely safe.

She had copied the techniques she had learned there as they began the climb up to the temple – she had used the rope to secure Ping to her waist – for she would lead. But it had been difficult to insure Ping's cooperation in what must be done.

Ping had had no idea what to do except cry and say that she could not do it. In the end Tatya slapped her and told her in a voice that brooked no nonsense that she was going to do this if she, Tatya, had to render her unconscious and carry her up over her shoulder, This Tatya did not want to do – this climb would be difficult enough with the burden of a senseless Ping to be carried.

Ping also objected to following Tatya up the mountain and to Tatya's amazement this was because Ping was horrified at the thought of looking at Tatya's bare buttocks the entire time.

"Oh, for God's sake!" Tatya swore. "Would you rather *I* looked at *your* bare ass? You have no idea how to get up this mountain and I do. And you can't close your eyes – I am not going to tow you up with magic as I shall need all my magic for what I have to do to climb and then for the ceremony in the temple. You looked at my ass while we were swimming – what is the problem now? We cannot give in to your outraged modesty! I am sorry, but that is the way it is going to have to be – unless you want to stay here and be found by those bandits and repeatedly raped? The next man they give you to may be even worse than that Lui! And I am NOT going to stay here and wait for a pack of rapists!"

With this Ping gave in and actually tried to be helpful, but she sobbed on and off all during the climb.

It was a difficult climb. Even sending the rope ahead magically and securing it firmly to an outcropping didn't make it easier. When she and Simon had climbed in the Cairngorms they had been wearing stout boots and thick clothing, as well as climber's gloves. Here there was nothing to protect their bodies from scrapes and cuts, nor cushion their hands from the rough rope. Tatya had removed her stockings and tore each one in half to make rough mitts for herself and Ping, but her stockings were sheer silk and were soon shredded. She did not dare expend too much magic for she needed it for the climb and what she had to do once they reached the temple. One of the first things Simon had taught her was that magic had its limits and there was always a price to pay for it. Very often that price was exhaustion and illness of the magician. Tatya was very worried that she would not be able to do what needed to be done. She was feeling increasingly fatigued – she had not slept or eaten properly in two days – and one of the cardinal rules of magic was never work on an empty stomach. Before the Witches in her Coven back in Dublin undertook a ritual they had a feast of foods that imparted energy.

They seemed to climb forever. It was rough rock surfaces they had to traverse, and Tatya could hear Ping saying over and over to herself. "What if someone sees?" between bouts of crying. Tatya could not imagine who Ping thought would see them, unless there were a party of gentlemen *voyeurs* sailing overhead in a balloon. At any rate, she had cast a the very useful 'don't look at me' spell and she was certain even the horrible Hong could not see past that.

At long last they reached the ledge that stood just before the temple. By now it was full dark and the moon was rising.

Tatya had to haul Ping up the last few feet as the Chinese woman seemed to have just about collapsed. Ping fell to her knees as soon as she was safely on the ledge and then

236

fell to the ground, where she curled into a fetal position, She was crying again.

Tatya bent and grabbed her by the arm. "Ping, you cannot give up now! We have to get into the temple where I can work."

"I am cold and my body hurts!" Ping said, hands covering her face. "I am all scraped and I am naked!" she wailed.

"You'll be warm in the temple. What I am going to do will warm us. Now get up," Tatya ordered.

"You are cruel," whimpered Ping, But she nonetheless came to her feet and allowed Tatya to untie the ropes about her waist. She followed Tatya into the temple, bent over, her arms crossed over her chest.

Tatya decided to ignore this and merely pointed to a corner where Ping could huddle in misery.

This building looked as if it had once been a dragon temple, long abandoned now, for there were carved dragons everywhere. Moonlight, which was now beginning to flood the roofless temple, outlined statues of all sizes of *lung*. Some were covered in vegetation which waved in the slight breeze making the stone creatures look almost alive.

This was a Holy place, Tatya felt when she sent out her sense to touch it. Although long disused it had lost none of its potency. It also sat on top of a huge node of power. Many ley lines converged here and Tatya gasped and reeled slightly as she felt its raw strength.

In the normal tradition of Witchcraft, females were not taught to use the ley lines – they drew their power were from other sources – the energies of woods and fields, of crystal and of the moon. But Tatya's first teacher had been Simon, a Wizard, and Wizards did use the ley lines. She hoped now that being able to tap the ley lines would make up for the other lacks in the ritual that she was about to perform.

"What are you doing?" Ping asked from her corner where she sat with knees up to her chin and her arms wrapped about her legs. She seemed to be trying to make herself as small as was possible. Her voice was full of tears.

Tatya had picked up a chunk of stone from the fallen roof and in an open place on the floor was inscribing a circle. There was but a small space to work in but, as Tatya reflected, there was but herself to work the Circle, not the usual thirteen Witches of a normal Coven Circle. Although there were many more than thirteen, usually, in a Coven, the ritual Circle was always Worked by thirteen.

"I am making a Rtual Circle," she explained to Ping. "First of all I will inscribe it, than activate it and begin the Ritual. Ping, it is very important that once I start you do not cross the line of this Circle. You could be injured, for I shall be working some very strong magic. I am going to draw down the moon and take her power into myself. So no matter what you see or hear, stay there and don't come into this Circle – no matter what! Promise me, now!"

Ping nodded. She had no desire to move at all.

Once the Circle was drawn Tatya began to inscribe the names of the goddesses of the moon – Artemis, Diana, Selene, Cybele ...., around the outside edge of the Circle, remaining inside it as she did so.

She missed her wand – putting the power into the Circle would be much easier with it. But that horrible woman had her wand as well as her jewelry.

"I am going to attempt to raise the Mists of the Moon," she told Ping. "It's just as well that I have no clothing, as this ritual must be done sky-clad."

"Sky-clad?" Ping repeated.

"Naked – most of our Rituals are done so. We Witches are responsible for the agricultural fertility of the British Isles and planting is done properly by the phases of the moon. We draw the goodness of the moon into our bodies and then into the earth through our dances and Rituals." Anticipating Ping's next question she said "And we have to be sky-clad, for the light of the moon is not as strong as that of the sun and not as easy to capture. Clothing gets in the way of absorbing it. Even the Wizards and the Druids, who draw the sun, wear but thin linen robes over their bodies." As she spoke she called power up from the ley lines. It flowed from her fingers in a blue arc, igniting the circle and the names she had drawn as if it were gunpowder and she had lit it.

"Our Rituals are done in sacred places – usually in a ring of standing stones which have been used for that purpose far, far back in time. That is why I wanted to get to this temple – it is a sacred place. And since the standing stones are out of doors and the climate is not warm much of the year, to keep warm, and to hide out sky-clad rituals from prying eyes, we draw down the moon and create a mist which shields us and warms us. Many non-magicals like to come and spy on us – particularly young boys and men who fancy watching a large group of naked women dancing. No Wizard or Druid, of course, would ever find anything the least bit titillating about a sacred Ritual."

"You dance naked in front of men?" Ping said in horror.

"Sometimes –" Tatya answered. "But there is no leering, Ping, for instance when we dance at our welcoming to spring – it is a religious celebration and is considered very sacred. And we are not compelled to do it – if a Witch does not wish to participate she is not coerced."

Ping shuddered. She thought it sounded horrible How could her friend speak so casually of such depravity?

The Circle was now alight, glowing softly.

Tatya knelt, facing the rising moon which now outlined her body in its soft sheen. She sighed with joy in its embrace. She lifted her arms and chanted:

Mortal though I be, yea, ephemeral, of but a moment
I gaze up into the night's starry domain of Heaven,
There no longer on earth I stand, I touch the Creator,
And my lively spirit drinketh immortality.

This had been written in the second century by Ptolemy of Alexandria, the great astronomer, geographer, astrologer and Wizard and had quickly been adopted by Witches everywhere, for it described exactly the feeling that came from communing with the moon.

"Forgive me, lady moon," said Tatya silently, "for coming before you impure, and unanointed as one of your daughters should be. But my need is great."

For of course, there had been no time or way to provide for the ritual bath of purification, nor the anointing with the proper oils, nor even the ritual libation of wine in honor of the goddess in all of her aspects. The Witches also wore silver bandeaus that placed the crescent moon upon their brows.

Tatya was also afraid that she alone was not enough — that there had to be thirteen supplicants. She remained kneeling, drawing on the ley lines, sunk back on her heels, arms outstretched and repeated to herself the words of the summoning, words that were usually chanted by the entire assemblage, not just the thirteen who had been honoured by being chosen for the Circle, but all of the sky-clad women in the Coven, who knelt around the Circle. All of these women fed their power to the Circle.

To her delight she felt the familiar warmth stealing over her. It was as if the moonlight caressed and warmed her body. Most Witches, after one of these rituals, went home in a state of arousal and many children were conceived on the night of a ritual. Tatya was certain that she had conceived Alan on the evening of her first ritual for she had returned home so very eager to be alone with Simon. He had said it was fortunate that there were good contraceptive spells, for otherwise there would be endless pregnancies and even a team of Wizard Healers would not be able to keep up with the birthrate from all the moon fertility rites.

Ping, watching, saw the moonlight around Tatya deepen until her friend seemed to have been dipped in purest silver. A mist began to rise around her and to spread out through the ruined temple and onto the hillside.

Ping flinched away when the mist approached her but she could not evade it. To her shock, it was not cold and wet but warm and soft. Suddenly she longed for Jian, and his touches when they shared the Ivory Couch in the women's quarters. She gave an involuntary "oh!" of pleasure.

"Fall into its embrace, Ping," came Tatya's voice. "It will warm you and raise your spirits. It is the goodness of the moon. It will protect us as well. And it will be the horrible Hong's destruction," she added in satisfaction.

240

29

Surrender

Si Wang did not sleep well for a long while that night. Her ego had suffered a severe blow. She had never thought that Hong would desert her for another woman – and a *fan qui* at that.

It was only after she succeeded in convincing herself that it was the lure of the Witch's strangeness that had taken Hong away that she was finally able to relax. He would soon tire of his Witch – how could someone like that compete with *her*? That insipid white skin and those large breasts – so like a cow's udder! Hong would soon come crawling back. The Witch more than likely would just lay there – not offer the keen participation that Si Wang knew Hong liked – so rough that it was almost a battle. Nor could the Witch handle a sword or a singlestick. Fighting naked, till sweat ran down their bodies, aroused Hong as much as it aroused her and when their bouts were over they fell into bed, almost clawing at one another in their eagerness.

Oh, yes, Hong would be back, Si Wang was certain. And at any rate, she had plans of her own that might very well involve a new lover. Let Hong indulge his passion for the strange for a while. He would tire of her and the Witch would end in one of the Houses of Pleasure in the village. Si Wang would see to it that it was one of the lowest that catered to the most decadent tastes.

Si Wang awoke at first light. She was not alone in the nest of blankets – mid-way through the night, when thinking of Hong had both angered and stimulated her, she had roused Chen Bo and invited him to her bed. He had been willing and eager, and Si Wang had laughed aloud when Ch'ang, who slept close by the fire as did they, picked up his blankets and moved away with a sound of disgust. The Sorcerer was an old woman!

She rolled out of the blankets, leaving Chen sleeping. She would let him sleep a while longer – he had pleased her last night.

241

In spite of the chill of the early morning air she did not resume her clothing. The cool air felt good on her bare body and she strode to the edge of the cliff where Ch'ang thought that the camp of the foreign Sorcerer might be and looked out over it. Ch'ang had said that there was a ripple of distortion in that area but that he could not see through it. He was not certain what it was – sometimes a sacred or Holy place had such a distortion – but he though that it might be their hiding place.

A wave of excitement ran over Si Wang, almost the same excitement that a man's touch brought to her. It finally looked as if all her plans would be coming to fruition. This morning might change the rest of her life.

Si Wang turned abruptly on her heel and went back to her place by the fireside. Rummaging around in the welter of discarded clothing and blankets, she found her breeches and stuck her hand in a leather pouch that dangled form the wide belt. When she found what she wanted, she closed her hand tight about the treasures and withdrew her fist.

She stood up again. The sun was now beginning to rise and its first rays gilded her body and caught off the glitter than lay in the palm of her opening hand.

The sun showed Tatya's necklace and rings.

Si Wang chuckled to herself as a slow, almost smug smile spread over her face. She closed her hand again and, going to where Chen Bo snored, awoke him by the simple expedient of kicking him in the ribs.

As was usual, Lakota woke first. The night air had been chill and even for a dragon it was comfortable to sleep by the steadily burning ley line fire.

Lakota had dreamed about home again last night and the dream was still with him this morning. He had been suffering increasing pangs of homesickness. Most dragons never went very far from their native soil – they liked it that way – and in less than four years Lakota had been to Russia and now to China. And they might be going to America next year, for Simon had told him that he had been invited to co-author an Encyclopedia of Dracophilology and that would mean several years, perhaps, living in Boston, Massachusetts in America. America would not be as strange as Russia and now China had been. For one thing, everyone spoke English and the American attitude towards dragons was much the same as it was in the British Isles. Nothing would be as strange as China! And Lakota had always longed to find out if he had relatives living in America still – he often envied those dragons he knew who had parents and siblings. Although he loved Simon and the rest of 'his' family dearly it would be nice to have dragons of his own blood to know, he thought wistfully.

Something suddenly drew his thoughts from home and the possibility of America. His acute senses felt the presence of something he had only felt back home in Ireland.

At this moment, the flap of the tent was lifted and Simon and Ash, followed very shortly by Tuan and Dr. Quong, emerged.

"Simon!" began Lakota eagerly."There's –"

"Look!" Ash interrupted and pointed to a cliff side above them. "They're waving a white flag!"

They all looked up above to se a figure waving the universal sign of truce.

"What do they want?" said Dr. Quong, puzzled. "Surely we have nothing to speak to them about!"

"Given what we know about that warlord woman she probably wants to bribe us to go away," said Ash cynically.

"Perhaps she wishes to have her Sorcerer meet us on the field in – what do you call it, young *Wu?*" Feng turned to Simon.

"The Duel Arcane," said Simon, rather grimly " Shall we parlay with them, your Highness?"

"Yes, for it is best to know what the enemy expects," said the Prince.

With a wave of his wand Simon broke the concealment spell so that they could be seen. He then took his handkerchief from his pocket and attached it to the end of his wand. He waved it back. "Lakota," he said in an under voice, "take T'a Ming and the panda away with you but stay close. I'd like to have you in reserve in case anything goes wrong."

"You have your dragon whistle?" Lakota said anxiously.

"Right here," Simon touched his chest where the dragon whistle and the little jade dragon hung under his shirt.

Looking anxious, Lakota aroused a sleepy Chao, who grumbled incessantly. T'a Ming, as was usual, looked frightened, but allowed Lakota to grab the panda and swing him onto her back. Then the two dragons took off.

Simon and the others walked towards the figure scrambling down the hill.

A they came closer they saw that it was the warrior woman herself. She was clad in black rhinoceros hide armor, which had been studded with dragon talons. Her breeches and shirt were red and her boots were black. A sword was slung across her back. She wore no helmet and a single long braid of glossy dark hair hung down her back. She was tall for a Chinese woman but she came scarcely up to Simon's shoulder. Her figure was very slim and lithe, almost boyish. But her eyes were hard and calculating. The cold dark eyes kept her face from true beauty for there was no softness there.

"What do you want, woman?" Prince Tuan demanded when they had come with speaking distance. "Do you surrender to us?"

"Surrender?" she gave a great shout of mocking laughter "No, it is you who will surrender to me! I want your Sorcerer, this foreign devil, to give himself over to me." She gave Simon an appraising glance.

"You must be mad!" said the Prince in amazement. "Why should he do such a thing? All the power is on our side – your Sorcerer is a coward who would not even stay and fight!"

"Oh, I think that you will find that *I* have all the power," she said complacently. "You see, I have these."

She pulled her hand from her pocket and slowly uncurled it to reveal Tatya's dragon whistle and her wedding and Cloddagh ring.

Simon stared down at the jewelry, feeling such a wave of anger that it almost swept him off his feet. A pulse began to beat in his forehead. "What have you done with my wife?" he said in a cold, low voice. "If you have harmed her–"

"She is safe – for now," Si Wang said carelessly. She laughed to herself. The Witch was probably even now underneath Hong, for the third or even fourth time. Hong was a lusty man and had learned tricks in the brothel to prolong ecstasy and that allowed a man to quickly recover and take a woman again and again. He might even be tired of her by the time Si Wang returned to Kwen-Lum. "If you do not do as I say I shall have her killed. My sorcerer is watching us – he will spirit himself to my fortress and kill her if you do not do as I say."

"What do you want me to do?" Simon said in a flat voice. He would take no chance with Tatya's life.

"Give me your magic stick," she demanded and held out her hand for his wand. When he handed it to her she stuck it into her belt. "And now you shall come with me."

"No!" cried Prince Tuan as Simon took a step forward. He grabbed at Simon's arm. "Do not bow to her demands!"

"She has my wife, Highness. What else can I do?" Simon said wearily.

"You would surrender so easily – for the sake of a *woman*?" Prince Tuan was outraged.

Intellectually, Simon could almost understand the Chinese attitude toward females – it was deep in their culture – but now it revolted him. A quick look at the faces of Dr. Quong and Feng Hu told him that they felt the same – they would probably sacrifice a mere woman as well.

"You aren't married, Highness-" Ash began. His glance at least was understanding. Not only was Tatya's Simon 's wife and much loved, but no English gentleman would stand by and let a woman be harmed while he could prevent it.

"I have three wives and five concubines," said the Prince. "I will give you all the women you wish, Dr. Stillfield! Do not allow this unnatural female to have her way!"

"You do not understand," said Simon in English so that the warlord would not comprehend and have further ammunition to use against him. "Tatya is the completion of myself – the pulse of my heart as we say in Ireland. Without her – I don't even want to think about that. And If I let her die needlessly I would never forgive myself – or anyone who kept me from doing anything I can to save her. I'll go with this woman, see what she wants and try and rescue Tatya. Don't try and stop me, Highness, not if you value your own life." He added in Chinese. "Feng, don't you try and stop me either."

"I bow to your decision, young *Wu*," said Feng, suiting his actions to his words.

" Good luck, Simon!" said Ash. "Lakota is your ace in the hole."

"Speak Chinese!" said Si Wang angrily. It infuriated her that she did not understand the foreign devil tongue.

"The rest of you," she ordered "will leave this place at once! Or he dies and his woman with him! He is powerless now that I have his magic stick! These mountains are mine!"

She had no opinion of Feng Hu – he was frail and ancient and hardly a danger. And she knew really little of dragons – to her they were a commodity and she never even regarded then as sentient creatures. She would take and kill those two that had flown away very soon.

Once more she felt a deep scorn for Ch'ang – he was a coward to fear the old man! And the young one had proved easily controlled. She had, again, shown herself to be more powerful and clever than any man.

From a ledge high on the mountainside Lakota crouched low with T'a Ming and Chao. He watched, almost holding his breath as Simon talked to the warlord and then after a brief conversation with the other members of his party, walked away with her. The two of them climbed the hill and then Lakota could see they mounted horses. Another man and the Necromancer waited at the campsite and those two remained behind, even though it looked to Lakota s if the Necromancer and the warlord had an argument.

Si Wang took off at a gallop as soon as they were mounted. To her private satisfaction the foreign devil, unlike

Ch'ang, sat his horse well and had no trouble keeping abreast of her at all, even though she had mounted him on Chen Bo's gelding, who had a reputation as a hard-mouthed, stubborn brute.

For a *fan qui* – and she had seen foreign devils in both Canton and Shagh'ai – he was attractive. He was tall and slender, not as broad as Hong, but she would be surprised if he were not a great deal stronger than he looked, for his hands were every firm on the reins and he kept that iron-mouthed horse well up to the bit with no apparent effort. She liked his hands: well-shaped with long tapering fingers. He had strange pale hair, like the silk of a thistle and slanted back brows. His round eyes were curiously coloured – she could not be quite certain what colour they were for they had darkened with anger as she had told him of his woman's whereabouts.

What would it be like to lay with a foreign devil? On her trips to the cities she had been tempted. She had a friend who owned a Green Bower Room in Canton where foreign men often went and she had more than once been tempted to play the part of a courtesan and entertain a foreign man. Something had held her back but she had wondered if they knew different techniques than did Chinese men. Her friend had complained that they were rough and impatient, with no true amatory skills. Si Wang was not a delicate, refined flower like her friend who had spent as many years learning to play a lute and to sing as she had learned the arts of pleasing men. Men did not want to listen to a woman playing a stringed instrument and singing! Men were only interested in one thing!

A shiver of delight went over Si Wang's body. Perhaps she might find out, very shortly if foreign men were different! She suddenly could almost understand why Hong wanted the Witch so badly.

247

30

Retribution

It was nearing dawn before Hong came.

Tatya had anchored the mist to the ley lines. This was done ordinarily by the Coven itself, to keep the mists covering and warming them until the Rituals they had gathered for had been completed. Sometimes a Great Ritual could go on until the early hours of the morning.

Sometime during the wait Tatya had fallen into a light doze, curling up in the midst of the Circle. Ping, too, lay asleep against the wall in the corner she sat in.

The mists had another curious property – as well as warming they magnified sound, warning the Witches if any unauthorized person had come to gaze upon them.

The sound of boots treading on rock woke Tatya abruptly and she sat up, all of her senses on the alert. Was this the horrible Hong? She listened carefully, holding her breath and wishing that her heart was not beating so loudly. She willed Ping not to wake, for the Chinese woman would probably start crying and give their location away. Even after sleep, Tatya felt so tired that she could easily had lay down and cried. She was afraid that she would only have enough strength to work the absolute necessities of magic – and that had to be dealing with Hong, not quieting and soothing Ping.

A night of fruitless searching had not sweetened Hong's temper nor abated his desire for the amber-eyed Witch. He had, probably foolishly, gone out by himself to search for the two women, but he wanted to deal with the Witch himself. As soon as he found her he would tie her up with the coil of tope fastened to his belt and take her, roughly, to punish her for evading him and making him wait for his release for so long. The other woman he would tie up as well but he was not concerned with her, although he might beat her to teach the Witch a lesson, since the Witch was so concerned about her friend. He would show the Witch who was master and that his wants and needs came first. She would soon learn to please him, but Hong looked forward to the no doubt many tussles he would have with her. It would take time, for he did not want to break her spirit entirely. Complete acquiescence would be very dull – perhaps he could train her to fight as he did with Si Wang. That would be very exciting – to see her pink and white body shining with sweat as they spared and those beautiful breasts, so much more rounded and feminine than Si Wang's...

Lost in these thoughts he did not notice the heavy mist until he was well into it.

He cursed loudly. Mist was a constant danger in these mountains, some of which seemed to be shrouded in its wispy tatters all of the time.

Hong had searched all of the places where he thought they might hide near the fortress to no avail. It was not until well into the early hours of the morning that he thought that they might have actually climbed the hill. It was rather more than he expected two naked and scared women to do. It earned his reluctant admiration and made him more determined than ever to have the Witch. She had a fierce spirit and once she gave into him – what passion there would be between them!

He felt his way cautiously through the mist – he knew these mountains very well indeed, and, moving slowly, he was able to remain safe.

He reasoned that they might have made for the ruined temple – seeking shelter and thinking that a temple might save them, being a sacred place of which he would not disturb the sanctity.

But Hong had no religion other than that of money and sex – that was all that mattered. As he remembered, there was a very useful altar in the dragon temple to which one could tie an unwilling woman.

As he made his slow way up the mountain, hand over hand, he found signs of their passage. There were signs that a rope had been used and, even more to his satisfaction, he found bits of blood and skin and even a long honey-brown hair. So they had injured their nude bodies on the rock, had they? Hong grinned to himself. hey would be in pain and hungry by now – as far as he knew they had had nothing to eat for over two days. They might even be eager to give into his desires in exchange for the food he carried in a pack. There were many interesting things one man could do with two women! He remembered this from growing up in the brothel, where his mother and the other women had catered to a wide variety of tastes.

He was almost to the temple when suddenly there she was before him – the Witch! Right in the middle of the trail.

Her body shone with the pearly mist, forming little beads of moisture on her skin.

She smiled on him, and beckoned to him. "I have been waiting for you," she said seductively. She ran her hands up her own body, and thrust her breasts at him. "I want you now – I was foolish to resist. Come and take me!" she said in a low, husky voice, dropping her head and looking up at him through long, long lashes, She ran her tongue around her lips.

Hong 's eyes gleamed as desire rushed over him. "Lay down for me," he said. "Right here."

"Come to the temple," she purred. "You can have both of us. We are tired of running and want to be yours."

He stepped forward, hands outstretched. Laughing, she eluded him, and arched her body suggestively. "Come to the temple," she repeated. "I can promise you delight beyond what you have known."

He lunged at her and – stepped out into nothingness.

In the temple, Tatya heard his scream and the hollow thud as his body hit the rocks far below.

The room spun around her and she fell back. That had taken a lot out of her! But it had worked – he was dead – no one could have survived that fall! She cut her connection with the ley lines and the mists began rapidly to dissipate.

"What were you doing?" came Ping's horrified voice. "Saying those immodest things and touching your body like a Pleasure woman!" Ping was not exactly certain what a Pleasure woman might do but what Tatya had just been doing struck her as indecent and extremely immodest.

"I was making an illusion – I conjured up an image of myself to make Hong chase it." Tatya levered herself up on her elbow as she spoke. "I had to look as if I wanted him to catch me, Ping, and the illusion mirrored my actions. What was I supposed to do? Wait until he was on us? I am very tired – I could not have fought long and he would have had us, probably raped us and taken us back down the mountain for the other men to use as well. Now he's dead. And he was so arrogant, it seems that he came after us all by himself! Now we can wait for Simon to come. He or Lakota will have noticed the mists of the moon and they will come looking."

She tried to sound more confident than she felt, for she had no idea what Simon was undergoing or how far away he was.

She and Ping were in a bad situation. They had no food – there was a small spring at the back of the temple, little more than a trickle of water and nights were cold here in the mountains. Last night she had been able to raise the mists to warm their bare bodies but tonight, exhausted and hungry, she would not be able to do it again. However, she could not voice these doubts to Ping. Tatya knew all too well what her reaction would be.

They arrived at the fortress of Kwen – Lum in record time. One of Si Wang's men sprang forward to take the bridles of the horses as they dismounted. He stared curiously at Simon but said nothing.

"Come with me, Sorcerer," Si Wang ordered brusquely.

"Where is my wife?" Simon demanded harshly, still standing beside his horse.

"You shall see her in good time. She is safe and well treated," lied Si Wang smoothly. She hoped that the Witch was howling her fear under Hong's rough handling. To Si Wang's regret this foreign devil sorcerer did not appear to be the type that would savagely take a woman for his own pleasure as she knew Hong would. "I would talk to you first. We shall break our fast and talk."

Simon was angry – and worried. He could sense however that this woman had a will of iron and would proceed at her own pace. He had to find out where Tatya was before he could proceed with a rescue mission. He could coerce her with magic but he did not know if he could hold off an entire garrison if she called for aid, even if he called Lakota. He had seen the cannon on the ramparts and he could imagine what that could do to his dragon friend if a shot came his way. And he had no idea what traps and protocols the Necromancer might have set about her. It was prudent to proceed with caution, although he burned to find Tatya as soon as possible. But he did not want to endanger her or even be the cause of her death. Perhaps he could bargain with this woman for Tatya's life.

"Come!" Si Wang gestured him into the fortress.

Following her, Simon took careful note of everything: the doors leading from the long dark corridor, the narrow windows, unsuitable for escape as they were mere arrow slits. He had noticed the heavily manned ramparts as they came in at the thick copper-bound front gate. There was also a fair amount of Cold Iron used here – Simon could feel it as a beginning ache in his body and bones that would soon settle into a nagging pain that could eventually cripple him. He had little time to act – perhaps an hour – and once more he was grateful that Tatya was immune to Cold Iron. If she was not, she would have been very ill indeed after just a little time in this place.

The room Si Wang led Simon into was large and lit by many brass lamps, and warmed by braziers. There was a table and a pair of stools. The rest of the furniture seemed to consist of cushions.

A very old man waited by the table and bowed low to Si Wang.

"The gracious lady wishes?" he said.

"Ring for food, Fan, and take my armor off," she ordered. She threw Simon's wand and Tatya's jewelry on to the table as Fan rang a bell that hung from a cord on the wall.

"Might I ask how you obtained my wife?" Simon asked as old Fan removed her sword belt and then unbuckled her breast plate.

Si Wang sank down on a stool and held out first one leg and then the other so that Fan could remove her boots. "I sent my lieutenant Hong to the Huang Lung, particularly to bring her here. When word arrived of foreign devils in the valley and we saw you, Sorcerer, I knew that taking the other foreign devils – especially the woman – would bend you to my will. I have observed in Canton and Shangh'ai that foreigners are silly and sentimental about their women."

Simon noticed with relief that Si Wang had not mentioned Alan. He could only assume that Tatya had somehow made certain that their small son was safe before they had taken her. Simon did not want to mention Alan if the boy was somewhere safe from this awful woman.

"I want to see my wife," Simon said abruptly.

"In time," Si Wang waved a careless hand.

The door opened and a servant came in with a tray of food and a pot of tea.

Heedless of Simon's presence, Si Wang let Fan strip her. The old manservant held up a silken robe of red, embroidered with a peony design and Si Wang slipped into it, Belting it around herself, she returned to the stool. "Sit and eat and refresh yourself," she said to Simon.

He sat, but did not eat – food would have choked him. "You said you wished to talk to me, now talk – and then give me my wife and we shall leave," he said, his voice hard.

She laughed. "Did you look when I was naked, sorcerer? Did you like what you saw? Here, look again!" she swept open the robe to show her body. "I can be yours – and I will share with you all the wealth that I have taken! Fan, the jewel box! Spill it out on the table!"

Fan brought an intricately carved sandalwood box from a corner and upended it on the table top.

There were jewels of every description – rubies, diamonds, sapphires, emeralds, pearls and gold and silver pieces as well. It was obviously a King's ransom worth of plunder.

"Close your robe, madam," said Simon coldly. "I have no desire for you or your loot. All I want is my wife."

Si Wang ignored this. "I am offering you the chance to be my consort – my Tang Wang Kung! You have fathered a son on your foreign devil wife – now you can do so on me!

Together we will make such a son – one who will rule China as did Genghis Khan – a Sorcerer and warrior!" Her eyes shone with excitement and her breast rose and fell rapidly.

"Once again, I will ask you, where is my wife? " Simon's voice had gone all silken and soft, his face white and set. As he looked at her his eyes blazed with fury. "I warn you, madam –" His temper was in shreds – he was sick of her games. He forgot his resolve to be cautious.

"What can you do?" she laughed. "I have your magic stick!"

"This!" Without standing, Simon waved his hand and pronounced in a voice of thunder "*Destruere!*"

And with a noise like a hundred avalanches the entire side of the fortress blew outwards.

High up on the mountainside Tatya heard the sound and knew that it could only be one thing. "Simon!" she whispered joyfully.

31

The Queen of the Genii

"I ask you once again," said Simon. "Where is my wife? Tell me at once or, by God, I will pull this entire building down around your ears and destroy every one in it!" His temper was in shreds – the time for caution was past. He was also insulted that this woman thought he would give up Tatya for a mound of jewels and a naked body he did not find even vaguely attractive.

Si Wang, for once, was silent. She looked at him with wide eyes as she shrank back from him. She had never imagined such raw power! As far as she knew Ch'ang could do nothing like that. "You do not have your magic stick," she said weakly.

"I do not need my wand to work magic; it is a tool, that is all. I am not about to sit here discussing magic with you, madam, I want my wife. Now do you tell me where she is or do I take down this place brick by brick?"

"My men – " she began, but never finished, for through the huge hole in the wall came a blue head on a long neck. "I thought that was your magic, Simon!" Lakota said cheerfully. "Feng had me come – he took care of all her men. Wait until you see what he did to them!"

"She has Tatya, Lakota," said Simon briefly and then turned back to Si Wang. "Tell me where my wife is!" he said slowly and deliberately, raising his hand towards her. Violet power flickered on his fingers. "I will not hesitate to use violence on you- even if you are a woman!"

"She is in the cellars – I gave her to Hong – he wanted to lay with her," Si Wang said reluctantly. "But you are too late – " she added with a flash of her former spirit. "He's probably taken her again and again. He stripped her naked before he took her below. We all saw her."

"You hurt Tatya?" Lakota said angrily. Steam trickled from his nostrils.

Simon got up and went to the door. Old Fan cowered in a corner and made the sign against the evil eye as Simon

255

passed him. "Guard her well, Lakota," Simon said as he opened the door into the hall. "If she tries anything, flame her."

Lakota pushed aside some of the rubble so that he could come further into the room. "Gladly!" the dragon promised. "I might just flame her on general principles! I don't like her!"

With one last look backwards Simon waved his hand again and Si Wang's robe, which had been open all this time, closed and belted itself.

Simon wasted no time. Magic tore the door to the cellars off its hinges and he ran down the stairs as quickly as had Hong, shouting his wife's name. If that bastard had mistreated her –.

Throwing open every door in the fortress's cellar showed him that there was no one there. Simon found the room in which Tatya had been confined for such a brief while – where a rope still dangled from the ring on the wall, but there was no other sign of anyone's having been there at all, for before Hong had left to search for Tatya he had told several men to remove Lui's body and throw it on the midden and to clean the torture chamber.

Simon went back upstairs in a towering rage.

Si Wang, for the second time in her life, and both times in the same day, felt real fear as she saw his face. The destruction of the wall had been terrifying enough, but now she felt that she personally, might be harmed.

"She is not there!" Simon said. "Stop playing these games with me! I have no more patience with this! Where is she?"

"But Hong took her there – I saw him go. I let him leave my camp in the hills to come back here and take her," said Si Wang. "Perhaps he took her to his quarters..."

"Lakota, search this fortress for Tatya or any trace of her. Rip open the roofs – destroy anything you have to." Simon scooped up his wand and Tatya's jewelry. Sunlight was beginning to pour into the room from where it was usually blocked by the thick stone wall. It caught and glittered on something on the floor. Simon turned towards the shine and held out his hand, calling it to him.

The shining object flew to him like a homing pigeon. The sun had caught in the large diamond focus stone at the end of Tatya's wand.

"Simon," said the blue dragon "I think I know where Tatya is – you didn't have a chance to notice this morning and I did not have a chance to tell you, but someone drew down the moon last night, from up in the hills. It has to be Tatya because, from what I heard you and Dr. Quong discussing, no one here knows about drawing down the moon."

"Take me there!" said Simon quickly. He slipped Tatya's wand and his own into the front of his shirt – since the day had promised hot he had worn no jacket – and the jewelry went in to the pocket of his white duck trousers.

"What about her?" said the dragon, pointing a talon at Si Wang.

"I'll just put her put of the way of any mischief," said Simon.

Si Wang found herself propelled through the air and plastered against the wall, some four feet above the floor. It was if she had been glued there. She began to struggle and curse. "Fan! Get me down from here!" she shrieked.

The old man ran forward to tug ineffectively at her feet.

Simon leaped to Lakota's outstretched foreleg and from there into the saddle, ignoring Si Wang and Fan as if they did not exist. Lakota backed from the room as Simon strapped himself in. Barely clear of the rubble of the wall, the blue dragon leaped into the air and with one thrust of his wings, cleared the rocky hillside and was at the temple.

Ping was scandalized. Tatya, in broad daylight, was standing in clear view of anyone who might look up from the valley. She had been standing there since the explosion had echoed through the hills. She insisted that the explosion had been caused by Simon and she was equally insistent that she wait for him – out there in the sun where everyone could see her nakedness! Her husband would be shocked and would probably put her aside for immodesty!

Tatya did not care who saw her. The horrible Hong was dead and Simon was coming. She knew that he had caused the explosion! Without any means of enhancing her eyesight she could barely make out the fortress below but a tell-tale plume of violet smoke was still wafting up from the scene of the explosion.

From here, on the edge of the cliff, she could gaze down and see, barely, Hong's body sprawled below. She had heard him screaming a long way down. But she did not regret leading him to his death. It was not only the insult her had offered her, but it was vengeance for all the people of the Huang Lung valley that he had killed and made homeless. She hoped that the girls had been able to free themselves before the robbers had their way with them.

She also realized what a distance they had climbed last night and what a miracle it had been that they had been able to do it at all. Her body was covered in scrapes and cuts and she was stiff with fatigue today. The height Hong had fallen and they had climbed was enough to make her head spin.

A great blue form loomed up over the edge of the ledge and Tatya waved and jumped up and down in excitement. Lakota made a neat landing and Tatya was running towards him as fast as Simon was sliding off his back.

They met halfway between the ruined temple and Lakota's landing place. Simons' arms went around her waist and her arms twined around his neck. He buried his face in her hair, swinging her off her feet, murmuring her name again and again. Then setting her on her feet, he kissed her, long and hard.

Ping, watching from the corner where she still sat crunched up was amazed. Where was his shock at seeing his wife naked on a mountainside? Why was he not censuring her for immodesty?

She would have been even more amazed if she could have heard their conversation.

"Is this some new fashion?" Simon asked teasingly. He was so glad to see her that he could have laughed aloud in wild relief. "If so, I like it – you should definitely wear it more often!"

"Everyone I meet wants to tear my clothes off!" she said. "Simon, I am so glad to see you! That awful woman's troops raided the valley–" Succinctly she told him what had happened, assuring him at once of Alan's safety.

He did not let go of her during this recital, only raising one hand to smooth back her hair that was blowing in the breeze. "I'm so proud of you," he said huskily when she had finished. "You rescued yourself and Ping, kept Alan safe and defeated your enemies." He gave her another long kiss.

"Ping was a pain in the ass," said Tatya, making a face.

Simon began laughing, which thoroughly convinced the listening Ping of the foreign devils' complete and utter depravity.

"If we ever have a daughter, " said Tatya, "she'll be raised to not be such a namby pamby and not to get so upset about a little nudity! Simon, give me your shirt – Ping will stay in that corner for the rest of her life if I don't give her something to cover herself. She's so silly – she'd rather freeze, starve or die than have someone see her naked."

Simon stripped off his shirt. Tatya was pleased to see her wand and to find out that he had her jewelry as well. She returned her rings to her fingers immediately. It was her turn to laugh when she heard that Simon had hung Si Wang up on a wall. She then took the shirt to Ping.

"What do you laugh about?" Ping asked as she slowly stood up, keeping her hands in place before her body to expose as little of herself as possible. She kept glancing towards the ledge where Simon stood by Lakota as if she was afraid they would look at her. "Don't worry, Ping," said Tatya dryly. "Even Lakota has turned his back."

Simon's shirt was very large on Ping – it hung down over her hands and as far down as her knees but she was decently covered. "What will you wear?" she asked Tatya.

"Well, I can't very well ask Simon for his trousers," said Tatya cheerfully. "I can emulate Lady Godiva and wear my hair!"

Ping did not understand this illusion of course.

She did not want to climb on Lakota's back either – she was afraid and she was still embarrassed by her attire or, in her view, the lack of it. She was further shocked when Tatya climbed on the saddle in front of Simon. "You cannot go like that down there with all of those men!" Ping exclaimed, outraged.

"Ping," Tatya said, trying to be patient, "practically everyone here has seen me naked – what are a few more? I'm hungry and tired and I don't want to stay up here any longer than I have to." She pulled her long hair forward over her breasts. It hung down well below her waist.

"When we land, Tatya," said Lakota,"I'll land close to a wall and then you may slide off my other side, and you can go beneath my wing until Simon can fetch you something to wear. I'm so glad you are back with us!" He gave a delighted wiggle.

"Thank you, Lakota," said Tatya approvingly. The dragon had more sense than Ping. She knew too, that he thought all this fuss about clothing was silly. Humans had to wear clothes to keep warm. But when it wasn't chilly, why bother? Lakota bowed to human custom, even if the customs were past draconic understanding.

After coaxing on Simon's part and impatience on Tatya's, Ping was persuaded to mount the dragon and they glided back down to the fortress,

No sooner had Lakota landed than Ash came hurrying up to them. Tatya slid off on Lakota's opposite side and with a squeak of alarm Ping followed her. Lakota lifted his wing and they went underneath. The dragon crouched down and held his wing so that it seemed as if they were in a little room, safe from prying eyes. "You had better find TWO outfits, Simon," came Tatya's voice. "Ping doesn't fancy your shirt at all!"

"Did you find her?" Ash demanded. From a distance he had not seen the two women slip from the dragon's back.

Very briefly, Simon told him of Tatya's kidnapping and her self rescue.

"She's all right though?" asked Ash anxiously.

" Yes – she'll be better as soon as I get her some decent clothing," Simon returned, knowing that Ash was actually asking if she had been raped.

"There's a large storeroom filled with things one level below where the warlord is – err – currently hanging about." A huge grin lit Ash's face. "Good show, that by the way. About those things – most of them are men's garments but I am certain that I saw a few women's things in there as well."

They began to walk back to the fortress, Simon calling out to Tatya that he had probably located some clothing for her.

"His Highness and I have been exploring – you cannot conceive the amount of loot these bandits have amassed! Gold, silver, jewels, silks and brocades, porcelain – it's like Aladdin's cave in most of these rooms. None of these bandits will have any use for their share now, of course."

"Is the Prince going to behead all of them?" Simon knew they deserved death – they had robbed, pillaged and raped the neighborhood for years – and Chinese law demanded that they pay for these crimes with their heads. But he felt sick at the thought of so much death.

"Didn't Lakota tell you?" Ash asked in surprise. "Feng Hu took care of them all. Look!" He flung out a dramatic hand towards the ramparts as they drew up to the fortress.

Where there had been men standing near the cannon and beside the piles of weapons, there were now terra-cotta figures. Each was unique, for each man had been caught in a different movement. They were still life-sized, looking as if they had come from the shop of the finest sculptor in China.

"Feng says they are frozen for all eternity and the Prince thinks it a fitting end to their villainy. He has yet to decide what to do with the warlord. He says that she deserves an evil fate."

More terra-cotta figures were in evidence as they passed in to the fortress. Servants, bandits – all had been caught by the force of Feng's spell. Only those who had shared the room with Simon had been spared It was a very impressive piece of magic.

Ash showed Simon to the storeroom, where he searched for and found two female robes of silk. These he took, as well as two jewel encrusted combs, out to Tatya and Ping and requested that they join the party in the main room as soon as they were dressed.

Ash and Simon found Dr. Quong, the Prince and Feng Hu seated at the table, drinking the tea that Si Wang had ordered for Simon. Feng had warmed it magically. Someone had found more stools and cups.

Feng, slipping his tea, sat staring at Si Wang. He raised his eyebrows slightly at Simon's shirtless state but said "I trust you found your lady wife in good health and spirits, young *Wu*?"

"Yes, thank you. She and Ping, who was also carried off by the bandits, will join us shortly," said Simon as he took a seat at the table.

Dr. Quong blanched visibly. "My daughter-in-law?" he said in horror. "She was carried off by the bandits as well? Was she dishonored?"

"No, Tatya prevented it but she was roughly handled," Simon answered as Feng poured cups of tea for him and Ash.

"Jian will have to put her aside if he has been in the hands of the bandits, and therefore defiled," said Dr. Quong. "Our family honor demands it."

"Jian should be glad that she is not dead!" said Simon sharply.

"Surely your honor demands that your wife is no longer fit to be your consort and the mother of your sons?" Dr. Quong asked, looking at Simon as if he could not understand him at all.

"Even if Tatya had been raped – repeatedly – or had had to give herself to some man to save her life or someone else's I would still love her and want her," said Simon. These idiots and their honor! What about the woman's feelings? Roughly handled, raped and then abandoned by the very person who should be offering support and understanding and love? He was suddenly homesick for his own people and his own land where everything was not, or so it seemed, so backwards and twisted.

Si Wang had been listening avidly to this conversation. Now she began laughing in a malicious fashion. "Is that what your woman told you, Sorcerer, that no one mounted her or the other woman? I am certain that Hong took her, just as Lui would have taken the noblewoman. They were both lusty men and stripped both of the women naked before us all and handled their bodies as well! You are a fool if you accept her lies, Sorcerer! Of course he had her" she added in scorn.

"Tatya and Ping escaped before that happened. And your man Lui and the other are dead. Tatya killed them," said

Simon levelly.

Si Wang was stunned. Hong was dead? She gave little thought to Lui – his great size would have made him an interesting bed partner for a moment but she knew his tastes all too well and she had no desire to be burnt or beaten to satisfy his perverted lusts. But Hong – Hong was different – no one else had ever managed to satisfy her as much as he had. The thought that she would never spar with him, nor lay with him again – it silenced her as nothing else would have done. She even forgot that she herself was probably facing death.

Under Lakota's wing Ping and Tatya dressed in the silken robes that Simon had brought them. The combs were the type that were used as hair ornaments but with a detangling spell from *One Hundred and One Useful Household Spells* Tatya was able to get most of the tangles from both her and Ping's long hair. The combs Simon had brought also served to anchor a twist atop their heads.

Ping had been looking more and more miserable as they dressed in long, heavily embroidered robes. "What did your husband say to you when he saw that you had no clothing?" she blurted out suddenly.

"He was glad to see that I was alive, that is all. He had been very worried," answered Tatya

"He did not censure you, or scold? Will he beat you for immodesty?" Ping queried.

"Of course not! Once I told Simon what had happened he understood why I was naked. He didn't think it was my fault that the horrible Hong ripped off my clothes."

Ping finished twisting up her hair into a knot, still looking troubled. "I must tell my father–in–law, as head of our house, of what has befallen me – of my indelicate and wanton behavior ..."

"*Your* indelicate and wanton behavior?" Tatya was outraged. "Ping, that man forced you – he stripped your clothes from your body, he was the one who touched you and tied you to that table. How is that indelicate on your part? And anyone less wanton I have yet to see! What were you

263

supposed to do – fend him off – he was four times your size! Or do they expect you to kill yourself rather than let him even look at your body?"

Ping looked at her through tear-filled eyes. "Yes, I should have killed myself before I dishonored the name of Quong."

Tatya felt a chill run down her spine. The woman really believed this nonsense! Perhaps at one time she herself might have felt so – even in a Western culture many women felt that death was preferable – rape was sometimes called the fate worse than death – but being dead was a great deal worse than being raped. Poor Ping did not have a husband like Simon, who would love his wife no matter how many rapists had taken her. They would work out the aftermath of such a happening together Tatya knew that she could count on Simon's love and support no matter what – and that of their family as well. Poor Ping had no such reassurances.

Tatya felt a wave of pity for the Chinese woman wash over her. Her ordeal was over but Ping's was just beginning.

"Hello!" she heard Lakota say above them. "Are you looking for someone?"

"I seek the *Wu* Feng Hu. He has summoned me," said a female voice.

"Who is it, Lakota?" Tatya called.

"It's a Faerie woman, I think," he returned, "Are you ready to come out now?"

"A Faerie woman?" Tatya queried. Lakota lifted his wing and Tatya, followed timidly by Ping, came out from beneath it.

The woman standing in front of Lakota did indeed seem to be at least closely related to the Faeries. She was regally slim with the narrow face and long slender hands that Tatya had learned to associate with the Elves and Faeries she had come to know in Ireland. She was also hauntingly lovely with Oriental features, a cloud of dark hair and skin of polished ivory. She wore bejeweled robes of peacock blue and a fantastic headdress of peacock feathers.

Tatya sank into a deep curtsey. One should always be very, very polite to Faerie persons. "How may I serve you, my lady?" she inquired.

264

"I seek the magician Feng Hu," the Faerie woman answered in soft musical tones. "He has summoned me to a judgment. I am the Queen of the Genii – Si Wang Mu."

Tatya and Ping looked at each other, shocked.

32

The Cherry Blossom Woman

In spite of his exhaustion Jian did not sleep at all well that night. He tossed and turned, thinking about Ping and about Gui. What was he to do about Ping? More and more he realized that he wished her back – he became aware that he both needed her and wanted her – he loved her, as he had never thought he would love any one but a son. In his culture, women were not valued, save as the mothers of sons that could carry on the family name and honor and show duty to the ancestors. He called the affection he felt for his daughter and, more so, for Hai, 'love' but as he lay there, looking up at the stars he realized that the feeling that swept over him for Ping was much more. He desired her – true, the hours they spent on the Ivory Couch together were sheer bliss – but he found that he would want her even if they could never have sexual relations again. He just wanted to be able to see her and talk to her and laugh with her again. She was so sweet and feminine and could make him laugh with her quaint observations.

Finally he decided, well after midnight, that he would keep her by him, even should his father object. Perhaps she could be his concubine if his honorable father thought her no longer worthy to be First Wife. But he was not going to return her to her father's house where he would never be able to see her or touch her again. It would be unbearable.

And what of Gui? Jian realized that the boy could very well be his son. The youth was sixteen or so – and seventeen years ago, when he was Gui's age, he had been a frequent visitor to the House of Pleasure in the valley. There had been one particular woman that he had always asked for – she had been little older than he was then – shy, in spite of her profession, and sweet. Of course, she was more experienced than he had been and she had taught him much – and given him much satisfaction when he had needed

266

release from the tension of studying for his Civil Service examinations. Sometimes he fancied that it had been she who had been responsible for the high scores he had achieved, for after an interlude with her he had been able to obtain a restful sleep rather than laying awake worrying over the examinations.

He would ask Gui in the morning about his mother. With these two decisions made Jian finally feel into sleep in the few hours remaining before the dawn.

Morning came far too early for one who had slept but little. Jian awoke groggily, to find the sun already peeking over the horizon and Gui busy about the campfire, making *jook* for breakfast. A pot of tea was steaming as well. Jian yawned and stretched.

"Good morning, honorable Magistrate," said Gui, with a short jerk of his head rather than a full bow. "There is water for washing there." He pointed to a basin on a flat-topped rock.

Jian stumbled from his tangled blankets and made his unsteady way to the basin. He had been on horseback at breakneck pace for nearly three days, with little or no rest and he was stiff and sore.

A splash of water in his face woke him somewhat and he made his way behind the bushes to an area they had agreed to use as a latrine.

When he emerged from the bushes Gui was ladling up *jook* into two bowls. "I have fed and groomed the horses," he announced as Jian joined him. The boy held out a bowl of steaming food which Jian took, and sat on a log near the fire to eat it.

They ate in silence until the first pangs of hunger were satisfied. Still in silence they drank their tea.

Jian felt awkward. He should not have, he thought, for as a magistrate he was used to getting to the heart of a dispute or making a ruling on problems .

But that was for other people! How ever did he tell this self possessed young man who did not seem to need anyone and who had already determined to go his own way,

that he, Jian, was probably his father? And what was the
family to do about this new relationship, if what Jian
suspected was true? But to have another son could be nothing
but a blessing.

"Who is your mother?" he asked Gui abruptly,
forgetting all about tact.

Gui, scraping the last of his *jook* from the bowl, looked
up sharply at this query. "She is the one they call the Cherry
Blossom Woman – because of the pale pink of her –"

"Yes," said Jian hurriedly. It was not proper that a
young boy know that about his mother! "But her name, her
real name, is Ai, is it not?"

"How did you know that, Magistrate? Have you had
her?" asked Gui mockingly.

"You will speak with respect of your mother!" Jian
said angrily. "She is a fine woman. She was sold to a House of
Pleasure by her parents when she was only twelve as they
were every poor. They thought it would be a better life for her
than starving to death on their small farm as there were too
many girls in her family and no money for dowries."

"How do you know of this?" Gui asked suspiciously. "I
thought that she had spoken of these things only to me!"

"I knew your mother before I married, years ago," said
Jian. "She was newly come to the Huang Lung Zhi, having
been sold from a house in Chengdu. She had hopes of being a
rich man's courtesan, but lacked talent in music and learning."

"Instead she ended in a house where she is abused by
camel drivers and peasants," said Gui bitterly. "My mother is
sweet and eager to please even the most jaded of tastes. She
thinks, Magistrate that one, even a pleasure woman, should
always give of her best."

"She was always loving and giving," said Jian,
remembering Ai.

"Why do you ask me these things?" Gui demanded.
"To remind me of my place as a man of no name and no
ancestors, because I spoke to you with disrespect yesterday?"

"I speak of this things," said Jian, his voice raw with
emotion, "because I am certain that I am your father."

For once, Gui, who was never at a loss for words, had
no answer to this statement.

They had saddled up and taken off, still in silence. Gui would not speak to Jian, in spite of all that Jian did both to coax and demand that the boy communicate with him.

The boy's face was set and stony and his mind obviously elsewhere. At length Jian had to give up trying to make him speak. They rode at a relatively brisk pace, cantering whenever possible to make time. Gui seemed to know where he was headed and Jian let him lead.

Midway through the morning a cloud of dust appeared on the horizon. Gui and Jian, by unspoken mutual agreement, pulled off the road, where they might not be noticed in a grove of stunted trees.

Within a few moments a small contingent of cavalry was visible. And to the surprise of both watching men, nine soldiers appeared. Each carried a passenger – a young girl.

"Jing Mai!" called out Gui. With happiness and eagerness in his voice, he sounded more as a youth of his age should sound. Gui put his heels to his horse and it leaped out on to the road in front of the soldiers.

"Gui! Gui!" Jing Mai shouted, and skid down from behind the soldier whose belt she held on to. She ran towards the boy who jumped from his horse even before it had slid to a stop.

They fell into an eager embrace, hugging one another. All the spectators could hear were breathless disjointed phrases: "I knew you would come for me!" "They did not hurt you?"

The leader of the soldiers rode up to Jian. "We were on our way to join Prince Tuan when we came across these girls. They managed to escape from the bandits with their virtue intact." He nodded at Jing Mai. "That is a clever girl – the others tell me that she enticed the guard and then killed him with a shrewd blow so that they could escape. The *fan qui* Witch loosened the ropes with a spell."

"The bandits had my wife and the foreign lady as well," said Jian anxiously. "Did they escape?"

The leader shook his head. "We have no sign of them – but my captain expected to meet with the bandits and deal

269

with them before we reached the Prince. These girls were kept at the rear of the bandit troop on foot while the officers of the bandits bore your lady and the foreign devil away. The girls do not know what happened to them. My captain detailed us to take these girls home in safety and do what we could to protect the valley."

"Thank you," Jian said dully, staring at nothing. Where was Ping? What had happened to her? Was she terrified? Was she even still alive?

"Come, Magistrate," said Gui's vice at his stirrup. "We go on to find your wife."

Jian looked down. The boy, his hand entwined with that of Jing Mai, looked up at him, his mocking smile on his face.

"You have recovered your woman," Jian said."Why –?"

"Jing Mai tells me I owe such a duty to my father. Is not filial obedience important, Magistrate?" said Gui. Jian was not certain as to whether Gui was making game of him or quite serious.

But suddenly it did not matter. Jian was very aware that he did not want to go on alone, afraid of what he would find. Therefore he made no more protest as Gui swung back on his horse, and helped Jing Mai to climb up behind him.

Zhang Bao, formerly a prosperous citizen of Canton, was now a fugitive from justice. At one time the wily merchant had borne a striking resemblance to Confucius, a similarity he cultivated by copying the philosopher's beard and mustache style and affecting antique style robes of azure and gold. Zhang Bao was rather stout of body as well, and over given to quoting the sage.

Now, however, he had squeezed his body into peasant dress, and was heading north, towards Mongolia. From there he intended to head for St. Petersburg in Russia, where he had many holdings, including a prosperous tea importing business. It did not matter that the business had been his for a number of years under an entirely different name. And with his face shorn of his Confucian resemblance he could leave the country of his birth behind and live elsewhere quite comfortably.

Getting out of it comfortably was another matter all together.

Zhang had fled Canton a bare hour ahead of the Emperor's troops who were coming to arrest him. Somehow they had found out that he had been trafficking in dragon flesh, skin and bones. Under the new laws that had recently come into effect his head was forfeit. In defiance of the Emperor's edict, Zhang had kept selling dragon remains illicitly. There was far too much profit in it to halt.

Zhang did not know who had betrayed him. He suspected that unfeminine Si Wang. She was a greedy whore – she probably wanted to cut him out and sell her draconic goods directly to the customers and pocket all of the money herself. True, Zhang marked up the dragon goods 120% over the exorbitant fees he paid Si Wang, but, he felt, this was not enough considering the risks he had been taking in marketing the goods.

Now he rode in the slowest of vehicles – an ox-cart – with as much of his worldly goods, meaning what was easily transportable, that he could bring in two rope-bound boxes. Both boxes had false bottoms and were there laden with jewels and pearls – as these weighed less than money. On top of the false bottoms lay simple clothing, some cheap porcelain wrapped against damage and some food, as a blind, in case the boxes were searched.

He thought that no one, looking for a rich merchant would bother stopping an old man in an ox-cart, an old man who told anyone who showed the slightest interest, that he was going to live with his daughter and son-in-law in the north. He had told this story, in garrulous fashion, to the driver of the ox-cart and to anyone who would listen, going on about his wife who had died of a wasting disease and about his daughter and her children. This would guarantee that all would avoid him – everyone, even while they respected his status as an elder, would avoid an old bore, particularly one who allowed a whine to creep into his voice.

And so it proved. Mile after weary mile passed. Several times troops of soldiers rode by and gave the cart and its occupants scarcely a glance.

271

When at last they stopped for the night – not in an inn but in a field – Zhang did not have to feign the whine. It was there in his voice as he dismounted from the ox-cart, feeling three times his age and stiff with pain.

The stopping place was one frequented by travelers, the poorer type who had to make due with sleeping beneath the stars and cooking food on an open fire. There were already other occupants of the campsite – three men, with two others tied to a tree.

Zhang's first thought was to curse. Now he would have to sit up all night guarding his boxes – those looked like bandits or worse, soldiers with prisoners.

Then he noticed that the two men tied up were *fan qui*. And he noticed something else as well – he knew the men guarding said foreign devils. He would go and speak to them.

"Lao Min!" he exclaimed when he reached their campfire. "What do you and your brothers do here?"

The biggest of the men looked up. "Honorable Zhang!" he exclaimed and stood to bow low. "We are on our way to Canton. We found these foreign devils," he waved a hand towards his captives "And we thought you might wish to hold them to ransom."

He was obviously burning to ask what his one-time employer was doing so far from Canton, shaved and in peasant garb, but he held his tongue.

"I shall not be in Canton for some time," said Zhang, not without regret, for foreign devils usually paid well for the return of other devils.

Lao Min looked disappointed. "But what shall do with them?" he queried. "I do not know how to collect ransoms from the foreign devils."

"Kill them or let them go – I care not. I would like to hire you and your brothers to escort me to the north," he added, struck by a sudden thought. Lao Min was loyal to him and always eagerly accepted any employment. What better escort than three bandits?

"Don't kill them here!" shrilled the old peasant who had driven the ox-cart who had followed Zhang out o f intense curiosity. "Their ghosts will haunt us! No – you must let them wander away to die on their own as they will surely do, being foreigners and strange to our country."

Lao Min was much struck by this and took out his sword. "I do not want any ghosts to haunt me!" he said.

When Tom saw the big man coming towards him with drawn sword he thought it was all over. They were going to be killed then and there.

Beside him, Faversham gave a gasp but surprisingly said, "Stiff upper lip, what, old chap? Dareswear this is it for us. But we'll die like Englishmen!" With this he stood up very straight with a look of defiance on his sheep-like features.

To their surprise the big bandit slit the ropes that bound them and then waved towards the road. It was clearly a "go" signal.

Feeling almost faint with relief Tom rubbed his wrists. Faversham, recovering, bowed towards their captors and said "Thank you!"

Tom was in no mood to be grateful. He pulled down the cuffs of his jacket and shrugged it into a better fit across his shoulders. After all of this time his jacket, like the rest of his clothing, was little better than a rag.

The lining suddenly gave way all at once and a piece of parchment fell to the ground.

With an exclamation of surprise the bandit bent and took it up, faster than Tom could move, for he was stiff from being tied up.

Ton's heart sank as the bandit opened the parchment and gazed at it avidly.

He had found the map. And only a complete fool would fail to realize what it was.

33

The Justice of the Genii Queen

"Will you show me where I might find Feng Hu?" the Faerie woman repeated.

Tatya curtseyed again. We are going to join my husband and Feng Hu will more than likely be in his company. I can show you the way."

The Genii Queen graciously inclined her head as Tatya then introduced herself and Ping. She walked along with them towards the main entrance of the fortress, first biding Lakota a polite good-bye.

"That is a strange *lung*," she remarked as they walked away. "He is winged, yet has no facial whiskers., but has the toes of a *t'ein lung*. I have never seen such a colour of *lung*."

"Lakota came with my husband and myself from our home on the other side of the world," said Tatya. "He is not a Chinese *lung*, but an American dragon."

It was evident from the look on the Faerie woman's face that she had no idea what Tatya meant by 'American'.

Ping reacted with shock at the first terra-cotta figure they saw. "I recognize him – he was in the hall when we were brought in to this evil place! How did he come to be made of clay?" she stammered.

The Queen of the Genii laughed softly. "Feng is up to his old tricks!" she said. "In ancient times he turned many into clay at the whim of Emperors who wished to bury themselves with an army, concubines, servants and horses, ready to serve them if they should ever walk the earth again."

"You are well acquainted with Feng Hu, ma'am?" Tatya inquired, as she opened the door of the fortress. It was so heavy that she need to give it a magical push.

The Faerie woman laughed again. Like the Elves Tatya knew, her laugh was like silver bells ringing. "I knew him well in every sense," she answered, "At one time we shared a bed. For a human he was a magnificent lover."

Ping blushed and could not look at the Faerie woman.

Tatya preserved her countenance. She was far too used by now, after nearly four years in Ireland and being in the company of Faerie creatures, to their sometime outrageous conversation and conduct. Some of them delighted in shocking the humans they knew.

Ahead of them Tatya could hear the murmur of voices. With another bow she opened the closed door for the Faerie woman

The Genii Queen inclined her head in acknowledgement of Tatya. And she gave a slight smile of approval. Faerie creatures much appreciated good manners and deference to their status, which of course, far outweighed that of any human.

Simon and Ash came to their feet as the three woman entered. Tatya went at once to Simon's side and handed her husband his shirt.

"Ah!" Feng came to his feet and went to the side of the Faerie woman. "You have come," he stated.

"Did you think that I would not?" she said. "What little you told me intrigued me. A black Sorcerer? Dead dragons? A vile usurper? And me to render justice? No, I could not stay away."

"Alas, I must report that the black Sorcerer has escaped my net – he fled in a bolt of lightning and I have yet to track him. And the young *Wu* here," he waved a hand at Simon, "has made certain that no more dragons will die, as have I. But there still remains the question of this usurper," He waved his hand again, this time at the female warlord who still hung on the wall.

Si Wang, still lost in grief at the thought of Hong's death, did not at first pay attention to the other people who had entered the room. But now she felt eyes upon her, hard, cold eyes that woke her from her stupor of pain and drew her attention outwards again. She lifted her head and stared into the eyes of a woman who looked not quite human.

"So, " said this female in a sibilant whisper. "You are the usurper who dared to steal my name, who dared to steal the name of my palace for this inferior hovel and even dared to covet the very name of my consort!"

"Who are you?" Si Wang whispered.

275

"*I* am Si Wang Mu, Queen of the Genii!" the Faerie woman announced. "She from whom you have stolen her good name, Zhong Ju! And the good Feng Hu has given it to me to pronounce judgment on your for your crimes, for not only have you besmirched my name, but you have robbed and pillaged and laid waste in my name." She waved her hand and the erstwhile SI Wang fell to the floor with a thump.

She lay there, now Zhong Ju once more, looking up at the Queen of the Genii, fear beginning to fill her eyes.

The Genii Queen studied the woman who lay before her. "You are used to ordering others about. You will therefore serve me as the lowest of the low – you will scrub the floors of my palace. Your head will be shaved so that men will know you have displeased me and you will be naked at all times but unable to attract a man to lay with you. From now on you will be celibate." As she spoke she waved her hand and Zhong Ju's hair fell to the floor, leaving her hairless. Her robe disappeared and for the first time in her life the warlord felt shame at appearing naked before men. The loss of her beautiful glossy black hair made her feel as if they looked on her with revulsion.

"Your body hair will be thick and coarse and your feet large – no man or creature of the Middle Kingdom will want you," the Genii Queen continued Compared to Western woman, Chinese females had sparse body hair and many of them shaved what little they had.

"And anyone less like a chrysanthemum I have never seen," Ash murmured to Simon, as, before their eyes, Zhong Ju changed to become what the Genii Queen commanded.

"I shall take her with me now," the real Si Wang announced. "She will serve me all her days and obey the slightest command given her, else she shall be whipped. She will sleep on a bed of rags and eat only the poorest of foods with no drink save water." So saying she went to the former warlord, and took her by the arm, "Come, slave," she said, and the two of them disappeared in a blinding flash of bluish white light.

"A fitting punishment," said the Prince in approval.

Simon and Tatya looked at each other, The warlord had been a horrible woman but to them this punishment seemed very harsh. The Chinese people in the room seemed to feel that this was just.

"And now, former daughter –in-law," said Dr, Quong severely to Ping. "you must tell me of your shame, of your wantonness in allowing these bandits and that woman to see you unclothed and thus dishonoring my family name. Did any of them touch you ?"

Ping hung her head. "Yes," she said miserably, and continued " I know that I must be put aside for the shame I have brought to your noble house and I shall return to the home of my father…"

"No! You shall not!" came a voice.

There in the doorway, his entrance unnoticed, stood Jian. Behind him were Gui and Jing Mai.

"What happened to Ping is not her fault, honorable Father, I am certain that she did not wish for the bandits to strip her or touch her, She has always been a good, modest wife and I – and I ," he swallowed hard and went on "and I love her and will not be parted from her."

Ping looked up, sudden wild hope on her face and Tatya said "Oh, bravo, Jian!"

Dr. Quong looked startled and then outraged that his son should be so lost to all filial respect as to contradict him. "She must be put aside!" he said angrily.

"I think we had better leave," Simon suggested to the others who were not involved in this family quarrel. "They had best settle this for themselves."

The Prince showed a tendency to want to stay and arbitrate, but Simon tactfully drew him away, leaving angry voices behind him.

Out in the hall they found the door open and Lakota's blue head, looking worried and anxious poke din the open door.

"Oh, Simon!" he said 'T'a Ming has gone missing! Not even Chao knows where she went!"

277

34

The Hungry Panda

Chao was hungry – while waiting on the ledge with Lakota and T'a Ming he had eaten the last of the bamboo, even though the large bag had been stuffed to bursting with the succulent stalks and roots. But since a full grown Panda ate 20–40 pounds of bamboo every day, even the massive amount that T'a Ming had gathered for him had not lasted even a week.

Pandas usually gathered their own bamboo – but Chao was afraid of heights – he could not climb the trees, nor even go to the altitudes where the trees grew – 5,000 to 10,000 feet up on a mountainside. For years now T'a Ming, his friend, had gathered the bamboo for his use, for of course a dragon who could fly had no fear of heights. Chao did not know why his senses swam sickeningly when he tried to go higher, whether up a tree or a mountainside, or why a paralyzing fear overcame him. He only knew that without T'a Ming's friendship and her willingness to fetch this essential food for him on a daily basis, he would have been long dead. He owed her his life – that was why he had insisted on coming along when the Celestials ordered her to make this trip. She was as afraid of this journey as he was of heights. He could understand that perfectly.

If he felt affection for anyone it was for T'a Ming. He had been orphaned as a cub and at any rate, Pandas, by nature, were solitary creatures. Chao had never bothered to search for a mate during the short Panda breeding season – he had been afraid any desirable female would laugh at a male afraid of heights, who depended on a creature of another species to feed him. It was this constant feeling of failure, of inferiority, that kept his temper short.

This morning, hunger also kept him irritable. He could eat small rodents and gentian roots as well as grasses, bulbs, and fruit. But there did not seem to be any of those things about at the moment. At any rate, he preferred bamboo to anything else.

The two dragons and the Panda watched as Simon rode away with the warlord. Lakota anxiously, paying no attention to the other two beside him.

They continued to watch as Feng Hu, with surprising agility for a man of his age, went up the hillside to Ch'ang and engaged the Necromancer in conversation. Whatever he said sent the black magician fleeing in a dark pinwheel as he dematerialized and disappeared.

Shortly after that a troop of soldiers appeared – the Prince's men at last had arrived. Then Feng called for Lakota to come down.

"Stay here," the blue dragon told T'a Ming and Chao. "I shall have to see what he wants."

They expected him to come back immediately but instead he flew off with Feng and the rest of their party in the direction of the fortress just as a mighty explosion rocked the entire area.

"Oh!" T'a Ming squealed, flattening herself on the ledge. "What has happened?"

Chao had stayed well back from the edge of the mountainside shelf they sat upon and if it meant going near that drop he did not care what had happened.

"It has nothing to do with us," the Panda growled. His stomach gave a loud rumble.

T'a Ming's head whipped around. "Oh, honorable Chao! I beg your pardon!" she said, bowing her head in embarrassment . "I am a poor friend – I have not attended to your needs. You hunger! I shall go at once and fetch some bamboo for you."

"They said to wait here," he pointed out.

"I saw a stand of your favorite type of bamboo not far from here," she said. "I may fetch it in but a moment. It is not proper that you go hungry when I and the others had a nice breakfast." The meal had not been swallows, but it had been dried meats and vegetable stewed with grain and honey – quite tasty.

Over his protests she lifted her *poh shan* and pumped it until she could fly away. Chao was uneasy – he did not like the fact that the Sorcerer had disappeared and they did not know where the man had gone. The Necromancer was a danger to them all – particularly dragons.

He became even more uneasy – even alarmed – as the time passed and she did not return. Below, the Prince's men were setting up camp. None of the humans seemed to notice that T'a Ming had gone missing. Nor did they seemed to have a thought to spare for Pandas stuck up on ledges. And the other members of the party – the human ones – had all gone elsewhere.

Chao had just about screwed up his courage to attempt the descent and try to communicate with a human when, with a thump, Lakota landed on the ledge.

To Chao's relief the blue dragon noticed at once that T'a Ming was missing. "Where has she gone?" he inquired, looking about.

"To fetch me some bamboo," ground out Chao. "And don't look at me like that – I didn't ask her to go – she just took off! How could I stop something that can fly?"

"How could she be so foolish?" Lakota fretted. "I must let Simon know and then I shall search for her."

"Take me with you when you go to look for her!" Chao demanded.

Lakota agreed to come back for him and took off again.

Within moments he had returned. "I'm to go look for her, "he announced, "if I find her in trouble I am to return and fetch Simon – they are all returning here."

"I'm coming with you," Chao repeated.

Lakota looked doubtful, He was still under saddle but Chao had required a great deal of help to mount T'a Ming and fasten himself in. However, he could crouch closer to the ground than she would or could and perhaps if Chao got up on a rock ...

In the end, they managed it and Chao was able to use some of the harness fastenings. Pandas had unique paws – one of the wrist bones was elongated and could be used like a thumb. Usually this enabled them to grasp the bamboo stalks and to climb trees. Today it enabled Chao to snap the safety harness used for the waist in place. The shoulder harness that buckled he could not manage. Lakota told him to pull out the handle on the saddle and hang on.

Chao had been used to flying with T'a Ming – if one ever got used to such a thing. He had grown accustomed to the way she rose straight off the ground and undulated through the air. Riding this dragon was very different. Even though Chao kept his eyes closed he could feel that difference.

First of all there was a powerful feeling of thrust beneath him and then they spiraled up in the air rather than rising vertically – the Panda would have been dizzy if he had been able to look and see the world going round. Chao was also conscious of the beating of the great wings. He seemed to notice the rush of wind – he did not know it but Lakota was going far faster than normal, using his long dragon sight to search for T'a Ming. Even from the air, a white Imperial should be easy to spot.

It did not take long to locate her – she was indeed at the edge of a bamboo forest – as bamboo grew too thick for her to get in amongst the trees – and she was in trouble.

It took Ch'ang but a moment to realize what Si Wang was up to, demanding the foreign Sorcerer come with her. She still cherished the foolish idea that she could have a son by a magician that would then be an unconquerable warlord – enough to rival Genghis Khan. She was a very stupid woman – surely she realized by now that she was more than likely barren? She had slept with dozens, if not hundreds of men and she had never become pregnant – not at least since Ch'ang had been with her – and in that time she had been intimate with so many men that Ch'ang had lost count.

He had tried to get her to give over this foolish plan – the foreign devil did not seem as if he was eager to cooperate but Si Wang thought herself irresistible and clever. The *fan qui* looked as if he would not tolerate her evasiveness as to the whereabouts of his woman for very long.

But she would not listen to his protests, riding off with the Sorcerer back to Kwen-Lum.

Then the old man had arrived and announced that Ch'ang might as well give up – he was defeated and his days of evil were finished. Even now the Prince's soldiers were arriving to arrest him and he would be tried for crimes against the state – he would be found guilty and beheaded.

Ch'ang had panicked and before he thought of any

plan, he dematerialized blindly and arrived at the first place he thought of – a grove of bamboo, where they had caught their very first dragon.

How it rankled that he did not have even one pearl! He dared not return to the fortress. The old man said that the young foreign devil would stop at nothing to have his wife returned. And as far as Ch'ang was concerned, that was a danger that Si Wang could face alone.

But he regretted those pearls – all that work for naught – he had still not unlocked their secrets. A copy of the *T'ai Ping Kwang Chi* was easily obtainable anywhere – but the pearls – it was a great, a tragic, an unfair loss. Now he would never be adviser to the Emperor, the wisest man in China and –.

His ruminations were interrupted by a noise. He had hidden himself within the thick growth of bamboo trunks and was well out of sight. Something large had just arrived and he peered out, carefully, keeping to the shadows.

He could not believe his luck! A dragon! A lone dragon, a white one, with the pearl gleaming at its throat.

Could he take it? Could he manage to kill it without the aid of Si Wang's young ropers, and the caterpillar that destroyed the brain?

He watched it for a moment – it was a female he decided and a fearful and timid one at that. She looked all about herself again and again, cowering at the slightest sound.

For some strange reason she was stripping bamboo from the trees and digging up its roots. This was odd behavior – as far as Ch'ang knew dragons did not ingest bamboo – but it mattered little. She was not a large *lung* either.

Ch'ang grew confident, this would be easy – and even ONE pearl was better than none – even one pearl could make him wise and wealthy.

He lifted his staff and a flock of swallows appeared in the sky. Just as he thought, the *lung* forgot what she was doing and lunged at them.

He cast his net of black energies.

35

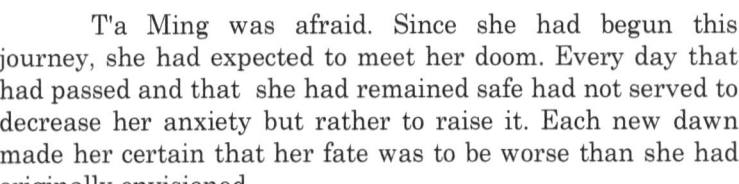

Amongst The Bamboo

T'a Ming was afraid. Since she had begun this journey, she had expected to meet her doom. Every day that had passed and that she had remained safe had not served to decrease her anxiety but rather to raise it. Each new dawn made her certain that her fate was to be worse than she had originally envisioned.

She was aware that to go off by herself like this was foolish but in one way she wanted to wait no longer – if her fate awaited her in the bamboo forest she wished to meet it. She was physically sick from worrying.

And at any rate, she could not let Chao go hungry. He was her friend and had been her friend for years. She did not begrudge in the least the time and effort it took her to gather bamboo for him. Instead, she made certain that she chose the choicest shoots, stalks and roots for him.

She had made quite a nice pile for Chao when the swallows burst from the bamboo wood. With a gasp of delight she lunged at them, hoping to catch five or six in her jaws. Breakfast had been a long time ago and to a Chinese *lung* there was nothing better than a swallow – or several.

When she felt the net close over her she knew she was lost.

The black energies were powerful and bore her to the ground. She did not even try to escape – the stories she had heard from the other *lung*, of how escape was futile filled her mind. This then was death.

She offered no resistance when the magician emerged from the shelter of the close-growing bamboo. She knew at once who and what he was.

Ch'ang surveyed her in satisfaction. She was not fighting the web, nor was she shrieking in rage. She crouched low to the ground, the net holding her down, and regarded him with large eyes.

"I am glad to see that you accept my mastery," he said approvingly, stepping close to her.

She lifted her head, as much as the enveloping net of black energies allowed. "Yes " she said in her low voice. "I am prepared for my fate."

Ch'ang considered her for a moment. He had no need for her flesh or talons or skin – he had no way to harvest them. "I shall let you live," he said abruptly, "if you give me your pearl. That is all I really want. Your pearl for your life – it seems a fair bargain."

T'a Ming stared at him. "But my pearl holds my *Tao*!" she said, in protest. "Where would I store my wisdom? And with my *poh shan* it enables me to fly! I would be a ground dweller without my pearl – and it cannot be replaced! I was born with my pearl – it is mine!"

"No," said Ch'ang, growing tired of her "It is now mine. I have given you your choice – give me the pearl freely and you shall live or I shall take it by force and you shall die."

A voice overhead said grimly "She will do neither!"

There was a great clap of wings and Lakota thumped down almost directly in front of Ch'ang. Steam was trickling from his nostrils and his ruff was fully extended around his head.

Chao, fumbling with the straps that held him on Lakota's back, finally slid to the ground with a growl of rage. A Panda's usual vocalization was a friendly bleating, rather like that of a lamb or a goat. They could also huff and bark and even honk, and Chao made all these sounds as he stood on his hind legs and waved his large paws at the magician threateningly. He could not remain in this posture for long and in spite of his impressive size he simply did not look dangerous.

But Lakota did look dangerous as he allowed a flame to shoot from his maw, where teeth as long as Ch'ang's arms gleamed white. His teeth were far more formidable than those of the Chinese *lung*.

Ch'ang reacted instantly – he threw another net of black energies over this odd-looking dragon.

To his chagrin it dissolved in the air before it even touched the blue dragon's back.

"That won't work on me," Lakota told him. "Nor will the caterpillar – I shall flame it! And I shall flame you unless you release her!" Another tongue of flame shot from his mouth, igniting the grass at Ch'ang's feet. "And you needn't think your magic will save you – I've flamed several magicians!" This last was sheer bluff. But Lakota reasoned, Ch'ang did not know this.

The Necromancer saw nothing for it but to escape before he was a pile of smoking ashes. Even obtaining the pearl was not worth it. Discretion was the better part of valor. With a curse, he once again disappeared in a swirling pinwheel of black and red energies. As he left, the net over T'a Ming fell to pieces.

Lakota wished he had a way to follow the magician. Simon and Feng Hu would be sorry that he had escaped them yet again. But T'a Ming's life was far more important.

He looked down – he had followed the sparkling spiral of the sorcerer's departure – and saw that T'a Ming and Chao were touching noses, even as the Panda was busily scolding her.

"Don't you ever do that to me again!" Chao said in anger, as he rubbed his nose fondly to T'a Ming's. "I have never been so worried in all of my life! When we were coming in and I saw that black net over you -"

"You saw me – from the air?" T'a Ming said in surprise. "You opened your eyes?"

Chao blinked and looked at her in surprise. "I did open my eyes! I was so worried about you that I must have opened them sometime on the way here!"

Lakota listened with interest. "Were you afraid?" he queried.

Chao thought a moment. "I don't remember being afraid –!" he continued, suddenly excited. "I wonder – perhaps I could climb a tree?"

T'a Ming was excited as well. "Here are bamboo trees you can climb!" she said. "Oh, do try , Chao!" She knew what a difference it would make to his life if he overcame this fear of his – he could be with other Pandas, find a mate and gather food when he needed it, not just when she could fetch it for him.

Chao lumbered over to a nearby bamboo tree and peered at it with a speculative look on his face. He put his front paws up against the trunk and then very slowly, he began to climb. He was slow and clumsy at first – Pandas were not noted for their grace – but he seemed to gain confidence as he went up.

"Look at this marvelous bamboo!" he exclaimed. "It is so fresh and green!" He paused to browse amongst the shoots, enthusing over the bamboo shoots he was able to get, completely fresh as they grew on the tree.

Fifteen minutes later, when Lakota said that they had to go or Simon would be getting worried. T'a Ming had picked a large bag of bamboo for her friend and Chao was a convert to tree climbing.

He rode T'a Ming back to the fortress and never once closed his eyes.

It was an atmosphere smelling of April and May, Ash thought. The fortress was full of lovers. Simon and Tatya, overjoyed to be reunited, the boy Gui and his Jing Mai and Jian and Ping.

He felt rather *de trop* – even Feng had a smile of reminiscence on his old face, thinking about his younger days with the Genii Queen, while the Prince was busily supervising the soldiers, who had begun arriving. Ash was the only one with nothing to do.

Both Tatya and Ping had been glad to learn that the village girls had escaped from the bandits unharmed and even now were on their way home.

Prince Tuan was pleased that the bandits were finished, at little expense to the kingdom. He had greeted Feng's suggestion of that the terra-cotta statues be buried in a deep trench with approval. "Perhaps, " said Feng with a sly smile, "someone will find them one day and wonder who they are and why they are there."

The only one not happy with the outcome of all of this was Dr. Quong. Although he was very pleased that his beloved *lung* need no longer go in fear of their lives, he could not approve of Jian's defiance in retaining his wanton wife. He was only mollified to an extent when he discovered that he had another grandson – one could never have too many sons or grandsons, even if their mothers were pleasure woman.

Tatya and Ping both were eager to return to the

Hunag Lung as they were anxious about their children.Tatya had the greatest confidence in Janus's abilities, but she was not as certain about Ping's servants – they had seemed silly and hysterical.

By the time that all the loose ends were tied up though, it was a little late in the day to leave for the Huang Lung. Lakota was tired – he would have to carry a party of six which was all that there was room for on his saddle. Gui and Jing Mai were going to ride back while the Prince was going to stay with the troops. He had decided that it would be well for the empire if the fortress were to be repaired and used as an outpost for Imperial troops to guard against more bandits in the area. The ill-gotten goods would of course go into the Imperial Treasury in the Forbidden City.

It seemed a long time to Tatya before she could finally be alone with Simon and they could really talk. There was so much she wanted to tell him and so much she wanted to hear about. She wanted to be alone with him for another reason as well. Drawing down the moon had had its usual effect on her.

Simon had laughed with pleasure when she whispered what she wanted and had obligingly taken her to the tent they preferred to stay in. Tatya had had quite enough of the fortress.

Afterwards, she lay in the crook of Simon's arm and sighed in satisfaction. "Perhaps we just made a brother or sister for Alan," she said dreamily. "I never wanted him to be an only child. If we have another child soon it will be old enough to play with him."

Simon agreed. His one regret about his childhood was that he was almost ten years older than his brother Stuart. It would have been nice to have a brother nearer his own age. "Tell me exactly what happened in the valley and how you ended up naked on a hillside having to draw down the moon. I only heard the bare bones outline," he suggested, when they had thoroughly discussed the possibilities of another child.

Tatya started from the beginning, giving every detail. Simon was angered by Hong's actions, she could tell and when he said brusquely, "It's a lucky thing for him that he is dead," she shivered a little, for his voice was very hard and cold. Hong had an easy death compared to what Simon and Lakota might have done to him – for the blue dragon had been just as angry as Simon was,

Dragons did not truly understand the concept of rape. A British or American dragon mated for life and would never think of taking an unwilling female, not especially a female that was mated to another male. Lakota was angry that someone had stolen Tatya from their family and that she had been treated badly but to him, the fact that Hong lusted after her and would take her whether she wanted him to or not was utterly foreign to draconic morals.

"In many ways, "said Simon, when they had discussed this, "our dragons are morally superior to man. They don't steal or lie – they do exaggerate for a good tale – and they would never think of taking a female by force. They can be too literal-minded, particularly when they are young, and they do hoard gold and jewels. But when they love, it is unconditional and they seem to be largely free of jealousy. Of course, they are not all like this – the Ice dragons in Russia were jealous, manipulative, and arrogant – much like our dragons might have been before Merlin changed them."

"It is too bad in a way I could have not set Lakota on Hong! I would have loved to see Hong's face if Lakota landed in front of him, breathing smoke and flames and threatened to roast him to a nicely done crispiness!" said Tatya wistfully.

"But at least he is dead," said Simon. "He was an evil man and deserved to die."

"He screamed a long time, falling down the cliff," said Tatya. "Perhaps it makes me bloodthirsty and unfeminine, but I am glad I killed him. He hurt so many people – not just me."

"I could not believe the height of that cliff!" Simon said. "However did you manage it with only a coil of rope and nothing save shoes to wear?" He had already treated her many cuts and scrapes with healing ointment

"I was just so mad at Ping – she had objections to being naked – as if we had *decided* to go climbing naked! – and to looking at my bare buttocks -"

"I am always happy to look at your bare buttocks," said Simon with a grin.

Tatya ignored him. "But it's all over now and we can go home!" she said. "I will be very glad to be at home again!"

Simon's grin faded. "We can't go home as yet, Tatya," he said, suddenly sobered. "We've got to find that fool Tom and his idiot employer. The Prince wants him out of the country."

Tatya lifted her head and twisted around to stare into his face. "Oh, no!" she said. "Do we have to be responsible for them? What abut the Necromancer – do you have to chase him down as well? "

"Feng insists that he will take care of the Necromancer but wants me to help him track the man down. And Tom is my kinsman – " Simon began.

Tatya made a face. "I still find that hard to believe – he is the last person I would ever suspect of being related to you! Very well, we will go after the awful Tom, and help locate the Necromancer, but Alan and I are NOT going to be left behind this time! I don't want to be carried off by another lust-crazed bandit!"

36
Jade Dreams

Ch'ang fled from the strange dragon, paying no attention to where he sent himself, going to the first place that came in to his mind – an action that Simon could have told him was foolish, for dematerialization was risky under the best of circumstances and if one did not know where one was going the consequences could be serious.

Ch'ang was fortunate – he came out of the spell to find himself sitting in a tree near a traveler's campsite on a road leading from the south – the very road he had traveled to reach Si Wang's fortress to the northwest. It was not particularly where he wanted to be – he had been thinking along the lines of Hindustan, where black magicians were appreciated – particularly in the cult of the goddess Kali – but any place was better than being in the company of the blue dragon who could breath flame and claimed to have burned magicians to a crisp.

Ch'ang's arrival did not go unnoticed. The traveler's area was full of people, for it was nearing the end of the day and in the heat, many had chosen to stop early.

Some of the peasants had fled, shrieking, in to the shelter of a grove when the fiery pinwheel had appeared and lodged itself in a tree.They did not wait to see it turn itself into a man.

Several persons were made of sterner stuff and watched with calculated interest as Ch'ang attempted to extricate himself from the tree's embrace.

A man dressed as a peasant gave a nod to a big man who came forward and handed Ch'ang down from the tree.

"Many thanks," said Ch'ang rather breathlessly, once his feet were again on the ground.

The big man, who, judging by the size of the sword that hung at his waist, the knives in his belt and the rifle and ammunition belt he wore was either a guard of some sort or a bandit, bowed and said. "My master presents his compliments and begs that the honorable Sorcerer join us for tea."

Ch'ang bowed in return, accepting the invitation. He could do with a cup of tea after the morning he had suffered.

He was conducted with grave courtesy to a campfire where four men sat, and near them, two foreign devils were tied to a sapling. Ch'ang frowned at this sight. He had no desire for the company of foreign devils, but as they appeared to be prisoners, he made no demur.

The big man introduced himself as Lao Min and the others his brothers Gang and Djan, and the peasant as his master Zhang.

Ch'ang was welcomed effusively and plied with a fine tea and a plate of stew. Zhang let him eat and sip at his tea until he remarked shrewdly "You present all the appearance of a man fleeing from something or someone."

Ch'ang looked up sharply. Was he so easy to read?

"Do not bother to deny it," Zhang said. "It is written on your face for all to se and in the condition of your robes and hair. But tell me, what could have so frightened a Sorcerer? For there is no doubt that is what you are – no ordinary man could travel in such a fashion."

As Ch'ang was not forthcoming, Zhang continued "We are all fugitives here. And fugitives who have come across what might be a very lucrative proposition, for which a Sorcerer might be very useful indeed. Would you like to be very, very wealthy, Sorcerer?" He smiled in an ingratiating fashion.

"Who would not?" Ch'ang said slowly. What had these bandits have in mind – for he now had no doubt that were bandits. Not more dragon captures! In spite of his regret over the loss of the pearls and of all his loot at the fortress, he had decided he was done with dragons.

Zhang reached in to the front of his tunic and withdrew a folded piece of parchment that crackled between his fingers. "This is a map," he said, "to a place in which the jade lies upon the ground for the taking. No one knows of this save us, for it is far to the north in lands long uninhabited and shunned by men."

Gingerly, Ch'ang took it and opened it. It did indeed seem to be a map of some sort but the writing upon it was indecipherable. "What foolishness is this?" he grumbled, looking up over the parchment to Zhang. "It is not readable!"

291

"It is in the foreign devil tongue, which I can speak but cannot read," Zhang explained. He waved his hand towards the two prisoners. "They, however, can, both of them, read it. And they will be useful as slaves when it comes to removing the jade from its resting place."

Ch'ang looked doubtful. His experience with foreign devils had not been fortunate. "Are either of them Sorcerers?" he asked suspiciously.

Zhang laughed heartily. "A foreign devil with magic? Such does not exist – they are too crude, too stupid to apply their small minds to the study of magic! They care for one thing – making money. That is why these two pollute the Middle Kingdom with their *fan qui* stench – to steal from us the stones of heaven that should be ours."

Ch'ang did not enlighten Zhang – he too well remembered a certain young foreign devil who seemed the have very powerful magic at his fingertips. But he said nothing, comforting himself with the thought that if these two foreign devils had magic they would not have let themselves be tied to a slender sapling and used as slaves.

He allowed himself to be persuaded into helping the what he was now certain were bandits. Zhang seemed to think that Ch'ang would be able to locate the mine easily and even transport the jade to a safe place to sell it.

Ch'ang was not about to correct this thinking – there would be time enough for that when they had located the jade. He intended to steal as much of it as he could and then either kill or abandon the bandits – for he had no doubt at all that they intended to do the same to him. The two foreign devils would be dead if they were not needed, and they would not long survive the finding and the exploitation of the mine.

Yes, he would play along with these bandits until he could assure his own wealth. And then he was for Hindustan where his knowledge of the black arts would be welcomed and the jade wealth he secured would make him a prince amongst Sorcerers.

The next morning Lakota flew his passengers to the Huang Lung Valley.

It was shocking to see the difference in the valley that had been wrought by the bandits' attack. Burned out ruins of homes were the least terrible thing – far more horrible was the amount of new graves. and grieving faces to be seen. "When they had landed at Dr, Quong's residence, it, too, was in falling-down shape.

Feng Hu said to Simon "You and I, young *Wu*, may repair these dwellings for these people but we cannot repair their hearts nor fill the empty places at their tables."

After a joyous reunion with Alan and a report from Janus as to how well he had behaved – as good as gold, the cat said. Simon had a serious talk with Dr. Quong. As Tatya had, Simon felt that they had brought the disasters upon the valley by coming here.

Dr. Quong would not hear of this.What had happened had happened. There was no telling, if even without Simon's family present, if the bandits might have come to the valley. The dragon's anger, which had so nearly caused the flood, would have killed many more people than did the bandits if Simon had not been there to prevent it. And Dr. Quong's own family would have been killed in the earthquake if it were not for Simon.

Dr. Quong was far kinder to Simon than he was to Ping.

"He treats her as if she were a prostitute!" Tatya fumed to Simon that night as they were preparing for bed. "Ping is exasperating but she does not deserve to be made to feel as if she belongs somewhere in a brothel! She invited none of what happened to her! That man who wanted her – Lui – he was an enormous, strong man – she could not more have prevented him ripping her clothes off and touching her that she could have prevented the flood! I don't understand these people at all! It's perfectly acceptable for a husband to take another woman, right in front of his wife, and her parents tell her that she should watch carefully for purposes of instruction, but to let another man see her naked and touch her body when it is no fault of her own and she can't prevent it – ! When we first came here I respected Dr. Quong, but now

I think he's a contemptible, hidebound, old idiot!" she finished angrily.

"I think he's wrong, too, Tatya," said Simon quietly, "but at least Jian is glad to have her back and perhaps in time Dr. Quong will soften towards her as well. We can't change the way he thinks. He, Feng Hu and the Prince were all shocked that I would let the warlord inveigle me into going with her – just to rescue you. Their attitude was that you were only a woman and I could replace you easily. Only Ash understood how I felt – how I would do anything rather than see a hair on your head harmed."

"I wish we were going home, *now* Simon," she said suddenly, allowing the brush she had been drawing hastily through her hair to drop. "Lakota told me he wants to go home as well, and Alan said today that he wanted to go and see his grandparents." Her voice was very wistful. She put the brush aside and went to lean against him as he sat bolstered up by pillows. "When we first married and we went to live in Ireland I thought I would never get used to it and I was so homesick for Russia..."

"I know," he said in a low voice, his hand coming up to rest on her hair. "I felt awful, taking you so far from everything that was familiar and dear to you."

"Everything seemed strange – even the weather –" she admitted. "But now – I think of Ireland as home, as if I've always lived there. And I am impatient to get back."

"Feng and I are going to do a casting for the Sorcerer tomorrow and Tom left behind a pocket handkerchief that I will use to locate him with a pendulum," Simon informed her. "And don't worry – Tom shan't come home with us – I shall see him and Faversham put on a British ship under close guard. We are to stay with Anatoly and Marushka on the way home, as well as with Dr. Swensen, and Tom is no one that I would care to introduce to our friends, much less claim him as a close relative! Hopefully, we shall be on our way soon and perhaps even able to move into the new house before Michaelmas Term begins."

"That would be wonderful," said Tatya on a sigh. "How I long for everything to be back to normal!"

Tom, too , was longing for everything to be back to normal. He finally admitted that he had been a fool even to leave England, and fervently wished himself back there, sitting in his club listening to a prosy old bore such as General Mandeville talk of tiger shooting in India. At this time of night the servants would be brining 'round tea and coffee, with a 'little something' before the members left for their homes or retired to the rooms upstairs, with such things as hot buttered toast, crumpets with orange marmalade or black currant jelly and potted prawns to spread on the toast.

It had seemed so easy when Faversham had shown him the map. Go to China with a rich fool and stuff his pocket full of Oriental jade – sell it and make a handsome profit. But nothing had turned out as planned.

Things were worse than ever now. The map was in the possession of this Zhang who smiled at them in an oily, knowing way that Tom did not like at all. The man's smile made a chill run up his spine. Zhang was dressed as a peasant, but the mere fact that he spoke and understood good English told Tom that this man was not what he seemed. The three Lao brothers were exactly what they seemed to be – professional thieves and probably assassins as well.

And now they had been joined by a Chinese Wizard – not a very good one in Tom's estimation – even Faversham had said "Oh, bad show!" when the Sorcerer had landed up in a tree. What were they planning?

And what was even more critical – how could he escape? For Tom cared very little about Faversham – it was his own skin that mattered to him. Faversham could bloody well take care of himself.

37
The Hunt Begins

Ch'ang had learned a trick which would be the envy of many a Western Wizard. He could actually transport one person with him when he dematerialized. This was how he proposed to move the entire party quickly to the approximate location of the jade mine in the north. The map was clearly marked as to landmarks and Ch'ang was quite confident that with the landmarks near the mine firmly fixed in his mind, as translated by the *fan qui* he would have no trouble traveling there via magic. When told that the guide hired by the foreign devils was unable to follow the landmarks he concluded scornfully that the guide – and the foreign devils – were morons.

To make certain of his notion, early on the next morning, he went it by himself.

And he came out exactly where he had hoped – in a field between the two major landmarks – a mountain shaped like a camel's two humps and a dead, forked tree. Whoever had drawn the map was very accurate. He hoped that the depiction of the whereabouts of the jade mine was as accurate – it was marked off in paces, and as close as they had figured, it was less than two miles from the field.

Upon returning to his new confederates he at once began transporting them, one by one.

It was a taxing undertaking for there were the three Lao brothers, Zhang and the two foreign devils to take to the location. There were goods to be transported as well – including Zhang's two rope-bound boxes.

This form of quick travel was hard on the magician, but Ch'ang had become used to the feeling of being torn apart, and the disorientation and vertigo engendered by the bending of time and distance. The Necromancer was merely completely exhausted when the task was completed, but his 'passengers' were very ill indeed. None of them could even stand upright and just lay about the field, where he had deposited them, feeling as if they might as well be dead.

After the last trip – for the supplies they would need – Ch'ang too, collapsed, fatigue making his limbs shake and his vision blur. He would recover by tomorrow, but looking at the rest of them – most of whom had been wretchedly ill and given up the contents of their stomachs – he doubted if they would be any good for anything for several days, much less going treasure hunting as they had planned.

And he himself was far and away too tired to play nursemaid and set up a shelter or even make some reviving tea. That would have to wait until he had recovered somewhat.

Leaving the others to their own devices Ch'ang turned his back on their misery and went to sleep. He would make tea when he felt better.

Simon was very interested in seeing how Feng Hu intended to trace the Necromancer. The elderly *Wu* had never heard of pendulum dowsing and was as eager to see this performed as Simon was to witness his methods.

The two magicians spent the early part of the day doing what they could to restore the valley. Lakota helped as well – the blue dragon tore down wobbling walls and dug pits to bury debris and even in some cases, bodies that were discovered in the rubble remnants of building. Meanwhile, Tatya worked on Dr. Quong's home. The Chinese Draco-philologist was overjoyed to find that his entire library had been saved from the bandits' depredations – Tatya had even stored the translation table and Simon's gift of his new manuscript in the room that had sheltered the maids and the children.

But some things could not be repaired, even by magic. Bedding was torn and stained beyond fixing and some porcelain broken in to naught but small shards. And in many homes, the bandits had made off with jewelry, pictures, coins and other easily transported commodities. Prince Tuan was sending scribes to make lists of claims of what had been stolen so that possibly precious possessions and needed money could be returned to their rightful owners. Simon also decided to contribute a sizable sum of money to the rebuilding effort. He could well afford it and still felt guilty that perhaps his family's presence had brought this tragedy to the valley, no matter what Dr. Quong said to the contrary.

When they had returned to Dr. Quong's home after a morning's difficult work, Feng looked fine drawn and pale, as if he had over extended himself. He seemed slightly revived after a light luncheon and tea, and insisted, over Simon's protests. on doing the ceremony that could trace the Necromancer.

He chose, as the place for this ceremony, the garden, in the now repaired pavilion near the lotus pool. He invited Simon to come with him, but wanted no one else to be present. He took a small gong, a tea pot, tiny cups and the makings of tea and a small brazier and incense with him.

The brazier was lit and the small brass kettle filled with water and the kettle put on to boil. On the edge of the pool Feng placed a cushion and this he sat upon, cross-legged, the gong nearby. As the kettle began to boil and the incense to send out a strange sweet fragrance, Feng began to chant in a sing-song, ancient tongue that Simon could almost, but not quite understand.

Lakota was nearby, dozing in the afternoon sun. He had repaired the garden as best he could but it was a sad reflection of its former beauty. it would take more than just magic to become again what it once was – it would take years of tender loving care as well.

As Feng continued to chant the blue dragon woke and stretched, with a yawn, and then cocked his head, looking at Feng curiously. "Why, that's Elfish!" he said at last. "It's different than what we speak, but it is Elfish, definitely!"

Lakota was right, Simon though in surprise. Little wonder it sounded so familiar. "You're summoning Faeries!" he said after listening carefully for several minutes.

Feng scowled at him. "You must not interrupt, young *Wu!*" he said crossly. "The beings whose cooperation I seek are shy and timid and do not help us readily. They must be coaxed, and served their special tea and..."

"Do you want to speak to the Faeries who live in the lotus blossoms?" Lakota interrupted. He stretched his neck towards the pool and said "Hello! Would you come out and speak with us, please?"

298

To Feng's shock a tightly furled lotus blossom began to open. The lotus bloomed in the early morning and closed by mid afternoon. Each bloom lasted but three days.

These lotus were known in the West as the Hindu lotus and were a deep pink in colour. The largest bloom unfolded and the petals began to spread. Each petal was revealed to be a creamy yellow at its base. And there on the golden stamen stood a little person, no bigger than Simon's palm.

Like her counterparts in the British Isles she had transparent wings, but hers were more like those of a butterfly than a dragonfly as was usual in the Six Nations. She was delicate in build with slender limbs and slim, long-fingered hands. A nimbus of coloured light – in this case pink, like her flower – surrounded her. Her features were Oriental and she was strangely lovely, in the inhuman manner of Faerie creatures. Unlike the Faeries Simon was accustomed to, she wore clothing. Most of the Faerie creatures he knew flitted about naked, no matter the season and most had skin the colour of leaves or flowers. This little Chinese faerie wore an elaborate robe such as a great Court lady of the Forbidden City might wear. Her smooth dark hair, too, was arranged in complicated fashion, with decorated orna-ments. Her complexion was the colour of old ivory and her black eyes were very bright as she studied them.

"Greetings, honorable Lah-koh-ta," she said, with a bow in the dragon's direction.

Greetings, Loi Yen," Lakota returned. with an answering bow.

"Of what do you wish to speak?" the little Faerie asked. Her voice was a sweet as a crystal chime heard from far away.

Feng Hu was stunned." But the summoning," he protested weakly. "I have not yet rung the gong, nor made the tea – "

Loi Yen said "I should like a cup of tea," with a an enchanting smile. "And such ritual is not necessary, venerable *Wu*. Perhaps in times past – but now one only need ask."

"Lakota has an affinity for Faeries," Simon explained. "I think he knows every Faerie in the British Isles"

299

"I met Loi Yen the very first night I spent in this garden," said Lakota happily "You should have told me, Feng Hu, that you needed to speak to a Faerie – I could have introduced you!"

"What is it that you want me to do?" the Faerie asked again.

Feng Hu had gone about making the tea automatically as Lakota made his explanation. "I need someone found, a magician like myself, who calls himself Ch'ang Hao."

"We know of him," Loi Yen said," but he is not a magician like yourself, for he is evil and we have named him false and dragon slayer. He is no friend to us – he has truck with demons. He sacrifices children to demons!" Her voice was full of horror and Simon understood at once that the Faerie peoples of China held children in as high regard as did their British Isles counterparts.

"Feng wants to find this black mage to punish him for having killed so many dragons," Lakota said.

Loi Yen looked at Feng in approval. "This is a noble undertaking," she stated. "We will do all that we may to find him. I will send out word this very night. We should know where he is by tomorrow afternoon. I should like my tea now," she added.

The little Faerie stayed to watch Simon do a dowsing with a pendulum.

Simon spread out one of the excellent maps supplied him in Canton as he explained to Feng Hu and Loi Yen that pendulum dowsing was a form of sympathetic magic. With the aid of something that belonged to the person he was searching for, the pendulum would search for that person's 'energy signature' which was unique to each person. This search was conducted through the ley lines and then would show the location on the map.

Simon wore an additional chain across the front of his waistcoat, along with his handsome hunter watch. It was a chain of Elfin silver – a wedding gift from Oberon, that ended in a very fine rose quartz pendulum, carved in tear drop shape.

Simon took a stool from the pavilion and placed it in front of the map. He tied Tom's pocket handkerchief just above the pendulum crystal. He then sat in a relaxed position and held the pendulum out over the map at about the height of his knees. He began swinging the rose crystal back and forth towards and away from himself. This was a neutral position he explained and he would ask the pendulum if it knew Tom from the 'signature' on his handkerchief, asking the question only in his mind.

After a few moments the pendulum, on its own, began to spin clockwise. "That means yes, it does know Tom," Simon explained it his fascinated watchers. "Counterclockwise would mean no."

The pendulum returned to its back and forth swing until Simon asked it another question: could it tell him where Tom was?

"Yes," it indicated and them began to spin faster and faster, until it stood almost straight out. Simon had to stand to accommodate its pull on him.

As rapidly as it had accelerated, it slowed and stopped over a remote region far to the north, near Mongolia.

"How did he manage to get that far in such a short length of time?" Lakota, who had watched the proceedings with interest, asked. "That is a long way from here!"

"They must have ridden those two horses that he stole into the ground," said Simon, frowning. "I'm going to cast two more times. The rule of three says that three times are the charm and always correct."

Twice more the rose crystal showed the same location without hesitation.

"That is where we must go, then," said Simon, as he returned the pendulum to his waistcoat pocket. "Feng, we shall wait until the Necromancer is found, and Lakota and I shall help you find him Then we shall go after Tom. After all, the Necromancer can wreak far more havoc than my cousin, who hasn't a magical bone in his body."

38

North Northwest

Lakota was increasingly impatient to be heading home. He did not see why they had to go after Tom – he could understand to an extent why they must find the Necromancer – suppose he started killing dragons again? – but Tom, the blue dragon felt, could be left to his own devices.

Therefore, the next afternoon, he was waiting impatiently in the garden near the lotus pool for the Faerie scouts to return.

Most of the humans were having tea in the pavilion. Only Tatya seemed to share Lakota's keenness to finish their tasks here and head home. And she felt as he did for the same reasons – she wanted to be back where everything was what she was used to. Even now, Ping still looked at her askance, no doubt thinking of their naked adventures and how brazen her Western guest had been. Tatya had talked it over with Simon and he had agreed she could have done little other than what she had done. But Ping's delicate sensibilities had been ruffled – although she was very happy that Jian had not repudiated her, she seemed to be slavishly apologetic to him and to her father-in-law, as if she was begging for their forgiveness.

Simon had told Tatya all that mattered to him was that she was alive, uninjured and with him again. He saw nothing to forgive.

And Tatya wanted to be back with people who would not be treating her as if she had done something truly dreadful. Ping could barely look at her.

Both Tatya and the dragon were relieved when several pink shapes flitted into the garden. A surprising amount of Faeries lived in the lotus blossoms and Loi Yen had sent some in each direction of the compass

A tiny Faerie, dressed as if he were a mandarin, flew up to Feng.

"Honorable Sorcerer," he said, hovering in mid-air as if he were a hummingbird and managing to bow deeply and

302

gracefully, "we have located the black magician. He is north and northwest of here, near to the border of the country you call Mongolia."

"That's where Tom is!" said Simon, puzzled. "However did that happen?"

"That simplifies things!" said Lakota happily. "We can take care of both of them at once. And then go home!"

"It's not quite that simple – " Simon began, but was interrupted by Feng.

"We will leave in the morning," said the elderly magician. "I wish to confront this evil as soon as is possible. We must make plans now. Where is that map?"

Only Simon, Feng and Ash, as well as Tatya and Alan (for she refused to be left behind again) would be going on this trip.

While Feng planned the route with Lakota, Ash and Simon had a low-voiced conversation.

"Is Feng up to this, do you think?" Ash asked. "Every day he looks more frail. I swear at times he looks almost transparent."

Simon, too, had noticed Feng's increasingly insubstantial air. It was if he was fading away and aging several decades each day. But his spirit was still strong, as was his determination. And he was adamant that he would be the one to deal with Ch'ang Hao.

Simon said as much to Ash. "I have no authority to keep him from what he wants to do," he admitted. "By taking him with us I can at least keep an eye on him and help him out if he needs it."

"I only wonder why he is so insistent on tackling this Necromancer by himself," Ash wondered. "He will only say that since he is Chinese he ought to take care of a black Chinese magician his own self."

Simon frowned. "There is something else going on there," he said slowly, "but I don't think Feng is willing to talk about it or will even reveal what it is until he thinks the time is right."

"He rather revels in being mysterious," Ash said on a sigh. "I own, I shall be glad when we have your cousin in custody and I am able to clap him and Faversham on a British man o' war and see them sailing out of Canton harbor."

"No gladder than I will be!" Simon said. "Cousin Tom is an added complication I never looked for. I wish he had stayed in England!"

Tom Stillfield was wishing the very same thing, and not for the first time.

First of all there had been the terrible trip to the location of the jade mine. Tom had never felt so ill in his entire life – and none of the others in the party had fared any better. He had been too ill even to try and escape – it was all he could do to lay on the ground and not wish for death. If that was how magicians commonly traveled he wished them joy of it – he never wanted to undergo that experience again. Only when the Chinese Wizard had made them some tea had he begun to feel as if he might want to go on living.

When they had recovered somewhat and located the jade field – the map proved to be accurate – the wily old Zhang had put them to work.

The magician was able to locate the jade with the use of a metal tool with which he struck the boulders. The pyroxene boulders containing the Stone of Heaven gave off a different sound – a more ringing tone – than did other boulders - and the blow could also expose the bloom of the jade – the 'pine needles' as it was known.

Jade was hard and normally painstakingly, patiently extracted with care and skill. But magic could locate and split the rock at the best place and lay bare the rich emerald green prize within.

Ch'ang did not wish to overextend himself so he confined his efforts to tapping and splitting the boulders. Tom and Faversham were set to digging them from the earth when the necromancer 'felt' the jade beneath the ground. The Lao brothers stacked it as the stones fell apart

Zhang, of course, did not dig nor do any work, other than greedily calculate how much wealth could be amassed from the sale of the stones. This was the finest quality jade – much of it just laying about in boulders on the ground. The magician said that there was a lot more in the mountainside and in the ground. Even a fast flowing stream nearby would yield small stones of excellent jade, suitable for jewelry

Zhang had questioned the foreign devils as to the source of the map – the one who resembled a sheep said that he had found it amongst his grandfather's papers – an ancestor on his mother's side who had been the captain of a ship that was in the Oriental trade. It had long lay hidden as his mother's people preferred to forget that anyone in their family had ever been in Trade – for such beginnings were shameful in society. The money it made was not shameful, of course, only the method of amassing the fortune. Such, in a generation or so, could be conveniently forgotten.

By nightfall of the first day they had a great deal of jade – such a large amount that Zhang could not believe it – even did he actually honor his agreement with the Lao brothers and with the magician they would all be very rich. And there was so much more to be taken!

This was a wild and desolate region of the country. There were no signs of any human habitation. Zhang congratulated himself on his foresight on leaving the previous campsite and going ahead to buy picks and shovels and supplies at a village – there would be no supplies here. Game seemed abundant so they would not go hungry and there was water – as well as a cave to use for shelter in inclement weather. The Sorcerer could be sent back for staples such as tea and rice, since he did not seem to be as physically affected by his mode of travel as did the rest of them.

Zhang had agreeable visions of an eventual full scale mining operation – he did not worry about the government here – it was too far from the Forbidden City – and they were so near to Mongolia that he might establish a trading route into Russia. The Emperor had a long memory so although Zhang himself could probably not return to China any time soon he could hire agents to sell the jade in the Middle Kingdom – the Son of Heaven would pay a long price for jade of this quality! Eventually, perhaps, Zhang could employ artisans who would carve the jade – increasing his profit – particularly if the artisans were slaves and were owed no wages.

When at last it grew too dark even for the magician's staff to light the holes from which the boulders were

305

extracted, Zhang allowed the work to stop for the day.

Tom and Faversham collapsed with exhaustion and shaking limbs. Neither one of them was used to the physical exertion that bending and lifting shovels full of dirt demanded. Their backs ached and their hands were covered in blisters. Zhang had allowed only short – too short – rest periods – and a very small luncheon of unleavened bread and dried meat, washed down by tepid tea. If they showed any signs of slacking, the eldest Lao brother had cracked a whip over their hapless hides.

Faversham, to Tom's disgust, seemed to think that Zhang would eventually let them go. Tom labored under no such misapprehension – when their usefulness was ended Zhang would have them killed. That was why it was so important to try and escape.

The Lao brothers were very cautious – Tom and Faversham were tied up tightly at night and well guarded even while they were working. One of the brothers even inspected the area in which they were tied for rocks with sharp edges that the heavy ropes might be sawed apart, or for other rocks that could be used as weapons. Which ever brother was on guard duty made both Tom and Faversham turn out their pockets before they were tied up again so that there was no opportunity to slide a knife like sliver of jade into a pocket for later use.

Tom furiously made and discarded plan after plan as he dug the boulders from the hard ground. Should he beat out the Lao brother's brains with his shovel and try and run for it? No – there were two other brothers, Zhang and the magician as well – who could catch him easily with a spell. And where would he run to? He had no supplies, no money and had no real idea where they were, so far to the north northwest as they were. His shoes and clothes ware falling apart.

It never occurred to him that Simon would come looking for him. Tom had no family loyalty and if the situation were reversed, he would have never gone looking for Simon.

That was why, when on the afternoon of the third day of digging, when a huge shadow glided overhead and violet and jade green bolts shot to the ground near the Lao brothers, he was as startled and frightened as were the others and, like them, dived into one of the holes for protection.

39

Hsien

"Look out!" screamed the eldest Lao brother, Min, as Lakota swooped down on them, both magicians sending out bolts of light towards the men.

Feng concentrated upon Ch'ang, who wasted no time in throwing up black waves of energy from the tip of his staff towards the diving dragon.

Lakota easily evaded Ch'ang's blasts of magic – he was too used to the dodges and feints of dragon-ball and he was amazingly quick at turning and rolling.

Only Simon and Feng rode the blue dragon. Simon had insisted on Tatya and Alan, guarded by Ash, remaining a distance away on the mountainside.

The Lao brothers had made a mistake. Only one of them – Min – was armed – they had been so confident that no one was about that the guns were laid to one side so that the brothers could concentrate on helping with the jade. Gang and Djan had leaped into holes to protect themselves from the dragon attack. Min, who had been making certain that Tom and Faversham did not stop work until they were told to do so, leveled his rifle and fired at Lakota.

Simon deflected the bullet with a wave of his wand and it loudly ricocheted off a stony cliff.

Faversham had stood there with his mouth open, looking at the dragon as if he had no idea what he was looking at. Tom grabbed at him as he dived into a hole, dragging the hapless idiot with him. If they were about to be rescued Faversham owed him a considerable sum of money and if his employer was dead there would be no way to collect it.

Tom could not believe his eyes – his cousin had actually come after him! What could have prompted such familial affection? In Simon's place, Tom would not have come. Cynically, as he watched the magical battle from his hole, Tom thought that the jade mine and its riches had proved irresistible to Simon after all. Perhaps he, Tom, still might come away from this misadventure with some riches, if he played upon Cousin Simon's sympathies, and pointed out how much he had suffered.

Ch'ang was exceedingly angry and threw black energies recklessly, not even troubling to shield himself. What was wrong with these people? Why could they just not let him be?

From the first he sensed that the real danger, for him, was from the ancient Chinese magician. He seemed to be concentrating all his jade green energy bolts upon Ch'ang and the Necromancer was forced to do use his staff as deflector again and again. The violet energies from the foreign devil magician seemed to be focused on keeping the Lao brothers from participating in the battle – one burst of light destroyed the guns laid near their campfire and another struck the gun from Min's hands.

If only that dragon would stop darting back and forth so! He rolled in the air, back-winged, turned at sharp angles and did impossible maneuvers that Ch'ang had never seen a dragon do before. It was difficult to get a clear shot at the creature and when he did manage a bolt up into the air it was exploded against a wall of violet light. The foreigner was protecting his dragon.

Finally Ch'ang had to dive into a hole when the jade green bolts came fast and thick, too fast to counter – and the necromancer was at a disadvantage – the dragon moved so quickly that he had no idea where the bolts might next strike at him. So Ch'ang, too, retreated to a hole and bobbed up and down, lobbing black lightning at the dragon and his riders.

Feng was riding behind Simon and said quite loudly in his ear, "It is time to finish this, young *Wu*! Have the dragon land. I will meet this black magician on his own terms."

Simon did not like the sound of this but he leaned forward in the saddle and asked Lakota to land.

The blue dragon landed well away from the scene of conflict, The Lao brothers were brave but stupid – as soon as Lakota was in the ground they rushed from their holes, shouting and waving their arms.

Surprised, Lakota turned his head and let loose a thin stream of flame – it ignited the grass in front of them in a loud burst and halted them in their tracks.

"Must you make things more difficult for me?" grumbled Feng as he accepted Simon's help to slide from the saddle.

The old magician looked as frail as a long dead autumn leaf – his ivory skin was heavily wrinkled and transparent – withered , thought Simon, was a good word to describe his looks and demeanor. "Take me to the fire, young *Wu*," he ordered Simon and leaned heavily on the young Wizard's arm.

Lakota's fire now separated the others – Zhang and the Lao brothers, Ch'ang and Tom and Faversham, from the dragon back party.

Using Simon for support, Feng tottered up to the edge of the fire and took a deep breath, which seemed to give him some measure of strength. "Do not aid me," he said in a low voice to Simon. "I must do this myself – it is more important than you know."

"But why–?" Simon began, anxious for the health of the old man. He was so enfeebled! Did he expect to fight the Duel Arcane in his condition? Ch'ang was a man in his prime. True, Feng's magic had been strong while he was sending it after the Necromancer but could he keep it up? Did he have the strength to finish this battle? That he had the will to do it, Simon was certain – but whether his body was equal to the demands of his spirit was another matter.

"All will become clear in time," said Feng calmly. He let go of Simon's arm and took another deep breath and a step towards the fire.

"Let me douse the fire –" Simon said hurriedly but Feng ignored him and walked right through the wall of flame as if it were not there. Simon and Lakota exchanged looks of awe – even they could not do that. With a wave of his hand Simon extinguished the fire and followed Feng. He could at least prevent the other men present from interfering. He doubted if any of them had magic – if so, they had not used it so far.

Ch'ang rose from his hole as he saw the elderly magician approaching. "What do you want, old man?" he asked in a hostile tone. "Why are you persecuting me? I am no longer hunting dragons – that is what you wanted, is it not? Why do you not go and leave me in peace? What I do now does you no harm!"

"You are a black magician – you summon demons and sacrifice to them. As such, you must be destroyed. And you must be punished for your crimes against the *lung*," said Feng evenly.

"And *you* are going to punish me?" said Ch'ang in tones of disbelief. "You can scarce stand upright! Or is that foreign devil going to lend you his magic?"

"This is between us, evil one," Feng stated. "And yes, I shall punish you – have no doubt – I shall do it."

Ch'ang raised his staff and pointed it at Feng, saying a WORD of power.

To Simon, watching intently as Lakota kept an eye on the Lao brothers and Zhang, a black veil seemed to fall over Feng, obscuring him from sight and bearing him to the ground.

Simon lifted his wand. But before he could do anything, the veil was torn asunder by jade green light in a strong, almost blinding flash.

"Is that all that your congress with demons has gained you, evil one?" Feng asked scornfully. "A power that an apprentice – a poorly trained one – could muster? Now feel my full power! And take the form whose name you bear!"

A pillar of green fire shot up from the earth as Feng spread his hands. It enveloped Ch'ang, pulsing and glowing, covering him from view, flaring high into the sky.

But they could hear him screaming.

The pillar seemed to shrink in upon itself and then spread out in all directions, like a ripple caused by a rock thrown into a pool. It was impossible to look at it – the brilliance was painful.

It died as suddenly as if had come.

At first Simon saw nothing where the necromancer had stood – only his staff laying on the ground, next to what appeared to be limb from a tree.

But as Simon watched the thick limb stirred and raised an ugly, hooded head, with flat,cold bronze eyes. As Simon looked at it, it grew larger until it was nearly eighteen feet in length.

It was a King cobra, a Hamadryad – the largest of all

venomous snakes, brown in colour and deadly. Hamadryads were noted for their menacing aspect and for attacking without motivation.

"Do not think, evil one," said Feng to the snake "that you may strike me and kill me. You have no venom. Without that you shall be King of the Snakes, Ch'ang Hao, for but a small space of time, for you will have no defense against your enemies. Now crawl away and find a hole to stay in for the rest of your miserable existence."

The cobra reared up, hood flaring, as if to strike. Simon raised his wand and Lakota took a deep breath, ready to flame.

Feng stared the snake in the eye, his gaze as unblinking as that of the giant reptile.

The snake looked away first. It fell heavily to the ground and slithered away, awkwardly, for it was far more used to being a man and walking on two feet that in crawling on its belly over the ground. It headed in the direction of the foothills.

Behind it, on the ground, the forgotten staff disintegrated into ash.

Feng watched it go for only a moment, until the snake was out of sight and then the elderly magician fell to the ground, like a marionette whose strings had been cut.

Simon sprang forward and threw himself on the ground beside the old man. "Feng!" he said in severe anxiety and lifted the old magician's head and shoulders onto his arm.

Feng seemed to have collapsed in upon himself. His skin was like parchment and his breath was so faint that he seemed to have ceased breathing.

His paper thin lids were closed over his eyes, now sunken in his head – which was rapidly assuming the aspect of a fleshless skull.

"It is well," he said in a thread of a voice. "I am dying, my young *Wu*. It had been a long time in coming and I am content. If I am granted the felicity I shall soon be what all we long for – I shall be a *Hsien*."

"A *Hsien*?" Simon repeated. It was obvious that the old mage was dying and there was nothing he could do for him. It was as if Feng's extreme old age had suddenly caught up with him all at once.

312

"Many years ago," continued Feng in that faint, faraway voice, " I was told in a heaven sent vision that I would be spared death, and go into a long sleep, only to awake and combat evil. And when I had done that I would achieve a state of transcendence – I would be as one with nature, as the great *Lao Tzu* book of the *Tao* promises us. I would leave my earthy body and become immortal – a *Hsien* spirit. It is the wish of all of us who follow the way of the *Tao*. I shall have a new body, refined and immortal – and I shall partake of the bliss of paradise. Do not grieve for me, my young *Wu* – I am content. The *lung* are safe – the black magician is no more. I have accomplished the task that was set for me so long ago."

He gave a sigh and began to fade from Simon's arms, as if he were smoke. Very soon nothing was left, save a tiny wisp that was born away on a soft breeze. Feng Hu was gone.

40

The Last Of Zhang Bao

"What happened?" Lakota whispered, staring at Simon in consternation. "Where did Feng go?" Out of the corner of his eye he saw one of the Lao brothers move and he swiveled his head suddenly to bend a stern eye on him." Do not move," he said in Chinese, "unless you want to go up in flames!" He allowed a small flame to spurt from his mouth and showed his gleaming large white teeth to the Laos. They froze in place.

Tom clambered out of his protective burrow, not waiting to see if Faversham needed any help out. He strolled over to Simon and said in a pseudo-hearty, friendly tone, "Well met, cousin! I never thought to see you here! Is it the jade that brought you or is this actually a rescue?"

"Neither," said Simon brusquely. He had become fond of Feng Hu, and had learned much from him – and would have liked time to learn more. Tom was unwelcome – Simon would like to be alone with his new and raw grief. Tatya and Lakota would understand how he felt but Tom did not seem to possess an ounce of sympathy. He wore a knowing, insolent grin on his face.

"I have come to find you and your employer and remove you to Canton," Simon said. "The Imperial family of the Qing want you gone from this place."

"Not without my jade," said Tom, his smile fading.

"It isn't yours!" Lakota said forcefully. "It belongs to the Imperial House!"

"It is mine!" said Zhang Bao in English, coming up to them. He was covered in dirt from having dived into a recently dug hole and looked far from, prepossessing. But on his face that so resembled that of Confucius he wore a look of grim determination. "I lay claim to all of this jade! I have worked too hard –"

"*You* have worked too hard?" Tom interrupted him. "Faversham and I did all of the work! All you have done is sit on your arse and direct the work!"

"I grow tired of you, foreign devil," said Zhang coldly. "You are my slave –"

"I'm nobody's slave!" said Tom hotly. "You had the guns and all the advantage. Now I have a Wizard and a dragon on my side –"

"I am on nobody's side," Simon began, but was drowned out by an increasingly acrimonious argument between Tom and Zhang.

Simon left them to it and went over to where Lakota stood. "I' m ready to go home," he admitted to the dragon.

"I'm so sorry about Feng," Lakota said. "Did I hear him say that he was to become a spirit?"

Yes," Simon began to explain what he had understood of Feng's passing. When he was done Lakota nodded and said "It's getting late in the day, Simon. Why don't I go back and get Tatya and Ash? Then we shall get Tom and his friend and head back to Huang Lung." They had left most of their baggage and the familiars behind at the house of Dr. Quong.

Simon watched the blue dragon lift into the sky feeling, all of a sudden, very tired. Going home sounded so good to him. He just wished that it was not such a long journey. It would be wonderful to be at home – to see the family, to see how the new house was progressing, to begin preparing for the next term, perhaps even writing a monograph on the Asian dragons to present to the Royal Society in the autumn....

Lakota returned in but a moment with Tatya, Alan sleeping at her breast, and Ash, who had one of the new high-powered rifled slung over one shoulder.

Simon went forward to help Tatya slide down from Lakota's back and foreleg. "Lakota told us about Feng," she said softly. "I'm so sorry, Simon. I know that you liked him."

He did not have a chance to respond to this for Ash gave a muffled exclamation and said "You've captured Zhang Bao as well? Good job!"

"Zhang Bao?" Lakota exclaimed angrily, his tail lashing. "The man who bought all the parts of the slain dragons? Is that him?" He pointed with one talon to the man still arguing with Tom.

"Yes – he's changed a bit, but I saw him far too often in Canton to doubt that it is indeed him," said Ash. "What he

315

is arguing about with your cousin?" he inquired of Simon, for the argument had grown quite loud and angry.

"Who owns the jade," Simon answered tiredly. Tatya gave him a glance of sympathy.

Ash rolled his eyes. "It's neither of them, I can assure you. The Prince gave me to understand that no traitor like Zhang Bao, nor a foreigner such as Mr. Stillfield, would be allowed to profit by this find – a very rich one, I should say from all of the evidence I see," he added, looking at the amount of gleaming green laying about.

Tom turned his head and looked at Simon, his face black with anger. Nearby, Faversham stood wringing his hands, bleating helplessly "Oh, I say! I say!"

"Tell him, tell this fool that the jade is mine or you will change him into an orangutan!" Tom demanded of Simon.

Zhang looked contemptuous, until he noticed the other figures beyond Simon. He discounted the woman but when he saw Ash he blanched. He recognized Ash as Ash had recognized him. And the presence of the foreign devil from the Legation of the British Isles did not bode well for Zhang's continued freedom.

Zhang panicked. He was not about to go back to Canton disgraced, and probably be beheaded.

He pushed up his sleeve and pulled out a dagger he always wore in a sheath strapped to his arm. No one ever knew it was there – it was an excellent insurance policy.

It slid into his hand and he lunged forward and pressed it into Tom's side. "Stop!" he cried. "One move from any one of you and I will end his miserable life!"

Tom tried to twist away but Zhang's arm snaked up and went around his throat, all the while the knife still pressing into his ribs. The old man was a great deal stronger than he looked.

"Oh, I say!" protested Faversham.

"I want safe passage to Russia!" Zhang demanded. "You" he nodded his head towards Simon. "You will take me there on dragon-back, with as much jade as we can carry. Promise this or I shall kill him!" He pressed the knife in closer to Tom.

Tom tried to pull away from him but only ended in coughing and choking.

Simon raised his wand, which he still held, and violet power spilled from it. He begin to bring it up, as if to level it at Zhang and the merchant lost his head. He thrust the knife into Tom, pushed his sagging body away and began to run.

Lightning swift, Ash raised the rifle and shot him through the back of the head. Zhang fell without a sound, dead on impact.

Simon and Tatya rushed forwards to Tom. He was lying on the ground, a look of surprise on his face. Faversham was already kneeling beside him. He looked helplessly up at Simon his sheep – like features distressed. "It's his lung," he said. "Is there anything you can do?"

"I'm not a Healer," Simon said, equally distressed. "I'll try –" he pulled aside the remaining rags of Tom's jacket but saw at once that there was little he could do.

Even as Simon examined the wound Tom began coughing and a tremendous rush of blood gushed from his mouth. He lay back and looked up at Simon. A crooked grin suddenly twisted his bloody mouth. Faversham bent forward and wiped his mouth with his grimy pocket handkerchief.

"I was going to be rich – to go home wealthy and pay Dick back for stealing from me," he said almost dreamily. "Who'd have thought it would end like –" He broke into another spasm of coughing.

"Don't talk!" said Simon urgently. "I'm going to try some magic-"

Tom shook his head. weakly. "Too late." He looked up at Simon. "I always hated you," he said conversationally and then coughed again, this time flooding the area about him with his life's blood. He then gave a terrible shudder and lay still, not moving again.

"He's dead," said Faversham numbly.

After that there was little left to do.

Simon pit a preservation spell on Tom's body and they used one of the blankets to wrap it in.

During the confusion the Lao brothers disappeared into the hills. No one could be bothered hunting them down – they were bandits, true, but the last glimpse any one had had of them showed them to be terrified of Lakota and Simon and obviously intent on getting as far away as possible.

Ash took an sample of the jade to show to the Prince and after Lakota dug one of the holes deeper to bury what remained of Zhang, they loaded Tom's body into Lakota's breast harness. His body would l be sent home to England, Simon decided. via the ship that would take Reginald Faversham back to his family.

Ash had removed the map to the mine from Zhang's body – this too would go to the Prince.

Faversham made no protest at being returned to Canton. He was in shock from all that had happened, Simon thought. Perhaps the long voyage home would help him regain his equilibrium.

They stopped briefly in the Huang Lung valley. Tatya was pleased to see that Dr. Quong was beginning to thaw towards his daughter-in-law, who was indulging his every whim, and making all his favorite foods her own self. Tatya and Simon were both happy that Jian was treating his wife with love and devotion.

In Canton, Tom's body was placed in a sealed coffin under a strong preservation spell. Simon's party would arrive in the British Isles before the ship could do so and Simon would undertake to see the family at the Grange in Norfolk and tell them of Tom's last days. This was a grim duty, but one he felt he must undertake.

After an orgy of shopping – presents for everyone at home and furnishings for their new home, the dragon-back party left China with many good wishes. Three weeks later, after an uneventful and pleasant journey, they arrived back in Dublin. And all of them were very content to be at home once more.

Epilogue

Summerhills, outside of Dublin, Ireland. Early June, 1835

Once again it was end of term and the Long Vacation lay ahead.

"What are we going to do this summer, Simon?" Lakota queried as they set down in front of the dragon pen.

"I'm afraid most of the summer will be spent in packing and moving to America," Simon said. "We shall have to be in Boston by August at the latest – that is when the work on the Encyclopedia of Draconic Studies will begin."

Lakota was silent for a moment and then said on a sigh, "It seems as if we have just returned from China and here we are going off again."

"America is a great deal like home, Lakota. I already have friends there and there will be many dragons to keep you company. Unlike the Chinese dragons, they will think and act as you do. I'm quite certain that you will like it there."

"Tatya said that this is too great an opportunity for you to pass up – that your name will be on the title page of this great encyclopedia that will be used in every university in the world that studies dragons." The blue dragon sighed again. "I hope that things do go better in America then they did in China. It's not that I did not like the Chinese dragons – well, some of them," he amended. "But they treated poor T'a Ming very shabbily indeed and I still think that Xiang was intolerably conceited!"

"Simon!" a voice called as Simon slid off the dragon, and he turned to see Tatya hurrying towards them "You will never guess! An enormous box with the Imperial seals all over it has just arrived from China! And there are letters – from Ash Pendleton and Dr. Quong! I'm having the footmen bring the box out here to the dragon pen so that you can see what it is, Lakota!"

A few moments later two of the Summerhills footmen, followed by Alan, Janus, Marinka, and Marinka's new litter of kittens, who were just now old enough to toddle about on their own and get into mischief, bore a large wooden crate out to the dragon pen.

"I'll be getting a crowbar from the stables, ma'am," offered one of the footmen." 'Tis something like that we'll be needing to open this box, I'm after thinking."

Further behind the footman, in stately progress, came Ô Failhbe, the Summerhills butler, bearing a number of letters on a silver salver, followed by nearly every servant in the house, for all were agog to see what came in the big crate with the foreign markings.

Simon and Tatya had brought home a number of pieces of porcelain, Chinese scrolls and paintings on silk from their trip to the Orient – enough to create a Chinese room papered in Chinoiserie silk in their new home – the servants were now used to Oriental *objets d'art*, but they never tired of seeing the odd and interesting things that arrived from Russia and now from China.

The footmen returned from the stables with a hammer and a crowbar began to carefully pry open and tear apart the crate as Simon took the letters from the salver.

He read the one from Dr. Quong first. "Dr. Quong is sending me – packed in this crate – the notes for his new book, which he thinks might be of use to the Encyclopedia," he announced, quickly scanning the letter. "Ping sends her greetings, Tatya, and Dr. Quong tells me that he has at last become reconciled to her adventures with you – because he has presented him with another grandson! Gui and Jing Mai have been married and she is expecting a child in the autumn – Dr. Quong is praying for a great grand son. And T'a Ming sends her warmest affection to you, Lakota, and says that Chao has found a mate!" He folded the letter and returned it to the salver, planning to read it thoroughly later.

With a final crack of splintering wood the crate gave way to reveal what looked like a pile of straw. A letter, on a pile of scrolls, lay atop it.

"Dr. Quong's notes!" said Simon eagerly and bent forward to scoop up the scrolls.

"They sent us a pile of straw?" said Alan in disbelief. He was now a sturdy and very precocious three-year-old.

"That's being too heavy for a pile of straw, Master Alan," said the footman.

Tatya took the letter from the scrolls and opened it with a fingernail, It was sealed with the Imperial Dragon Seal.

"It's from Tuan! He says: *The contents of this box are from amongst the first fruits of the jade mine that you helped find. Please accept these small offerings as tokens of the continued gratitude and esteem of the House of Qing.*"

Janus jumped to the top of the pile of straw and dug her paw in deep. "There's something here!" she announced. "Alan, come dig this out."

Alan dug eagerly through the straw and a good sized paper wrapped bundle emerged. With his parent's permission he tore the wrappings off.

It was an exquisitely carved jade Chinese dragon.

All in all there proved to be twenty-five pieces of carved jade – animals, flowers, even an Imperial war chariot and a phoenix rising from the flames of its funeral pyre. There was jade of all colours, but in particular the rich, deep green.

"This is a treasure trove!" Simon said reverently. "This is an heirloom collection!"

"There's more, sir!" The older footman interrupted.

At the bottom of the box was a large flat package. It opened to reveal a jewel case and a enormous dragon-sized collar of carved jade in the form of lucky bats. There were also horn adornments, talon sheaths, and forehead jewelry, all of gold and green jade. Lakota was thrilled and had to try it on at once.

A smaller jewel box held a delicate human-sized necklace of tiny dragons, with matching earrings. And there were two jade dragon tie-pins as well, as well as jade collars for two felines.

"I shall scry the furniture shop and order a display case," said Ó Failbhe in approval. No other house in Dublin or its environs could have such a magnificent collection of jade.

It was not until much later when all the excitement over the jade had died down and it had been given a temporary home in the library that Simon remembered they had had another letter – from Ash.

He and Tatya were in the library, admiring the jade yet again. "Such a generous gift!" she said. "We shall have to write a very grateful letter to the Prince, Simon." She reached up and touched the jade dragons at her throat. They had changed for dinner and she had chosen a gown of Irish green silk that set off the jade jewelry to perfection.

Simon agreed absently as he slit Ash's letter with a letter opener

He read for a moment in silence and then said "My cousin Richard has written to Sir Perceval thanking him for trying to dissuade Tom from going on his hare-brained quest. The letter took almost a year to reach China."

"That was nice of Richard," Tatya said. "I was agreeably surprised by Richard, Simon. If we did not plan to be in America I should have had no hesitation in accepting their invitation for Christmas. His wife is a charming girl as well."

Simon had felt it his duty to meet Tom's coffin when the ship bearing him home arrived at the Port of London. Dragon-back, they had arrived back far before the ship.

He took his cousin's remains to Norfolk, not knowing what sort of reception he and Tatya would have – for she insisted upon accompanying him.

As Tatya had said, it was an agreeable surprise. Richard had changed amazingly. He was now a prosperous solicitor and the owner of the Grange. The property was unentailed and Dick had purchased it outright from Tom when it became obvious that Tom was only intent on wringing every groat he could from the property to spend on riotous living. Although Tom had been given a fair price he had persisted in thinking that Richard had cheated him.

Now Simon remembered Dick saying rather bitterly "It was never enough for Tom. No one could ever do enough for him. He always thought that he was entitled to more and always took the easy way." But Richard was grateful that Simon had brought Tom home to lie in the family plot.

Simon and Tatya stayed for the funeral and met James, who was a doctor. John and Robert had gone out to Canada and were doing well as farmers on Prince Edward

Island.

Letters had begin to be regularly exchanged and this past spring both Dick and James and their families had visited in Ireland. Simon doubted that they would ever be truly close, for there was a gap between magical and non-magical people that was sometimes difficult to bridge. But it was satisfying to not be on the outs with them and Simon had been given a bundle of his mother Elfrida's papers and jewelry and even a small portrait of her – this meant more to him than anything else.

Now Tatya said, "I shall never forget China – parts of that trip were horrible but we made some good friends."

"I hope you like America as well, Tatya," he said seriously. "I feel badly, taking you and Alan from home again – so soon. It seems as if we have scarcely settled in here and now we are leaving for a least a year."

Tatya looked thoughtful for a moment and then murmured "As long as we are all together." Her finger stroked one of the jade dragons at her throat. "Is it true, Simon," she asked abruptly, "that if a child is born in the United States he is automatically an American citizen?"

"I think that is so –" he replied and then it struck him what she was telling him. "When?" he asked joyfully.

"It is very early days yet," she cautioned. "But I saw a Wizard Healer today and they, you must know, can tell almost from the moment of conception. Sometime after Christmas – Alan will not be an only child after all!" she added in satisfaction.

Simon jumped up and put his arms about her. "Should you be standing up?" he asked anxiously. "Wait – should you undertake a trip to America?"

"Oh, nonsense!" she laughed. "I am perfectly fit! My physician has already given me the name of an excellent *accoucheur* in Boston who trained at Edinburgh. I shall be fine!"

And so it proved and Ivan Robert Stillfield was born in Boston Massachusetts in very early January of 1837 with little trouble to his mother, who had enjoyed a healthy, happy pregnancy in spite of a long journey over the sea.

The End